George in London

*A true account of young George Washington's adventures
and romances in England in 1751
as recorded by his companion, master mariner
and son of African nobility,
Darius Attucks
of New York.*

I0547982

By Tim Queeney

Front & back cover by Shannon Perry
shancore@gmail.com

George in London is a work of fiction and any resemblance
to any person or organization either living or dead is purely
coincidental.

Web
www.TimQueeney.com
Facebook
www.facebook.com/timqueeney.author
Twitter
@timqueeney

Books by Tim Queeney
www.TimQueeney.com

The Perry Helion Thrillers
Available now
The Shiva Compression
The Atlas Fracture
The Ceres Plague
Coming soon
The Proteus Evasion

The Perseid Collapse Kindle World
The Borealis Incident

Humorous historical fiction
George in London

For Wendy
My lovely companion
on life's adventure

Contents

Introduction
by Professor Edward G. Portobello,
Department of History, Custis College

GEORGE WASHINGTON made one short trip to Barbados as a young man. He returned to Virginia and never again left America. Or so we Washington experts have long believed.

That view was shattered into a million little pieces recently when I discovered a manuscript hidden in the foundation of Mount Vernon. My spectacular find has turned the world of Washington studies upside down. Every historian, indeed, every American, must rethink the great man's life.

I was not looking for anything unusual on that misty, cool March morning when I descended to the cellar of Mount Vernon. My intention was to view restoration work then underway on the oldest section of the mansion's basements. It is true I was not a member of the restoration team. However, as a noted academic at Custis College and acclaimed writer on the subject of George Washington, I felt entitled to lurk on an unofficial basis.

Dr. Eugenia Ball, a former colleague and friend, led the restoration efforts. Dr. Ball is a history professor at The Washington Institution and Substitute Teacher's College of Northeastern Central Virginia and the author of the bestseller *While Washington Slept Here.*

Once in the basement, I spent several minutes listening to the lively banter of Dr. Ball's team while I crouched behind a huge stack of paper towels. Eager to examine some of the recently completed work, I crawled on my belly to the foundation wall. It was then that I noticed a silvery coating on the foundation stones. Believing this to be a modern material, such as epoxy or cooking spray, I moved quickly to protect the authenticity of Mount Vernon. With my bare hands I made an effort to wipe away the coating.

A simple action had far-ranging consequences. When I pressed on the wall, two stones shifted to reveal a hollow.

Resting inside was a tightly wound tube of paper. Concerned that the sudden change of environment might damage the paper, I thrust the tube down the front of my pants and sprinted from the cellar. I was able to find a temperature- and humidity-controlled archival room nearby: my office at Custis College, a short two-and-a-half-hour drive (depending on traffic and how you catch the lights) from Mount Vernon. I carefully examined the manuscript over a bottle of wine and realized I had made a major discovery.

The manuscript was written in 1751 by an African American named Darius Attucks. Born a slave in New York City in 1727, Attucks showed a natural gift for navigation and seamanship. Because of these skills, Attucks' shipowning master decided to educate the young slave. Attucks received extensive tutoring in reading and writing, as well as history, rhetoric and mathematics. He developed a style in expression far exceeding that of young George Washington, who received only a rudimentary education. Attucks' master left instructions in his will to free his slaves on his death. As a free man, Darius followed the life of a merchant sailor.

Attucks' manuscript is a first-person account of the 24-year-old seaman's and the 19-year-old Washington's transatlantic adventure. Of course, when Attucks wrote the manuscript in 1751, he could have no idea of Washington's later importance.

Why has no hint of the manuscript's existence ever come to light? There is no mention of Darius Attucks in any of Washington's papers. This is not surprising, however, once we know more about Washington, the man.

Washington in his later years was deeply concerned with his place in history. He hired several of his Revolutionary War secretaries to review his wartime correspondence and censor or rewrite anything that might reflect poorly on him. Moreover, Washington instructed his wife Martha that on his death she was to destroy all correspondence they had exchanged during their marriage. True to his wishes, at his passing in December 1799, Martha made a bonfire at Mount Vernon. She torched a historical treasure so vast the flames threatened to set the mansion itself alight.

Washington's concern with posterity may well explain why he did not reveal his friendship with an African American former slave nor discuss the man's revealing manuscript. As for Attucks, it seems likely that his friendship with Washington ultimately overrode his desire to publish his work.

In any case, the Attucks manuscript is a Washington treasure that was lost for centuries. I have now singlehandedly recovered this gem for all people to study and enjoy [for speaking engagement dates and prices, and all the latest merchandise offers please go directly to my website: www.PortobelloGiftToHumanity.com].

Prof. Edward G. Portobello
Custis College
Pargiter, Virginia

Chapter One
Heaven Favors our Undertaking

A VIRGINIAN NAMED George Washington drowned in my arms today. The young man departed life on this date, May 1, 1751, aged but 19 years.

The immediate cause of the squire's passing was water infusion of his lungs. The greater agent was a monstrous storm that o'ertook our ship, the *Mary B.* She was a pretty vessel and I, Darius Attucks, was pleased to sail aboard her as second mate and navigator.

When the storm struck we were 30 days out of Bridgetown in Barbados, bound for Bristol, England. We had made the crossing of the Atlantic in good order and were off the coast of Cornwall by my reckoning, on course for the Bristol Channel. That afternoon, the sky in the east lowered and grew dark with veins of hammered pewter. By the turn of the watch the storm was upon us. The wind spit thick and the waves peaked in great watery cliffs. Not able to make sail in the tempest of wind, we struck all canvas and ran before the storm under bare poles.

For some time we scudded helplessly downwind. I could make no sense of our position in the wave-tossed dark and feared we might come to grief upon the coast.

The shriek of the wind was great, overpowering all else. We did not hear the crash of the waves upon the rocks as we neared the shore. When the ship grounded hard upon the reef, we were suddenly thrown to the deck. I shouted to young Washington to assure him, "There is no worry! The ship is strong. She will hold together."

Terrible was the tearing as the hull was ripped to pieces. The *Mary B.* spewed her guts into the waves. Her bow and midships sections stayed in the grip of the rocks. The stern piece, to which George and I clung, was carried into the shallows. We were but 100 feet from the sand — but a great maelstrom of foaming surf blocked our path. A sodden line of ship's rats swam to the stern, each hopping aboard in turn. Following the last of these vermin from the water was a fellow crewman, a mute sailor named Simon

Gull, who had joined the ship only hours before we sailed from Barbados. I was cheered by the mute's arrival in the midst of the disaster, as I had seen none of the other crew. "Can you assist Master Washington to the shore?" I shouted.

Gull vigorously nodded his agreement, his red hair spraying water like a dog. And then he leaped into the sea and made for safety, the rodents following his lead.

So it fell to me to help the young Virginian through the churning waves to the land. As we clung to the shattered deck, he voiced some small feelings of apprehension as to getting ashore safely.

"We will surely die," he bellowed.

As we had little time for argument, I calmed his fears with my fist.

He collapsed into my arms. I dumped his gangling frame into the surf and leapt after him into the boiling sea. The waves and the cold water hindered my efforts as I struggled to drag him to safety. He was torn from my grasp and driven deep under the frigid water. With aching hands I hauled him back to the surface, only to lose him again. When he had suffered three such immersions in the frigid surf, I knew he had expired. Even the gloom of night — frequently split by great bursts of lightning — could not hide the sad truth.

How could I, a mere mate on a trading ship, so easily conclude the lad was dead? Firstly, I have seen other cases of drowning. I am a man of the sea, with 15 years aboard ships both great and small. Secondly, I have made bookish study of the medical arts. I consider myself as near a physician as possible, though I have not had leave to sit for the examination.

Though he was now a mere corpse, I was aware that young Washington came from a Virginian family of some means. They would certainly desire the return of the young man's remains (perhaps for some consideration of money). I, therefore, did not relax my grip on the body, but rather heaved it up onto the sand. Working quickly, I dragged Washington's remains above the tide line so no wave would return it to the hungry sea.

Glimmerings of light heralded the dawn. The clouds had thinned in spots and the glow from the rising sun aided my efforts to recover what I could from the wreck. I scurried about, plucking valuable items from the surf. I rescued a tin of biscuits, a box of plug tobacco, a magnum of claret, a small barrel packed with cheese, a blanket, a greatcoat, a rucksack, a small wooden box with the captain's writing implements including a roll of parchment, and a hatchet. I piled these behind a rock to keep them out of the wind. I then spied my shipmate Simon Gull, who had snatched up a bottle of brandy rolling in the surf. He motioned to me to follow as he strode toward the ridge that fronted the beach. He climbed and crested the ridge, motioned again and was gone. But I could not abandon young Washington — that is to say, his body.

I turned back toward the corpse to ensure it had not been washed away. I have nothing but respect for the dead, especially in such a case. I was shocked, however, to behold a most amazing sight: young Washington sitting upright. I wondered if this was merely a reflexive action of his muscles, the last act of his fleeing spirit. But then he coughed, spit seawater and moaned. Then I knew Washington's posture was no cadaver's twitch.

The immediate stab of monetary loss was countered by a profound sense of wonder. This young Lazarus, whom I was sure had expired, was now sputteringly alive.

I realized in a flash this was the work of Heaven. The thought was confirmed by a sunbeam from on high, a shaft of golden light that enveloped young Washington as if to say, "Brother, behold thy brother." Clearly, this fellow was blessed by Heaven and was destined to live, perhaps to some good purpose.

Given this portent, my task — indeed, my responsibility — was to stand by this young man. I was filled with awe. I was the Almighty's chosen instrument in saving the Virginian. Clearly, I must accompany him on his travels. These orders from above both humbled and filled me with a solemn trepidation. The least of my thoughts — which I mention only so as to give a complete inventory — was the prospect of the gold and silver that might fall to me from assisting him.

I approached the young man and cheered him on his survival. I also explained that I had been the agent of his deliverance. He seemed focused, however, on a single aspect of his rescue.

"You miserable bastard! You punched me!" he shouted over the still powerful wind and crashing waves.

I agreed that I had applied my fist to his face. But I argued that it had been the most Christian blow ever landed. "I only struck you to save you from the tempest," I said, nettled by his ingratitude. "And my efforts were a success."

"I don't see how knocking me insensible aided in the rescue of my person," the colonial replied hotly. "It was more likely to speed the process of drowning."

"So you are a physician?" I replied. "You are well-versed in the ways of Hippocrates?"

"I've never met anyone named Hippockra Tees," he said. "I am speaking of simple common sense. If one is not awake, one cannot swim."

This was a fair point. Still, I held the ultimate card. "But you must agree that you are indeed alive."

He rubbed his chin and grumbled it was true. "But surely," he added, "there are better lifesaving techniques than beating a man. Besides, it is unseemly for a man such as yourself to put his hands upon a man such as myself."

I suspected the young Virginian might raise this point. "Because I am of African blood and you are of English?" I asked with force.

He looked at me for a long moment, as if to reconsider, before giving a hesitant nod.

"Would you fancy that I never manhandled you, yet your lungs were full o' water?"

He raised his eyebrows quickly in concern. "Well, perhaps my complaint is of little consequence given that I am alive, but there's no call for saying I was manhandled. Please do not repeat such a thing."

About to make a reply, it only just then occurred to me that I had not seen any of my shipmates, save for Gull, nor any of the ship's passengers on the strand. I gazed across the waves to where the broken pieces of the ship lay exposed on the reef. The hammering blows of the waves would soon leave not so much as two planks joined together. Everyone aboard the *Mary B.* — except ourselves and Gull — had surely been dashed to a bloody end upon the rocks.

Two stinging truths were now evident: We were the only survivors and I needed to purchase a new seabag.

It was pointless to remain on the beach. We needed to

get warm, to eat and drink. I gave young George the blanket for warmth. As I wrapped myself in the greatcoat an arm inside its right sleeve dropped thickly onto the sand. Drained of all blood it was marble white, like the arm of a statue. "That is surely the arm of Gus, the bosun," I said. "He swung a proper cudgel."

"I believe you are mistaken," Washington replied. "That truly is a muscular hand, but I swear it belongs to one of the passengers, Mr. Stine. Observe the gold ring. Did the bosun wear a ring such as that?"

I was impressed with his powers of observation. "You are correct," I admitted, removing the ring and slipping it into my pocket. "For safekeeping," I explained. I was somewhat pained that the young fellow knew my own ship's company better than myself — and that I had missed gold in plain sight.

We sat down behind the rock to eat. We were so hungry we ate the biscuits without first striking them against a rock to remove the weevils. We wolfed the moldy cheese and shared the brandy in chin-dripping gulps.

"Hadn't we better be getting on?" the Virginian spoke after he stood up, one arm on his hip, one leg braced outwards to make a better sight of himself. He was posing — as if Mr. William Hogarth himself had come down from London town to paint his portrait.

"Quit your poses, eh? There's no person here to see you but me."

The young man's countenance fell. He crossed his arms across his chest. "I just thought we might as well get moving," he said sheepishly. "To discover what part of the coast we've fetched up upon. Then I hope we may procure transport to London."

This was a solid plan. But first we must follow Gull over the brow of the ridge. The wind would be lessened there.

I hefted the bottle of wine and he picked up the hatchet. The other items I piled in the rucksack, which I slung onto my back. We left the sand and climbed. It occurred to me that we should determine what names to call each other. I was clearly destined by Heaven to guide this young man in matters of some importance. A special name for him seemed fitting.

"Your name is long and I have not got the breath to say 'George Washington' on every occasion it is necessary. Therefore, a nickname would suit." I paused and considered. "I will call you 'Geo.'"

"Geo?" the young man puckered. "Whatever for?"

"Well, your name is George and an oft-used shortening of this name is its first three letters. More than that," I noted, "you are a surveyor, he who sketches the face of the earth. And from which sketches comes the study we call geography. Thus, Geo." I admit I was happy with the nickname. Having read some few lines of Homer and Ovid, I think it is far to say I am nearly an expert on items poetical.

Geo showed less enthusiasm. "It's not particularly becoming. I confess I fancy something more ... heroic, perhaps?"

"So you are a hero? Destined to kill dragons and topple kings?"

Geo smiled shyly. He met my gaze for a moment, then turned away. "I never thought too much about it."

I laughed out loud. "Oh, you're lying to me now, Geo. On our passage from Barbados you let everyone know about the man you met in Barbados, your new friend the German baron. You talked plenty about your big plans to join him in London. You surely thought about it."

Geo grimaced and nodded. "All right. So I did." Then he quickly spoke of me as if to divert attention from himself. "What shall I call you? 'Mr. Attucks' or 'second mate' seems wrong now that we are on land. What about your Christian name? I never heard it."

"That's right you didn't," I said. "A ship runs on orders and the crew needs to know who gives 'em. A captain or mate on a ship must keep his distance. Sailors won't respect nor follow him otherwise. Just remember that. You never heard my first name on a ship and you rightly never will." Maybe I was a too severe with him, but on this topic I had my mind set.

"But what is it?" Geo asked. "Your name?"

"Oh ... I suppose that since we are on land now, I can tell you. My name is Darius, like the king of the Persians. And that is right, too, because I come from African nobility. My people were kings, once."

"King Darius of Africa," Geo said. And he said it with

a humble regard that made me feel good. I felt as though he heard me, somewhere down deep. Not a feeling I knew much, and almost never coming from a white man.

"Well, Darius, anyway. But you can call me D."

"Simply 'D'? Not the full extent of your name?"

"Aye, D alone. That'll do."

The clouds in the east were shredded now, revealing the morning sun. The wind was dropping, the storm blowing itself out. We rested in the grass near the crest of the ridge.

"If we wait here a bit," I said, "we can be sure to see any of the others. If any of them survived the calamity. Don't know where that odd fellow Gull has gotten to. Maybe he is of more help on land. He wasn't much good as a sailor."

Geo nodded and inched higher on the crest to get a better angle downhill to the sea. I looked him over as he dutifully scanned the beach. He wore a nut-brown jacket and a faded green waistcoat with brown breeches and worn leather boots. His hat had been lost to the clutches of the sea and with his long hair falling across his face, there was much of the eagerness I first saw in him when he came aboard my ship in Bridgetown some weeks ago.

I admit I liked him from the start. Geo was a young man itching to make his way in the world. His business associate, the German baron, had no doubt told the Virginian to keep his affairs to himself. But Geo was too thrilled by his prospects to stay quiet. He had shared with me something of his expected good fortune.

The details of Geo's business in London were not altogether clear to me — not the least because Geo himself did not know the full particulars. The enterprise turned on the sale of land in the west of America, across the Allegheny Mountains, along the river known as the Ohio.

As a younger son, Geo had no family fortune to support him. The money, land and chattels went to the oldest son on the father's death — in Geo's case his older, half-brother Lawrence. Thus, the death of Geo's father, Augustine, when Geo was but 11 years must have been a crushing blow. Young Geo, his eyes wet with sadness at his father's abrupt departure, found himself with no captain to rule the logbook of his life, no shipmaster from whom to receive his night orders. Without a firm hand upon the wheel, a ship may hit the rocks. And without the benefits of fatherly love and direction, a boy can go astray.

Nor was that all. As Geo grew he learned that he must earn his living by the sweat of his brow. So Geo did that thing most unpleasant to British men inclined toward the nobility: he acquired a trade. Apprenticing himself to a surveyor, he learned to measure land. He walked and he walked, covering mile after mile. It was hard labor. Scorched by the sun, stabbed by thorns, blistered by flies — all the while chopping through woods as thick as any Adam cut when the world was new. And throughout it all Geo recorded the numbers of every step.

I'm a man of the sea; I know the importance of measuring and marking. I measure and mark the heavens, the positions of the sun, moon, planets and stars. And I can use them to find where my ship is on the open sea. Geo, he measures land and draws out the grids on which nations grow. Empires ride upon the very act of measuring — on sea and on land. So Geo, he chose his profession wisely.

The Baron saw right away that Geo knew plenty of the western lands of Virginia. (Ask a Virginian and he'll say their land goes clear to the other side of the earth.) The Baron knew that Geo could talk firsthand of the lands along the Ohio River. So he signed up the young man to help him sell those lands in London town.

I looked across the grass at Geo. What gentleman of commerce would not want a strapping young man like Geo as his associate? He stood six feet and two inches tall, bigger than most men. He had light brown hair and blue eyes the color of the ocean at noon. His broadness of shoulder and of hip, with long legs and general muscularity of frame, suggested a strength and toughness not commonly found in a young man of 19 years.

Geo wanted the world to see him as a great man, like an Alexander or a Hannibal — a man of dashing action, outwardly courageous, proclaiming by voice, countenance and posture his eagerness to joust with fate. All this and more I learned while on our journey across the Atlantic.

Sitting on the ridge, I decided I wanted a quid of tobacco and asked Geo if he'd like to join me. His answer was yes and he held out his hand. I bit off a piece for myself and moved to give him the rest. Then I saw a look in his eyes. He let his hand fall and he turned away.

Geo shared a bottle of brandy with me when he was cold, wet and thirsty. But now, after the shipwreck had passed, taking a plug of tobacco that had touched my African lips troubled him. Well, to hell with him. Heaven says he had better get used to me.

Geo and I spent some time on the ridge waiting for other survivors of the shipwreck. We rested and I began the writing of this account. We waited and we waited. But it was clear enough that only we had lived through the wreck of the *Mary B*. Seaman Gull must have set off on his own and there was no sense in lingering for him. I had been chosen and I was not a man to keep Heaven waiting. We began walking.

By these events, I threw in my lot with Geo. I was to be his sideman, his second in the affairs of honor and his trusted confidant (and partake in any monies that might come my way).

It was a rough track through the fields. The sun climbed and the day grew warm. We found a road and followed it alongside thick stands of grain divided into small plots. In the distance lay mist and mountains. There was no town in sight, only small, whitewashed dwellings. We saw not a soul as we walked. With their weathered thatch and overgrown yards these houses looked as though their people had fled.

Now I am a man of sound limb, but I breathed hard in keeping up with the long-legged Geo, who surged ahead of me in his excitement. Geo, head down, counted his paces under his breath. "That's one rod," he said.

"What rod? You found something in the grass?" I asked. I took the opportunity to stop and rest.

"No ... well, yes, I found a distance. Six of my easy paces is one rod."

I looked at him, still not grasping his meaning.

"One rod is 16 and one-half feet. A rod is used by surveyors to measure the ground, to set boundaries and enclose acres."

"That means nothing to me. I'm a man of the sea — I use feet, fathoms and cables. I don't use rods except for keeping a sailor in line with a blow across the back."

Geo thought about this and began walking again. "Let

us come together on a compromise, then," he said. "How many feet in a fathom?"

"Six," I answered as I strode to catch up.

"Hmm, six doesn't go amicably into 16 and one-half." He thought again as he paced off rods for some mythical estate. "Yes, of course, six feet goes into one chain. A chain is four rods, or 66 feet. So, four rods is one chain, which is the same as 11 fathoms, which is 66 feet. Does that help?"

I had to think on it a bit, but then answered, "Yes. It will serve." Geo noted this and we continued on in silence. Perhaps we had reached a kind of compromise, a translation between the ways of measuring earth and measuring sky — and perhaps a bridge between two men of different stations, different occupations and different ages. There was much to separate us, but this formula — from rods to fathoms — perhaps spoke of a way to transcend it all.

The mist cleared from the far mountains, revealing them as lonely and untamed. I wondered if indeed we had landed in England, or had come ashore in some other, wilder, place. We came to the top of a small rise and saw a crowd of men gathered around a few barrels in a field, making a great commotion. As we drew closer, we saw these men were not sturdy English yeomen, but instead a disheveled and threadbare lot. They roared and swore, responding to a man on a horse. He rode back and forth, exhorting them with a booming speech. In the grass around them lay the most pitiful sort of weapons, from hay forks to spades to hastily made pikes — many of these little more than sharpened sticks. A precious few of the men had muskets and even those looked old and rusty.

Having made our way amongst them, we could hear their speech and now had no doubts as to their homeland. These were not English men, but Irish. I was most aggrieved to realize that my navigation had been off and instead of the west of England, we had gone ashore in the east of Ireland. I hoped Geo wouldn't take notice of my error. But Geo was engaged in watching the leader of the Irish, who sat his horse and waved an officer's sword as he spoke. We stood at the edge of the crowd and listened.

"Men of Kilkenny and Waterford, of Wexford, Arklow and New Ross, I salute you," the horse rider yelled as his mount pawed the turf. "It falls to you to begin the rising that will spread like flame in the parched grass. I salute you who fight the English lords; who fight the climbing rents and the wicked ejections of the folk from their homes. You will start a rebellion throughout Ireland. We will throw off the English yoke and live as free men."

The crowd shouted their approval of their leader, a firebrand named Rob McKeown. He was a portly little man but whose very manner sizzled like bacon in a pan and whose voice made men see possibilities.

When Mckeown finished, the rabble in arms took notice of us. For bloody rebels, they were a friendly lot — smiling, laughing and slapping our backs, so eager to welcome us to their cause they did not even ask our names. The truth be told, neither Geo nor myself could understand much of the sweaty Irishmen's speech. And we wanted no part of an Irish rising. But once we were within their circle, the Irish would not let us go on our way.

Crude wooden cups were thrust into our hands. Thirsty from our morning march, Geo gave his thanks for the water and drained his cup. He coughed so hard he couldn't talk for a minute or so. The Irish were not drinking water. 'Twas a whiskey with the evil Gaelic name of "potcheen" — a spirit so strong it burned the throat and watered the eyes if you could get it down at all. I spit my first swig back up in a gasping spray. The coarse revolutionaries bellowed and pointed, laughing at our weak-kneed efforts to drink their foul liquor.

The rebels' high spirits were short-lived, however. An ominous sound arrived on the wind: the beating of drums from the eastern edge of the field. It grew louder like the rumbling of an approaching storm. In brisk order, a unit of the king's infantry appeared. They came into view rank by rank as they ascended the rising ground. The regiment of foot, some 300 scarlet-coated soldiers, came on with fearful precision. The drummers beat time as the fife players ripped into "Liliberlero" — a song that is said to enrage Catholic Irishmen. Flags waved lazily in the dying breeze as the scarlet wave broke upon the field. The regiment's officers, their coats trimmed in bright brass buttons and their wigs freshly powdered, drew their swords — an action that caught the morning sun with a dazzling flash.

The rebel McKeown spurred his horse and galloped

round the Irishmen, herding them like a sheepdog. He demanded they take up their arms and resist the scarlet beast that approached at a stately march. "Show 'em who we are, me boy-o's. Let 'em come on. We're ready for 'em, ain't we? We know the prophecy, we do. When we beat the English in open battle, a free Ireland will follow." Irish ardor cooled as British muskets drew closer. I decided the time was nigh for Geo and I to melt away. Except, our way was blocked and we were each handed a rude pike.

When the soldiers were four rods, or 11 fathoms, from the muttering crowd of rebels, the regiment halted. Its commander was a prosperous colonel with a tubby face. A jovial smile seemed the natural set of his mouth and he displayed a good-natured manner that suggested either a charismatic charity or a simpleminded jollity. Sitting alongside him was a major, who by his size, shape and general appearance seemed a younger version of the older colonel. Save that while the older man presented an air of affable good nature, the younger officer wore a pervasive scowl. Adding further interest to the scene was a horse and rider positioned behind the regiment. 'Twas a woman in a scarlet dress, the very color of the officer's and soldiers' red coats. She was of ample proportion and watched the proceedings with a spyglass.

The colonel approached the rebels and spoke thus: "Men of Ireland, throw down your weapons and we will call this rebellion done and finished. 'Tis a fine day and a good field. We could be happier running foot races or throwing cannon shot. It is a contest of games I propose, not the waste of war. What say you?"

A contest of games? — I decided the British commander was clearly possessed of a simple mind.

McKeown laughed and spurred his horse forward and shouted to the British officer, "We say that we are free men of Ireland, who will not live under your English king. We will bash your noggins and use 'em for our drinkin' cups."

The smiling colonel even took this brazen insult with evenhanded good humor. "Very well," the colonel said, "But I think we could have had a lovely set of races and perhaps some javelin throws." He and his younger companion turned and cantered their chargers back to their unit. An order followed and the scarlets fixed their bayonets atop their muskets with the clack of mating metal.

"Buck up, me boys," McKeown shouted. "Their first shot will be heard throughout Ireland and 'round the world as the first volley in our fight for freedom. Long live Eire!"

The British advanced again, now drawing to within 30 yards. The ranks of soldiers stopped and raised their muskets. The sour-faced major barked a short, sharp order and the soldiers loosed a volley of lead ball. The roar of the guns was answered by the screams of men. Finding body and limb, eye and hand, groin and brain, the musket balls harvested the men in the field. Many of the Irish went down, writhing and yelling, their blood pooling in the dry, trampled grass. The red-coated soldiers charged, their mouths' wide with rage. Geo and I, we ran as fast as we could go. It was no cowardice to get out of there. That was no battle but a slaughter. And bravery had no place in it.

But our escape was blocked. The cruel-faced British major wheeled his horse in front of us, his saber high. Then he closed his eyes and slashed at Geo, the saber tip hissing past the Virginian's neck. The major advanced and it was clear the next blow would cut Geo asunder. I picked up one of the rude pikes and swung it into the British officer's chest, unhorsing him. The fallen officer glared hard at us as we fled.

A shadow o'ertook us as we ran. We saw McKeown ride past us. His body low, McKeown's short arms clutched the horse's neck and the mane flew in his face. He called out to us: "This way. Follow me." We followed him into a hole in the trees. It led to a narrow track along a stream. He turned to us as we caught up to his bleeding horse.

"The English are a bloody sort, are they not?" McKeown said, his voice low, but with a jaunty tone still.

"How can you urge your ill-equipped men to stand against such regular troops?" Geo gasped between breaths. "That was little more than a massacre."

"'Twas perhaps not the day for us, truly spoken," replied McKeown. "But there'll be another day and another after that. We'll never give up our dream," said McKeown as he plastered mud on his horse's wound.

"They will bloody more than your horse should they catch you," Geo said. "How can you escape?"

McKeown snorted, "See them hills on the far horizon?

They'll never catch me up there. They love their drills and their formations too much. They will never crawl on their bellies to follow my track. No, me and some of my men will live on. And the spirit of rebellion will live with us. To beat 'em, you just have to outlast 'em. May take a long time, but we'll win in the end. Just remember that." He flashed a mad smile and nodded in certainty.

Geo was rubbed a bit raw at the Irishman's offered advice. "I am not Irish. I have no need to fight the king's men."

McKeown smiled wide. "Aye, I'd guess so. You look a proper gentleman. Just do us a favor, will you?"

Geo was grudging with his nod.

"Tell 'em nothing of Rob McKeown's whereabouts and the blessings of the little people will be with you always."

"See here now," I piped up. "We don't believe in any little people — well, save for Happy Sally in Boston, who is small and can hang from a rope while she — "

"Don't worry," Geo interrupted, "we will keep our mouths shut."

"Then the blessing will be yours, whether you believe it or no."

The bloody rebel told us we were in southern Ireland, with Wexford not more than a day's walk. Then he galloped off down the stream, his horse spraying water and mud in the dappled light.

"A man in his situation, how can he have such a sanguine temper?" Geo marveled. "Perhaps there is something to what he says. Might keeping the flame of rebellion alive be enough to defeat so strong a nation as the English?"

"I am a man of the sea," I said. "But I suppose even the English could lose interest in a bloody war without end."

From our hiding place we could hear the victorious shouts and laughter of the English troops. They were drawing closer. "We had better move," I said, "or we'll end up in Davy Jones' locker — or whatever fly-ridden swamp surveyors go to die."

Chapter Two
At Bayonet Point

GEO AND I FOUND the sun hot for early May. Doffing our coats, we crept through the bushes and tall grass and along stone walls to get away from the soldiers. We came to a road that showed no sign of the red coats and walked in a direction we supposed to be the port of Wexford. Finding a stream that ran clear, I stooped down and drank. While Geo drank, I stood and was satisfied to see my reflection in the water. I have had many compliments on my pleasing face, with its strong nose, noble mouth and pure ebony eyes. 'Tis true that some of the good words were from whores well paid for my pleasure, but others came from women with no incentive to say so save their appreciation of a handsome man. Not as tall as Geo, I am yet a man of stature, finding myself easily as tall as most people I meet. My well-formed arms and legs speak of an active life aboard ship. I was a man used to living out of doors, accustomed to making my way in the world.

But there were differences betwixt us, of course — including that most obvious difference that dogged our relations and from which we could never be completely free: I was the older man.

Geo was born in Virginia; me in the city of New York. He is a surveyor and a gentleman, I a mariner and a man of humble origins. Geo's forebears came to the new world from England, with axe and spade, sword and musket, ready to conquer, to build, to hold. My people also came to America with implements of metal, but they were the iron of manacles and chains. My people were African royalty — my mother whispered to me tales of kings and queens — my forebears arrived subdued, to build and to work, not for themselves but for those who called themselves "masters."

My mother was a slave in the household of a Dutch ship owner, a man named Jan van Seeher. In 1706, while a young man, van Seeher left Amsterdam and landed in New York. He quickly prospered, coming to own three ships and much land. As I grew, van Seeher named me Darius for the great Persian king. When I was age eight, he put me aboard his ship *Raritan,* as a cabin boy. The truth of it is that I am a natural sailor, a seaman to my bones. I learned every part of the ship, every sail, every line, every gasket and brace. And not just the sailing of it, either — I was born to command a vessel at sea.

I learned to navigate better than the captains or mates with which I sailed. I kept my own logbook, with my own figures. Soon, I had ship's officers asking me for the ship's position. And my navigation was right, and so my navigation became the one to guide the ship. They kept their own logbooks for show — but I was the navigator.

Word of my feats reached my master and van Seeher brought me back to New York. He was childless, a lack that vexed him. When a horse fell upon his wife and killed her, he became a different man. He gazed out his parlor window for many an hour and left the running of his estate to others. One day he resolved that I should be schooled and learn the ways of a proper young gentleman. "You shall be a ship captain and a man of means, Darius. You will see." Perhaps it was the shock of his wife's death that warped his mind — an African slave could not be a gentleman anywhere in New York. Putting no stock in the customs of his wealthy white neighbors, van Seeher enrolled me in the local academy. But a crowd of angry parents made to set the school ablaze if I did not leave at once.

"They block us? Then we will sail around 'dem," van Seeher reassured me. And to that end, he hired a tutor to teach me in the confines of his house. I learned fast and well. There was reading and writing and history and philosophy — I already had a good feel for numbers from my navigation studies. Van Seeher fitted me out like a proper East India company ship: fully decked in fine clothes like a vessel pressing forward under full canvas.

It all ended quickly, however. My master was in Jamaica and caught the yellow fever. He died straight away in the streets of Kingston; and then again aboard ship a week later when it was discovered he had not died properly the first time.

In New York, important men gathered for the reading of my dead master's will. I was to be barred from the meeting, on the grounds that I was a young African man of no consequence. But I was determined. They would not keep me from the last thoughts of the man who saw me schooled and gave me hope. Assisted by a household slave, we removed my master's body from his coffin. As he had died some days earlier and was now overripe, we propped him up in the privy, its noisome vapors masking somewhat the stench of his body. I climbed into the empty coffin just before the men entered my master's private library for the reading.

On the reading of his will, I heard that my master wished all his slaves to be set free upon his death. The important men, however, disliked this point and conspired to ignore it so that the commerce of my dead master's shops and warehouses, ships and farms might continue. I was aghast. Flinging open the coffin, I sat up and demanded justice. The sight of a black man rising from van Seeher's casket was too much for the reader of the will, who fainted dead away. The other men were so taken aback, they capitulated to my moral fervor and agreed that we slaves would be released as per van Seeher's wishes.

Thus I was a free man at the age of 17. My mother had died two years before. I knew not my father, as he was sold away when I was but a boy. I had a twin brother, who my mother called Jabbar. But he died when I was a very young. I never knew him, though my mother said he would always be with me, even if I could not see him. Sometimes, when I am alone I do try to see him. But 'cept for a shadow here or a curl of smoke there, I've never seen him. Would make me feel good to have Jabbar at my side. Even a ghost would be right company sometimes. With no other person to love me and give me support, I was on my own. I was not sure what would become of me.

I remember I stood frozen halfway down the steps of my master's house. I watched the newly freed household slaves departing to seek their fortunes. A few turned and beckoned me to join them. I wished to do so, since I am an African the same as they. But I looked up at my master's house, ran my hand across my fine clothes and somehow could not move. I only stood and watched as they skipped down the muddy street, laughing and shouting at their rebirth. At that moment I felt my situation most keenly — suspended between two worlds and feeling not at home in either. I wished my mother was alive to guide me with a kind word, with the warmth of her hand in mine. How I missed her then ... and yet still do.

Presently, a ship captain, just returned from sea, came to call upon Van Seeher. I informed him that my master had departed this life. His face fairly lit up and he asked if I would sign aboard his ship. He had heard of my skills at navigation. So I put away my fancy clothes and signed on. I then moved on to other ships. Ships that sailed to St. Kitts and Martinique, to the Canary Isles and to Madeira, to Gibraltar and Lisbon, to Portsmouth and Deptford, Brest and Boulogne. I would sign on as a cabin boy or a steward, then work my way up to one of the mates. My navigation was as sharp as ever and captains made good runs when they followed my chart. A fast, safe run makes money and few captains or ship owners care so much about the color of a man's skin when they can make more money.

Many times at the end of passages I found myself paid off in the town of Boston or New York. In this way I sailed out of New York and Boston and found myself at home in both cities. On one ship I became friends with a half-African, half-Indian man from Boston named Attucks, who spoke of liberty and independence for the colonists of America. He believed that Americans should have their own country, free of Britain altogether, where slavery was forever abolished. I was struck by his passion. When I first went aboard ships, I took my master's name, sailing as Darius van Seeher. But I was so swayed by Attucks that I took his name for my own.

The ship Geo and I had recently escaped with our lives, the *Mary B.*, had been my home for nearly four years. I had worked my way up to second mate aboard her and was displeased that I must start the climb anew.

Geo and I sat down for a rest under a shady tree and Geo took off his boots to rub his feet. Then any thought of signing aboard another ship left my mind. I saw something out of the corner of my eye — the steel edge of a bayonet. Cracking twigs and quick feet brought more bayonets and muskets and red coats. Five British soldiers and a sergeant surrounded us.

"Well, well," the sergeant said with a chuckle. "I think we done captured us some Irish rebels."

"And, look, Sarge, one of 'em is a blackamoor," said a short private, with a smile more gap than tooth.

The happy crew put their muskets at rest while the sergeant produced a bit of rope. "Alright, up with you then; on your feet. I've got to tie your wrists."

"You are mistaken 'bout our allegiance, sir," I said quickly as Geo grabbed his boots. "We are no rebels," I continued, "but loyal subjects of the crown."

"If that be so, you Moorish knave, then why were you just on yonder field of battle?"

"We but stumbled upon the rebels while walking from the sea," I replied. "Our ship, the *Mary B.*, was wrecked upon the shore this very morning."

"Why is a black fellow like yerself speaking for a white man?"

Geo considered this and then stated weakly, "He saved my life. I suppose that gives him a sort of leave."

The sergeant raised one brow and scowled. "Well, then do ya live in this county? Are ya Irish with livings here?"

"No, we are not," Geo replied.

"Then you are not honest citizens but rebels come here to make trouble for the crown."

"He's got some kind a' Irish way a' speaking," the nearly toothless private said.

"I hail from Virginia," Geo replied.

"You're Irish rebels and fit to swing from a rope," the sergeant snapped as he finished binding my wrists.

"But, Sergeant ... ah, what is your name?" I asked.

"Chivers."

"Sergeant Chivers, we are not Irish but from America. We have no reason to fight for Ireland."

The sergeant paused a moment, then pushed back his tall soldier's hat and scratched his head. The short private piped up. "Hey, Sarge, if they are from the colonies, then the darkie has got a good point."

"Shaddup, Hopkins. The colonel wants all prisoners brought to 'im."

"Especially those that can run fast and who have strong arms for throwin'," Hopkins added.

Chivers turned his head. "Hopkins. Didn't I tell you to shut yer gob?"

"Right, Sarge."

The sergeant finished the knot on Geo's rope. "C'mon, we're off then."

"Don't forget what the colonel said 'bout jumpin' high." Hopkins added. "They also should be able to jump high."

"Hopkins!"

"Right. I ain't saying no more."

"You better not or you'll feel my boot up yer arse!"

"I ain't said another word, Sarge," Hopkins offered. "You can count on me. I'll be quiet as a bleedin' mouse, I will. I know how to follow orders. Ain't I done that the whole time I been in the regiment? Ain't I been a good soldier, Sarge?"

Chivers rolled his eyes and the party marched off down the road under a bright Irish sun.

I watched Geo closely. I thought I saw certain signs of fear and trepidation on his face. He must have taken that statement about swinging on a rope to heart. As we trudged on, though, I saw a change in him. His earlier fear faded and he showed something different. Not resignation and defeat, but more a stoic acceptance — perhaps even a hint of noble authority.

We turned round a bend, where an old elm stuck a weathered arm above the road, and came upon a worrisome scene. A rope hung over the branch and a man sat upon a horse underneath it, surrounded by a clutch of soldiers. Directing the affair was the cruel-faced British major whom I had unhorsed during the battle. Alongside him was the ample woman in the scarlet dress I had seen observing the battle with a spyglass. She was middle-aged and wore a fashionable wig with a large hat. She inclined her head and smiled tenderly when she saw us approach. I soon realized the man on the horse awaiting execution was none other than Simon Gull, my mute shipmate from the *Mary B*. More astounding still, he opened his mouth and spoke.

"I ain't got nothin' to do wit' no rising," Gull protested loudly. "I'm an Englishman. I ain't no potato-eating Irish."

The major adjusted the hanging knot around Gull's neck. "Th-th-that's not too tight, is it?" the major asked Gull solicitously. "N-n-no need to be discomfited til the final drop, eh?"

"Quite right, dear," the woman said with an approving nod. "We must treat our fellow man with as much good will as is within our power. Oh, and Francis, that knot has one too few turns. Fix it at once."

The major looked at her, sighed and said, "Y-y-yes, mother."

He directed a sergeant to retie the rope. When he finished, it had the correct number of turns for a proper noose. "Just so," she said sweetly.

Then the young major espied us approaching and his mood turned happier.

"Aahhhh! M-m-more Jacobites for battlefield justice," The major now had a quite sunny disposition. "I sh-sh-shall dispatch you *en masse*."

"Francis, you fail me," the woman said. "It is exceedingly rude to simply hang them without a few introductions. You must remember, dear."

"B-b-but, mother," the major objected, "g-g-getting to know these Jacobites serves little purpose as they will soon depart this earth."

"True enough," she agreed with mellow tones. "But a British officer always displays his good breeding, no matter the situation."

Geo and I presented our names with a slight bow. She received them graciously before announcing, "I am Lady Frances Chase, mother to Major Sir Francis Chase whom you see before you."

"D-d-delighted," Sir Francis mumbled.

The niceties completed, Major Chase called for more rope. Soon Geo and I were in similar straits as Gull: sitting on horses with ropes fastened 'round our necks, surrounded by a squad of soldiers.

Geo whispered to me, "What is a Jacobite?" He was utterly confused as to the nature of Jacobitism but kept his voice low as he did not wish to appear a provincial bumpkin.

"Is it not obvious that a Jacobite is a follower of the grandson of King James II of the house of Stuart?" I replied. "Jacobites desire the overthrow of the royal house of Hanover, of which the present King George II is a member." Geo shrugged his shoulders as if what I had told him made no sense — young people these days!

There is nothing like the prospect of swinging from a rope to clear one's head and mine was now horribly unsullied. I tried another gambit. "Sir, that man was aboard my ship and was a mute. Yet now he speaks. Is there not something incredible about this? Should we not take the time to inquire further into this miracle?"

The major shook his head. "N-n-not at all. 'T-t-tis a well-known fact that the nearness of death has unexpected powers and such last-minute 'cures' are often observed. The occurrence of such a cure is to be celebrated, as it only lends further luster to the administration of British justice."

"How is it that you can now speak, Gull?" I shouted across at the chatty fellow.

Gull shook his red-haired head but refused to meet my eyes. "Don't know. As you say, a bloody miracle."

With the ropes in place and we prisoners ready to drop, I saw the need for further discussion on several points.

"If I might ask another question?" I said to Sir Francis.

The major was sorely vexed at the prospect of additional time devoted to conversation.

"Francis, you must honor his request," Lady Chase prompted him. "It would be un-British to be so rude." She looked us over approvingly. "Besides, they are both such handsome men. 'Tis a shame they can't be spared."

Sir Francis grimaced and shook his head. Then we heard it: the sound of drums and soldiers marching. Sir Francis heard the noise as well. He ordered the execution to proceed forthwith. To the major's chagrin, however, the regiment's commander, Colonel Sir Charles Chase, who was his father, rode up with his aides-de-camp.

"Francis," Colonel Chase called out. "What are you doing?" Then to his wife, "Good day, dear." Lady Chase nodded at her husband.

"F-f-father, these are dangerous Jacobites who would destroy the peace of the kingdom and overthrow the King. I am protecting the realm."

"But you can't execute those men, my boy. They are well suited for my special interests. Cut them down immediately." The colonel looked upon Gull, Geo and myself with giddy anticipation.

"B-b-but, Father," the major protested, "I caught these Jacobite devils. I really should be allowed to dispense with them. It's only fair. I was very polite to them. You can ask mother."

"He did require some prompting," Lady Chase said. "And he was quite testy in allowing for final questions from the prisoners."

"I l-l-let *him* — " Sir Francis pointed at me, "ask a final question. But then he asked a second question. I don't see how he is entitled to two questions. That clearly goes beyond the bounds."

"But overall," Lady Chase continued, "I would say he is making steady progress, Charles."

Major Chase reluctantly complied with his father's request, and we happily escaped the hangman's noose. I was anxious to speak with Gull, but no sooner had we been released from the ropes, than Gull grabbed the ear of the Colonel. The conversation was highly animated, but I was too far away to hear its import.

That night, Geo and I and all the captured Irishmen were locked within a barn. The last we saw of Gull, he was riding out of camp with the Colonel at his side. I couldn't think where they were going, or how Gull had made the jump from prisoner to commanding officer's companion. Perhaps there was more to his miraculous cure than I had first supposed.

The Irish prisoner, who lay all around us in exhaustion and a generally bad temper, smelled worse than a crowded fo'c'sle in the tropics.

The next day we were brought before Colonel Chase and Major Chase in the front room of the Colonel's regimental headquarters, an unassuming Irish farm house with a pig rooting by the kitchen door. Lady Chase, who we discovered from Private Hopkins was generally known as Fanny, was also there. It seemed Fanny Chase would occasionally accompany her husband in the field. She spent most of her time in London tending to her custard shops. Of middle age and not possessed of fine-featured beauty, Lady Chase somehow presented a friendliness and warmth that did much to commend her. She was of a prosperous girth — no doubt a side benefit to owning a London custard establishment.

While we talked with her husband, Lady Chase wrote in a small leather volume and smiled at us often.

Colonel Chase was a bit older than his wife, but his cheerful face and the youthful, almost girlish bounce to his step made him seem younger even than his son. Sir Francis, by contrast, seemed awkward, stiff and uneasy. To see them side-by-side, the family resemblance was striking. The colonel's ebullience, however, differed sharply from the younger man's sour expression.

The Colonel looked us over closely before he clapped his hands together with glee. "These fellows are first rate."

"Oh, yes," Lady Chase added enthusiastically. "I must agree," she added with another warm smile.

"They will make great sport for us," Sir Charles declared. "I cannot wait to begin."

Now many an African man and woman have been subjected to the most barbaric behavior from the white men who steal us from our homes in Africa and transport us across the sea. But I never heard anyone take such glee at the prospect of hanging a man.

"Colonel, sir," I said. "We are no Irish rebels and do not deserve to swing."

The colonel's face fell. His constant smile vanished. Now that his good feelings had fled I wondered if he would have the hanging ropes fixed at once. But no, a look of surprise and even hurt occupied his features. "My dear fellow, if I had wished to hang you, I should have done it yesterday. No, indeed, I would have you earn laurel wreaths of victory. By the way, are either of you fleet of foot? You'll pardon me, I hope, were I to ask you to run down to that haystack yonder and return?"

I looked at Geo, but he merely shrugged. "I will run as you ask," I said.

Upon returning, the colonel was most solicitous. "You are quite swift. This will be one of the best races the regiment has ever run." Turning to Geo, he asked, "And what is your specialty? Running? Jumping? Perhaps throwing shot?"

"I thought that was what cannon was for," Geo said.

The colonel, eager to win us over, agreed quickly, "Yes, yes. Cannon are superb for it. But there is an event in the ancient games wherein the athletes would throw heavy stones. It works well to use six-pound shot, rather than searching high and low for stones of suitable size and equal weight."

"I am not fast, but am fair at throwing stones for accuracy, if that is acceptable to your Excellency."

After considering this, the colonel nodded. "Certainly. We may add such an event."

"Colonel Chase, are you proposing an athletic contest like the ancient Greek games played at the foot of Mt. Olympus?" I asked.

The colonel's face lit up. "Precisely, sir. That is the very essence of it. And you are one of the very few who has grasped this. You strike me as a man of some education and even, may I say, refinement."

"And you are surprised that an African man can have any such thing as refinement?"

The colonel nodded. "Yes, I suppose I am. I have not met many such dark men as yourself, but I salute you for your knowledge of athletics. You see, given the chance, I would recreate the ancient games in all their glory. My fancy is a team from every nation and people in the world competing in a series of athletic events."

"Even Africans and the peoples of the East?" Geo asked.

Chase nodded enthusiastically. "Indeed, yes."

"Would they compete for prize money?" I asked expectantly.

"Why, no," the colonel replied, a bit distressed at the question, "they would compete for the glory of athletic endeavor, of course."

"Oh, I see," I replied.

"Now, combining you with other Irish prisoners, I think we could get a proper set of events going."

We walked outside to see four of the Irish rebels under guard at the edge of a farm field. Three were fierce-eyed men, sporting bloody bandages. The fourth rebel was a mere boy, no older than perhaps 12 years. I was lined up with the four of them at one place. The colonel ran lightly to the starter's position and stood with his lace handkerchief at the ready. He dropped the handkerchief and I started running, easily outpacing the four rebels. Yet they gamely continued on. Every 20 yards or so we passed another English soldier standing guard round the track. I gained a considerable lead on the rebels and glanced back to check on their progress. They were just passing a thicket of trees, halfway between two guards, when all four made a hard turn and disappeared into the trees. The nearest guard raised his musket and fired, but the rebels were shrouded by the verdant growth. I coasted in to an easy victory.

"Well, I dare say that was a different way to run a race," the colonel said with as much mirth as he could muster through his obvious disappointment.

His son the major muttered, "'O-o-olympical games — what utter rot."

"Francis," Lady Chase spoke up. "It is most impolite to speak in such a manner."

Sir Francis pursed his lips and looked away.

"Hey, Sarge," asked Private Hopkins of Sergeant Chivers, who stood nearby, "aren't they supposed to run on the course? How will we know who won if they run into the trees?" Hopkins waited for an answer, but Chivers just shook his head.

Then it was Geo's turn to compete in a stone-throwing contest. He battled against the colonel. They sent two Irish prisoners into the field with long sticks topped with flags to indicate where the stones fell. The colonel threw first. It was a respectable distance and the colonel drained a small cup of claret and waved his handkerchief in celebration. Then Geo let fly and his stone bounced quite a bit farther than the colonel's. The two Irish rebels trotted out to mark the spots with their flag sticks. Both Geo and the colonel were excited when they saw how far out the Irish lads had gone.

That is, until the rebels dropped their sticks and kept going. British muskets barked again, but the two lads were four strides from a stone wall. Over it they went and were gone.

An embarrassed silence was broken by the colonel, "A fine bit of vaulting, that, really quite impressive. We should add a vaulting competition to the list."

"Yes, sir," Hopkins chirped. "Reminds me of the time...." Chivers shot Hopkins a withering look. The private went quiet.

"Well, then what's our next event?" the colonel asked.

"Actually, sir, other than these two," Chivers motioned toward Geo and I, "We've right run out a' prisoners."

"Oh, is that right? Hmm, well, that *is* a problem. Perhaps we ought not to have killed quite so many rebels during the battle." Colonel Chase snapped his fingers for more wine in his silver drinking cup. After tossing it off, he announced, "I suppose that will be all for today." And then, a bit crestfallen, the colonel and his lady returned to the farmhouse.

Before Major Chase retreated to his tent, he glanced over at Geo and me with a look of foul enmity. I shuddered. If given the chance Sir Francis would finish the job of hanging us.

Geo and I were now alone in the barn. We were happy men when private Hopkins came banging through the heavy barn door, bringing us some milk, bread and a bit of cold mutton.

"Imagine you're tired after all that runnin'," Hopkins said as he delivered the victuals. The prospect of food cheered Geo up. He had grown quiet and sullen.

"Thank you," Geo said. His voice was so quiet it seemed strange coming from a big fellow.

"The colonel, he likes you two," Hopkins announced. "Don't think he's gonna hang you even after his ancient games. Must be good news, eh? Stompin' round Ireland, raisin' rebellion, cursing the King, inciting sedition and such, and you get away with your necks. Luckiest Irish I ever saw."

I looked at Geo and the big fellow met my eyes with a shrug.

"We're not Irish, Hopkins," I said, feeling some sympathy for Sergeant Chivers. "We come from America."

Hopkins looked at Geo and then at me. "Are you sure? I know an Army mate who grew up in Bristol and he swears there are Irish blokes what are blacker than you."

"Well, bring him in then and let him look at us."

Hopkins shook his head, his light brown eyes wide. "Can't do that."

"Why not?"

Hopkins lowered his voice and looked around before speaking. "He ran off to London to appear in the theatre."

"Doesn't he fear for his life?" I said. "Deserters get

executed, do they not?"

The private nodded. "That's right. But the Army is looking for a *man* that deserted. They might not 'ave too much luck with that, if ya' know what I mean."

Geo looked lost, but I understood — a sailor sees many odd sights in the ports of the world.

"Anyway, I expect Sergeant Chivers has got some work for me to do. I'd better go make a pretence of doing it, eh?" Hopkins gave us his gapped grin and took his leave.

The visit by the private seemed to cheer up Geo for a piece, but he suddenly turned glum again.

"Yo, ho, Geo, what's ailing you?" I asked.

"I am sorry to be such poor company. However, my excellent prospects decline each day. The baron gave me instructions to meet him in London, if I do not show my face, he may choose another to help him."

"Fret not, my young friend. He was set to depart Bridgetown after us, on a ship not nearly as swift as the *Mary B*. The Baron may arrive in London no sooner than we. And where in London will he find a young man like yourself with your experience of the lands across the mountains of Virginia?"

Geo agreed, and he showed some better humor as he slid off to sleep.

Young Geo's prospects were bright indeed. On the long voyage from Barbados to Ireland, I spoke often with the young Virginian. I learned his story, filling in the blank spots by later questioning.

Geo traveled to the island of Barbados due to the dread disease of consumption suffered by his older brother Lawrence. The tropical air of the island is well known as a marvelous curative to consumption. While on the island, Geo and Lawrence often dined at the governor's house and there they met people of every station.

Officers of the garrison, wealthy local planters and even people of fashion and breeding on their way to Jamaica or headed back to England; all would would attend at the governor's invitation. One such man was Geo's German baron. He told us he was returning to the continent after profitable business dealings in the Caribbean. His Lordship Meissel von Mulct, the Baron Mowenholtz, was a nobleman of the German principality of Farkenheine-Ausgas — one of the myriad principalities, duchies, electorships, and free cities infesting Germany. The governor introduced the baron to the assembled group, most of whom were happy to meet a representative of German nobility. The only sour note was sounded by Colonel Dunderhurst, the commander of the garrison.

"I must say that I have never had the occasion of meeting anyone from Farkenheine-Ausgas before," Dunderhurst intoned. "Nor, indeed, have I ever happened to hear of such a place. And I strongly believe that geographic knowledge is the very cornerstone of a British officer's training."

The baron smiled earnestly at Dunderhurst and agreed that his homeland was surely the most frequently overlooked of all the fractured multitude of tiny German states. The baron stated Farkenheine-Ausgas was not so far from the German province of Hanover as you might imagine but not nearly as close as you might think. "I can assure you that, though small, it does exist," the baron retorted. "In fact, if it did not, zen I would not be standing before you now." This remark brought titters of laughter to the group, with even Dunderhurst joining in after he heard the laughter of the others.

Geo related to me that in appearance the baron was a thin fellow of energetic constitution. He exhibited a steady movement, almost a tremor, of his hands or feet whenever he was required to sit for any length of time. He had entrancing eyes and a fine, aquiline nose that suggested his noble breeding. A man of developed tastes, most notably in his attire, the baron wore his hat or his wig at all times.

The baron quickly sized up Geo as a promising young man. Indeed, when he heard that Geo had experience surveying in the wild western lands of Virginia, he was most impressed.

A few days later, as the baron was leaving the premises of a local scrivener, he chanced to meet Geo on the street. The German invited Geo to dine with him at his lodgings. Geo agreed and they had a merry and convivial meal after which the baron put a business proposition to Geo: come to London with him as his assistant.

"What would be the nature of my assistance to your lordship?" Geo asked.

"By my various business arrangements, I have come into ze possession of a substantial portfolio of land claims in America. These are parcels in ze areas of vestern Virginia, across ze mountains, an area that you yourself have visited, very near ze Ohio River."

"My brother Lawrence is involved in just such an Ohio enterprise," said Geo with pride. "With several Virginian men of property and renown."

"Ah, yes. Und your brother has included you to a profitable degree in this?" the baron asked. "He haz made you a full partner in zis enterprise?"Geo paused.

"But certainly he haz done right by you? You will realize a substantial financial gain, yes?"

"Well, not in so many words. However, I think — "

"Ahh," the baron interrupted. "It is not unusual for ze eldest brother to take everything for himself, ja? Zat is too bad, as zese Ohio lands are very beautiful und very rich. But, if you do not wish to work with me, I understand."

Geo knew the rules of inheritance. And he had tried his utmost not to resent his older brother. There were times, however, when his goodwill wore thin. To have this German, who he barely knew, point out how his brother took everything for himself was galling and embarrassing to Geo. He was angry with the baron. Geo also realized, however, he was upset with Lawrence that much more. He decided he must make his own way, he could not hope for Lawrence to show him the slightest advantage. "What duties would I perform?" Geo asked solemnly.

The baron paused to smile warmly at the young Virginian. "You will assist me in the sale of these deeds to gentlemen und ladies of character in London. Your personal testimony of the value, beauty, und the improvability of this land will be highly persuasive. Due to the machinations of fate, the details of which I am not at liberty to divulge, I am in a position to sell these properties at a very reasonable rate. Further, I must say that, as my assistant und partner in this enterprise, you stand a very good chance of not only securing good monies, ja, but could well come out of zis with a personal title, say, baronet or viscount, und a country estate of some considerable extent." The baron patted Geo's hand. He could see that Geo was intrigued by these ideas.

As a younger son Geo had to make his own luck. And

what the baron suggested to him was the possibility of a lifetime. Geo, who had determined the only proper way for a young man was decisiveness and heroism in all things, decided on his course of action.

"I would be honored to assist you in London, your lordship," Geo said, as calmly as his racing heart would allow.

Since the baron required several additional days to complete some work with the local scrivener, he determined that Geo should proceed to England on his own. The baron would leave soon thereafter and the two would be reunited in London.

And so it was that Geo came aboard my ship, the *Mary B.*, in Bridgetown.

Geo and I stirred from our straw beds at the very crack of the Irish dawn. As prisoners of the crown we expected hard work and harsh discipline. We knew there would be nothing but bread and water for breakfast and then ceaseless toil until sundown — with a few beatings thrown in for good measure. In a state of uneasy distemper, we waited for our cruel-hearted jailors to appear.

And we waited.

After some time, we lay down and went back to sleep.

Finally, by mid-morning we were exhausted with rest. We rose and dressed. To keep occupied we cleaned the barn.

Soft Irish weather had come again and the sky was gray with a fine rain. When one of our jailors did appear in the barn, it was the talkative Private Hopkins. He told us that Colonel Chase had called off the running and jumping and throwing, what he called his "Olympical Games," on account the weather offered poor footing. Hopkins reported that the colonel was busy with what he called "his rainy day endeavor." It seemed Chase was working on a new British army uniform. He had come up with a design he planned to present before Parliament. "One of us soldiers stand still as a statue," Hopkins said, "while 'e drapes bits on us — different lots of cloth, buttons and the like. He gets excited as a March hare and jumps about, lookin' at his designs from round about and making all manner of comments. It gets damn tirin' to stand still like that. But the colonel, he has a real gift for drawing up clothes, a real gift."

"So you favor the look of his new uniform?" Geo asked.

Hopkins looked around and then leaned in close to whisper, "Naah! It's bloody awful."

Since the colonel wasn't going to hang us and we weren't Irish rebels anyway, I had an idea that I presented to the colonel as he ate his breakfast.

"Colonel, sir," I said with Geo's assuring stature beside me, "seems like we could stay here and run and jump and throw shot. And that would be fine enough, but I suggest that we, Mr. Washington and myself, could take your ideas to London. Surely a man of your accomplishments must know influential members of Parliament and have important friends at court?"

"Charles, your chin," Lady Chase admonished.

Colonel Chase wiped a yellow tear of yolk from his chin and opened his eyes wider. "Yes, yes, of course. My son Francis has been named commander of the Prince of Wales' Life Guard — we received the dispatch only this morning. The safety of young Prince George, the future king, will soon be in his hands."

I nodded in appreciation of this. "He will be a man of note, then."

Chase warmed to the idea of his son's budding importance. "Yes, and that is not all. He will also be a gentleman of the Prince's bedchamber, master of the prince's privy codpiece, knight of His Majesty's foot bath, Lord Chamberlain of toenail shears and much more, no doubt."

"Well, sir, this news only confirms the value of my plan," I said.

"It does?" asked the colonel. "Pray, tell me." He leaned forward, ignoring the last of his eggs.

"Since we two have competed in your Greek games, we are the perfect envoys to introduce the concept. And your son, given his important and august responsibilities, and the fact that he has the Prince's ear, can smooth the path for your ideas of a revived Greek games. They could be held in London, with the Prince himself as their patron."

"Marvelous!" the colonel clapped his hands like a

schoolboy. "I must own that I had not considered that possibility."

"The plan only requires that you provide us with papers of free passage to London. When we arrive, we will report to Sir Francis once he has taken up his post."

Chase nodded happily and was ready to begin immediate dictation to his secretary when Sir Francis joined us. After the colonel outlined the plan, Sir Francis made a fateful change to the arrangements. "Th-th-there is no need for papers of safe passage, Father. I am prepared to depart for London on the hour. I will escort Mr. Washington and his associate to the capital myself." After he secured the colonel's assent to this arrangement, Sir Francis displayed towards us a seeming affability. Behind this friendly pose, however, I suspected wicked designs upon our persons.

Soon we were ready to depart the regimental camp. We were joined on our journey by other travelers. Sir Francis asked the colonel to include a soldier to ensure we acted honorably. The colonel asked Sergeant Chivers which of his men he could spare. Chivers seemed quite animated by this idea. "Now, if I have to give up a man, let me see …" Chivers made a great show of considering his options by ticking off imaginary candidates on his fingers. After some display of careful deliberation he settled on his choice. "Hopkins, sir. Private Hopkins. I hope he will as great a help to Major Chase as he has been to me, sir." Off-duty soldiers playing cards or cleaning the dried blood off their muskets looked up briefly, but stuck to the tents to avoid the gossamer Irish rain. Chivers, however, came out to see us off. Though his coat soaked up the rain, he beamed and offered us his good wishes. We made our way out of the camp past two sodden sentries.

Geo and I sat in the rear of a small wagon, while Hopkins drove and Sir Francis rode his charger alongside.

"Yoo, hoo!" Lady Chase called to us from the open window of her coach. "What a lovely day to begin our journey!" Now quite wet ourselves, we merely nodded politely. Fanny had decided to accompany her son and return to London. Apparently, she had devised a new plan to increase the revenues of the custard shops she owned in the capital and was eager to put the scheme into operation. Her coach driver was a slight fellow bent to a sagging "C" to avoid the rain. He took no notice of any of us, only interested in quick nips from his flask.

That is how Sir Francis, Private Hopkins, Lady Chase, Geo and myself came to make our way toward London, which was, after all, the goal of our efforts since we departed Bridgetown. My worries were threefold: 1) The major's need to punish Jacobites, 2) his insistence that Geo and I were members of that dangerous conspiracy and 3) that Lady Chase's prattle on the subject of custard might drive us mad.

Chapter Three
Phantom Firkins

WE DID NOT HAVE far to travel, as Wexford was reasonably close aboard. The road was poor, however, and we bounced mightily. Private Hopkins made to keep up with Major Chase, who set his horse at a brisk trot. Lady Chase followed behind, her coach driver in a dripping funk. Clouds hunkered overhead and washed us in a steady drizzle. I wished more than anything to be aboard a ship smoothly taking the seas rather than bobbing in a wagon on a rutted Irish road.

We had no sooner left the sight of the regiment than the major halted the wagon and ordered us to be fettered.

"H-h-hopkins!," Sir Francis barked. "D-d-did you bring the short lengths of rope?"

"Oh, yes, sir," Hopkins replied with a satisfied smile.

"Th-then t-t-tie their hands. The coddling of Jacobites ends now."

Hopkins tied us quickly. Since he was a soldier and a landsman, his knot work left much to be desired. I was fairly sure Geo and I could easily escape our bonds.

"Did you offer your prisoners some refreshment?" Lady Chase asked Sir Francis when her coach drew abreast of the wagon.

"M-m-mother, they just had their breakfast. They n-n-need not eat nor drink."

"A parsimonious hospitality reflects very poorly upon the host, dear," Lady Chase remarked disapprovingly. "A bit of biscuit and some water would suit, Private Hopkins." The private promptly carried out her order.

"B-b-but Mother, these are my prisoners," Sir Francis protested. "F-f-father gave *me* command of this expedition."

"If only," she mused, "I had some of my custards to provide." Then to Geo and me, "You *do* favor custard, do you not?"

"Yes, ma'am," we replied in unison.

"Then you must visit my custard shops in London and partake of our signature flavors — lime-strawberry, vanilla-mint, molasses-mustard, beef-liver, radish-turnip, parsley-mushroom ... there are so many from which to choose. I'm sure you will find several favorites."

Geo and I again nodded politely and were thereafter happy with musty biscuit and water.

Soon we finished our victuals and continued our journey. As we rolled along I saw Sir Francis use his spyglass to examine each hill as we approached it. None seemed to meet his requirements.

"Major Chase," I began, wiping the soft rain from my eyes. "It is most kind of you to escort us to London in this way. We could have not asked for a finer guard of honor on our way toward fulfilling your father's scheme. However, these bonds hardly seem necessary, since we are not prisoners, but, instead, emissaries of athletic good will." I tried to impart this little speech with as much humility, yet manly good cheer as I could muster.

"N-n-nonsense, you two are d-d-deadly Jacobites," Sir Francis answered abruptly. "The bonds remain. B-b-but do not fret, you shall not have need of them for long." After checking again with the spyglass, Sir Francis pointed toward a hill with a substantial tree on its summit. "H-h-hopkins, that is our next stop."

As we approached the hill, I believe I saw a figure scramble down from the tree and disappear into the underbrush, but I was unsure, given the rain that dripped into my eyes. Irish weather can quickly change: shafts of sunlight suddenly shot through the clouds as the rain abruptly ceased. We bounced up a narrow sheep track — slow going for the wide army wagon. On reaching the oak that reigned at the summit, we saw the town of Wexford spread below us. Beyond the town was the Irish Sea and the mountains of Wales appearing and dissolving in the distant mist.

"P-p-private, you did equip the wagon with two long ropes?" Sir Francis asked.

"Yes, sir. They're in the back —" Hopkins frowned and then began to frantically search the back of the wagon. "Well, they was right here. I swear it, sir."

Geo looked at me and hid a smirk. When I first climbed aboard the wagon at the camp, I saw the ropes. I kicked them to the back of the wagon. Geo saw this and after we departed the camp, he casually nudged them overboard onto the ground.

"W-w-well, Hopkins, you must go down into the town and secure some rope. We will await here. B-b-be quick about it, man."

The wind shot through the gnarled oak and its leaves rustled like a thousand sails. Yeasty clouds rose and the sun again disappeared. Fine sheets of rain peppered the ground as the major, Geo and I waited for Hopkins to return. Geo and I sat with our backs to the trunk of the oak, Sir Francis remained on his horse, his back straight and his gaze clear. As for escape, there was little chance of outrunning the major's mount.

Lady Chase's coach creaked into our midst after a long, slow climb up the hill. She opened the coach window and waved to Geo and me. "Yoo-hoo. Hello there. Are we all enjoying ourselves? I must say I am. Though I wonder if I might have Mr. Washington join me here in the coach? I am in need of assistance in devising new flavors of custard." She beamed expectantly.

Nettled that his mother wished to put one of his prisoners to such frivolous employment, Sir Francis ordered Geo to remain where he was.

"Sir Francis, if I might, sir?" I asked. The major nodded, so I asked my questions. "What is the likelihood of Jacobites in America? Do you know of any American Jacobites, sir?"

"N-n-no, I do not. And that is why vigilance is essential to prevent the contagion of Jacobism establishing itself in the American colonies. There is no telling what American Jacobism might lead to — an American pope, an American king, even such fevered notions as an independent America. That would be unnatural, of course."

"I think you forget our allegiance to King George, sir," Geo said with some feeling. He was obviously offended by such talk.

"Yes," I added. "We are British citizens, after all. Why would we take so precipitous a leap as to declare our independence?"

"R-r-rebellion is a tricky thing," Sir Francis said. "Like a water mold rotting the trunk of a seemingly healthy tree. Let the rot grow unchecked and even a small breeze could fell the tree. And I have heard that you Americans are a contentious and difficult lot, prone to fitful winds."

"'Tis true that Boston can be a town of fitful winds," said Geo, smiling at his own joke.

I confess I felt some despair. How could I convince Sir Francis to release us? I was taken aback when he asked *me* a question.

"W-w-what about yourself, Attucks?" Sir Francis said. "I am most surprised and impressed to meet a dark fellow who has such command of the language."

"Why should it surprise?" I replied hotly. This was a subject that instantly put me in a temper. Some of my own African people disliked my learning and my use of proper English. And yet, though I speak as well as any English officer, the English, too, find fault with me.

"I received instruction at a fine school in New York," I retorted. "Until I was thrown out of it for my African skin. But my master was a man of strong convictions and he paid handsomely for a first-rate tutor. He was determined that I be educated and so I am. Are Africans less able to learn from good teachers than men of lighter skin? Do you think there is something that hobbles us from learning? Or should not an African man use the King's English? Would you feel more at ease should I say, *'Alltwo dem man done fuh smaa't'* or should I rather say: 'Both those men are smart?' Well?" I demanded, "Which way *should* an African man from America speak?"

The major was flustered. "I-I-I d-d-do not know. I-I-I confess I had not thought too deeply on the subject. But 'tis a fair point, you make, Attucks. A fair point."

"Got the ropes, Major!" Hopkins reported with a satisfied shout. We had been so engrossed in our discussion we had not seen him climb the hill. The rain had again ceased and the sun struggled to break through a fleet of reaching clouds.

"Well done, Hopkins," Sir Francis said. "Did you requisition the lines from a chandlery in the harbor?"

"No, sir. I just walked me down the 'ill and a strange old Irish fellow approached me. Said his name was Peter Bird and asked 'ow he might assist a soldier of the king. Soon enough he gave me them ropes. Even suggested we use this old oak. Said that main branch gave a lovely view of the town."

"V-v-very thoughtful of him," the major said." You may proceed with the execution, Hopkins."

Before long Hopkins had everything arranged. The twin ropes hung from the long branch of the oak o'erlooking the town. The wagon was in place directly below the ropes — Lady Chase had provided helpful advice on the proper alignment of the wagon. Hopkins had us standing in the back of the wagon, hands tied and with nooses around our necks. I noted a distinctive odor coming from the rope. It was an acrid smell, but I could not place it.

It was now real to me that I would die in Ireland, far from my humble beginnings in busy New York town. For Geo the prospect of death must have been especially bitter. He was not a seaman like myself. We sailors face the possibility of shipwreck and death with every voyage. It is our lot and we become accustomed to it. But Geo had come aboard the *Mary B.* to acquire a fortune in London, not to die on an Irish hill.

"We're ready, sir."

"I must protest this treatment, Major," Geo spoke up. "We have told you time and again that we are not Jacobites. And indeed know of not a single Jacobite in America."

"B-b-but you could *become* Jacobites," the major retorted. "The fact you participated in a Jacobite Irish rising indicates your possible Jacobite leanings, even if you are presently unaware of them. Put your feelings aside for a moment and think of *my* position. I have become fond of both of you. However, my duty to protect the king overrules petty personal considerations. I don't like it any more than you do, but I'm afraid it must be summary justice for you both."

The major turned his back to us, took out his spyglass and surveyed ships on the Irish Sea. A large flock of sheep approached him, but he took no notice. Still facing out to sea, Sir Francis waved his hand to Hopkins. He wished Hopkins to go ahead with the hanging.

The moment of death is frightful. At least that is what I have read in books. I had passed close to it on many occasions during my eventful years at sea, but had never stood in the spot where circumstance and fate coincide. I very nearly began to cry. Yes, I'm quite sure I did weep a few bitter tears.

Geo, however, became very quiet, even relaxed. He no longer strained against his hand fetters and did not shoot furious glances at Hopkins. It was a most impressive display of a cool head under fire. Lady Chase busied herself with writing in her notebook.

Hopkins stood behind us in the wagon. He reached up and grabbed both ropes, intent on giving each a sharp tug to ensure both were ready. To all our amazement, both ropes parted in clouds of rotten manila. A loud *crack* followed and the oak branch to which the rotten ropes were attached shuddered and crashed to the ground.

Furthermore, something or someone unsettled the horse that was harnessed to the wagon. The frightened steed bolted, charging down the hill at breakneck speed. As it sped off, Hopkins lost his balance and toppled out of the wagon. Geo and I, meanwhile, fell *into* the wagon. As we rolled down slope we saw Sir Francis gamely attempting to mount his horse, but was prevented from doing so by the great herd of sheep that now engulfed him.

Our wagon just missed colliding with Lady Chase's coach. As we passed we saw her look up from her writing and cheer us with a friendly wave.

The wagon caromed down the hill, drawn by its crazed horse and the pull of gravity. Geo and I were little more than spectators to this, as we could not move forward nor grab the reins. The horse and wagon rolled onto the main road, clattering past the buildings of the town. Finally it slowed as it entered the town square. A swift-moving Irishman ran out from a doorway, grabbed the horse's reins and brought the wagon to a stop. Another man, clad in the woolen clothes of a fisherman, appeared. With a sharp knife he cut our bonds and motioned for us to follow him. We climbed down from the wagon, still a bit dazed from our headlong descent, and made ready to flee. A lazy rain again began to fall as the Irish weather changed its unsettled mind.

Major Chase, while not of the strongest stomach given his inability to watch an execution or, indeed, any violence whatsoever, was otherwise an energetic and resourceful officer. He had extricated himself from the flock of sheep and followed the wild path of the wagon through the town. Astride his black charger — which we learned was a mare named Pip — he came galloping down the main street toward the square, his sword drawn. It seemed Geo and I would once again be his prisoners.

As he clattered across the cobbles, something most unexpected occurred. A flurry of small barrels flew from the upper window of a house bordering the street. These firkins dropped in graceful arcs, landing just ahead of Pip. The casks shattered, releasing their contents of creamy Irish butter across the cobbles. Pip lost her grip in the slippery mess and fell. Sir Francis slid off his mount, dropped his sword and rolled for a considerable distance in the golden lard. Geo and I and our fisherman guide laughed out loud, even though we would have been better served to run.

Pip popped up, apparently unhurt by her slippery slide. Sir Francis groaned and stirred. He rose unsteadily to his feet and, his head down and his hands on his knees. Chase slowly gathered his wits. Then Private Hopkins come into view at a dead run. Just as Sir Francis stood again to his full height, Hopkins hit the pond of rain-soaked butter and lost his balance. Like one of the woods in a game of bowls, Hopkins slid on his back into Sir Francis. The major fell in a jumble with the private. They struggled to get up but no sooner had Sir Francis got waveringly to his feet, than Hopkins pulled him down; when Hopkins was nearly standing, Sir Francis capsized him. And so they traded places in a stumbling perambulation.

Following up the rear, Lady Chase arrived in her coach. She grasped the situation immediately and called out to Sir Francis, "Mind the butter on the road, dear."

Our fisherman guide, a Mr. McPeek, insisted we depart. He led us down to the waterfront and onto his small fishing sloop. Raising sail, we cast off and soon were making our way across the Irish Sea. The rain stopped. The sun poked holes in the clouds, showing us golden stepping stones toward Wales.

We carefully scrutinized every vessel astern of us, sure that Sir Francis would pursue us all the way to London.

Chapter Four
The Beast of the Thames

"GEO, YOU WERE A PICTURE of calm with that noose around your neck," I said. We were aboard the fishing sloop of Mr. McPeek at evening twilight, crossing the Irish Sea. A fair northwest wind drove us smartly towards the Welsh coast. Our plan was to clear St. Govan's Head in the light of the waxing moon and make Bristol the following day.

Geo smiled. "Was I brave?"

"Aye. You laughed in the very face of death." I handed him the small cask of water from which I had just swigged.

Geo hesitated, his eyes fixed upon the cask where my lips had touched. Then he looked at me, laughed, and drank heartily.

"I knew there was little chance of being properly hanged," he said. "We might get a bit of a burn from the rope, but we would not die."

"Pray how did you know it?" I asked.

"When I stepped upon the wagon and Hopkins put the noose around my neck, I saw an old Irishman. He stood in the cover of some trees. He waved furtively toward the trunk of the large oak. And then I saw."

"Saw what?"

"A fall of sawdust upon the ground. Remember that as a surveyor I am also a woodsman. So I knew there was sufficient dust to indicate that the branch had been nearly severed where it adjoined the trunk. Only the smallest tug was needed to bring the branch down."

"And the old man?"

"When I looked back to the spot where he was standing, the old fellow was gone."

"'Twas one of the little people, it was," observed McPeek.

"Yes," said I, "one of the little people with a very sharp saw."

With few funds in our possession, Geo and I could partake only of simple fare and engage meager lodgings as we made our way to London. After thanking McPeek, who refused any payment, we went ashore at Bristol.

On our way to London, we walked, rode in wagons, danced with a troupe of traveling balladeers and even went for a few leagues by boat on the River Thames. Geo and I spent a considerable time together. Nothing was spoken between us concerning our relation to each other, but I could sense from the turning of a head, the readiness of a smile, the offering of a hand for help up a riverbank, and many other small signs, that an understanding of sorts was evolving between us: That we had in some way become less two men thrown together by circumstances and more compatriots and shipmates.

On at least one occasion we became aware that Sir Francis Chase was no more than a league behind us and was actively seeking our trail. Thus, our trip from Bristol to London was a story of many adventures, narrow escapes and much vexing privation. That, however, is a tale for another time, as I seem to have misplaced that portion of my account.

Upon our arrival at the edge of London town itself, our small amount of money was exhausted. We were once again walking with little hope of a roof over our heads.

A passing wagon, driven by a man with rounded shoulders and drooping head, stopped to pick us up. Geo and I, eager to accept this stranger's good deed, swung ourselves up into the wagon. We settled ourselves as best we could on its load of fresh mule hides. Even the foul smell of the skins did not chase away my happiness at riding instead of walking. I was a man of the sea and used to riding the strong back of a ship, not endless slogging through mud and dust. The man, stooped and worn by time and hard work, told us he was named Argus MacGloam.

"Bless you for letting us ride with you," I said, not expecting more than a grunt in response.

"Not at all, boys. Happy to be of service." MacGloam replied with a spirit that contradicted his years. Certainly so ancient a man would not speak with such vigor.

"Have you worked hard upon the land in your long years?" I asked, in respect of my elders.

"Nonsense," MacGloam snorted. "Only last Saturday was I given to drive this wagon. I am but a youth of seventeen."

Neither Geo nor I said a further word to him. We were both amazed to see a young fellow who had been worked so hard that 17 looked like 67. "'Tis a testament to the vibrant nature of the British economy that so much work could be squeezed from a fellow so young," Geo said with some pride.

For Geo and myself, this ride with MacGloam was unexpectedly glorious and inspiring. The wagon crested the top of a small hill and we beheld a wonder. Spread out before us, extending to the very edges of our vision, was the city of London. Though I had beheld many sights in my sea voyages and had visited great cities before, the overwhelming expanse, richness and industry of London was one that nearly took my breath from me. And for Geo, he who had experienced nothing more grand than the muddy streets of Williamsburg in Virginia, the moment was one of nearly perfect awe.

London was a prospect unmatched. Mere words did not render it justice: the spires of uncounted churches, the towers of royal palaces and ancient fortifications, the massive dome of St. Paul's, the elegant mansions of the peerage, great expanses of shops and houses, markets and squares, courts and parks, the Thames bridges, the hundreds of boats and ships, armies of horses, carriages and wagons and the jostling, yelling, fighting, stealing, whoring, toiling people by the hundreds of thousands. There was nothing like the great breathing, growing beast of London. This beast sucked in water and oats and beef and flour and tea and rum and ale and sugar, and breathed out great billows of coal smoke and steam, piss and shite, blood, gold and glory.

"You surely have arrived now, Geo," I said as the wagon passed the top of the hill and the brief glimpse of London was blocked by a jostle of half-timbered buildings.

Captivated by the fortune presented by the massive city, and with a new feeling of apprehension he had perhaps not expected, Geo struggled to reply.

"I have arrived," he finally managed to repeat with cold conviction. It had lately occurred to him that the great city, which he had imagined he would conquer in one bold rush, might not only be indifferent to his efforts, but even implacably opposed to them. And further thoughts, no doubt, troubled him. Like the beast it was, the city sucked in not just provisions and victuals, chattel and fuel, but people, as well.

Some the city smiled upon and glorified, others it discarded, issuing forth their corpses like so many stripped beef bones.

With a gentle tug on the reins, MacGloam stopped his wagon and announced that he had arrived at his destination. "Goodbye, Mr. Washington and Mr. Darius," MacGloam said. "Was honored to serve your honors. Happy to give a ride on the morrow."

"We are staying in town," Geo replied.

"Still and all," MacGloam said. "Would be pleased to have you ride with me."

Geo nodded his head and gave me a wink. "Right. Tomorrow then."

"I'll be looking for you."

"Yes, good man. You do that. But if you don't see us, you'll continue on your way, won't you?

"Aye. That I will. But I'll be pleased to give you a ride."

Geo and I climbed down into the road, now quite eager to walk.

"Yes, yes. Goodbye, then," Geo said. We were back on foot. In only a few ticks of a clock, however, we heard a horse clip-clop alongside us. Geo sighed at MacGloam's persistence. But it was not MacGloam at the reins, but another man who looked aged. And he was accompanied by an aged woman, who sat close by him, eying us with the satisfaction of a falcon who has spied a sparrow.

"Pray, forgive our intrusion, but we noted your name was spoken by the fellow in the wagon yonder. We also noted your tall stature and a purposeful stride that could well have been honed by long surveying trips into the wooded wilderness whence you learned the value and comeliness of the lands that lie to the west of the mountains of Virginia in the American colonies." The aged man paused and then added, "That is to say, might ye be Mr. George Washington?"

We sized up the old fellow and his companion. The man was tall of stature yet thin of constitution. He had a wizened aspect to his face, which was frosted with two wild white eyebrows and topped by a drift of snowy hair. His companion was a plump woman of dark complexion, who exhibited a nervous agitation; she repeatedly adjusted her shawl across her shoulders and swiveled her head to take in her surroundings.

"Yes, I am he," Geo answered. "Whom are you to inquire?"

"Who else could we be?" the woman shot back. "We are Prudence and Hawkins, sent by the Baron Mowenholtz to meet you and take you to his house on Julian Square."

Geo and I were happy at the prospect of a ride to No. 4 Julian Square. Though we knew the street name and the number, as to where the house actually sat we had little sense. How these two servants knew where we would be was almost as much of a mystery to us as knowing the way to Julian Square. I asked Hawkins as much.

"We knew you was coming from Bristol. 'Tis a big country, true, yet there are only so many roads by which one can travel. And the time required for the trip is well established. Besides all of that, the baron sent word you were close."

Prudence, for her part, was less sanguine about the ease of the meeting. "We been three days waiting here, sleeping in the wagon in the park. Was enough to drive a soul mad, it was."

"We are most happy for your efforts," Geo said diplomatically. "We have no experience with a city this vast and would be hard-pressed to make a good account of ourselves."

"That's why the baron sent us!" Prudence countered. "He don't want you wandering round from Westminster to Whitechapel. Ya' wouldn't find Julian Square before Candlemas."

"Yes, ma'am," Geo and I chimed.

After meeting us in a place called Knight's Bridge, we rolled past the large green expanse of Hyde Park, and then by a series of turnings we traveled through a very handsome section of town, which Hawkins identified as St. James Square. Thence we proceeded through Charing Cross, past the towering house of the Earl of Northumberland. In the road at Charing Cross was set up a pillory. A crowd here heaped derision and obscenity upon the two criminals locked within the pillory's wooden fingers. A few of the mob punctuated their comments by tossing rotten apples or a dead cat at the men. The crowd laughed and drank ale until another dead animal could be procured.

From thence we passed onto a wide avenue of great throngs of people. Gaudy and colorful signs hung above each place of business. We saw the gold-gilt coaches of the wealthy with their retinues of footmen in rich hues of cobalt and green, crimson and gold. Most of the footmen rode upon the rear of the coach, but in the front of each of the grander coaches were two running footmen. They kept pace with the horses and each carried a small flag with which to wave away the mob of people that pressed into every corner.

And as far as the eye could see were the turning wheels of commerce. So crowded was the road and walking pavements with chair repairmen and pickle barrels and cobblers and firkins of butter and booksellers and milkmaids and common peddlers, that there was little room to squeeze by. In response to a question, Prudence was quick to tell us that everyone knew the street was called "The Strand" and why were we asking?

And there were the smells that surged like waves; of wood smoke and beer brewing, beef roasting and bread baking, leather tanning and fabric dyeing, the low tide reek of the Thames mud and the sweaty shirts of the porters and chair men, rotting fish and the putrefying carcasses of horses and rats, sheep's heads and cats.

All the while, Hawkins, who claimed he had lived all his life in London, attempted to describe for us some of the principal aspects of the great imperial city. He had time aplenty, given the slow travel caused by so many horses, wagons, drays, carts, chaises, carriages, chariots and coaches; and the hurrying tradesmen and postmen and bread sellers and whores and beggars and those selling hot and cold viands and the cutpurses, sharpers and mountebanks playing their fiddles and organs and hurdy-gurdies. Such multitudes of people and wagons and coaches often got bunched and jammed as to bring travel to a complete standstill. At which time danger lay in the fights that erupted between coach drivers and the prospect of a cut from their hissing whips.

The noise was unimaginable: milk-girls crying out, chimney sweeps hawking loud, coal men with a rough shout, newspaper sellers blasting on their tin trumpets and still more — card match vendors and apple men, boot-blacks, pie men and ballad singers. It seemed every soul was shouting about something they were selling or buying or just because noise was the right and privilege and duty of every Londoner.

"London is a prodigious machine of many people all scurryin' about," Hawkins intoned as they rolled along, his voice and manner displaying a theatrical air. "A vast beehive of streets and avenues and lanes and alleys and yards and mews and courts, a mighty encampment which expands with every year. That is to say, 'tis big." Warming to his subject, Hawkins continued, with suitable corrections and additions delivered by Prudence in her agitated manner.

"Observe that if ye were a bird flying high overhead, you'd see the river tracing a shallow letter 'M' below you. The left leg of the M is where the river flows north past Westminster, the first crest of the M is where the foul waste of the Fleet ditch empties into the river as it heads east. Then the great stream dips south, just beyond the Tower. The second crest of the M is found at Shadwell, and finally the right leg of the letter is where the sea-seeking water flows south, hard by the Isle of Dogs. Many hundreds of thousands reside in the grasp of the river, within the bills of mortality, and to each of them must come the sustenance of life, their daily portion, their bread and meat, their cake and milk — that is to say, victuals."

"Aye, we all must eat," said Geo.

"Well then, your fish can be had at Billingsgate," Hawkins continued, "your apples and plums at Covent Garden and the Borough market — "

"Nor forgetting the fruit market at Three Cranes Wharf," said Prudence.

"And corn at Bear Quay and Queenhithe, chickens and turkeys and geese and eggs at Leadenhall, and the great stinking cattle and sheep and horse pens at Smithfield. What of food for these animals and the many others?" Hawkins asked as he reached forward to give a friendly pat to one of the wagon's horses. He lost his balance and nearly fell off the wagon seat. Prudence only saved him by deftly grabbing his waistcoat and yanking him back aboard.

"So, yes, as I was sayin'," Hawkins resumed, "what of the food for the beasts? Well, there is hay for sale at Smithfield, Whitechapel, the Borough and, with respect, at Haymarket."

"London is also a great port," I said, feeling that I must put in a word for my fellow seamen.

"Aye, that it is," Hawkins replied, pleased for the show of interest from his audience. "Ships sail all the way upriver from the sea. 'Tis only the great mass of London Bridge that bars their progress further upstream. So the ships swarm the river east o' the bridge. All the coal the city burns for warmth comes by sea from Newcastle. And what else is unloaded at the docks? Everythin' you can imagine: cheese, meal, timber, corn, cherries — "

"Whiting," interjected Prudence.

"Herring," replied Hawkins quickly.

"Sprats," countered Prudence.

"Mackerel."

"Oysters."

"Sole."

"Turbot."

"Codling."

"Flounder."

"That is to say, much fish," said I.

Hawkins winked at my summation. "Aye and what sort a' people eat all this fruit of the sea? Well, there's the high and mighty — the king and queen, the Prince of Wales, a fine lot of dukes, earls, countesses, viscounts, baronets, knights and such. But there be many others, too: bankers and men of capital, shopkeepers and clerks, clockmakers and metalsmiths, mechanics, tailors, carpenters, weavers and wig makers, brewers, bakers and cheesemongers, washerwomen, coal heavers, lumpers, tanners and toshers, mudlarks, bone pickers and the nightsoil men, to name the least. There is not an occupation nor trade known upon the earth not found here in town."

Finally, he warned Geo and I of dangers: "Do not stop to listen to the ballad singers, they work with the pickpockets, who can effortlessly slide your sword from its sheath or take your coin purse from your pocket. Beware, as well, of tall porters carrying baskets on their shoulders, 'specially near twilight."

"Whatever for?" Geo asked earnestly.

"Inside the basket sits a young boy. As the porter passes by, the boy pops up from within his sanctum and plucks off your wig, disappearing back into the basket before you even see him. Do not be fooled by what seems real, but is only a ruse. Take note, by example, of beggars who seek money from carriage owners, claiming the horse has bitten them. The gruesome wound they display 'tis only an artificial sore made with unslaked lime, soap, and the rust of old iron, sprinkled on the back of their hand. Yes, and there are many more such diversions and distractions, confusions and sleights of hand, tricks and snares — that is to say, take care in London town!"

By and by the Strand turned into Fleet Street and we passed the great cathedral of St. Paul's, a towering vault into which one could fit every church in humble New York. From thence we swung round onto Newgate Street and continued what I imagined was north, but cannot say with certainty. With some considerable embarrassment for a navigator like myself, I must confess I was lost entirely and could not follow the progression of turnings, crossings and windings, which brought us to a narrow passage whose name was Bull Pure Alley. This narrow conveyance, Hawkins informed us in a stage whisper, led directly onto Julian Square.

At the alley he and Prudence took their leave, as they had other tasks to perform whose nature they cared not divulge. Hawkins bade us to make our own way to No. 4. The baron was not currently in residence, as he had business in Kent, but he would arrive soon enough.

Geo and I walked on and soon the square hove into view. It was a crowded assembly of houses, some grand in extent, all arranged around a small central greensward. Many of the houses had seen hard service and were clearly in need of drydock and a refit. The neighborhood, while pretending toward a gentile civility, had more the air of creeping squalor. Cracked paint went untouched, green shoots grew from chimney pots and eaves, and shacks huddled in a few back yards, housing those unlucky people sliding downward from honest work toward beggary and crime. The impression of decline was further heightened by the herds of sheep and goats that were regularly walked through the square toward the Smithfield sheep pens — the animals left their black calling cards spread across the cobbles.

Number 4, the house the baron rented, was in the process of renewal. It was an ample residence, a four-decker with many rows of portholes — those openings of air and light that landlubbers suffer to call windows. The building extended well back from the street and ended in a fenced yard.

We entered and found a crew of workmen toiling at repainting and plastering and other repairs. We inquired with the workmen as to the whereabouts of the baron. Immediately we ran afoul of Boyle, the foreman.

"Who are you?" Boyle grabbed me by the front of my sailor's blouse and lowered his large, ugly face toward mine. He was a brute of a fellow, with coal eyes and a crooked nose. The fish from his lunch announced itself with every word.

"I am Darius Attucks, master mariner and companion to Squire George Washington of Virginia." I nodded toward Geo, who nodded back.

"Where is that dog, von Mulct?" the foreman asked. "He has not paid us for a fortnight."

Geo took a step forward. "Do you mean to enquire as to the whereabouts of Meissel von Mulct, the Baron Mowenholtz?"

Boyle let go of me and turned to Geo. "Yeah, that's right. The baron. Where is he?"

"We had hoped you would know," Geo said quite reasonably.

"Oh, ... did you now?" he said with some menace.

"Yes, we have just arrived from Ireland," I said quickly. "We were told to meet him here."

"So you two are friends of the baron? Attucks and Warrington?"

"That's Washington," Geo corrected cheerily.

"Don't cut in when I'm talkin', lad." This admonition was delivered harshly, with a raised arm and the threat of violence.

"But I must defend my name, sir," Geo explained.

Boyle's face grew radish red. He glared at Geo and it seemed the large foreman was losing his temper. I had no idea what he would do if he became truly enraged.

A quarter hour later, when dirt had ceased to fall on the box, I stressed to Geo the importance of not giving in to panic — he needed to maintain a stoic calm. This was not advice that he took easily. I suspect that may have been due to our somewhat vexing situation.

"D, we're buried alive!" he yelled as best he could given that we were cramped inside a wooden crate. Boyle and his workers had pushed us into the box before shoveling dirt atop us. While Geo was right we were indeed buried alive, I didn't think it was helpful to dwell on the point.

"Yes. We are. However, I think our best course of action may be to remain calm."

"But we will surely die!" Geo hissed.

"This is the second time you have declared your death," I said. "It does lose some force with repetition."

"No. Surely, this is the first time I have proclaimed it," Geo replied.

"You don't remember the wreck of the *Mary B.*? You were positive you would perish in the waves or be dashed upon a rock. I did not allow it to happen then nor will I let you die now." I didn't reveal my feelings of divine commission to protect and shepherd the young man. Sometimes there are no words to discuss those thoughts we hold most deeply. I had not sensed the nature of Geo's devotion to the almighty and so I left that discussion to another time when we would talk of my pay.

"Truly I am indebted to you for the shipwreck rescue," Geo choked out, "however, I am unsure how the second will be effected. As it appears that you are as deeply buried as I am."

This last observation by Geo was indeed a troubling one. I had not yet puzzled out an answer to give the anxious young fellow.

"You are as clear-eyed und upstanding a fellow as I could hope to accompany my dear friend und associate, young Mister Washington." The well-dressed man said in his shimmering German accent. "I zalute you, Mister Attucks." The man who spoke to me was none other than Meissel von Mulct, the Baron Mowenholtz himself.

He stood before us in a jaunty fashion, one hand upon his hip and the other hand out thrust out, resting on a gilded cane. His clothes were most splendid: a scarlet waistcoat with delicate gold brocade, a golden yellow jacket faced in white silk, yellow silk breeches, the finest linen hose, and supple black dogskin shoes with round buckles. His exquisite wig was expertly powdered and atop it, like a frigate riding a wave, was a large, scarlet tricorn hat edged in snowy owl feathers. The color of his hat perfectly matched the hue of his waistcoat.

I was at a disadvantage to reply to his greeting as I was still bound and lying in the wooden box with Geo. The formerly murderous foreman Boyle was now solicitous, stepping down to help Geo up from the box that only minutes before had been his coffin.

"There ya' are, young sir," Boyle cooed. "I'll have these ropes off straight away." Boyle's workmen freed me as well and soon we were clear of the box and out of the cellar of the baron's house.

The burying incident, Boyle later explained as he playfully clapped me on the back with one of his massive hands, was nothing more than a simple mistake. "Not a bit of ill will was ever intended," Boyle assured us in his thick London accent. "Was all a misunderstandin', it was." Boyle explained everything: he had assumed we would pay him what the baron owed for the renewal of the house. When we were not forthcoming with the proper monies and when Geo corrected the foreman on Geo's proper name, Boyle became vexed.

When the baron arrived only minutes later, he settled up with Boyle and ordered our immediate disinterment. Once explained, the matter faded to insignificance. The baron paid for one of Boyle's workers to fetch a copious supply of ale and wine and soon our little band was quite jolly. Whilst the workers and their foreman toasted to the long ties of good will between Britain and the baron's principality of Farkenheine-Ausgas, the baron took Geo and I into one of the alcoves of the entrance hall for a more discrete discussion.

"It is quite wonderful zat I am seeing you again, young George," the baron said warmly. His Teutonic-tinged speech did take some getting used to as he was sometimes a bit hard to understand. However, one could only feel friendship for a German who had made the effort to learn the proper language of civilized discourse.

He was a comely man and his fine clothes only added to the general effect of a prosperous and robust nobility. Of average height, the baron was thin of frame and wiry of limb.

His wig fit him perfectly and only his reddish eyebrows gave a hint to the color of his hair. His aquiline nose and fair-skinned face showed both intelligence and a sanguine aspect that spoke of his great breeding and character. In every way he was a model of those traits most prized by society.

The baron's eyes were of a most unusual green tint. Add to this rarity the dulcet tones of the German's voice and his effect can only be described as strangely entrancing — like a cat at the edge of a fire, eyes blazing of another world. Or, as Gullah people say, *"He be stonish wil'cat."*

I will admit to liking the baron immediately — I'm sure his rescue of Geo and I from premature burial had no bearing on this. He was a nobleman with the common touch.

Events were soon to suggest that the baron may not have been entirely reciprocal in his feelings toward me. But that episode is revealed below. I must not fail at my task of chronicler by relating the events out of their natural order.

Chapter Five
Our Convivial Assembly

SO GREAT WAS our revel with the foreman and his
workers that the next morning we awoke lying in various
groupings across the floor like the slain citizens of a sacked
city. A clutch of women lay scattered among the men,
further testifying to the general air of celebration and good
cheer occasioned the previous night. As the women awoke
they demanded payment from the still-sleepy workmen. And
like paid-off sailors on a newly docked ship, the women
trooped down the gangplank — the bright morning sun less
kind than the evening glow of wine and candlelight — and
headed back to Gropecunt Lane.

The baron's upstairs apartments had already been
completed and so he had ample opportunity to dress. He
descended the stairs arrayed as resplendently as the day
previous. Stopping five steps from the bottom, he turned to
show himself to us.

"Surely, fine clothes are one of the great joys of life,
ja?" he exclaimed from his perch, a wry smile betraying both
his good nature and his fashionable sense of proper
appearance.

Geo and I nodded in agreement, with Geo quickly
looking down on his worn and dusty brown coat, waistcoat
and breeches. They had been only of medium quality in
Barbados. Now, after our shipwreck and journey from
Ireland, they were dirty and tired.

"Ja, ja, my young friend, George. From your
smallclothes to your coat, you are in need of refitting. That is
the furst thing we must do to get you started properly in
London."

Geo smiled and nodded at this.

From Geo, the baron turned to me. I was still wearing
my sailor's slops: loose canvas breeches ending at the knee, a
blue striped blouse, my oilskin coat and a wool tam o'shanter
on my tightly curled black hair. I was every inch a man of the
sea. On viewing me, the baron's expression soured. "You,
Africa man. We must get you fit to appear before a better sort
of people, ja? We are off to ze tailor!"

With several turnings here and crossings there, the baron, Geo and I soon left Julian Square behind. I was hard pressed to follow as city navigation is not my strongest suit, but I hoped that the young surveyor Geo was even then laying out a map of the town in his head.

We followed the rapid stride of the baron as he nimbly avoided washerwomen and street vendors, sedan chairs and sword-dangling fops. Von Mulct led us across the busy precincts of Holborn Street and to the downstairs premises of a tailor named Jedediah Pratt. Mr. Pratt outfitted us with an assortment of serviceable enough clothes: A black coat, a faded blue waistcoat and brown breeches for Geo; a lavender coat, a mottled black waistcoat and grey breeches for me. When we had left the shop, Geo noticed a hole in his coat the size of a musket ball. My waistcoat, meanwhile, looked as if it had been inexpertly dyed black, as if to cover up a large red stain. While we pondered these discoveries, we stood aside for two undertakers. Between them they carried a fully dressed corpse down the stairs. Before long they returned to the street with a naked body, only its loins wrapped in a cloth.

"These clothes have been previously owned," Geo remarked sharply as he put his finger through the hole.

"Ja, I do think so," said a voice from behind us.

We turned to see the baron, resting on his cane. "We need to get a fast start, ja? And this way, ve don't have to wait a week or even two for London's slow-moving tailors to cut you a suit of clothes."

Geo was about to protest, but then nodded reluctantly.

"Come, ve will go to the nearest coffeehouse to plan our great enterprise."

Once again, Geo and I trailed the swift-of-foot German nobleman who could navigate the streets, alleys and back passages of London as if he knew them by heart.

When we arrived at tiny Burnhampton Court, there was a sedan chair waiting near the entrance to an establishment called the Janus Coffeehouse. The four chair bearers were thickset men with burly arms and barrel legs who seemed strong enough to tear down London Bridge. They meekly withdrew, however, as the baron approached.

As he came abreast of the sedan chair, von Mulct deftly wheeled around to face us. He opened the door of the chair and stepped aside — as if he had rehearsed the motions for the stage.

Geo and I watched in anticipation. A female leg, immodestly exposed to the calf, reached out and set down on the cobbles. What followed the shapely leg was a tall woman of most pleasing proportions. She was fitted out in a richly appointed blue dress of some lustrous fabric, a fashionable set of hair ribbons and a wig of aristocratic refinement. The woman's mature face matched the handsome assemblage of her clothes and suggested intelligence, perspicacity and wit. Her effect on Geo and myself was to produce delight and admiration, as if a goddess had descended from Olympia to stand shining before us in the fetid confines of the close courtyard.

"I present to you, Lady Antonia Montagrave," the baron intoned, "of London, Sussex and Edinburgh."

Geo stood rooted to his spot, transfixed. He got moving after I landed a well-placed kick to his shin. Then, forgetting his Virginia training in dance and gentlemanly composure, he lurched forward. When he stood before her, he doffed his hat and bowed. "I am honored, my lady." Her smile in response was even more handsome than her composed visage.

"And I am pleased to meet *you*, Mr. Washington." For a woman of her obvious refinement, I was surprised to hear a touch of gravel in her voice, a counterpoint to her graceful clothes and charming face. "And who is the Moorish fellow you have with you? Is he your slave?"

"No Lady Montagrave. He is — "

"I am Darius Attucks, my Lady," I completed Geo's sentence. "I am no slave but accompany Mr. Washington and act as his advisor and second."

She looked me over right then, giving me the approving tilt that I have seen from many a wharfside doxie. She liked the cut of my topgallants, is what I mean. But it was readily apparent that Geo was the prime focus of her interest.

As we followed the baron and Lady Montagrave into the Janus Coffeehouse, Geo shot me a reproachful look. "I

never named you my advisor or my second," he hissed.
"No, but *I* did."

Our little party was gathered at the end of a table in the least noisy corner of the coffeehouse. The baron and Lady Montagrave both sipped on cups of the acidic Arabic liquid. Geo and I chose tea, the more patriotic drink. By way of further introduction, the baron related to us that Lady Montagrave had been married to Henley Montagrave, the third Earl of Letchinwood, who was killed when a hayloft he was inspecting collapsed. A house maid who was accompanying him during the inspection lost all her clothes in the accident, but in a stroke of great luck was not harmed.

The coffeehouse was crowded with men who drank lakes of coffee, smoked their clay pipes, shouted about matters of the day and on the most effective methods for making money. Over there was a pudgy broker who worked at the Royal Exchange and wore a waistcoat too long and coat too short; just here was a dandy shipowner in perfect fashion who shouted rudely; across from him was a banker who pointed with the long stem of his pipe, nearly blinding his fellows. The discussion became heated on a number of topics:

- Whether the Whigs were doing their very best to ruin the country or whether the Tories could not do a much better job at mucking up affairs if given a chance;
- If the coming reform of the calendar, which would result in the loss of 11 days, would cause business to grind to a halt or be a boon for the printers of calendars and datebooks;
- If the ongoing craze for gin represented the utter corruption of British civilization or its highest achievement.

The passion reached such heights that at times coffee cups were emptied on opponents' heads, benches upended, clay pipes broken and wigs tossed under tables amid general tumult and dissension.

No such display disrupted our convivial assembly, however. The baron gathered us together to explain the method of our London enterprise. It seemed that the Baron Mowenholtz held deeds and other necessary legal appurtenances to an attractive assemblage of land parcels upon the Ohio River and its immediate environs and tributaries. He announced that he would offer this portfolio of land parcels in the valley of the Ohio to select members of London society. And in the process of this offering, he would also introduce them to George Washington, surveyor. The young man's firsthand knowledge of this expanse and his stories detailing the richness of the land on the far side of the Alleghenies would suffice to answer any questions and thus, it was hoped, induce them to purchase holdings of this land.

"Do you understand your role in this great endeavor, Mr. Washington?" Lady Montagrave asked tartly.

"I understand that I am to act as witness to the beauty and economic potential of these lands. And by doing so, aid in their sale."

"Lovely," Lady Montagrave purred, her half-lidded eyes fixed on Geo.

"For which service," Geo added, "I am to receive a just reward."

There was an awkward silence. I was about to speak when Geo added, "Mr. Attucks will also be recompensed, suitable to his efforts."

A cloud seemed to pass the baron's face at the mention of my name.

"Ja, ja, that is right," the baron said with a pleased nod to Geo and a darting glance toward me.

"Pray, tell us, when are we to begin this campaign of commerce?" I asked.

"Ve shall eat here, and then ve are off to our first appointment."

"Shame we couldn't get started a bit earlier," said Lady Montagrave. "We could have popped by Bridewell and seen the women and girls whipped."

"What is Bridewell? " Geo asked.

"'Tis a prison," she replied. "Of course, we could always go see the lunatics at Bedlam or perhaps view a hanging at Newgate ... if you prefer."

Geo tried to smile pleasantly, but he seemed aware that he was in unsurveyed territory.

The baron announced business should come first and

the enjoyments of Bridewell, Bedlam and Newgate would have to wait. It was then I noticed some vibrations in the air below the table. By the slight motions of Lady Montagrave's dress, I quickly determined that she was causing the sensation of motion. I peeked under the table and saw Lady Montagrave sliding her foot, sans shoe, along Geo's lower leg in a bold display of interest. From what I could discern, Geo was not displeased by this attention from the handsome noblewoman. He made no move to arrest the rhythmic stimulation.

The baron's first potential buyer was one Robert Smithson, ninth Earl of Claywich. As the baron related it, only a few years previously the earl had owned a large and well-appointed house in Westminster. A combination of gambling and artifact collecting had nearly bankrupted him, however. Possessing an insidious love for cards, Claywich spent long hours at the gaming table. On a particular occasion he became so engaged that he refused to leave the game and take sustenance. As he grew faint with hunger, he had a flash of inspiration. The lord whispered to his servant and the man disappeared. When he returned he presented Claywich with an ingenious new type of food that allowed the earl to stay at the gaming table while eating: a piece of bread in between two slabs of mutton. His gaming companions were so impressed with this invention, they dubbed it the "Claywich" and asked their retainers to bring them a similar meal. All except for one earl, who refused the culinary concoction, lost badly and left muttering about things being "quite wrong."

Claywich had a second great love. This was not, alas, his wife. (She was said to have left him for a French chevalier who regularly won large wagers playing tennis against French nobles at Versailles.) After gambling, Smithson's ardor was for collecting zoological specimens. Stuffed birds, fish and other animals filled a warehouse along the Thames in Blackfriars. Claywich sold his Westminster house to a newly-rich tanner for a very profitable sum. The amount not only saved him from debtor's prison, but allowed him to purchase the warehouse for his collection and also provided some ready capital for his gambling and wenching exploits.

The baron, Geo and I walked to Blackfriars to meet with the earl. Unfortunately, Lady Montagrave was unable to join us for our call to the earl; she had returned to her lodgings to privately discipline one of her footmen who, she claimed, was known for the worst sort of immodest behavior.

In the street we were joined by another associate of the baron, Sir Gerald Compliss. A solidly-built man, Sir Gerald was square-jawed and possessing of a serious, even sinister demeanor. Several scars peppered his face, marks that looked very much like sword cuts. Contrary to the dissipated appearance of so many in his class, Sir Gerald's physique was brash and imposing. To a man of the world such as myself, Compliss seemed a fellow not to be crossed. While the baron was charming and wry, Sir Gerald was his opposite in bearing and deportment. It was a wonder two men of so different manner remained friends. Such associations seem to appear often in the pursuit of money and commerce, but are seldom witnessed in the realm of social relations.

"Mr. Washington," the baron said while touching both their arms, "may I have the pleasure to introduce you to Sir Gerald Compliss, my very good friend und associate."

Sir Gerald sized up Geo with a hard look and then slowly smiled, but with none of the warmth one associates with that expression. "I understand from the baron that you are most knowledgeable regarding the western lands on the Ohio. I do hope you are a reliable witness."

"I have surveyed in these lands, sir, and am acknowledged by Lord Fairfax of Virginia to be a most reliable scout and surveyor." Geo answered with much pluck.

Sir Gerald seemed to weigh Geo's response and his smile waxed warmer. "I am quite sure you are as you say." Then the big man's gaze turned to me. He seemed neither friendly nor hostile, but rather like an astronomer gazing into his glass at a distant planet, trying to discern what, if anything, its significance might be. "And what of this dark man? What part has he to play in our little drama?"

Not waiting for the baron or Geo, I spoke up forthwith. "I am Darius Attucks, seaman and mate, lately attached to Mr. Washington as his advisor and second. As such, I am humbly at your service."

"I must say, I have never conducted a business

transaction whilst having a blackamoor in a position of trust," Sir Gerald said. "And I am not entirely convinced that it is wise to do so. Mr. Washington, do you warrant that this fellow is to be taken at his word? Or should we rather take him down to the Fleet Street auction blocks and sell him for a tidy profit?" The Englishman punctuated his question by placing his hand on his sword.

Sir Gerald was as hardened a character as any flog-happy captain I ever sailed with; here was a man who bore watching at all times. I noticed, via a speedy glance at the baron, that the German was observing the proceedings with a hard, judicial prospect — as if Sir Gerald's question was not his alone.

All eyes now fell on Geo, awaiting his response to Sir Gerald's query. I was not the least of the three in my expectation of his reply. The young Virginian drew a deep breath and composed himself. "I would guess there is not a better gauge of a man's mettle than his behavior in the hour of dire extremity. By that measure, I can attest that Mr. Attucks is a man of reliability and, indeed, honor." It appeared to me that Geo's resounding response as to the honor of an African man such as myself surprised even Geo. It seemed he had not expected to say what he did.

Meanwhile, a significant nod passed between the Englishman and the German. Thus, it seemed a bridge was crossed. When the baron said, "So, to business, then, ja?" I was included in the group that traipsed up Lord Claywich's stairs.

One might think that to a man of the sea such as myself, the vast collection of animal specimens surrounding us in the Earl of Claywich's warehouse would mean little. Indeed, the average sailor wouldn't give a ha'penny for dusty old polecat pelts and hedgehog skulls. But, the truth is that I had made a study of natural history via several books on the subject. Though I had not received any formal schooling on the subject, I considered myself very nearly an expert on such matters.

Through much of the proceedings, the earl and Geo jabbered on 'bout this animal or that bird, or some such snake. It was apparent that Geo's accounts of bears and beavers and other beasts made Lord Claywich increasingly excited so that, at the right time, the baron had only to produce the portfolio and Claywich fairly jumped at the chance to purchase several of the Ohio parcels. The baron required half payment on signing a letter of intent to purchase and Claywich, who apparently had done well lately at the tables, scratched his noble name upon the documents and produced a bag of guineas in payment.

After the sale the baron was clearly pleased with our efforts — we did not walk back to Julian Square but rode in a hackney cab. Sir Gerald took his leave. Meanwhile, Geo, the baron and I climbed aboard the hired carriage. If Geo had any doubts about his role as the baron's business partner, those thoughts departed in the time needed for a small purse to arc across the cab and land with an intriguing jingle in Geo's hands. The Baron nodded as Geo opened the bag to reveal a clutch of coins, each a shiny gold guinea. The effect upon Geo's countenance was pronounced: His eyes glowed and his mouth broke into a self-satisfied smile.

"Yours und Mr. Attucks' share of our recent business. Should ve be lucky, there will more such payments in the future." The baron smiled in the afternoon sunlight. "Perhaps many more, ja?"

Geo nodded eagerly as he cradled the purse. A wealthy and titled future as an English gentleman rolled out in his mind's eye.

We met with another prospective buyer the following day. Mr. Porfert Tubbs was a man without a title. However, what he lacked in nobility, he made up for in gold. A successful banker, Mr. Tubbs' most pressing problem appeared to be keeping his spending up to the pace of his income. Unlike Claywich, however, Mr. Tubbs had no interest in things that crawled, creeped or crapped. "I should think it a great boon to humanity were all such creatures hunted down till they disappeared entirely, thus providing more room to humans for the increase of commerce," Tubbs intoned when asked what his natural interests were concerning the western lands along the Ohio.

"My two concerns in a purchase such as this are: was the land properly surveyed and deeded to prevent legal tangles and will such land provide sufficient income upon resale? If you cannot assure me on these two points, gentlemen, then the chances of a sale are darker than that fellow's face."

Tubbs spoke this last with a cursory wave in my direction. Because he had received us in his rooms while he underwent a therapeutic bath of the finest Sussex mud alloyed with sodium salts and barley malt, his hand motion was sufficient to fling a ploppy stripe of mud across Geo and myself. Maintaining his even keel, Geo smudged off the mud with nary a foul look. At that moment it seemed to me that the young Virginian had a natural bent toward stoicism. Perhaps his best approach was not the dashing rogue but rather the steady rock, the unmoving pivot around which all things turned. I resolved to discuss this idea with Geo at my first opportunity.

"On those points I don't think you should have any problem, Mr. Tubbs," the baron replied. "My associate, Mr. Washington, can attest to some considerable knowledge of ze latest in surveying techniques."

Geo nodded in agreement. "'Tis true that I am quite knowledgeable of both the theory and practical particulars of surveying land."

"I suppose I am pleased that you are well situated vis-à-vis the profession of surveying," Tubbs responded. "Yet, you did not answer either of my questions."

Geo hesitated. Having not participated in the surveying of the baron's land nor even having looked over the documents, Geo was loath to say that he had. So I felt it was my duty to step in. "It is only his modesty and solid breeding that prevents Mr. Washington from boasting as to the skill and accuracy with which not only the survey work was accomplished, but the legal arrangements as well. You may rest assured that there are no problems nor pitfalls in these agreements."

"And who are you? You sound rather like a solicitor, which is a good thing, I think — if you are a solicitor. However, if you are not, I should think you would keep your mouth shut." Mr. Tubbs shifted his considerable weight in the bath, producing a rude sound as the mud shifted to escape his bulk.

I took no outward offense at Mr. Tubbs' admonition,

but merely looked to the baron. Mowenholtz spoke up immediately. "There is no issue as concerns ze legal aspects. I can, of course, produce a complete legal documentation if you so desire."

Tubbs seemed placated on the first question. "And what of the resale value?"

This time, Geo was on firmer ground, as the question called not for specific statements of fact, but rather for speculation. So Geo felt safe in hazarding an answer. "The parcels are rich in farm land, in water for crops and transportation, in timber and in minerals. Its value will only increase. Of that I am certain."

Tubbs asked further questions, but Geo answered each one with steady good nature. Soon Mr. Tubbs was sufficiently convinced that he agreed to purchase.

For Geo and me, this meant another hackney ride home with a bag of guineas.

There were other triumphs as well:

— We met with an aged widow, a Mrs. Elwyn Duskerhilt, whose dead husband had been a merchant with a seat at the Royal Exchange. Mr. Duskerhilt had amassed sufficient gold from his business enterprises that he had been forced to found his own bank. After his passing, Duskerhilt's widow had moved into the vault, piled high as it was with gold ingots and coins, so as to be closer to his memory. She was required to spend at a prodigious pace so that the steadily accumulating gold from his hugely successful business interests did not fall down and crush her. The baron took a special interest in Mrs. Duskerhilt and often worried aloud as to her health and safety. He related to her that death by pressing, especially being pressed by a great weight of gold, was widely acknowledged as the most painful manner in which to die. Evidently it also carried a spiritual danger, as the baron said it was well proven that when crushed by gold, one's soul was known to be squeezed from one's body just as juice is pressed from a lemon. The baron's tender mercies toward her were most heartfelt as he remarked on how much she reminded him of his own beloved mother in Germany. Under the baron's thoughtful guidance, Mrs. Duskerhhilt purchased many parcels of Ohio land.

— Admiral Viscount Algernon Tydalwaide, the elder, was a former Royal Navy commander whose fame resulted from a series of heroic voyages of exploration. The admiral, having determined that the search for the Northwest Passage to the Indies was too crowded an endeavor, had instead searched for several less-famed passages: the Southeast Passage, the North-by-West Passage, the South Southwest Passage and finally the Passage to the Left of the Alley Inclining Toward Masham Yard, East Spittalfields. While Admiral Tydalwaide was not successful in attaining the objective of his explorations, he was lauded as a true British hero. With each expedition his fame grew such that Parliament showered him with commemorative gold medals and monetary rewards in the tens of thousands of pounds.

We met the admiral in the great rotunda at Ranelagh Gardens. Ranelagh and Vauxhall Gardens were the principal pleasure gardens in London, wherein members of the monied class and the nobility paid an entrance fee to stroll the lush lanes, view statuary, listen to music, drink wine and ale, eat their supper and engage in private assignations in the small pavilions provided. We walked round the Ranelagh rotunda only twice before the great explorer became quite insensible of direction and had little idea where he was. Tydalwaide was happy to purchase land along the Ohio simply so the baron would allow him to sit down and regain his bearings. He was so relieved after signing the papers he even offered to mount an expedition to search for the Ohio River. Geo tactfully pointed out, however, that the Ohio's whereabouts were fairly well established.

— Sir Robin Teeter, a young baronet, was also a buyer. Sir Robin, wearing a heavy sword and a large tricorn hat that slid down his face and obscured his eyes, was ascending Surrey Stairs, having just crossed the Thames from a night of decadent leisure at Vauxhall Gardens. The baron, Geo and I met Sir Robin to finalize his purchase of some Ohio parcels.

We waited on the stairs for the young man to alight from the boat that had ferried him across the river. In a stroke of malign fate, however, the waterman's boat surged on a passing wave and Sir Robin was nearly tossed into the wet. Geo adroitly snagged the young baronet's coat to prevent his plunge. Rather than express his gratitude toward Geo, however, the young man flew into a rage that a colonial upstart had dared to lay his hand upon him who was half-brother to an earl, cousin to a marquess and bastard to a duke. Teeter pushed up his hat and with one of his gloves he struck Geo full in the face. This maneuver, however, caused the young fellow to mislay his foot and slip on the slick stairs. He spun and tottered into Geo and the two fell headlong into the bilge of the nearest boat. Sir Robin lay atop Geo, howling something that was muffled by the tangle of his coat. When the young man emerged from his swaddling he exclaimed, "Do not kill me, Mommy. I will pay anything!"

After the baron had a talk with him, the young bastard made good his frenzied promise by purchasing an extensive group of Ohio parcels.

– Mr. Zebulon Pencewit was an avid visitor to the gambling entertainments at that sweaty favorite of common folk, Hockley-in-the-Hole. The opportunities for wagering were many, viz, bull baiting, bear baiting, cock fighting, dog fighting, sword duels, cudgel matches, wrestling, boxing matches and even boxing between members of the fairer sex. On the day we visited Mr. Pencewit — a black-haired, well-snuffed man whose activities remained behind a shroud that we were not to disturb with any questions — we saw a mad bull dressed up with fireworks, lighted and turned loose. Then a dog dressed up with fireworks all over was also lighted and turned loose with the bull, and these were joined by a bear. Not to forget that the bull also had a cat tied to its tail. The firing of the explosives and the mad state they promoted in the animals made for a lively scene. 'Twas during this bit of sport that we were happy to conclude some very lucrative sales of the baron's parcels. And tho' the cat and bull and dog did not survive, Mr. Pencewit faired well in the pocketbook and was happy to help us prosper as well.

After these and other successes, Geo and I were quite happy with our entrée into London business. We had not been in the city long and yet had already amassed a considerable sum. I thanked Heaven for the rewards it had heaped upon me, its humble servant. We naturally felt we were destined for continued success, that, indeed, no other outcome was even remotely possible. We had no idea that events would soon take a dangerous turn.

Chapter Six
Bombazine and Bondage

GIVEN OUR NEWFOUND monies, the baron took Geo and me to yet another tailor — his own. The new suits we purchased were powerfully expensive. Made of fine fabrics, fancy buttons, elaborate embroidery, colorful piping, silk and linen linings, they had many details of which a simple sailor such as myself had no experience. But I must say I found learning about fine clothes to be far more engaging than I imagined I would. 'Twas like when I was a boy and I learned the names of the sails — course, topsail, topgallant, royal, studsail, jib — on a full-rigged ship. Is there not a perverse joy in man to possess exclusive knowledge? I suppose the desire to reside within the innermost circle is the cause of much unrest and does damage to men's souls.

My new suit of clothes was composed of a dark green wool coat with buff waistcoat and sedge green breeches, a white linen shirt, white wool hose and brown cowhide shoes with brass buckles. My cheap, bob wig was replaced with a proper rig with a cue and ribbon. A buff tricorn hat and canary neckcloth finished me most pleasingly. As my brothers in New York would say, "I be smokin' sharp."

The baron also chose well for Geo: a dark blue bombazine silk coat with crimson facing, basket buttons and crimson-piped mariner's cuffs, a crimson waistcoat with silver filigree embroidery and silver buttons, a crimson cravat, dark blue velvet breeches with white linen hose and silver-buckled black dogskin shoes. On his head Geo now flew a well-made horsehair buckle wig and atop it rode a dark blue Kevenhuller hat with a spray of eagle feathers.

And no more cheap swords for us, both Geo and I spent lavishly on finely made Dresden swords. So comely was the Saxon metalwork of the handles and hilts and the etching along the blades, that we both agreed t'would be a shame to sully them with a man's blood.

After we were newly attired, the baron departed and I composed a rhyme for Geo's good entertainment, viz:

A young Virginia fellow in dark blue

Strolled London town like a man made new
His sword cut a fine swath of bombazine cloth
As the noble eagle of his fortune upward flew.

Geo said he liked it, "especially the line about my
fortune being on the way up." It was late May, London was
abloom with spring growth, many beautiful women (both
high-born and availably low) were everywhere, and our
prospects were as bright as the ever-lengthening days. The
increase of sunlight seemed a perfect symbol of my and
Geo's happy ascent of the ladder of British prosperity.

We walked all that day. We marched down the Strand,
lingered in Charing Cross, and strolled through St. James
Park. Geo and I were happy to show off our new finery to
every lady — or least to all the prettiest ones. While in the
park we saw a procession of cavalry guards leading a fancy
coach and a retinue of servants in livery. Watching the
soldiers and coaches were a knot of young women, who
smiled and waved at the solemn horsemen. The women drew
us towards them in close observation. I was admiring the fine
lines of the ladies when Geo tapped my arm. He pointed at
the officer leading the troopers. It was none other than Major
Sir Francis Chase. Sir Francis had clearly assumed his new
post as commander of the Prince of Wales life guard — the
horsemen who followed him in perfect order.

Geo and I attempted to melt into the shade of a tree, but
Sir Francis, too, had cast his eyes upon the ladies. In the
process thereof, he captured us in his gaze. Obviously
alarmed, he instantly wheeled his horse toward us. Geo and I
turned and beat as dignified a retreat as was possible, not
wishing the ladies to think less of us.

Geo dropped his hat with the eagle feathers and was
forced to double back to sweep it up, just as Sir Francis came
thundering up to him. Geo spun and ran for the entrance of
the park. Sir Francis attempted to turn his coal black charger,
Pip, to follow.

When Sir Francis left the cavalry formation, his entire
command of 24 troopers followed his lead, scattering the
ladies and other onlookers as they trotted off after their
commander, leaving the coaches unprotected. Sir Francis'
sudden change of direction in pursuit of Geo put Chase on a
collision course with his men, who still rode along Chase's

original line of advance. The resulting melee of horses and swords and spurs provided a perfect opportunity for our escape. Geo exited the park at a full run with me only a step behind. We made our way into city streets, panting and sweating with exertion. As we stopped and laughed at having shaken off Chase, the man himself galloped around a corner. We nearly fell in our surprised efforts to flee again. Turning and speeding up the street, we barely dodged the throngs of commerce-obsessed Londoners, some of whom cursed us with the jaded malice of one who is often jostled and hurried.

In my flight, I passed a brooding, dirty building, hardly noticeable among the many commercial establishments — except for the familiar smell its smoke brought to my nostrils. As a sailor in the Atlantic trade I had smelled it before, both cooking in the Caribbean and baking in Boston. I waved to Geo to follow me as I turned to my right and ran through the gate into the walled yard. Sir Francis saw us turn and dutifully followed. Ahead, inside the cavernous halls of the building sat a large wooden tank, from whose top came the steady, sweet vapor of heated molasses. A sturdy ramp led to the apex of the tank where a scaffold provided footing for workers scooping buckets of the sweet liquid before heading back down the ramp.

I yelled to Geo to meet me in the far alley and then I ran up the ramp, much to the upset of the fellows working. I bumped them right and left as I sped toward the top. My hopes were realized when the major spurred Pip after me, her hooves drumming on the loose planking, her breath coming in hard blasts. There was little room for anything but the horse and as it climbed, workers fell off to alternate sides, their buckets spewing the warm molasses in all directions. The general tumult in the molasses factory reached deafening proportions, with workers, foremen and clerks running everywhere shouting and gesturing.

Sir Francis gained on me. He drew his sword and brandished it aloft with vigor. I reached the platform at the top and jumped upon the edge of the tank as his horse made up the last few feet. He moved to strike me with his sword when I grabbed an overhead rope and swung away from him as I had done so many times in the rigging of ships. With his body leaning into his sword strike, with his eyes closed, and with the forward momentum of Pip, Sir Francis could not prevent himself from flipping o'er the edge of tank. The warm molasses parted with a treacly splash. He went under and then surfaced like a candied porpoise. Covered in the sticky black liquid, he swam ably to the edge, where a clerk attempting to help Sir Francis fell in himself. I believe several others also fell, but I did not tarry to observe.

I climbed down the far side of the tank, doffed my new hat to an astounded foremen, and scampered into the alley to meet Geo whence we swiftly departed. I would not normally ascribe sweetness to a man such as Sir Francis, but in this particular instance, I can make a notable exception.

Upon our return to the baron's residence in our new, though now soiled, clothes, we were told to make haste to the baron's private cabinet. During our brisk walk to Julian Square, we discussed the need to reveal to the baron our regrettable encounter with Sir Francis. We would need to disclose that the king's officer was in London and had lost none of his determination to lock us up ... or worse. This was a serious matter that could potentially sink our business activities. Geo, in his forthright way, wished to tell Mowenholtz immediately. I favored a less obtrusive approach, viz, we would only discuss the matter should the need arise. After considerable debate, Geo very reluctantly agreed with me.

When we arrived in the baron's private office, we saw that Sir Gerald, Lady Montagrave and the baron awaited us with glasses of claret and the finest snuff. A fan of papers covered a side table — possibly some business had recently transpired. The papers were hastily gathered together by the maid Prudence, who clutched them to her chest and briskly walked out.

"You look suitably prosperous," Sir Gerald offered in an apparent compliment but which seemed more a rebuke. He was so focused on Geo he did not notice the splashes of molasses that marred my waistcoat and breeches.

"Yes, I should say so," Lady Montagrave purred. She was dressed in a riding habit, with tight leather stays under a close-fitting lambskin jacket. As she gazed at Geo, she tapped her riding crop against her gleaming top boots.

"You are pleased with ze business conducted?" the

baron asked. "You have made good money, ja?"

Neither Geo nor me had ever made so much money. I had worked for 10 years for mariner's wages. Even as a first mate, I never had many coins to rattle my purse. But the pile we two had collected in the past few transactions had swelled us up with greed for more. I was beginning to understand why some folk who are rich work so damnably hard to get richer still. Oddly, satisfaction seemed to recede with each crown of gold.

For myself, joy had never been born entirely of money. I also took my pleasure from what the world gave me: making a timely landfall from measuring the sun and stars; the beauty and awe of a pumpkin moon bobbing on the horizon's glow; the joy of the ship running downwind on a breezy day; the attentions of the doxies in a new port; and the smoldering satisfaction that I was a better sailor and ship's mate than any man I ever met.

All these things had seemed like a sort of riches to me. But after meeting the baron, I was not so sure. New clothes and the clink of coin in the pocket was a fine thing to a man in London — a place where anything could be had for a price. Such was the power of money, as Geo and I now discovered.

"We are most pleased, Herr Baron," Geo replied with every measure of dignity he could muster, so as not to show himself too eager.

"Well, I should say to you that these sales of land that ve have completed are, as yet, only a small number of the many sales ve can expect. Indeed, it will be a long line of glittering successes. That is good, ja?" The baron's eyes sparkled and his smile was warm.

"Yes," Geo let a grin cross his face. He was such a puppy. I was able to maintain the air of weary detachment I had so recently learned from Londoners.

"So, there is an important aspect of this zat I must point out. Given the enormous demand these lands are bound to elicit, ve must move fast before matters get out of hand. We would not wish widespread public knowledge und thus a speculative bubble. True gentlemen do not use the forces of the market to price their product beyond the reach of their peers. To avoid such an unseemly situation, it is necessary to maintain discretion and only offer our product behind closed doors and to a selected clientele, ja?"

"Yes, certainly," Geo agreed.

"So you will not discuss these sales with anyone. Und you will let myself and Sir Gerald arrange for all the prospective buyers."

"We are in complete agreement."

"Excellent."

"Baron, may I speak with you alone?" Geo asked.

The baron shot a quick glance at Sir Gerald, who tossed his head as if to say, "What of importance could the whelp have to say?" He and Lady Montagrave withdrew. As she did so Lady Montagrave threw Geo a last smoldering glance.

"Is Attucks to stay?" The baron asked.

Geo looked at me with a touch of surprise, as if he had forgotten about me. "Yes, I suppose he can stay. It would appear I am to have no secrets from him."

This last remark appeared to give the baron pause, but he said nothing.

"I wished to ask about the possibility we discussed in Barbados of my obtaining a title and an estate. As these sales appear to have a successful future, I would like to think there is a suitable chance of my request — "

"And *your* promise, Baron," I interjected.

Geo nodded, "Yes, and your promise, being granted."

His brows knit in concentration, the baron did not immediately answer, but rather tapped his cane on the floor in an absentminded rhythm. Then he slowly spoke.

"Yes, … indeed, … that possibility is greater with every passing day. I am engaged in discussions with very influential members of the nobility, the court und members of Parliament on this question. I think it is very probable, yet it will take time to secure such things, ja?"

With that, and with Geo's buoyed hopes, the conversation was concluded.

Not long afterward, Geo expressed his colonial joy: I heard the steady thump of his axe against the trunk of a tree in the baron's garden. Geo had a positive affection for the work of a sharp axe on live wood. This was a harmless enough preoccupation in the limitless primeval forests of America, but here in London cutting trees was another thing entirely. Geo had already felled a small tree in the rear of the baron's garden. We two had successfully tossed the trunk into a passing wagon and covered over the stump. Neither the baron, nor Prudence, nor Hawkins, had mentioned a word of the missing ornamental. I admonished the tall Virginian to cease his bad habit of cutting down trees, but there seemed no way to break him of the vice.

And here he was at it again.

I walked briskly toward the back of the house and encountered Hawkins overseeing a young servant who polished brass door handles in the hall.

"Ah, there you are," Hawkins remarked as I hove into view. "Grab a rag and join young McGinley here."

Hawkins regularly mistook me for one of the servants. "No, you are mistaken, sir. Surely you remember me? I am Darius Attucks, Mr. Washington's associate."

"Sometimes we do not see what is right in front of us, sometimes the many-threaded plait of the world's cares can weigh us down most grievously, sometimes a man makes a mistake that haunts him for a lifetime." He paused. "That is to say, Mr. Attucks, I am sorry," Hawkins made a rudimentary bow. "I believe you will find Mr. Washington in the back garden." Hawkins, it was said, worked some years as a gilder in the goldsmithing trade. Many older goldsmiths get a bit "touched" in their minds. Some say the effect is caused by the mercury used in goldsmithing. But I knew this could not be so. Mercury is well known as a pleasing and practical metal.

Prudence, unlike the sometimes airy Hawkins, was a whirlwind of energy and seemed unable to sit down or, indeed, direct the rest of the staff with the least coherence or economy. Yet, no matter their failings, the baron had an undiminished affection for the old couple.

"Thank you, Hawkins."

"I am your most humble servant, sir."

I strode into the garden eager to prevail upon Geo to cease his infernal whacking. I was surprised by the sudden appearance of the foreman Boyle — the very man who had attempted to bury Geo and me alive.

Boyle gave me a great big grin and then . . . darkness.

When I awoke, I found myself in the fo'c's'le of a

merchant ship riding to her anchor in the Thames. In some district of London east of the Tower — Wapping, I supposed based upon my previous visit to London as a sailor. My head had a large lump and throbbed with a suffusion of pain. As I attempted to rise, I found I was lashed to the fore bitts and could not stand. Needless for me to record here, but I was jammin' mad and wanted only to stove in the head of the first man that showed himself.

As I had hoped, Geo soon noted my absence. It seems the baron had taken Geo to dinner at a fashionable new restaurant, The Heifer's Demise, on Piccadilly Street. Sir Gerald and Lady Montagrave were already installed at a table when von Mulct and Geo arrived. Not wishing to break away from an intimate moment with Lady Montagrave, Sir Gerald was less than pleased to see Geo and the baron. He made a face and guzzled his wine, ignoring them to the last possible second.

Once they had taken their seats, Geo asked as to my whereabouts. The baron seemed surprised at the question. "Oh, I had imagined he discussed his plans with you. He appears to have gone back to sea."

"He signed aboard a ship?"

"Well zat is what I would think, as he is a man of the sea, ja?" the baron explained helpfully. "They often will disappear at a moment's notice, called by the ocean to voyage once again."

The first course of calf's head soup and larks on a skewer arrived hot from the kitchen. The baron and Lady Montagrave both remarked favorably on the robust taste of the soup and the delicate meat of the larks. Sir Gerald, however, said nothing. He tucked right in, slurping his soup and tearing apart the birds like a street dog.

"But what of Darius?" Geo asked. "I really would prefer him as my second," Geo insisted as politely as he could manage.

"Don't be silly. Sir Gerald can be your second. He is more than man enough fur it. He once tore off a man's arm and beat him senseless with it."

"Quite right," Sir Gerald managed to say with stuffed cheeks.

Lady Montagrave smiled wickedly at this and addressed Sir Gerald. "You tore off the sleeve of his coat trying to break your fall into a pile of shite. His arm stayed quite well attached. And it 'twas he who beat you about the head."

"Really?" Sir Gerald replied, a bit surprised at this. "I was quite sure I triumphed. Perhaps I had been drinking."

"Perhaps," Lady Montagrave retorted, "the sea is salty."

Geo, however, would not be dismissed. He pressed the baron. "I must insist. I want Darius sought out immediately. Before the turn of the tide and before his ship sails."

A significant look passed between Sir Gerald and the baron.

"Look here, pup," Sir Gerald began, wiping his greasy fingers on the tablecloth. "You have no further need for that blackamoor. He will depart and resume his life as a sailor. You have important business here in town. And if you do not wish to continue as our able associate in this endeavor, we shall have no choice but to cut you loose and find another."

For Geo, it was an awkward moment. Three pairs of eyes regarded him with cool curiosity: Sir Gerald with his elbows planted on the table, fist in hand; the baron swirling the wine in his glass; and Lady Montagrave sucking languorously on a lark bone. Geo knew this was a watershed. Perhaps he should knuckle under to their will. They were people of substance, living at the very seat of empire. Meisel von Mulct was a baron of Germany; Sir Gerald Compliss, a British knight, clearly of fine family and the beneficiary of manly training; and Lady Montagrave, a noble woman of distinction and breeding. And who was he? Geo of Ferry Farm, from the undistinguished side of a second-rank family in the rude colonial world of Virginia. He was a younger son, a man of no accomplishment, little money and few friends. To stand up to these three meant the ruination of what could be his only chance at making his fortune.

The wrong choice could consign him to a wandering life of surveying in the Allegheny and Ohio wilderness: wading icy rivers, cutting mosquito-infested swamps, eating cold victuals and always in danger of losing his head to the aggrieved Indians, whose land he was marking off for dismemberment. He would forever be the hired hand with no land nor position of his own.

The logic of the situation was clear: forget the African seaman, do the baron's bidding and he would be rich. Listen to his British betters and he would profit handsomely. An estate here in England and a title could be his. Or he could return to Virginia with sufficient funds such that he could buy a bigger estate than his brother Lawrence's Mount Vernon.

Yet, somehow, giving in to the baron and his friends was repugnant. Geo felt a new spirit rise in chest. It emerged from within, as if it resided there all along in his Virginian heart — in, what he realized, perhaps for the first time, was his American heart. Cool personal calculation dictated to him that he should simply go along with the baron. But a mad, unhinged emotion swirled in him. If he were to follow his stated sense of himself as a man of dash and daring, he must obey this emotion's devil-may-care directives.

"Sir Gerald, I must insist that you do exactly that," Geo said firmly.

The big man squeezed his brow and leaned forward. "Do exactly what?"

"Find yourself another assistant. If you will not use your resources to bring Darius back within our circle, then I must bow out, sir."

The baron, who had just started to swallow a healthy slug of wine, suddenly spit the wine across the tablecloth in a vivid ruby shower. "Pray, sir," the baron said after he had cleared his throat and wiped his chin, "take no hasty positions. Let us have a proper dizcussion of this matter. I think ve can come to some agreement on this."

"Get Darius back as my second and I will be happy to discuss any situation. Those are my terms."

The baron looked again at Sir Gerald and Lady Montagrave then he turned back to Geo. "We are impressed that you have the strength of character to stand up fur yourself. It appears that you have an independent streak, my young friend." The baron trailed off and became silent for a moment.

Then his face brightened and he burst forth, "Of course, we knew this all along! That is the main reason that I chose you to join us in this venture," the baron said with growing conviction. "You bring a unique air of honesty und propriety to our endeavor. Of course, Sir Gerald will look for your friend. We can't promise results, but we will look with great vigor." With that, the baron turned to Sir Gerald, who took a moment to register the Baron's recent announcement.

"Ah, yes, yes," Sir Gerald suddenly piped up. "We will look for him."

As Sir Gerald sat fixedly in his chair pouring himself some wine, the baron continued his steely gaze. After some further rumination, Sir Gerald finally grasped the situation, made a face, put down the bottle and rose rapidly to his feet. As he did so, a pewter pitcher on the table was disturbed and fell with unfortunate accuracy upon Sir Gerald's foot. He cried out in pain and sat down again, holding the wounded extremity. The baron again looked at him sternly. Not wishing to further brook the baron's displeasure, Sir Gerald stood up, this time carefully, mumbled his goodbyes and hobbled off.

"He is a wonderful man in some respects," the baron observed. "In some respects."

Following their supper, the baron and Geo saw Lady Montagrave off in a hackney then repaired to the home of Baronet Wilfred Hippodrome Wyde-Parke, a prospective purchaser of Ohio land. The Baronet Wyde-Parke had a fondness for formal gardens — indeed, the interior of his home near Red Lion Square was cluttered with drawings, paintings, renderings, sketches and scale models of possible public gardens. Wyde-Park believed these gardens would greatly beautify the city of London and its environs, even if the installation of these seas of grass, shrubberies, and serpentine paths would require nearly half of the city's inhabitants to move to some other place.

"It is my desire that London be the world's most beautiful city," the baronet intoned. "Nothing but wide greenswards and sublime vistas."

Like Wyde-Park, the Baron Mowenholtz was a man of refined taste. More than that, the German was also a quick study when sizing up people. He connected with the most cherished ideas of his clientele. And as he did so, he led them to the successful conclusion of a sale.

"I am nearly undone by your plan to transform

London," the baron announced. "In many ways, it neatly mirrors a similar plan I have long considered for my city of Raubstadt in Germany."

Wyde-Park was clearly flattered. He smiled broadly and eagerly started to explain important features of his plan.

"Not only that," the baron cut him off, "but I understand you have plans for an even grander garden in ze New World?" the baron asked. Even though interrupted, Wyde-Park beamed. "Yes, I certainly do." He scurried to a pile of rolled drawings, knocking most to the floor as he dug deep. After some searching, he found one roll of parchment and returned to the middle of the room. When he rolled it out, I saw it was well-marked with tea and jam stains.

"Und this is?" the baron asked as he studied the plan.

"My plan to build the largest formal garden ever conceived. It will be along the south bank of the Ohio River in the colonies. It will stretch for exactly 100 miles," Wyde-Park exclaimed triumphantly. Geo, taking his cue from the baron, nodded approvingly.

"Und we have the deeds fur the land," the baron said. "That is an amazing example of fortuity, iz it not?"

Wyde-Parke readily agreed.

While the baron and the baronet finalized terms, Geo walked around the room, examining the various plans and drawings, until he came to a ship model mounted in a place of honor on a wide windowsill. The ship was quite complete with rigging and sails, but half of its hull was removed such that it was possible to view the cargo in the hold. That cargo, very accurately displayed, was not a mundane item such as coal, or grain, or iron manufactures. The freight was humans — black Africans stacked up 'til not another could be crowded within. So tight were the conditions in the hold that pairs of black wooden feet stuck out between the exposed ribs of the ship. Each little slave had been carefully carved and painted by an expert model maker determined to accurately render every detail of the African's ordeal, including lash marks and pools of blood.

Tho' the entire oppressive scene was only a representation in wood, Geo was wholly unsettled by the sight of the slave ship model, its lugubrious captives and their suffering. I cannot say whether his association with me had aroused his Christian feelings of empathy for Africans as fellow beings. But his indignation was apparent. He turned and barged into the business deal to pose a question. "Why is this ship model given a prominent place?"

The Baronet Wyde-Parke, enmeshed in proceedings with the baron, asked Geo if he would be so kind as to repeat himself. Geo did so and Wyde-Parke answered proudly that the ship model was commissioned by his father. The elder Wyde-Parke had owned a fleet of slave ships that had made his fortune.

Geo snorted and replied that it would be much more seemly "had you kept this revolting display in storage, rather than show yourself the benefactor of so dishonorable a trade as the gathering and transporting of slaves."

Wyde-Parke was so utterly taken aback by Geo's comments that, at first, he had no reply. He stood up slowly and gazed at Geo as if he were a curious artifact from a distant continent. Then he stammered out, "Am I mistaken in understanding that you are from Virginia?"

"You are not mistaken."

"Well, surely someone from a province so wholly dependent upon slaves has little call to question the honor of a deceased shipping merchant who also happens to have been my beloved father."

"Pardon me, I did not mean to question the honor of a man who is not present to defend himself," Geo said calmly. The baron seemed to relax a bit at this statement. But Geo was not finished. "It is *your* honor I question, sir."

The Baron Mowenholtz was disconcerted by this and made appropriate noises of polite protest.

Wyde-Parke, meanwhile, was now angry. When he spoke, his voice was several octaves higher. "Then I must demand satisfaction from you," Wyde-Parke squeaked.

The baron agreed, as affairs of honor required he must, to a duel between Geo and Wyde-Parke. He also suggested that since the baronet's victory was assured, there would be no problem with him signing the sale papers now. Wyde-Parke assented to sign, but would only part with the advance payment after the duel was completed. The day and time of the duel was arranged and Geo and the German departed.

Once they were in a hackney cab and the horse was trotting, Geo announced he would not duel without me on the field as his second.

"Do not fret, we will do our best to bring him back." Then the baron chuckled. "It is a bit odd, ja? That you would take offense to the son of a slaver. Does not your family own slaves?"

Now removed from Wyde-Parke's house, Geo felt a degree of discomfort at his behavior. "Yes, my half-brother Lawrence and my mother are owners. Though, I must state that I cannot be said to own any slaves directly."

"Ja, I see," the baron replied with a nod.

"Do you know the baronet's weapon of choice?" Geo asked.

"Ja, pistols."

The baron was then entirely happy to sit quietly and leave Geo to his thoughts as the hackney made its way back through the press and noise of London's streets to the leased house on Julian Square. Geo realized that by giving free reign to his emotions he had almost certainly signed his death sentence.

Chapter Seven
Falling Inn

FETTERED TO THE FORE BITTS of the ship on which I had been dumped, I only learned later of the arrival of a thick-set, brutish fellow. He came aboard very early in the morning and was ushered to the captain's cabin with a well-placed shilling to the sleepy cabin boy. As a prisoner in the fo'c's'le of the ship, I was naturally limited in seeing my surroundings.

Yet, many years experience as a sailor and mariner gave me a deep knowledge of a ship's creakings, squeaks and groans. I could determine, for example, that the ship was still in the process of loading cargo and the noises that had echoed through its hold the day before said she was not yet half full. So the ship would not depart for at least two days, given the size of the ship (which I could estimate from the size of the fore bitts, the thickness of the anchor rode and the general dimensions of the fo'c's'le), the state of the tide (I could see through the hawse hole and view the current streaming past buoys in the Thames) and the time of day (I could see daylight outside through the hawse).

It was obvious from the visits of the crew to the fo'c's'le that the ship was a few hands short of the number needed to weigh anchor. I was also able to query the sailors who entered and left the fo'c's'le and from their answers garner yet more knowledge. It was in this way that I learned of the arrival of the heavyset man aboard. Indeed, it was not long before the brute and the captain were clumping their way forward to where I lay, the light from the approaching lantern swaying in the passage.

"Is this the man?" the captain asked in a Yorkshire accent.

"Aye."

"Then untie him," the captain ordered. In one hand he held a club well-dimpled from tapping sailors' noggins. The captain watched as the brute unbound me. Before I was released from my bonds, while the brute was freeing the last knot, the captain stepped forward and cracked the man across the head. The large fellow gasped and fell to the deck.

Immediately, two sailors appeared and, with mariners' dexterity, tied the brute to the anchor bitts in the same manner by which I had been held captive.

The captain looked at me with casual disregard. "Well, be off with you."

"But why am I released?"

"This fella' here has paid to let you be. Go on, now."

I knew the answer before I asked. Yet I asked, "Who sent him?"

"Don't know."

"Why did you ill use him so?"

"'Tis a long fetch to India. I need every man jack I can get. He will take your place. Now, get off my ship or I'll bind ya' again and you'll sail with us."

I needed no further inducement and was down the gangplank and onto the quay faster than a starving rat. A pair of strolling doxies, who smiled brazenly and showed a bit of leg, looked very fine to me after my imprisonment in the fo'c's'le. I was sorely tempted to engage both of 'em for an hour or two of pleasure. In the tangled streets near the docks, however, I was in danger of being snatched by a press gang and loaded aboard one of His Majesty's ships. That was a life to be avoided at all costs.

The pay aboard Royal Navy ships was less than that aboard a merchantman and, perhaps worse, there was the danger of being torn apart by French and Spanish cannon balls. Impressment, forcing seamen to sail for the Royal Navy, is a crime against liberty and the rights of English subjects, but I was in no position to fight it. I had to find my way back to Geo.

I was responsible for the Virginian. I could have simply walked aboard another ship, signed on as an ordinary seaman and been away to sea. But should I be drowned or take ill and die, what would I say to my maker when I saw him face to face? How could I explain turning my back on Heaven's clear dictate? There was no chance Darius Attucks would ignore an order from the greatest captain of them all. And besides, my pocket had been picked and I did feel unnaturally light. Back to Geo I did go.

The sun squared away for dawn as I arrived in Julian

Square. The baron's windows flickered with moving candlelight. A coach waited at the curb, one of the horses stamping and snorting in the mild morning. In the waking city, the creak of handcarts, the rustle of wagons and the cries of street vendors rumbled like waves on a distant shore.

As I reached the threshold, Geo appeared in the hall, a black cloak thrown across his shoulders, his visage drawn. The change in his features was a sight to behold. Though Geo styled himself a dashing man of hot emotions and ready action, he more nearly showed the reserve of a lawyer considering a difficult case.

I was filled with joy to see Geo's care flee with a genuine smile when he saw me. In moments of despair in the ship's fo'c's'le, I admit I had doubted him.

"D! Pray, tell me where you disappeared. And me in need of you!"

"I was waylaid and clapped up in a ship. But I have been set free," I responded excitedly, as I was certainly as happy to see the tall Virginian as he was to see me. "What need do you have of me? Where are you off this morning?"

Geo laughed. "I have insulted Baronet Wyde-Parke. He took offense and so we must duel in St. James Park."

"What was the manner of your insult?" I asked in amazement. Perhaps Geo was more the hothead than I credited him.

"I told him he was a man of no honor on account of his father's business interests."

"Does not seem the most cutting of remarks, hardly worthy of a duel. He is powerfully touchy."

"His father owned a fleet of slave ships," Geo replied quietly, some of his confidence seeming to desert him. "I called it a dishonorable profession."

"As a man of Virginian society, your principles seem odd."

Geo's back was up immediately. "You find it odd?" he said with raised voice and knit brow. "That I am born of a slave-holding society, 'tis true. Yet you must think me different from Lord Fairfax, surely."

"I do not know this Fairfax," I said.

"He is the wealthiest man and largest slave owner in Virginia."

"And how do you differ from him?" I asked pointedly.

Geo seemed genuinely confused and perhaps hurt by this question. "I own no slaves! And I certainly don't find running slave ships honorable." It seemed to me that perhaps Geo was saying this and, indeed, had staked out his position of moral certitude as a juvenile defense of my interests. If so, I was ready to cut him down a notch. Going into a duel, he needed his wits about him. A sniffing sense of superiority would do little to help him attend to the deadly business. "Do you find me dishonorable, then?"

"I have no reason to," Geo shot back.

"But well you should," I said. "I sailed aboard a slaver."

Geo's face withered. "You worked a slave ship?"

"Aye. I needed a ship and could find no other berth in Jamaica. The ship on which I signed carried sugar and molasses to Boston. When we made port, 'twas my intent to find another vessel. Before we bobbed Boston Light, though, the captain recognized my navigation skills and made me third mate. We carried rum and glass beads to the Gambia River where we traded 'em for African people — my people. The passage to Jamaica was the worst of my life. At night I could hear the moaning and cryin' out of the people, the clink of chains and the death rattles of them that didn't make it. In Jamaica I ran from the ship and was lucky to find another. I am not proud of it, but I don't ever want to forget it."

Geo was silent after my story. The baron had appeared in the hall, but when he saw us, he turned and retreated. "So you would have me celebrate the owners of slave ships?" Geo said.

"No I would not. I'm just sayin' that life is not always so simple as the good fellows right here and the bad ones over there. They've got a nasty habit of mixing round — sometimes you can't tell which is which."

"Than should I offer my apologies to the baronet?" Geo asked.

I smiled at him. "Not at all. Put a ball into the bastard."

"Good advice, ja," the baron had returned to the hallway. "Let us be off."

Geo nodded at this, his brow again furrowed in thought.

The first rays of the rising sun reddened the mists in the trees of St. James Park. The dueling ground lay where the park's lines of trees converged near water called Rosamond's Pond. Across the pond to the west, sat Buckingham House, its roofs outlined in delicate washes of sunrise pink.

Baronet Wilfred Hippodrome Wyde-Parke had already taken the field of honor as our coach drew up. He looked pale and dour in the chilly morning air, wrapped in a deep purple greatcoat. He wore a flat brimmed hat — more suitable to a Devon ploughman than a London man of means — pulled low on his head. Almost as if he was ready to flee incognito into to the countryside at the first opportunity.

The formalities were quickly dispensed as a brace of pistols was unboxed, loaded and set at half cock. As dueling was an illegal and unchristian activity, it was vital for the affair to be completed before the full light of day chased away the mist and laid open our activities to prying eyes.

Wyde-Parke's second was Mr. MacSwilly, a squat man with bushy red eyebrows and a guttural Scottish rasp. He took the flat hat from the baronet and gave him a proper black tricorn with a stiff yellow cockade, which Wyde-Parke set upon his head with his own hands. MacSwilly brushed a bit of lint from the baronet's shoulder and then handed over the flintlock pistol. Wyde-Parke ably grasped the pistol's burnished cherry wood and clicked it to full cock.

MacSwilly suddenly seemed ready to make an announcement to all of us, thought the better of it and then stepped away. Drawn up with his pistol at the ready, the baronet waited for the signal.

"I have chosen the ground well, eh, Baron Mowenholtz?" Wyde-Parke asked as he waited.

"Ja, it suits, I think," the baron replied.

"Though," Wyde-Parke added, "I would have planted some ornamentals along the edge of the pond, perhaps."

"You mean along there?" the baron pointed with his cane to the misty far side of the pond.

"No, no, there," Wyde-Parke pointed in turn with his flintlock.

"Oh, so you mean over there?"

"No, right here."

"Along the back edge, ja?"

"No, along the front edge, right here."

The baron scratched under his wig and then shook his head. "I am afraid I am not seeing it."

"Well, look, it's quite simple really," Wyde-Parke insisted. "If you follow the near angle of the pond around to where there is a small hillock, then you will see where I mean."

"I see some bumps."

"You see the three hillocks? It's the one on the right, next to the berm."

As this continued, I walked with Geo to his place. The Virginian was the picture of steady composure — though the color had drained from his face in a most alarming manner.

"You know, perhaps, that dueling pistols often have different triggers?" I told him. "MacSwilly chose first. You can be sure that he gave Wyde-Parke the smoother, more predictable trigger. Yours will, no doubt, be feather-light and will fire at the slightest touch, a trick to make you miss."

Geo nodded.

"When he is to fire, stand sideways, thereby presenting a narrower target to his ball."

Geo shook his head. "I will stand facing him."

"Aye. That is what I thought you would do. If, after the first set of discharges, you both have missed, then the baron will ask Wyde-Parke if he has received satisfaction."

Geo nodded again. His physical composure was impressive, even if his coloring ghostlike.

"Are you ready?"

Geo raised the pistol and brought the hammer back to full cock. I had my answer. I tried to nod my encouragement, but felt a chill at the thought of losing my tall friend. I reluctantly stepped away to join the baron and MacSwilly in neutral ground.

"Baronet Wyde-Parke," the baron called out, "as the aggrieved party, you may fire first."

Wyde-Parke, looking deadly in posture and manner, brought his pistol up to aim at Geo. For his part, Geo did not flinch, but showed admirable courage concerning his person, keeping his shoulders square in the face of Wyde-Parke's yawning muzzle.

Though Wyde-Parke started the well enough, he suffered a sudden and shocking transformation. He lost all nerve at trigger time. His pistol hand began to quiver and then shake; he blinked hard, as if to remove sweat that rolled into his eyes. After an eternity of pistol shaking and blinking, the gun suddenly erupted in smoke and flame, seeming to catch even Wyde-Parke by surprise.

We looked to Geo and he still stood, his shoulders square. Wyde-Parke had missed entirely.

Geo then leveled his gun at Wyde-Parke, taking careful aim. The baronet immediately turned sideways, dropped his pistol, placed his hands on his head and closed his eyes in fear. After a few moments of threat, Geo lowered the pistol and fired into the ground well short of the baronet.

Wyde-Parke, who had held his eyes clamped shut and had not seen Geo's action, fell immediately to his knees, "I am shot," he wailed. "I am dead." Falling over onto his side he clutched at his ribs, kicked his feet and rolled this way and that in paroxysms of pain.

Geo looked at the baron and shrugged. "I'm quite positive I missed him."

"Perhaps it was a ricochet?" the baron suggested helpfully.

Wyde-Parke continued to writhe on the ground wailing and shouting, "I am killed. I am dead — aaarrgghhh!"

With an air of pained resignation, Mr. MacSwilly made his way to Wyde-Parke's side. He stolidly knelt down and whispered in Wyde-Parke's ear.

Wyde-Parke suddenly ceased his writhing and became quiet. He lay still on the ground, the newly risen sun framing him in golden light.

The baron cleared his throat and called out, "Have you achieved satisfaction, Sir Vilfred?"

From his position lying on the turf, looking up at the morning sky, the baronet replied, "Ah, yes, I believe that will be fine, Herr Baron. I'm sure I am quite satisfied." Then he said to his second, "Mr. MacSwilly, would you be so kind?"

MacSwilly rose and walked to me and handed over a small leather bag. I took it, noted the hard edges of coins within, and handed it to the baron. After a quick peek inside, the German said, "Thank you, Sir Wilfred. I will have your deeds sent over immediately."

Still lying on his back, seemingly ready for a nap, Wyde-Parke raised a hand and waved cordially to us. Geo, the baron and I climbed back into our coach and rolled away.

The baron divvied up the spoils. Geo and I looked at each other and made ridiculous faces, driven slightly mad by the weight of money. The baron took in our impetuous glee with a smile.

"Your lordship," Geo said, "you seemed entirely prepared to lose my services should the baronet have wounded or killed me."

The baron pursed his lips and gave a quick shake of his head. "There vas never any real danger. The Baronet Wyde-Parke has never even winged a man in a duel. He goes to pieces each time. He has been lucky to face men of principle such as yourself." The baron turned and looked at us with a wicked grin. "Do you think I vould leave anything to chance?"

In a mood to celebrate, the baron directed our coach to the precincts of St. James. We invaded the public room of an establishment called the Falling Inn, named after its proprietor Jeremiah Falling, a friend of the baron's. We toasted our good fortune with glasses of flip and shrub while eating steaming pigeon pie and stewed carp. Soon our happy party was expanded with the arrival of Sir Gerald and Lady Montagrave — who must have started celebrating whilst the duel was still in progress. Normally a grim fellow, Sir Gerald became a man of giggles and guffaws when he was well into his cups. Lady Montagrave fairly burst into flame at the sight of Geo, endeavoring to sit alongside him no matter where he moved on the benches.

All manner of people came into the pub and some heeded the call to join us in a toast ... or three.

"To King George!"
"To the Prince of Wales!"
"To the Duke of Cumberland! May the Bonny Prince rot in Hell!"
"To Jenkins's other ear! And to his nose and prick as well!"
"To Lord Chesterfield's missing days! May they all be jolly!"

Some time into our muddle of a midday meal, the

baron took his leave and repaired to the Inn's entrance hall, claiming to have to an important appointment. From Geo's position tottering on the end of the bench, pressed by the insistent hips of Lady Montagrave, Geo had a superior view of the baron and whomever he was to meet.

As I watched him, Geo suddenly perked up. It was obvious that the meeting was on, and evidently with someone of importance, given Geo's reaction.

Geo saw the Baron speaking with a young woman. She was taller than the German, and so Geo could see her face clearly. What he saw wholly captured him. She was lovely, with flinty blue eyes, glossy raven hair, a nose of fair proportion and an exquisite, full-lipped mouth. From her dress and accoutrements, from her beauty and her bearing, from the restrained way she spoke and the refined way she listened, Geo could see she was a noblewoman of some considerable birth and breeding. Throughout the brief time the baron spoke with her, Geo's eyes never strayed, nor did his attention flag. He beheld his Helen of Troy, and she launched a thousand ships of devotion in his heart.

With a toss of her head, she turned and walked out of the inn, down its front steps to the street. Geo was on his feet in a flash, moving toward a window that faced onto the road. The window's 12-pane lower sash was raised and Geo put a hand on the sash as he leaned out the opening to garner another view of the young beauty. As she drew abreast of the window, she turned her head to look up at the tall Virginian. She gave him a glowing smile and then walked on — a solitary thread quickly lost in the fabric of people, animals and vehicles crowding the London streets.

Geo stopped the baron as he returned from the hall and asked him urgently, "Who is that woman?"

The baron pursed his lips and looked back into the empty hall. "Which woman?"

"That woman," Geo repeated urgently.

The baron swiveled his head again to survey the hall, "Where?"

His exasperation boiling over, Geo blurted out, "My dear baron, the young woman with whom you just conversed in the hall."

"Oh, I see. That woman."

"So, what is her name?"

The baron paused, raised an eyebrow and tapped Geo with his cane. "We are associates on this Ohio River land sale, ja. However, as you must imagine, that is hardly the extent of my commercial interests. Do not presume to intrude into my other business endeavors. Is that clear?"

Geo was not deterred by the baron's efforts to brush him away. He stumbled slightly and placed his hand on the baron's chest to steady himself before urgently stating, "I must know, my lord."

The baron chuckled at Geo's ardor and his tipsy state. "Perhaps you will meet her sometime, ja? Until then, ve have more work to do."

And work we did, though the ornate ball the Baron held at his Julian Square house was far from the hard, rain-swept labor to which a seaman or a surveyor is normally consigned.

Chapter Eight
In the Forest Primeval

AFTER SOME WEEKS of work, the baron's rented house on Julian Square was transfigured. It changed from a building of sagging roof lines, crumbling brickwork and rotting window sills to a manse whose maladies had been rendered nearly invisible by the ready application of roof slates, mortar, shoring timbers, plaster and paint. From the street, the house looked only passably repaired. But to proceed beyond the front hall was to behold a house that gleamed in its furnishings, suggesting that one could no longer trust one's eyes, as if the exterior view one had just beheld belonged to some other house altogether.

The baron was pleased by the work of Boyle and his band of builders. So pleased that he announced that a ball would be held at the house. A ball that was to take the shape of an elaborate fantasy, the particulars of which were not discussed, but became apparent once the preparations began in earnest. Boyle brought in a second wave of workers who toiled all hours of the day and night, rendering sleep nearly impossible.

One aspect of the work I found intriguing was the baron's laudable ability to speak with common English workers. How a German noble ever developed this rapport is a mystery. I recalled those few captains I have sailed with who could command with iron discipline and yet gain the crews' hearts as well. Von Mulct's easy affability with the workers seemed yet another example of the nobleman's superior character.

The baron's grace was further in view when I questioned him regarding the attack that led to my imprisonment aboard the India-bound ship. I met with him in his cabinet and informed him I was quite certain it had been Boyle who had knocked me cold. The baron, however, claimed no knowledge of the attack. And he was most agitated at the idea that Boyle was involved. "Boyle is a hothead at times. That is no excuse, though. I will swear out a complaint against him before ze magistrate if that will help, ja?" The Baron absentmindedly tapped the floor with his cane, so excited was his disposition. He insisted on bringing Boyle in for questioning.

When confronted, Boyle was deeply apologetic. "I'm sorry, Mr. Darius. I didn't know it was you. I swear it. I thought you was some cut purse or somethin', and since you people all look so similar, I can't make you out one from the other. Begging your pardon, Mr. D."

Boyle insisted that after knocking me out, he had dropped me into Bull Pure Alley. How I might have ended up tied to the fore bits of a ship off Wapping quay, he claimed to have not the least knowledge. "I couldn't rightly say, Mr. D," Boyle replied as he glanced quickly at the baron. Von Mulct seemed to ignore Boyle's unspoken query. He only tapped his stick and nodded sagely. Boyle looked back to me and added with clear earnestness, "Won't 'appen again, Mr. D. You 'ave my word."

As I have read some extensive tracts on the subject of eliciting truthful testimony from witnesses, I consider myself something of an expert on the subject. It was quite clear to me that Boyle was giving completely truthful answers and so there was nothing else to discover from him. Thus, that was where I left it — though I was determined to avoid Boyle as best I could in the future.

The battalion of workers brought in to prepare the house accomplished their task quickly. Soon the night for the ball was nigh. Geo and I dressed in our fashionable clothes — since thoroughly washed after our escape from Sir Francis Chase. We walked through the house to examine the particulars of the fantasy. I noticed Geo taking a gander at himself every time we passed a looking glass or polished surface. I confess I took a few looks at myself, too.

Upon making an entrance, the guests saw an interlocking bower of linden branches in the front hall. The bower was plentifully adorned with clusters of grapes and wild flowers. This led them to the left and into the sitting room. The room was unlike any in London, however. Every bit of furniture was gone and the room was arranged with trees, bushes, grass and flowers to suggest an American woodland. The effect was further heightened by the installation of a rocky stream that flowed through the very middle of the room. At the far wall the water fell down through a hole in the floor. The water dropped into the basement and settled in a trough, where a hardy team of servants operated a chain pump — similar to that found aboard ships to empty the bilges. This pump raised the water back up to the start of the stream, and so the brook flowed continuously.

Prominently situated in the center of the room amidst the trees was a brass transit, an optical device used by surveyors. Other surveying tools were located in other parts of the room; a measuring chain here, an elevation rod there. The baron informed Geo that during much of the festivities he was to remain by the transit and explain the methods of surveying. Geo was to answer any questions the guests might have as to the methods employed to assay the baron's American properties.

Following the glimpse of American nature in the woodland room, guests next entered the drawing room, similarly cleared of furniture and replaced with Indian habitations called wigwams. Recruited to play the savages were Scottish Highlanders. Following the battle of Culloden, the Duke of Cumberland had evicted this lot from their ancestral lands in Scotland's hills. Some of the unfortunates found their way to London. The baron engaged a few to play the hut-living savages — a role not far removed from their previous lives in the Highland glens.

Red-haired, blue-eyed Indians seemed strange to Geo and me, but not to the many Londoners who had never been more than 30 miles from the waters of the Thames. They considered Scotland and America to be the same as the farthest reaches of Africa and Araby — all equally savage. So wigwams inhabited by pale-skinned Scots were deemed entirely authentic.

Next after the wigwam room was the library, which was converted to a map room. Maps and prints were stretched out on boards and hung from the largely empty bookshelves. Many of the maps and printed pictures were of America and American scenes: Boston Harbor, a plantation in Georgia, the cliffs above the Hudson River, a fanciful view of the Ohio River with the spires of golden cities in the distance. The baron, however, had mixed in other views to heighten the exotic appeal: a woodcut of a bear surrounded by Russian dogs, a mezzotint of an Arab sultan before the domes of Cairo, drawings of Laplanders hunting seals, prints of African tribesmen brandishing shields and spears.

Ever the man of commerce, the baron reserved one table for the signing of contracts. Alongside it sat a strong box for the banking of cash down payments.

Finally, and of most interest to Geo, was the dining room, which was now the dancing room, its expanse of floor cleared and ready for dancers. In the butler's pantry sat a cramped string quartet. The doors between the pantry and the dining room were removed to greater facilitate the suffusion of music to the dancers. The back hall nearest the kitchen was provided with several long tables and lit by four candelabras. Across the tables was arrayed a rich selection of sweet meats, roasts of beef, quails, pigeon pie, cold mutton, veal chops, Colchester oysters, ox palates, pickled whiting, turtle soup, peas, boiled potatoes, leeks, apples, oranges, plums, cheeses both white and yellow, loaves of bread, cakes, syllabubs, Atholl Brose, fruit pies and tarts. To drink were bottles of cherry wine, a bowl of brandy punch, fustian punch, mulled wine, French claret, Madeira Sack, heavy port wine, porter, ale, gin and rum — as this last was a sailor's spirit, I fancied the baron had provided it for my benefit and so availed myself aplenty.

Prudence and Hawkins, along with all the servants in their charge, scurried everywhere in preparation. Much ado was made of the smallest details. London was a town of opulence and excess, and the baron's refreshments paled by comparison to the efforts expended by the lords and ladies of the greatest houses. However, the fantasy and its associated victuals were not a thing of which a host need feel ashamed.

For a brief moment, the baron, Sir Gerald, Lady Montagrave, Geo and myself were in serendipitous congregation in the front hall beneath the linden bower. Sir Gerald grunted forth instructions to Geo and I to nobly comport ourselves, while Lady Montagrave took the opportunity to squeeze Geo's arse and give him a knowing wink. Geo pretended to be surprised by this behavior, but he was flattered by her attention.

The baron gave no strict admonitions or hasty last-minute instructions, he merely raised his hands as if in benediction and spoke personally and with affection, "My friends, enjoy yourselves. This celebration is fur you as well as the guests, ja?" He took each of our hands in turn and clasped them in his. Then he added forcefully, almost in another voice, "Also, remember that we will do business in the library. Direct all those who wish to buy to zat table."

Then the front door opened and the invited guests arrived to warm greetings from the baron, Lady Montagrave and even Sir Gerald. We were in good position to see each guest enter the house and thus judge the nature of the ball. We could not tarry long there, however. The baron dispatched Geo to his position at the brass transit in the woodland room, while I was instructed to assist Prudence with the pouring of drinks — a happy duty as I saw it.

In no time the house was thick with wealthy Londoners. These were well-dressed in the manner of those whose ready money made it impossible to consider wearing anything but the newest clothes fresh from the tailor. While outwardly feigning indifference, they studied the clothes, shoes, wigs and jewelry of their fellow guests as intently as a thief eyes a money bag.

The reaction of the guests to the American woodland theme was better than the baron could have hoped. Jaded Londoners closely examined the wigwams and questioned the "Indians" as to the nature of their lives in the wilderness of America. The guests found the Scots' answers about Glen Buchat or Loch Killin exotically fascinating.

Most popular with the women, however, was Geo standing tall in the woodland room, nearly as shiny and pretty as the polished brass of the instrument alongside him. A gaggle of women surrounded him, eyes wide and lips wet. He demonstrated the geometric principles inherent in the operation of the transit, and briefly touched upon the use of rods and chains in measuring distance. One guest offered that she'd like some "private instruction in the use of the rod." The other women laughed and giggled, causing the tall, strapping Geo to blush crimson. This change in coloration only served to goad the ladies into further remarks expressing their own desire for intimate instruction with Geo's tools.

As the guests drank, they became happy, the dance floor filled, the musicians sawed away and the baron, Sir Gerald and Lady Montagrave could be seen in close and fervent conversation with numerous guests whom the trio steered toward the business table.

After some time explaining surveying and receiving many lubricious remarks, Geo found his way into the dancing room. As Geo reminded me often enough to cause offense, the young Virginian loved to dance. He paid for his own lessons a few years previously and adored dancing of any sort. He was soon out on the floor and never did he seem at a loss for a dancing partner. For a powerfully built young man, he moved with equal parts grace and precision. And while Geo presented a visage of reserved probity at most other times, whilst dancing he smiled and was attentive to the smallest aspects of his partner's performance.

After many minutes of sustained play, the musicians needed time to rest their arms and fingers and lips, so a halt was called.

As the music died out, the house rumbled with low vibrations from deep within its structure. Some of those present noticed the noise, but most talked and mingled, enjoying themselves and showing the effects of drink in its usual progression. Meanwhile, the baron appeared in the doorway and set a course across the room, found Geo and brought him to the map room. I lingered at the German's elbow and heard him explain to the young Virginian how his assistance was required. A wealthy widow, Mrs. Gemma Woodlot, urgently requested a private discussion regarding the physical aspects of the Ohio lands. The baron led Geo upstairs to a small bedchamber and reminded him of the necessity of keeping the customers happy. Von Mulct then opened the door and gestured Geo through.

The widow Woodlot sat at the edge of the bed, her face brightening to see Geo standing before her. "Before I can bring myself to make a down payment on one of the baron's American parcels," she explained, "it seems I am in need of further persuasion. The baron said you would ... give it to me."

She stood up and came close to him, putting her hands on his strong chest, sighing slightly as she did so. Geo was surprised at her actions, but he did not pull away as he remembered the baron's admonition that the customers' happiness came uppermost. While more than a decade and a half older than Geo, the widow Woodlot was not unattractive and the proximity of her body, the scent of her perfume and the pressure of her hands as they slid down his torso and found their way to the laces of his breeches were all powerful inducements for him to remain still. Seconds later, she had deftly collapsed the knot and loosened the laces. His breeches sagged open to reveal his small clothes and the fullness of his nature. It was at this moment that Geo remembered a particular fact that caused some hesitation. He beat a hasty tactical retreat.

"Pray, would you excuse me for just a moment, ma'am? I must make an inquiry. Please take your seat upon the bed and I shall return presently."

Before she could voice a protest, Geo turned and was gone, gathering up the laces to his breeches so as to avoid the garment's imminent collapse to his ankles.

After a quick search through the downstairs throng he found me in one of the wigwams. I was demonstrating to a curious young London woman the American frontier technique of surviving winter conditions by bundling naked under animal skins. She remarked this was her first time lying with an African man. Since I was loath to upset her, I admitted it was my first time with an English girl on Julian Square in a wigwam during this particular ball.

We were alone in the wigwam because the Scots play-acting as Indians had found a few bottles of whisky. They abandoned their role as American natives and adjourned to the rear garden. They set a roaring bonfire and were jumping naked through the flames while bellowing indecipherable Highland oaths.

Geo excused the interruption and dragged me from the wigwam. I grabbed a wool rug on my way out to cover my African nobility. This unusual attire caused little notice as most of the guests were fully in the embrace of Bacchus.

Geo drew me aside. "I am upstairs with Mrs. Woodlot and she desires that we fornicate."

I slapped him on the back and suggested he get back to it before Mrs. Woodlot's ardor cooled.

"Yes, of course, but there is only one thing that holds me back," Geo said with obvious discomfort.

I looked at him with surprise. "You can't get your yardarm to brace up properly?"

"No, no, that's not it. It's rather that I ... well, I ... "

Suddenly I understood. And I laughed out loud. "You

have never ... ?"

"Well, in a manner of speaking ... that is to say... no."
Geo was clearly discomfited by the subject.

I laughed again and leered and made silly faces for
some time before falling oddly silent. I realized I was baffled.
"What is your question?" I asked.

"It occurred to me that perhaps there is some technique
or maneuver I should employ?"

I looked at him with utter disbelief. "You are applying
too much worry to what is, at root, entirely a natural
operation. Have you never seen dogs, cattle, nor sheep whilst
in the act?"

"Naturally. But this is different."

"Shite!" I exclaimed. "There is no special maneuver
nor technique. A bull knows what to do, and so do you. Get
back up there, you fool. The baron will be distressed at your
dallying."

This last argument galvanized Geo and he departed
immediately. For my part, I resumed my instructional efforts
in the wigwam with Miss Betsy, or perhaps was it Miss
Betty? I did not hazard to ask at this climactic stage of our
association.

Retracing his steps, Geo again found himself in the
bedchamber with Mrs. Woodlot. To Geo's surprise, however,
the widow was not alone. There was another fellow at the
helm of Mrs. Woodlot's ship and he was steering with
considerable vigor.

Seeing that his presence was no longer required, Geo
made a quiet exit. Though initially dejected at disappointing
the Baron, when he reached the dance floor and immediately
found a willing partner for a lively gavotte, his mood
brightened considerably.

But duty called and the baron sent Geo back to the
woodland room to answer any lingering surveying questions.
I returned to the Wigwam room and then strolled to the edge
of the foyer to spy if any further guests were arriving. I
nearly fainted when I saw who strode through the linden
bower. With his sour expression and resplendent uniform, it
was none other than Sir Francis Chase. Accompanying him
was his mother, Lady Fanny Chase, the custard proprietor.
Geo and I last saw Lady Chase in Wexford, Ireland,
following our escape from hanging. Sir Francis wore his

officer's uniform while his mother was swathed in a dress that could only be described as the color of her favorite after-supper dish.

I retreated as rapidly as I could, making a direct line to the woodland room. Geo was engaged in conversation with a matronly woman. I hid behind one of the trees and motioned to Geo that he should cease his conversation. I needed not have bothered as I saw his expression of alarm when he cast eyes on Chase, who stopped just inside the door to examine the flowing stream.

Geo spoke his apologies to the matron and bowed out. I joined him as we walked hastily to the dancing room. "What is our plan?" Geo asked.

"We should get out of sight," I replied. "Let us make our way to the baron's private cabinet. Then we may exit via a window directly into the alley."

Once inside the baron's private room, we felt decidedly safer. Hidden from the dangerous Sir Francis, we could make our escape. I tried to open the lower sash of the window, but could not move it. I have often had to haul a line by myself when aboard ship, and am something of an expert on applying leverage to lift heavy cargo. Thus, I gathered my strength and heaved. The window moved not a fraction of an inch.

Geo meanwhile, was examining the items on the baron's desk, particularly admiring a brass model of an Egyptian obelisk, some sort of ancient monument to a great Pharoah. "Geo, stop rummaging and help me with this window," I scolded.

The big fellow joined me and together we attacked with straining muscles. There was not a morsel of movement. "Again," I commanded, "two, six — heave!" The sash scraped upwards perhaps a quarter inch. "If we had still another set of hands, we could open it."

"Perhaps if we used some sort of lever?" Geo offered. "What if we use that thing?" he said, pointing to the obelisk.

"Perhaps, but I'd rather rig up an anchor burton and use the mechanical advantage of a line running through several blocks."

"A lever would work just as well."

"I've been aboard ships great and small. I know how to lift heavy items."

"But we are not aboard a ship right now, are we?" Geo said.

"No," I snapped. "But the principles still apply, you oaf!"

"A lever is simpler and, thus, preferable, you ass!"

So consumed we were with our discussion, we did not hear the door open behind us, nor the tread of footsteps entering the room.

"C-c-could I be of assistance?"

Geo answered, "That's very kind of you." He turned around whilst I studied the problem of the stuck window.

"Ah ... D?" Geo said quietly. He poked me with his finger.

I was too busy studying the window frame. "I wonder if we might take off the trim and thusly move the sash," I ruminated.

"D!"

"What is it?" I asked. Geo's incessant poking in my ribs caused me to turn around.

Chase stood behind us. He had discovered the baron's cabinet and followed us within. With some flair, he drew his small dress sword and demanded our surrender.

"W-w-what a curious turn of fate," Sir Francis remarked. "I a-t-t-tend a household ball and who do I chance to see skulking through the ballroom but the two of you. I h-h-had hoped for a simple night of diversion but it seems I must do my duty and finally bring two outlaw Jacobites to justice."

At this juncture I must admit I thought we were done for. Geo, however, leaped into action. On the wall above him was a small shield bearing the Baron Mowenholtz's coat of arms. Crossed beneath it were two swords. Geo grabbed one and threw the other to me. It seemed quite light in my hand, but since it was the baron's own, I imagined it was of the finest and lightest German steel.

Sir Francis, seeing our intent to put up a struggle, charged forward. With closed eyes he swung his blade at mine. When the swords met, mine instantly splintered. My weapon was little more than a wooden fake. With another swing, Chase destroyed Geo's false sword. Sir Francis' blade continued its arc and hit the wall, the impact knocked the shield with the baron's coat of arms to the floor. The shield did not bounce with a metallic clatter but shattered — it was apparently made of nothing more than cheap plaster.

Our situation was now grave. We could not retreat through the window and the way forward was barred by Chase.

"I have caught you at last," a voice proclaimed. Geo and I agreed this was surely the case and threw up our hands. However, the voice did not come from Sir Francis as we imagined but from someone behind him.

We leaned around Sir Francis and saw the baron standing at the open door. He strode into the room with Lady Chase and three young women. The doxies all possessed comely good looks and were fashionably dressed. Sir Francis's mood changed immediately. He lowered his sword and turned to gaze earnestly at the three women, clearly undone by their charms.

"We have been following you through the house, " the baron announced. "Trying to find you und introduce you to these young ladies eager to meet a young army officer, ja?"

Lady Chase beamed at this interest in her son. "Francis, you must tell these young ladies of your courageous exploits in Ireland."

"Of   c-c-course,   mother," said   Sir   Francis. "Immediately after I arrest these Jacobites and b-b-bring them to the King's justice."

A wider grin stretched across Lady Chase's visage. She nodded politely and then said to the baron, "If I might have just a moment." She walked over to Sir Francis and said quietly. "Francis, dear, it is most impolite to attend a ball and then arrest the hosts. A British officer would never engage in behavior so unspeakably rude. You will put up your sword and enjoy yourself with these wonderful young ladies."

"Y-y-yes. Mother," the officer replied.

Lady Chase then spoke to the women. "Now, don't forget you are all welcome to come and have a tasting portion of custard for no charge at one of my shops."

The three women surrounded Sir Francis and lavished him with attention. His face changed from its usual sour dimension. When he smiled, his likeness to his mother was immediately apparent. "Y-y-yes, we will have custard," Sir Francis babbled.

Geo and I used this occasion to slip past him and stand

by the baron. "Perhaps, ve should leave them?" the baron said to us *sotto voce.* Without a word, Geo and I departed the cabinet. The baron took Lady Chase's arm and guided her out. As he closed the door, the baron told a passing servant to supply Sir Francis and his new friends with all the wine and spirits they wished. Then he turned to Lady Chase.

"My lady, would you favor a dance?"

Lady Chase tittered before replying, "Perhaps one with you, my lord baron," she tittered again, "then a turn with Mr. Washington?"

"Ja, ja. That would be fine. And then I would speak with you on a matter that I think a women with your commercial instincts will find most profitable."

As we entered the crowded ballroom, Geo spied amongst the crowd a raven-haired beauty leaving the room. Was it the woman who spoke with the baron at the Falling Inn? She briefly turned her head and Geo caught his breath - 'twas surely her.

Geo pushed after his Helen, hoping to cut off her line of retreat by slipping behind the wigwams. She was moving faster than he reckoned and he failed to rendezvous with her there. Hurrying, he crossed the hall to the woodland room, saw dark tresses and pounced. "Excuse me, miss," he said as he stepped around to face her.

The woman he stood before was in her later years, her face long ago ravaged by the pox. She smiled at him and somehow in his shock, he fell back upon his manners and nodded to her.

Glancing over, he saw the object of his desire gliding through the Linden bower toward the front door. Geo gave chase, racing down the steps into the street. But she had disappeared in the warm Julian Square moonlight.

Despondent at only getting a glimpse of his beautiful Helen, Geo went to the woodland room and found his hatchet. With expert strokes, he V-cut a tree erected there. It fell over with a crash sufficient to draw the attention of a man in a French cap. The fellow was sketching the woodland scene with charcoal.

"That was most impertinent," he said to Geo. "I am capturing this scene. Now you have disturbed it."

"Why would you draw it?" Geo asked.

"I wish to capture its rustic American feel."

"If you wish to capture America, go there. Do not rely upon this farce."

Hogarth nodded. "What would you know of America?"

"I am from that place. Virginia, to be precise."

"Ah, you must be Mr. Washington, the young surveyor of the American wilderness?"

"Indeed. And who are you?"

"William Hogarth, the greatest artist in England. And I wish to paint you. As an American you carry the essence of that wilderness in your heart, in your very bearing. I will capture that. Come to my studio. I must paint you, and afterward you shall be forever famous."

An hour, perhaps two, later, the mainspring wound down. The guests had, for most part departed, with only the drunken cries of the Scots around their dying bonfire to disturb the late-night calm. The baron was in a jolly mood. He hailed three of us, Geo, Lady Montagrave and myself. Sir Gerald was not part of our happy group as he had succumbed to a surfeit of gin and lay snoring in a corner of the map room. We gathered on the dance floor for a quick tally from von Mulct. "We have signed more contracts and procured more down payments than I could have hoped. You were all vunderful tonight." The baron turned to Geo and gave him a cuff on the shoulder. "Und you did your duty, ja? Mrs. Woodlot seemed quite satisfied. She signed und paid promptly."

Geo said nothing, merely nodding and accepting the credit. I must say I was proud of him for not exhibiting his usual infernal honesty.

Moments later we were treated to the most amusing sight of the besotted Major Chase. He was being carried from the house by several servants — the group of them ably directed by Hawkins. So heavily was he under the sway of drink that he could not stand up nor put one foot before the other. The servants put him in a hackney cab and sent him to St. James Palace. Lady Chase had departed earlier, still aflutter following her dance with Geo.

For me the night was young. I tried to persuade Geo to accompany me out on further revels, but he claimed to be fatigued and would have none of it. He retired to his cramped room in the attic.

No sooner was he lying abed, however, when the door opened in the darkness. "D, leave me alone," Geo snapped. "I do not wish to go out upon the town." The portal scraped shut and light footsteps crossed the floor. A form climbed into Geo's bed. He was about to call out in surprise when the person unknown kissed him quite passionately. Geo moved to push the interloper away but his hands came to rest on a woman's breast.

"Aren't you the familiar one?" laughed Lady Montagrave before kissing him again, longer and more deeply this time.

"Lady Montagrave?" Geo asked in surprise.

"So you have guessed. So you are every bit as clever as they say," she said. Again they kissed.

"But what of Sir Gerald?" Geo gasped when their lips parted.

"What of him? He lies asleep in a drunken stupor," she crooned in his ear, "but you will find that I am *very* much awake."

Chapter Nine
Cornered by the Press

BY THE TIME Sir Gerald stirred from the map room floor, Lady Montagrave had dressed and departed the baron's house. Still, Geo felt Sir Gerald's bloodshot eyes watching him suspiciously.

"Where is Lady Montagrave?" Sir Gerald demanded.

"I believe she is not here," Geo replied.

"She had better not be," Sir Gerald said as he shuffled off, wincing as he did so. His head hurt powerfully from his prodigious gin consumption of the previous night. As Sir Gerald walked away, Geo mimicked the gimpy bull, step for step. Geo's mocking walk made me laugh out loud. Sir Gerald turned and grimaced. Geo smirked in return, which only further angered the big man. Sir Gerald, however, was hurting too badly to manage any counterattack to Geo's youthful insolence.

The baron had booked no appointments for Geo that day, so we decided to walk to rooms let by the artist Mr. Hogarth on Water Street near Dorset Stairs. He had invited Geo the previous night to attend him there. The butler Hawkins had some business along our route and so he joined us for a stretch.

I was concerned that after his visit of the previous evening, Sir Francis might seek out number four Julian Square. I asked Hawkins if he thought Chase would return.

"'Tis not likely. Freely did he partake and freely did his mind depart him. He will remember little of last night. I will be amazed if he remembers that the number four Julian Square even exists."

Happily reassured, we made our way from the baron's house southwards toward Fleet Street and the River Thames. We passed beggars red with runny sores, old broken-down shoe-blacks, coughing coal heavers, impudent harlots and doxies with their lewd solicitations (a few of which I rather fancied), fruit sellers, ballad singers, bone pickers, pickpockets, mountebanks and drunks — these last lying in the filth of the streets, some surely dead but as yet unnoticed since the odor of their decomposition had yet to o'ertake the stench of the choked roadways.

According to Hawkins, one of London's most infamous gutters ran south from Fleet Bridge to the river: the Fleet Ditch. "'Tis a great trough whose foulness is only concealed by the hard freezes of winter; a festering sore upon the fair countenance of Lady London; a sea of corruption flowing into Thames water — that is to say, it stinks." What centuries ago must have been a lazy stream flowing into the Thames was now a miasmic channel of filth, sewage, and the leavings of tripe dressers, sausage makers and catgut spinners.

In a book of verses I found in the baron's library — none of which volumes seemed ever to have been opened — I read a few lines written by the great wit Jonathan Swift on the condition of the Fleet Ditch following a hard rain:

"Sweepings from the butchers' stalls, dung, guts and blood,
Drown'd puppies, stinking sprats, all drench'd in mud,
Dead cats and turnip-tops come tumbling down the flood."

A weeping rain had begun an hour previous and the purulent flow of which Swift wrote was already gurgling down the ditch. As a man of the sea, I am altogether unmoved by the smell and stench produced by men living in close quarters. Yet even I must admit, my head felt light and my eyes stung from the vapors arising from the foul trench.

Hawkins, in his roundabout way, made an effort to help us with the challenge of living in the capital. Before he parted from us he remarked on the need to demonstrate discretion concerning the Ohio land sales. "Remember that although Mr. Hogarth is not a man of means himself and would have little chance at purchasing one of my master's land parcels, he moves among the propertied classes. He has the ear of many men and women of place and rank; lords and ladies, bankers and merchants and men of money — that is to say, keep your traps well shut." Hawkins fixed us in his stare and then backed away into the great flow of humanity that swept along the street like a tidal bore.

Geo told me of his first conquest of womankind —
though it sounded more to me that Lady Montagrave had
been the conqueror.

"Funny, ain't it?" I observed. "Until last night you
were a virgin from Virginia."

"True enough, D," Geo replied. He moved with a
confident step this morning and while I would be the last to
discount the buoyant effects of a night of rigorous rutting, I
sensed there was more to his good humor than merely the
pleasure of firing a broadside or two. Then, as if he knew my
mind, he spoke of it.

"This time in London has been very good for me, D. I
am a younger son. My half brother Lawrence is given all that
my family could bestow. And though you may think me from
a family of great wealth, the truth is we are only a few steps
above the rudest farmers and are nowhere close to the
moneyed position of Lord Fairfax, the richest man in
Virginia."

"It may be true that you are not the wealthiest family in
the colony," I said, "but you do have something that some in
America can never earn."

"What is that?"

"Your freedom. For the slaves in Virginia, and in New
York and elsewhere, freedom is a pearl beyond price."

Geo nodded and grew silent. Then he started up again,
saying sharply, "You needn't remind me of that. I am aware
of it." He paused, then, "Are we not friends?"

"Yes, of course. I say we are."

"Then may I speak to you as a friend, or must we
discuss all things in the terms of the English and African
races? If that be so, then perhaps we are not friends at all."

I was left momentarily speechless. It seemed to me that
Geo had just given me both a sharp rebuke and a most
heartfelt compliment. "Alright, then. I am corrected. You
were discussing your very own situation, not the state of
freedom as it exists or does not exist in America."

"Exactly so."

"Although you will admit," I added, "it is a subject of
great weight that is never far from my mind."

"D? What did I just say? Must we speak of it in every

discourse?"

"Very well, you are correct. We are friends and needn't bring it up every time."

"Alright then," Geo said.

There was a pause.

"But I must make it clear that freedom for slaves is a vital issue."

Geo was utterly exasperated. "D!"

"Yes, of course. Friends." I tried to sound as accommodating as I could.

Geo remained quiet as we walked, save for the need to refuse the advances of a doxie, to apologize for knocking someone down in the crush of people, or to demand the return of his purse.

"Shall you continue?" I asked him finally. "I am ready to hear you as a friend."

Geo turned and thumped me on the chest with one of his big hands. 'Twas as solid a whack as I have had. "Alright then," Geo said with a smile. "Serves you right."

I was about to remark on an annoying habit of white folk to strike African folk, followed by an explanation as to why the blow was for the good of the African. But I refrained from voicing this point.

"I was saying that my half-brother Lawrence, who is eldest, gets everything of value yet I, as a younger son, must shift for myself. I have always worried how I would make my fortune, starting, as I have, with so little. Yet, now I possess some money and I have great prospects. Baron Mowenholtz has assured me that a title and even a country estate with a regular income is within my grasp."

Though I could have made many points about his great advantage of being born into a family of Virginia gentry, I did not. Rather, I was genuinely happy for Geo. It was his desire and his ambition in life to become a man of means and importance. Who was I to critique a view he held so dearly and with such fervor that it served as his guiding star? There was something, however, that troubled me. I sensed that though Geo welcomed the idea of a minor title such as baronet, he would never be entirely happy. He would press upward for greater acclaim and an augmented income. But there were many members of the nobility in England, and they would not stand aside and let a colonial become their equal in title or wealth. It seemed that for Geo to reach his goal of great success, he would have to find some other route than the one he now so eagerly pursued.

One aspect of our talk was pleasing to me. Whereas, I had originally seen my assistance to Geo in the pure light of divine responsibility, I now viewed him in a more mundane, yet satisfying, fashion. I now counted him as my friend and business associate. Of course, an African man such as myself must always exercise caution as to the true nature of friendship with white folks. Partners who conduct an enterprise on nothing more than a handshake should not entertain sharply diverging definitions of common words like partner, profit and freedom.

The light rain continued throughout our walk. I did not have the oilskins I normally carry aboard ship and I was well soaked as we approached what we thought was the place of Mr. Hogarth's painting studio. So intent were we on finding the right way, I was not wary of one of the capital's prominent dangers: the Royal Navy press gang.

We turned into Two Block Alley and found ourselves staring at just such a gang of bully boys. These men were well armed with clubs and were led by the biggest, meanest fellow I ever saw — a Royal Navy chief petty officer crossed with a giant. The chief's eyes lit up when he saw the two of us, "Yo, ho. Lookie here, lads. We got ourselves some fresh chickens." The group turned and eyed us like a pack of wolves.

"We must flee," I remarked to Geo as calmly as I could.

"Who are these ruffians?"

"A press gang," I replied softly. "They will beat us senseless and then drag us aboard one of his majesty's warships," I said as I backed away. The gang started a slow advance toward us.

"Is that not illegal? It amounts to little more than kidnapping! I will have a word with them," he said strongly.

I grabbed his arm to stop him from leaving my side. "Nay, you will not. They have the king on their side. You have only me to back you."

We were in a narrow street crowded with carts of fish,

eels and prawns. I turned and scampered. Geo, finally grasping the true lay of the land, followed. The press gang pursued as best they could, but the rain had made the cobbles slippery. As I passed one of the carts, I grabbed a hold of its yoke and heaved upward. The two-wheeled wagon dumped its load of slimy herring across the street.

As far as the press gangers were concerned, Geo and I were two bags of coin with legs. Should they nip us, they would be rewarded with bounty money. Given this highest of motivations, they and their chief were in no mood to stop on account of a few little fish, but resolved to plow through the dead school.

The first sailor who reached the herring carpet slipped, went down and slid sidelong into a 20-pound sack of flour, bursting its seams. The roiling cloud of flour dust o'erspread the street like the smoke of a broadside and hid us for some seconds. In what I surely accorded the status of a miracle, we heard cursing and commotion as our pursuers, blinded by loaves of dust, fell in the multitude of fish.

We had almost passed round the next corner when one of the gang emerged from the flour fog and spotted us. The press ganger shouted out, and those who could still run followed. In this new alleyway, however, there were no carts to tip over. Worse than that was the brick wall that marked the alley's farthest extent. We had reached a dead end.

Freedom was to be ours no longer, it seemed. Our lot was to be the cruelty of the lash, the servitude of orders and the dangers of battle.

Chapter Ten
Lord of the Dance

A CITY of London's extent is a habitation with many practical problems. Water must be provided and food made available. After these two are combined, there comes an inevitable by-product: a material disagreeable in every way a material can be deemed so. This dross must be removed or the city will be overwhelmed by its own filth. In London, the night soil men are the means of its removal. They labor to gather the night soil from cesspits and cart it to regions outside the city's boundaries.

As luck would have it, no sooner had we arrived in the cul-de sac than a party of night soil men exited from one of the buildings into the alley. Their hand-cart was piled high with the foulest, most odiferous, stomach-turning load of shite I have ever had the good luck to smell. And the men themselves were well smeared with the brown and black stains of freshly excavated crap. At the appearance of the shite men, the press gang recoiled and I saw our deliverance. We mingled with the night soilers, who were happy to have any man treat them as an equal. They embraced us and we walked with them. The press gang was loath to approach the shite procession and though they growled and grumbled, they let us disappear round the corner. And so we escaped the clutches of the press via the exegesis of excrement.

We visited the artist Hogarth, but were not well-received in our shite-smeared clothes. We were given some clothing that Hogarth had in his studio for the use of those posing for paintings. Geo wore a blue satin collection, while I donned a suit of bright green.

Hogarth insisted on painting Geo standing up in a rowboat, a position that anyone with the least nautical experience would recognize as thoroughly impractical and prone to capsize. I was included as one of his hardy rowers. We thereafter took our leave of the mercurial painter. We departed without changing back into our own clothes. Once we realized this, we doubled back to Hogarth's studio. The painter had departed, however, and the door was locked. We had no choice but to return later to fetch them.

Thus, we let our path be governed by no government at all, but instead followed the serendipitous hand of fate. We walked London's streets, occasionally returning to Hogarth's studio. Each time we found it empty and locked.

On our ramble we stopped at a street side fortune teller. She was an African mystic named Mother Geechee, though, in fact, she appeared no older then perhaps 15 years. She threw the bones and prophesized that Geo would live in a large house by a river and possess a title of greatest importance.

To me she suddenly announced that I had the sight, that with the help of my dead twin Jabbar, I could see the future. I was frightened by her words. My hands shook at the mention of my dead twin. I denied any such gift or that I ever had a brother. Mother Geechee only silently stared at me, ignoring my denials, damning me with her eyes. "You can deny with your mouth," she said, "but I see what is inside. Jabbar will lead you and your gifts will grow."

Geo professed to place no stock in fortune tellers. "How could a man of action put his confidence in such a thing?" Geo scoffed.

"Some do believe in them," I responded as we hurried away. My voice quavered and my step was heavy. "Perhaps the hand of fate reveals what is to come?"

Geo shrugged. "I would wager Mother Geechee tells the same fortune to a hundred people a day. Besides, she is no mother. I doubt she has ever given birth to a child."

"Hmm, I'm sure you are right." I said it only to feel better.

"Of course I am," Geo said firmly.

We made yet another circuit back to the studio. Again, we had no luck as Mr. Hogarth was clearly on some extended errand. Whilst walking, Geo suddenly asked, "Did she say 'a *big* house by a river' or 'a house by a *big* river?'"

"I am positive she said 'house by a big river.'"

Geo knit his brow. "No, no, you are mistaken. It was, 'big house by a river.'"

"Very well."

After another few moments, he spoke again. "And did she say I would have 'a title of greatest importance?'"

I stopped and surveyed him. "I was under the impression that you did not believe in fortunes."

Geo stopped as well. He stuffed his hands in his pockets and rocked on his heels. "Well, I don't see any reason to needlessly offend fate. I will remember Mother Geechee's prediction as a courtesy."

Just then I looked up. The sign on the shop where we paused read: "The Custard Chase."

"Ah-ha, this custard shop must surely belong to Lady Chase," I said.

"But I saw the same sign on a custard shop not half a mile away."

I considered this. "Perhaps Lady Chase's idea is to have a number of custard shops selling the same flavors of custard all over the city. Such an arrangement would ease the minds of customers, as they could be sure each shop had the same flavors and the same quality."

"That is a foolish way to undertake commerce. Such a scheme would never work."

We enquired inside the shop for Lady Chase, as we desired to present our good wishes. The man inside, however, said that while Lady Chase was the owner of the custard shops, she was aware of her position and did not lower herself to toil behind the counter of one. After ensuring that no one was watching, he gave us each a bowl of custard at no charge.

Following a long day of wandering London streets and having had no luck in retrieving our clothes, we repaired to a pleasant supper in an establishment called The Two Lanterns, a crowded tavern suffused with clay pipe smoke and noise. Geo and I then intended to amble our way back to the house on Julian Square. Unfortunately, our meal was too pleasant. Geo tossed off many glasses of wine and I indulged in my love for ale. Perhaps we were stumbling when we left the tavern.

I am a nautical navigator and I struggle somewhat when ashore. Geo, of course, was unerring going overland. This night, however, Geo's compass was all a-spin. He led us very far a field from the familiar precincts of Julian Square.

His misnavigation started immediately after we left The Two Lanterns. As we walked along a gloomy street, we saw the yellow glow of fire reflected off windows ahead. We came upon a rough gathering of common people. A great mob filled the street, many holding crackling flambeaux.

These torches ringed the larger tongues of a raging bonfire. From the upper windows of an old brick row house, men were throwing clothes, bedding, mattresses and such down into the fire. Other members of the mob were dragging nearly naked women out into the street and jeering and laughing at 'em. The sullen mob raised a "HUZZAH!" as each feather mattress hit the flames.

Geo, still in his cups, shakily asked a bystander what the women had done.

"Oh, them's Frenchie whores what cheated some sailors," he replied with a low laugh. "The boys are showin' 'em who's got the upper touch."

"That's bar — barbaric," Geo slurred. "I m-m-must stop this!"

The bystander looked at him with surprise and then a nasty chuckle. "Right. I'll just tell the lads you want to talk to 'em." The fellow worked his way into the crowd, and spoke with several of the mob. He pointed at Geo. The bulls he alerted began to push through the crowd in our direction, eager-faced in the firelight.

I grabbed Geo's arm and pulled him back. "We must depart!" I demanded. "They will beat us grievously." We turned and hurried away; passing from the roar of the mob and the yellow glow into dark, empty streets.

Now shrouded by the full darkness of the night, with only the crescent moon for a drip of illumination, it was clear that we were lost.

"Now you've done it," I said. "We're way off the rhumb line, you know. No way to get back."

"Hussssshh! I am not without resources."

Ahead of us, at the end of the street, a ship of light lay at anchor. The great house, most certainly the city dwelling of a Duke, blazed from every window and lively notes of a bourrée drifted across the cobbles. A celebration or a ball was clearly underway. At the one end of the building a small crowd was gathered. But at the other end the garden gate was open and unguarded. We blithely walked through, across gardens fragrant with late spring blossoms of lavender and rose amid a winking congress of fireflies.

Unchallenged, we approached the nearest of the tall windows. We saw the house's great room was populated by a smattering of fashionably dressed ladies and gentlemen. One tall, young fellow, who seemed no older than his teens, stood in the middle of the floor. He was terribly bored. An older man lectured and then moved through a series of dance steps. The assembly waited patiently for the young man to follow along, but the fellow only executed the steps half-heartedly.

"He's a dancing instructor!" Geo yelled. "They're teaching that lad to dance."

"Yes, of course. That much is clearly obvious."

"Well," Geo replied testily, his voice rising, "I didn't hear anything from you about it until just now. Maybe it was not so obvious!"

"It was so obvious that I didn't feel the need to say anything! That's what happens when things are obvious!"

"I don't think you knew it was obvious in the least," Geo replied hotly.

"You're the one who didn't know it was obvious. If you knew, then you would have said nothing, but since you spoke, it is obvious that you didn't know it was obvious."

"That is not obvious!"

"Yes it is!" I said.

"No, it's not obvious that what you said is obviously so obvious is, in fact, obvious at all!"

"But I said it was obvious because ..." I stopped and scratched my head. "I'm lost. Where was I?"

Geo opened his mouth to speak but then shut it and shrugged.

"Gentlemen!" a voice boomed out.

We turned to see a man in an exceedingly fine set of livery standing in the wash of light from an open door. "You must be the fellows requested by the Duke."

Geo and I said nothing.

"Where is the rest?"

I looked myself over from head to toe. "This is all there has ever been of me," I said.

"The rest of your party, I mean to say."

"Oh, ... ah, they shall be here presently, I'd imagine," I answered.

"Very well, then. Come ahead." He indicated that we were to go inside. The servant stepped aside to let Geo stride through the doorway. But when I stepped into the light and he saw that I was of African blood, he was less sanguine. He caught my arm and said to Geo, "Is he one of your party?"

Geo turned and looked back. "Obviously."

The servant released my arm. "You may proceed."

We entered the great room where the young man was receiving his dance lesson. It was a tall room topped by a coffered ceiling with gold-leafed cherubs floating at its corners, handsome patterned wallpaper and thick wool rugs from the east. The gaggle of women in attendance were drawn up in a line on one side, while the handful of men stood behind the young man and the dancing master. Six musicians were perched in one corner, resigned to playing the same bourrée again and again. The liveried servant announced us by bowing toward the boy, "Your Highness, here are the men who were requested."

The young fellow turned to look at Geo, who still wore the suit of blue satin the painter Hogarth had provided. I was still clothed in the preposterous green.

"Ah, fresh blood. And a blackamoor, as well. Isn't that amusing. Is this all of them?"

"So far, your Highness. More are said to be making their way."

At this point, I surmised that the lad was none other than Prince George, Duke of Edinburgh and — with the recent, untimely death of his father Frederick — the newly installed Prince of Wales. This young man, only 13 years of age, was next in line to sit upon the throne now occupied by his German grandfather, his Most Britannic Majesty George II. This young George was a plain fellow, but not unpleasing. Tall for his age with a ruddy complexion, he had a weak chin and large blue eyes. Whereas, when viewed from outside the window, he had seemed bored and not a little irritated at this dancing session, now with Geo's and my arrival, the young Prince was enlivened.

"Let's have it again, shall we, Monsieur Le Fatineau?"

The monsieur, a spindly Frenchman with a fancy wig and a permanent glower, agreed with a shallow bow and the music began. As I had no local knowledge of these waters, I stepped back and let Geo show his wares. He performed well with an older lady of the court, who initially was sniffy and aloof at the sight of the shiny-suited young man. As the dance progressed, however, and she observed the felicity of Geo's steps and the grace of his interaction, she was charmed sufficiently to allow an approving smile to surface.

Prince George, as well, noted Geo's excellent acquittal of himself. When the dance had finished, the prince remarked, "Perhaps we should release Monsieur Le Fatineau and engage that fellow there." He pointed at Geo. The monsieur did not find this remark amusing and tossed a look Geo's way. The prince added: "Though we would clearly not ask his advice regarding fashion."

As the entire company laughed, Geo bowed to the prince, his face reddened.

At that moment, an army officer in a bright crimson coat, much gold braid and a sour, haughty air strode into the room. Geo and I needed no introductions. Nor did Sir Francis Chase, who had been promoted from major to lieutenant colonel. When he saw us, he stopped and put his hand to his sword.

"Y-y-your Majesty, those men are dangerous J-J-Jacobites intent on insurrection."

The prince looked at us and then turned his gaze back to Chase. "Really, Chase, you see Jacobites under every bed. These are two fellows helping us to dance. You are forbidden to cut them in two. In fact, we wish them to come here again tomorrow and assist us."

"Y-y-your Highness, w-w-we are to depart for Windsor in the morning. The king has requested your presence on the morrow. We must return to St. James in preparation."

Young Prince George immediately rejoined, "But we are now enjoying our dance lessons. Did our grandfather not request that we learn to dance properly?" He pointed to Monsieur Le Fatineau, "in the French style?"

"Indeed, y-y-your Highness. However, this royal request supersedes that one, I am afraid."

"We must protest this treatment, Chase. You are a lieutenant colonel and commander of our life guard, but we are a prince and heir to the throne. How is it that you may order us around so?"

"'T-t-tis only as my role as a loyal servant of my king. When it pleases God to take the king to his bosom and you are crowned, I shall serve you with equal fervor and loyalty, your Highness."

The prince snorted. "When we are king, we shall make you master of the royal night soil. How would you fancy that?"

"It w-w-would be my honor, your Highness," Colonel Chase answered dryly. "And n-n-now we must return to the palace."

"Alright then, we shall attend to my grandpa. But we want these fellows to visit us tomorrow in Windsor. We must find out how that one has so mastered the grace of the dance." Prince George walked quickly out. The assembled group bowed in unison and then scattered.

Sir Francis turned to Geo. "D-d-do not think I have forgotten your Jacobite rebellion in Ireland, nor your fleeing from custody, nor the ruination of my uniform by immersion in molasses, nor your other escape from my grasp which I somehow cannot quite remember. I shall bring you two to justice for all three of those incidents."

"Four," I corrected.

"B-b-but I cannot recollect a single detail of the last one," Chase said.

"Still, you do remember something happened."

"S-s-so?"

So, you should count it."

"D-d-do you think?"

"Of course, it represents one of the set of incidents, and even though you do not recollect every detail, the mere fact you have even the haziest memory means it must be included. Otherwise it could cause your mind to experience waves of discomfort that —"

"Enough! All right, then, f-f-four incidents. Three or four or ten, it does not matter. I shall still see you two at the end of a rope."

Geo gathered his wits and stated, "Both Darius and myself are now under the protection of the prince. You may do nothing to us while this is true."

The anger and displeasure on Sir Francis's face confirmed Geo's analysis. With the greatest effort, Sir Francis asked where he might have a carriage sent to pick us up.

"We are staying here in town. Do you not remember?"

"Why would I have any knowledge of your Jacobite lodgings?"

Geo just looked at me and smiled. Chase did not remember the location of the baron's house on Julian Square.

"No matter," he held up his hand. "Be at St. James

Palace tomorrow morning at dawn. I shall have a coach for you. And you had better wear something a bit less macaroni."

Geo was about to ask a question, but Lieutenant Colonel Chase was already on his way out. Geo and I were under the protection of the prince. What evil could befall us?

Chapter Eleven
A King's Right

KICKING UP a cloud of dust, Geo and I rolled down the road toward Windsor in a royal coach. Like princes of the royal blood, we rode in a coach adorned with the royal seal, with liveried footmen in attendance. Townsmen and country folk curiously regarded the coach as we passed. Some tried to peer inside, supposing its passengers included the king, Queen Caroline or Prince George. Geo clearly enjoyed the attention of the people during our grand progress to Windsor.

Geo took to waving at the upturned faces of onlookers and remarked that though he had not thought on it before, the prospect of being a king had its appeal. It was a shame, he said, one needed to be born into the job. What if, he mused, one accomplished some great feat and were offered kingship by acclimation?

Before our early morning departure, the baron and Sir Gerald sat Geo and I down and tutored us on the royal House of Hanover, the proper way to act in the presence of the king and the prince, and most important of all, the need to remain silent on the question of the baron's business affairs. If asked, we were to say that the baron was engaged in the importation of German specialty items, such as pork jellies, pickled herring, and oil of cloves. When Geo pointed out that the baron was not involved in the importation of any such items, the baron chided him.

"Not everyzing that I do is fully known to you."

"But why may we not speak of the sale of the Ohio parcels?" Geo pressed. "I am proud of my work opening the land beyond the Alleghenies."

The baron laughed. "Ja, Ja, it is stirring work, to sure. But, the answer is simple, no? The king and the prince are members of the royal family, but they also have business interests of their own. Should they find that we have been selling these very attractive pieces of land without having first offered them a chance to participate, it vould look very bad und they would be embarrassed. So, to protect them, the best approach is to keep the entire affair private, ja?"

We naturally agreed that the king and the prince should be protected.

As the ride was a long one, Geo found that he needed more stimulation than merely playing the royal. When we stopped to water the horses, Geo hopped out, gathered handfuls of walnut-sized stones and dumped them inside the coach. On the second half of our journey, he took great amusement in throwing a stone out the open door of the coach. He did this when a target, such a tree, well or cow came into range along the road.

Most of his missiles found their mark, except for a notable stone he threw as we passed through Windsor castle gate. It flew wide, missed a raven on the parapet and fell toward the stained glass windows in the castle chapel. The stone crashed through a colored glass panel that depicted the great piety of King Richard as he slew Saracen warriors during one of the Crusades' expeditions to bring Christian forgiveness and love to the heathen Arabs. Geo and I crouched low in the coach and hoped that no one noticed.

Ushered to one of the agricultural gardens, we were told to wait for the prince near what appeared to be a thick growth of bushes. We stood patiently, waiting for the young royal to appear. A voice called out, "We say good day to you, gentlemen." Though Geo and I were sure it was the voice of the prince, we could not place where he might be.

"Do you not answer your Royal Highness?" the prince's muffled voice spoke again.

"Where are you, your Highness, that we might answer you?" Geo replied.

"Why, we are right here alongside you."

"Though that might be, but we do not see you, Highness," Geo said.

The young prince now began to laugh. Finally, a section of the nearby bushes revealed itself to be a door as it swung open and Prince George stepped out, smiling broadly.

We bowed and the prince explained the serious thinking that lay behind his hideaway. "'Tis a privy, but one that has been expertly disguised to make it appear as a bush. We designed it to be used in the field during army operations. A privy such as this will allow officers to relieve themselves in comfort, while at the same time remaining hidden from the depredations of the enemy," he explained. "We have been horribly selfish in naming the invention after ourselves."

We smiled and nodded and the prince beamed proudly.

"We welcome you to Windsor Castle. It now occurs to us that due to the unusual nature of our meeting, we find ourselves unaware of your name or the name of your slave."

Geo saw me draw up in anger. He put his hand on my arm to calm me. "I am George Washington of Virginia, your Highness. And this is not my slave, but a freeman, Darius Attucks of New York. He has sailed as first mate on numerous merchant ships and is acknowledged by true sailors as a seaman of the first rank."

Prince George looked me over. "If he is that accomplished, perhaps we should direct the Admiralty to name him master and commander of a sloop of war?"

Unsure of the proper response, I simply bowed and murmured, "Your Highness."

"This is most auspicious that you are from the colonies. We are especially interested in Indian fighting. Do you know anything regarding the fighting methods of the American savages?"

Geo nodded vigorously. "Yes, Highness, I do. I have some experience in lands across the mountains, in the great basin of the Ohio River."

"Oh, this is the hand of the Almighty at work, to be sure. We are undone at your lucky arrival. You must teach us forthwith." The prince ripped off his fine jacket, tossed his hat aside and removed his wig — a small cloud of white powder from it caught me in the face. Once readied, he put his hands up in a fighting posture.

"Well," the prince said to Geo, "make yourself ready for hand-to-hand combat."

No sooner had Geo doffed his wig than the prince lunged at him. Geo was able to partially sidestep the big 13-year-old's attack, but the two young men soon fell into a heap on the ground and became engaged in a titanic struggle — at one moment Geo had the upper hand, the next, Prince George was in ascendancy.

Finally, after a long struggle, Geo was better able to use his leverage, perseverance and patient application of pressure to force the young prince to capitulate.

While they were still on the ground, Lieutenant Colonel Chase suddenly appeared on the scene. He was accompanied by Prince George's aide-de-camp, Lord Blathingwell, a fellow not much older than Geo. Impeccably dressed and of refined sensibility, Blathingwell was the son of the 12th Earl Pratterton. The main calling of the young noble's life was to wait for his elderly father to die so Lord Blathingwell could become the 13th earl.

An agitated Chase reached down and grabbed Geo. "How dare you put your hands on the person of his Highness the Prince? Do you see, your Highness? This is just the sort of attack I feared from this Jacobite."

As he got up, Prince George waved off Chase. "Sir Francis, you are thoroughly mistaken. Unhand Mr. Washington at once. We were wrestling at our royal request. Washington was showing us Indian techniques of combat."

Chase released Geo, ostentatiously shaking off his officer's coat from the supposed grime imparted by the Virginian. Geo and the prince dressed themselves fully again. In a moment of confusion, Geo mistakenly took Prince George's royal wig and put it on.

"That was monstrous good fun, wouldn't you say?" the Prince bubbled.

"You are a superb fighter, your Highness," Geo admitted. "I would hate to face you in a real fight."

"Nor we you." The prince then turned to Blathingwell, "Are the Indians and American settlers ready?" When the young lord answered "yes," the prince was further agitated.

"We must attend to our maneuvers at once," Prince George remarked.

For my part, I was most excited, as I have made some extensive study of all things military and I don't think myself the least bit boastful in stating that I am something of an expert on army affairs.

In a fallow field nearby the castle stood a replica American village. Milling around the village was a group of British soldiers attired to play the role of American frontier settlers. The costumer of these players, however, was perhaps not a recent visitor to America, as the playacting villagers wore the severe black clothes, white collars and tall buckled hats most favored by the Pilgrim settlers of Plymouth some 130 years ago. Still, the buildings of the mock village were generally up-to-date and the soldiers carried the correct arms and equipment.

Standing upon a small hill overlooking the faux village were the Prince, Lord Blathingwell, Colonel Chase, Geo and myself. Our position provided us with an excellent view. "Before us lies a typical village in the wilds of colonial America — in Pennsylvania, perhaps," the prince said. "Little do the happy residents of this town realize that savages will soon attack." At the word "attack" a young aide near us lowered the fluttering flag he held.

Through the trees a wave of "Indians" soon appeared. Unlike the erroneous clothes of the settlers, these Indian were correctly and truthfully costumed with deer leather cloths, feathers and painted faces. The only aspect of their appearance that rankled was their wig-powder white skin, freckles and fair hair.

Still, they came on at a rush, with tomahawks and bows and arrows looking remarkably deadly. With blood curdling yells they closed on the village, looking to destroy it and savagely attack its inhabitants. Even standing on the hill I felt the anxiety of the moment. The playacting soldiers in the town clearly had equally authentic feelings of fear at the sight. Those with their muskets at hand formed up in ranks and let loose a volley of sound and smoke into the body of the charging Indians. As the guns were not charged with ball but fired mere wadding, the volley had no effect and the Indians continued their charge. A second volley also did nothing to hold back the attackers and they were now at the edge of the village.

The realism of this piece appeared too much, however, for the soldiers who played the settlers. In the press of the moment, a well-drilled soldier ceases to think, but falls back upon his training. And so the British regulars fell back. They formed a line, fixed bayonets and counterattacked with cold steel. A bit too late, the infantry major who was in command of the mock battle saw the danger of the soldiers' actions and ran forward ordering the soldiers to cease their bayonet charge.

The wave of emotion and reaction induced in the soldiers was not so easily stemmed, however. Surging forward, the line of soldiers made contact with the Indians and bayoneted a number of them to their death. The other Indians, realizing that this had become combat in earnest, dropped their weapons and ran pell mell, screaming for help.

So infectious had the spirit of destruction become, however, those Indians equipped with torches lit the buildings in the village and a roaring fire sprang up, fanned by a gusty west wind. Great swirling clouds of smoke now descended upon a scene of utter chaos. Indians screamed, soldiers charged, officers shouted, villagers fled, and all staggered and stumbled from the suffocating effects of smoke.

"This won't do," the prince fretted. "This is far too confused, we cannot see what is happening." The prince coughed as the first tendrils of smoke reached our position. "This is what comes of using amateurs. If only things had gone just according to plan, like in a real battle."

The choking pall soon swept over us, driving us off the hill to seek clearer air.

Some minutes later, Lieutenant Colonel Chase and Lord Blathingwell informed Prince George that three of the playacting Indians had been killed and four badly wounded. This news put the prince in a philosophical temper as he wiped his face with a fresh towel provided by a servant.

"'Tis a shame that the poor fellows should die, of course," the prince explained. "But we should remember that this mock battle did provide a measure of realistic training for British regulars. And besides, the three dead men —"

"F-f-four, your Highness," Chase corrected. "Another one of 'em just expired."

"Alright, four then. Anyway, they were only some wretched fellows we hired from the poor house. They weren't anyone important. If these four fellows —"

"F-f-five, your Highness," Chase broke in again. "Another's gone."

"Goddamn it all, Chase. Stop interrupting us."

"Sorry, your Highness. You were saying, 'if these five fellows —'"

"Yes, if these five fellows provided us with a sense of war on the frontier with the Indians and the French, without all the confusion, of course, then so much the better. After all," young George opined, "someday soon we shall be king and we shall be the decider of such things as war and peace. And as decider we must decide. If we decide that war is what we want, then war is the right thing, since a sovereign always wishes the best thing for his people. We are sure that learned and clever men will devise a very convincing-sounding reason why war is just and right. Then this reason can be printed in newspapers and broadsheets and hand bills and distributed to the people so they can support their king in whatever war we decide to start. According to my grandfather, a first-rate example of this is that war about Jenkins' ear. Is that not so, Blathingwell?"

"Indeed, your Highness," Blathingwell said contentedly.

Geo was curious and hazarded a question, "If I may ask, your Highness, what about Captain Jenkins and his ear? Every patriotic Englishman knows Jenkin's ear was cut off by the scurrilous Spanish who boarded his ship on the high seas. 'Twas the very act that started the War of Jenkins Ear."

The Prince smiled. "Not precisely. Blathingwell, please explain it our colonial friend."

Blathingwell bowed slightly to the prince then addressed Geo. "Captain Jenkins' ship was not boarded by the Spanish in the Atlantic. And thus, they did not cut off the poor fellow's ear, though most believe it to be so."

"Pray, how then did it happen?"

"'Twas his wife that severed his ear upon discovering the good captain abed with a whore in Ludgate Hill. We made use of the sliced ear to goad members of Parliament in the correct direction. When Captain Jenkins held his ear aloft in Parliament and cried foul, they were putty in our hands. And there was little doubt that the British people would follow Parliament's lead, which they did. We soon had the whole country screaming for satisfaction and Spanish blood. And we had our war. A neat package all around."

Geo and I were too startled to speak.

"You must realize, of course, that the prince has entrusted you with a national secret," Chase warned. "You are not to speak of this to anyone. Though, if you did so, not a soul would believe you, so certain is the populace that a Spanish grandee, not a jealous wife, cut off the famous appendage."

"Now that we have discussed the ways of statecraft," the Prince said, "there is the small matter of explaining the unfortunate deaths of these unfortunates. We will petition our grandfather and see if he can make things right."

"He has gotten your Highness out of every tight jam in the past."

"Yes," young George smirked. "So he has, big George helping little George. Well, the time has come for us to say our goodbyes to Mr. Washington and his seafaring friend."

The prince clapped Geo on the back and proclaimed him a fine fellow. Just then, the thick clouds began to rain. This would certainly help to extinguish the nasty fire that burned the mock American village and which threatened to torch the nearby wood.

"It is raining, your Highness," Blathingwell offered.

"Just a moment. We are bidding farewell to this fellow."

"It is raining quite hard now, your Highness."

"Yes, Blathingwell, do you imagine us to be mad? That we have not the sense to seek shelter from the rain? We are exchanging farewells with Mr. Washington and we mean to finish them."

"Yes, your Highness," Blathingwell replied meekly.

The prince turned to Geo. "That was marvelous fun wrestling and discussing Indian tactics. Will you return from the colonies to visit us when we are king?"

"I certainly will do my utmost, your Highness, to pay my respects following your coronation."

The prince patted Geo on the arm and then disappeared inside the walls of the castle, followed quickly by Blathingwell, who seemed upset at what the rain was doing to his fine silk coat. For me, alas, there was no princely farewell.

Before he turned to follow the prince into the great fortress, Lieutenant Colonel Chase gave Geo and I a stern look that suggested anything but friendly regard. Geo spoke up, "Colonel, there is the matter of your father and his athletic games. He wished us to put the issue to Parliament."

Colonel Chase grimaced. "M-m-my father becomes increasing foolish as he ages. And his strange imaginings of a naked athletic competition are an embarrassment to himself and my family. D-d-do not speak of him again. Though I cannot yet prove it, I am sure of your Jacobite plotting and intend to find you out." With that he was gone into the castle.

We returned to town, all the while considering the deceptions, misstatements, subterfuge, underhandedness and lies a king is forced to undertake merely to do what is good.

When we once again found ourselves on the streets of London, I could tell Geo's mind had returned to the issue which lately had consumed it: the raven-haired beauty from the Falling Inn.

Chapter Twelve
Who to Win a Woman's Favor

AS I SAT in his room, high in the attic of the old house,
waiting for Geo to waken, I listened to the creaks, groans and
shudderings of the house at No. 4 Julian Square. The
renovation work performed by Boyle and his gang of
laborers had been almost entirely for the benefit of the eye.
The structure underneath had barely been touched — even
though all manner of extra walls, jury-rigged roofs and added
rooms had been tacked on. The entire dwelling had become
strained and out of sorts. As time passed, the house became
more outspoken.

Finally, Geo roused himself sufficiently to sit up in
bed. As he did so, I handed over a note left for him by the
baron. Geo broke the seal and perused it.

We were, the note announced, to appear, within the
hour, at the home of the great composer himself. Since the
death of the German Kapellmeister Johann Sebastian Bach
the year before, there could only be one music scribbler in all
of Europe worthy of such a distinction: George Frideric
Handel. His fame rested on his piece called "Music for the
Royal Fireworks," which was well-loved by all because it
occasioned a spectacular fireworks display during which time
the eye and ear were delighted by colorful explosions,
flaming rockets, spinning flares and flashing smoke. All this
boom and color rendered the music largely incidental and I
was of the opinion that during such a show the musicians
should put down their instruments and enjoy the celebration.

Hawkins accompanied us on our visit to Maestro
Handel. On arrival, we were ushered inside the composer's
Brook Street house. His large sitting room had been
transformed into a well-equipped music hall. There were
several harpsichords, a collection of violins, a harp, various
wind instruments and a beautiful pianoforte at which sat a
thin, middle-aged man who bobbed his head and hummed as
he pounded the keys.

Next to the pianoforte was a young woman who sang

beautifully. A handful of people stood listening attentively to her song. Geo grasped my arm as we entered, furrowing my flesh with his strong grip. When I looked to the young woman and noted her face, I saw that she was none other than Geo's Helen. With her dark hair made up into curls and long tresses, like the standing rigging on a French frigate, and her blue eyes, like the grandest stern lantern on a ship of the line, she was indeed beautiful.

Geo stood as if held by a magus's spell, gazing at his Helen with a longing that bordered on abandon. I would not wonder to see him burst suddenly into flames like a Maltese fire ship.

The small gathering parted to reveal a superannuated man. He wore an out-of-fashion full peruke wig, its cascades of black curls falling to his shoulders. His clothes, also, betrayed an affection for an earlier age: his brocaded coat too long, his dark purple waistcoat cut too full. The old man walked with a cane and he dragged one leg noticeably. He was none other than Handel, composer of the fireworks music, and also a recent choral work called "Saviour" or "Redeemer" or some such — it hardly mattered as it will soon be forgotten compared to his unmatched fireworks composition. In fact, it had occurred to me that an excellent business proposition might be for Mr. Handel to sell the sheet music for the fireworks piece in a crate well-stocked with fireworks. In this way the music would always be associated with the wonder of exploding munitions and would gain an even wider popularity. I decided I should attempt to speak with the maestro regarding this idea and offer my services.

Geo's Helen ceased her singing as Handel entered, but he bade her to continue. She did so adroitly, catching up with the piano player, who seemed unaware of anyone in the room and had continued to plow ahead. I later learned her song was called, "Who to Win a Woman's Favour," one of Handel's many songs written while living in London.

Handel was helped to his seat by two assistants, who lowered him slowly into the grand chair. He listened to the song, moving his hand to the music. When the woman finished, she went to Handel and offered her hand, which he took and patted, nodding his head. "Wonderful, my dear. However, your pitch was not entirely correct at all times."

"I shall work on that, maestro," she replied gracefully.

As I had occasion to learn both the playing and the composition of music while a youth in New York, and had thereafter increased my knowledge by serious study of a number of books on music, I felt I was very nearly an expert on the subject. I was on the verge of providing the young woman with a detailed critique of her performance when the Baron Mowenholtz swept in and took command. He spoke German to Handel and then took the dark-haired beauty by the arm and squired her across the room, directly toward Geo. Hawkins followed along behind the baron and the beauty.

Not moving, not breathing, Geo could not believe that his desire to meet her was to be fulfilled. When he was alone in the flickering candlelight of his attic room, Geo penned a multitude of dashing lines for her, each more sparkling than the next. But now, with the object of his desire approaching him, his paper was as white as a blizzard.

Geo held out his hand, removed his hat and bowed deeply. The baron, however, guided Helen right on past Geo. He never met her eyes, as Geo was bent over in his lowest bow. When he came back up and saw she was gone, he looked at me with utter surprise, as if a wallowing merchantman flying a Neapolitan flag had suddenly run up the French ensign, hardened smartly on the wind and run out 44 guns. Hawkins, mistakenly thinking Geo's bow was for him, reached out to shake the young Virginian's hand. A dazed Geo limply returned Hawkins' hearty greeting.

As the baron reached the hall he stopped, the raven-haired beauty at his side, and spoke with a man there. Geo detangled himself from Hawkins and walked at a measured pace toward the baron, with Hawkins again following. Geo's way was blocked by a boy carrying an armload of music folios. Before the Virginian could get past him, he spied that the baron and the beauty had moved on to two matronly ladies. Squeezing by the servant boy, Geo was almost at the baron's elbow when the German moved again toward a minister of the church. Momentarily delayed by a question from one of Handel's guests as to when dinner would be served, Geo broke free again to pursue his quarry.

Now the baron spoke to a big fellow near the front door. Feeling foolish, Geo suddenly realized the man was none other than Sir Gerald. Not risking the chance of the

Baron and the beauty slipping out the front door, Geo marched over to where the Baron stood. Hawkins kept close company to Geo's person, following along meekly.

The baron saw Geo coming and turned suddenly to address him, "Ah, my good friend und business associate, Mr. George Washington of Virginia. May I have the pleasure of introducing to you Sophie Antoinette Mouette, the Countess de Abbeville."

Geo tried to make his mouth work. "Yes, I had noticed that you were here when I first saw you, that is to say, when I first arrived, I noticed that you had also ... arrived and were here already, before I arrived, I mean." Geo said, too mesmerized to be embarrassed.

While he spoke, the countess watched him with the amused expression one might have for a puppy that had peed his master's shoes. I thought her attitude toward him exceedingly gracious as he sounded every inch a damn fool. But, to give Geo some scope on his anchor road, it was true that the Countess de Abbeville was so luminous as to be unnerving to some (though not to a man of the world such as myself). It was an effect made even more pronounced by her proximity, with the fair scent of her perfume and the rise and fall of her bosom so close to hand.

The baron rescued Geo from his tongue-tied opening gambit by brusquely reminding Geo of pressing business. "I am most sorry to remind Mr. Washington that ve are now due at an appointment."

"How unfortunate that you must leave," the countess replied in fine English, only lightly brushed with a French accent. The Baron Mowenholtz took her hand and kissed it.

In a hasty attempt to match the baron's noble manners, Geo awkwardly reached for the Countess' hand but missed entirely and grabbed a bit of her dress. When he raised his arm, he pulled up her dress and revealed her small clothes underneath before realizing his error. He quickly released the fabric and it sank into place like a sail released to a soft breeze. The countess could barely contain a laugh. She briefly covered her mouth to stifle it. Then with some effort, she said to Geo, "Perhaps we will meet again?"

Geo, chagrined at his *faux pas*, mutely nodded.

She turned to von Mowenholtz, "Baron, I know I shall see you again."

"I will wait for it with eager anticipation, ja?" The baron was the picture of gracious nobility.

The young Virginian then regained his wits somewhat and said in a rush. "I hope to hear you again and see your beautiful voice."

She suppressed another laugh and managed to merely smile. "Will you attempt to lift my dress on that occasion, as well?"

Geo maintained his composure and quickly retorted, "I hold you in the highest esteem, your ladyship."

The countess frowned a bit and said ruefully, "Not in too high an esteem, I would hope."

Putting his arm on Geo's shoulder, the baron turned Geo away and headed for the door. Geo, however, turned his head to look at the countess even as the baron and Sir Gerald led him out. The countess kept her eyes on Geo as well.

For the next appointment, Geo and I walked behind the baron and Sir Gerald, who each rode in a sedan chair. The day was overcast, tending toward cool and the sidewalk vendors had adjusted their wares accordingly, hawking the best stew, tea, hot brandy, chocolate, pigeon soup and meat pie ever made. A fair was underway in Smithfields and the streets were crowded with jugglers and jesters, puppet shows, ballad singers and acrobats. Booths were set up, like small theatres, where people could sit on hastily constructed benches and see bawdy shows for a few pennies. The large number of drunks face-down in the gutters suggested the fair was a great success.

"You sounded like a right idiot talking to the countess," I chided Geo as we followed in the wake of the chairs and their rough bearers. "As if you have never spoken to a beautiful young woman before."

Geo rolled his eyes. "I suppose such a thing is commonplace for you? That you are the picture of wit in the presence of a lady?"

"I have been around," I admitted. "I can sweet talk a wench."

"If you have 'been around,' then answer me a question."

"I'll do my best," I said with a smile.

"Why did you not utter a word, not so much as a peep, when the Countess Sophie stood not two feet from you? Do not tell me you weren't cowed by her beauty."

I can only say that we finished our walk in silence. And for my part, I wondered why God would force me to serve as companion and second to a young man as unpleasant and disrespectful as Geo.

The baron, Sir Gerald, Geo and I were to have our next commercial appointment in a well-established gambling house in an older section of the great city. The house, which went by the name of Monmouth's, was in a drab building no one would imagine for a house where vast sums were won and lost. Though the time approached the hour of the noon, the well-heeled gamblers gathered around candlelit, green-baize-covered tables had no notion of noon nor any other hour. The rooms' few windows were darkened with thick bolts of black canvas such that it was impossible to determine day or night. And many mirrors had been placed upon the walls, producing multiple, receding reflections at every turn.

As we discretely made our way past the tables of card and dice players, it was apparent how our little party had gained entrance to this gambling den. From nearly every table came cries of recognition and salutations towards Sir Gerald. He waved off all entreaties and we soon found ourselves at a table occupied by a handsome woman in a red dress who played a game of cards against a single opponent. On our arrival, the other player retired and the baron was able to speak with some privacy.

The woman was known to us only as "Lady S." She had put perhaps 40 years under her keel, and though she did not look young, she had retained a large measure of her good looks and would still be a handsome woman for some time, I wagered. Her husband had died face down in an oversized bowl of oyster stew following a record consumption of brandy. Lady S. was enjoying the money he had inexplicably failed to take with him. The baron sat and quietly chatted with Lady S. whilst Sir Gerald slipped away into the glimmering constellation of candlelit tables. Geo and I merely stood by in our role as camp followers. And since we were still angry with each other for the Countess Sophie meeting, we did not wish to speak.

In no time the baron had Lady S. leaning in close to hear every German-accented word about the vast potential of owning an estate in America along the Ohio River. Soon Lady S. was nodding and smiling and holding the baron's hand in hers. Every few moments, however, the lady would shoot a glance over the baron's shoulder at Geo. Indeed, I was almost positive I saw her wink at the strapping Virginian.

After a time the baron finished his conversation with Lady S. As we started out of Monmouth's, we passed a large, dimly lit room. I peered inside and I believe I saw Sir Gerald and some others engaged in lewd acts with a goat. This was intriguing as Sir Gerald was a rumored member of a group of libertines known as the Hellfire Club. Other reputed members included the Earl of Sandwich, the Duke of Wharton, Sir Francis Dashwood, even our recent associate, the painter Hogarth. Hellfire activities were said to include wild bacchanalian gatherings of the most depraved kind and possibly even the summoning of demons. But as it was not my province to make judgments on rumor and conjecture, I hurried to catch up with Geo and the baron, making note of Sir Gerald's tender affection for animals.

I knew the baron's meeting with Lady S had been a success when the baron ordered up a carriage for our return to No. 4 Julian Square — we never walked following a successful sale. However, the baron chose not to speak and Geo and I both refused to give the other the satisfaction of speaking first, nor, indeed, to even look in the other's direction. Thus, the ride across town was most dreary.

Upon our return to the groaning, creaking house on Julian Square, the baron insisted that we celebrate properly. We agreed, provided that the German first divvy up the lustrous coins that he had just received from Lady S.

Von Mulct smiled broadly and raised his arms in benediction, insisting that Geo was like a son to him. As for me — given my African skin — the closest connection he would agree to was distant step-cousin. He insisted we could perform base duties like counting money later. Geo replied that he thought of the baron as a father as well, but that he would feel even more devoted if the coins were counted out now. The baron finally agreed and divided the money forthwith.

The butler Hawkins was called to the parlor, where the hole in the floor from the baron's fancy ball had not yet been repaired. As he walked in, Hawkins came perilously close to the yawning pit. The baron ordered up three glasses of brandy.

After a quick toast in German (an insufferable tongue), the baron, Geo and I drained our brandy. Hawkins was admonished by the baron for not bringing the bottle with him, such that we might have another round. Apologizing profusely and a bit nonsensically — I thought I heard him say something about the sun — Hawkins backed away from us to return to the spirits locker. I raised a cry of alarum, having seen greenhorn sailors step into open hatches and plummet three decks to the bilge, but alas, it was too late. Hawkins fell through the hole into the cellar, his silver tray performing one complete rotation as it followed him down.

Since having met the Baron I had never seen him move so quickly. He was at the edge of the hole calling down into the murky cellar almost before I left my chair.

"Hawkins, Hawkins, you alright, then?" The anguish that showed on his face was surprising. It was a touching display of empathy for the lower classes.

A muffled reply floated up on the musty air. The house rumbled, as if also answering the baron's urgent entreaty.

"Are you injured?" Geo shouted.

"My person has not suffered the breakings of bones," Hawkins replied weakly, "nor can I say that any amount of blood has escaped from veins, nor has the fall seen to diminish my mental facilities; that is to say, I believe I am alright."

Prudence came running from the kitchen screaming bloody murder. She called down to Hawkins in the hole. He answered her, and she ran off again.

While the baron, Geo and I clustered around the hole and continued to shout questions at Hawkins regarding the state of his health, Prudence had the immediate good sense to descend the cellar stairs with a candle. As candlelight revealed the scene, we were astonished.

Hawkins had not been injured because he had landed

upon a soft forest of mushrooms. A thick stand of them had grown up from the dirt floor, some nearly as big as Hawkins' head. This fungal cushion, no doubt fed by all the water from the stream that had flowed during the baron's ball and the nearly perfect conditions for mushroom growth in the cellar, has been sufficient to buffer the butler's tumble.

Amidst the confusion, one of the other servants came to the baron to report the recent arrival of a porter with a message.

"Well, what is it?" Mowenholtz snapped. "Read it to me — quickly."

"Sir, the lady who saw Mr. Washington today wishes to see him again tonight. Her coach will be waiting at eight o'clock on the east side of the Marybone Basin, just north of Cavendish Square."

"Yes, yes, I know where Marybone Basin is. Very well, I will send a reply when I am done here, ja?"

Since I was standing alongside the baron, I heard every word of the message. I knew Geo would find it most interesting.

"You are quite sure he said that?" Geo asked excitedly when we convened on the back steps.

"I can hear a man break wind while he sits in the maintop during a gale. I can most certainly make out what a fellow is saying while he's standing alongside of me!"

"Yes, of course. It's just that I cannot believe it, that she wants to see me again. I am undone. She is the most beautiful woman I have ever met or, indeed, even seen. And her fine manners and wholesome character only amplify her appeal."

Geo was all anxious excitement. Finding his hatchet, he headed to the rear yard of No. 4 and found a small tree, one of the few left he had not already felled. With an intensity that supposed he could clear the continent, Geo attacked the trunk. Its final crashing demise had a salutary effect on the young colonial. He seemed a new man and calmly readied himself for his assignation with the beautiful French countess. It pleased me to think that given the endless supply of trees in America, neither a crazed chopper like Geo nor the multitudes of his descendents could ever hope to cut them all.

When the time came, Geo and I were quickly out the door and on our way to Cavendish Square. I had taken the liberty of writing a quick positive response to the lady's entreaty in the baron's learned hand and sent it off with the waiting porter, suspecting that perhaps the busy baron would forget.

Chapter Thirteen
Nearly into the Breach

BY A SERIES of clever short cuts suggested by Geo but over which I had the final say, we made excellent time to Cavendish Square. The sun had just set and the western sky still glowed with an ethereal crimson and gold — as if the world would end in good will with all things made right again.

As we advanced toward the still water of the Marybone Basin, the sight of a stationary coach along the right side of the basin became apparent even in the condensing gloom. Geo turned to me and placed his hand on my shoulder. "Hold," he said.

"But the time is nigh, we must go on lest the countess supposes that you did not come."

"'Tis true. But ..."

I saw the signal flags of doubt in his eyes. "Are you apprehensive of seeing her?"

Geo did not wish to say, but I knew it was so. The object of his desire sat in that carriage and his heart rested on a knife's edge. In a moment she could dash his hopes and send him away forever. Or she could gather him in, like a sailor happily furling a sail as the doxies of the town call to him. As I am a man of the sea and nearly always on the move, I had never surrendered to any woman as Geo now contemplated his capitulation to the countess — with the possible exception of Caldonia and perhaps a few others. At any rate, since I was unaffected by the anxiety he now suffered, I proposed an idea.

"The dark of night approaches and soon we will hide in the folds of its cloak. Since I carry none of the emotion that burdens you, let me speak for you. She will stay within the coach while I converse with her. Given the quality of my education, my facility for English rhetoric is excellent — certainly better than your own. She need never know that it is me who speaks to her. You will wait and when she bids you enter, so you shall."

"It does have a certain genius," Geo admitted. "Though I must protest the assertion that you speak the King's English better than me."

"How could the son of a pig farmer from the swamps of Virginia have better speech than a man educated at the finest school in New York City? The idea is preposterous on its face."

Geo grudgingly conceded my point and soon we were in place near the lady's coach. The coach lanterns were weak and the footmen who attended the countess were happy to see the tall, young figure of Geo step into the light. They had been told of his arrival, so they quickly repaired to the far side of the coach to commence games of dice and to drink gin. Geo then stepped back into the shadows and I stepped forward.

A female voice called out through the yellow curtains that masked the coach windows. "Who is that without?" The timbre of the voice was rather different than what I had expected from the countess, but there was no time to delay.

"'Tis I, my lady," I replied.

"Ah," she gurgled contentedly. "I am most pleased you have come."

"How could I do otherwise? To gaze once again at your beauty would draw me from the farthest reaches of Araby or even from darkest Africa." Geo frowned at my mention of Africa, supposing perhaps that I might give myself away, but I waved him off. He could be such a dolt.

"When I saw you today, I was taken with your manly prospect," she said. "Little did I realize you also had a tongue of silver."

"As you say, my lady. I possess a tongue of silver to sing your praises, ears of diamond to hear your wishes, a heart of gold to treasure your love and a root of the firmest British oak with which to be of service."

She laughed and her hand started to open the curtain.

"Pray, my lady, wait further before drawing back the cloth," I said quickly. "I am sensible of great delight in prolonging the moment of first entry."

She was not adverse to my suggestion, though she pretended to be so. "Shall we banter like this all night? I grow warm here in my coach."

"It would be a pleasure unsurpassed simply to continue this intercourse 'twixt us 'til old Sol peeked over the world's edge," I said.

"Would be pleasant, true, but I'd be consumed by the heat of my blood, which rises apace. You must climb aboard and make bodily plain the sweet ecstasy of your words. Do you so mercilessly tease the girls of America?"

"In matters of Venus, as in matters of Mars, there can be no quarter given. First must the citadel be besieged and made ready for the final thrust. When the wall is breached, then the attack can be consummated."

"Oh, indeed," she sighed. "You have most assuredly effected a breach, sir, and my inner keep lies open for your triumphal entry."

I smiled in the dark at her eagerness. "Even now my forces strain forward, tight against their constraining trenches. The trumpet is up, ready for the final signal."

A sigh of frustration came from within the coach. "Damn it! You must rush forward into the breach now! I will brook no further delay!" With this, she flung open the door and leaned forward with her arms outstretched.

I had expected to see the pretty young face and comely figure of the Countess d' Abbeville. I was instead confronted with another woman entirely. She was older and rather more shopworn than the countess. Leaning forward with an attitude of lustful abandon, a position underlined by her loosened clothes, bare skin and flushed complexion, was none other than Fanny Chase. My surprise was so great I found myself momentarily struck dumb.

And to be fair, the surprise for Lady Chase must have been equally great. Instead of a tall, dashing young white gentleman, she was confronted, instead, with a shorter, somewhat more weathered (though I like to think still dashing in my own way), African man. Though she knew me as well as she knew Geo, Lady Chase reacted as if she had seen Beelzebub himself. She screamed wildly as she attempted to quickly tighten all the items of her clothing that she had loosened.

Her cry of surprise shook loose the footmen who had settled in for a night of gaming and drinking on the far side of the coach. They had doffed their coats, hats, waistcoats and shoes. Now they ran about with a lantern in mad confusion as they tried to sort out who belonged to which piece of livery. They yelled at each other and shouted inquiries to Lady Chase as to the nature of her health.

As for me, I somehow regained my composure, though I was not aided in the least by Geo grabbing my arm and yanking me into the shadows. But not before he saw for himself that the woman in the coach was Lady Chase and not the Countess Sophie.

"We must fly from here," he hissed.

"I am agreed."

"You may have gotten her a bit too riled up," Geo admonished.

"Again, I am agreed."

"You are a lecherous bastard with the morals of a dog," Geo said with a measure of admiration.

"I am most *certainly* agreed."

No sooner had we jumped to our feet to make haste in our departure than a voice boomed out, "S-s-stop, y-y-you Jacobite fiends!" In the darkness it was nearly impossible to make out this man's features, but it did seem he was wearing a cockade in his tricorn hat in the manner of an army officer and his coat seemed to be army scarlet. And there was a distinct vocal pattern to his speech that was familiar. My query was answered when Sir Frances Chase stepped into the light, a pistol leveled at us. "Y-y-you despicable demons. P-p-pray you have not harmed her." Sir Francis opened the door of the coach to reveal Lady Chase. "M-m-m-mother?" he asked in confusion.

"Francis, I think it more polite of you to first knock upon a door before opening it." Lady Chase had rapidly set herself to rights and no longer suffered the night air upon her exposed skin.

"B-b-but this is the coach of my aunt, Lady S. W-w-what have you done with her?"

Geo was quick again. He grabbed ahold of me and we dove under the coach. We crawled under — through a generous deposit of road apples left by the horses — and emerged on the far side where the footmen still milled and shouted. Sir Francis was not faint of heart, either. He followed us under the coach, emerging nearly at the same time we did. This was his undoing, however. While we managed to surprise the footmen by rising from the earth like skeletons from dragon's teeth, our pursuer had not such luck. Whereas we ran off unimpeded, our passing had set their triggers. When Sir Francis emerged he was set upon by the scrum of footmen who grabbed his pistol and knocked him to the turf.

"I am L-l-l-lieutenant C-c-colonel Sir Francis Chase. I am protecting my aunt — and my mother. You fools! Let me up! They are getting away." The footmen relented and Sir Francis was on his feet. He commanded one to stay behind, while the other three followed him in pursuit. Though it was utterly pointless in the darkness, Chase discharged his pistol in what he thought might be our general direction. I was distressed to hear an angry hornet pass close to my ear.

Geo and I ran south into Portland Street and turned left at Oxford Market, dodging among the shop stalls shuttered for night. We startled a threesome of thieves pouring over their loot by lantern light. We ran past 'em and headed east. In some minutes, we became convinced that Sir Francis had lost our trail, but since night had fallen and the watch was about, we walked at a measured pace, changing streets, ducking down alleys and bye-ways, creeping across yards, mews and courts where we could.

We needed not only to avoid the men of the watch, but gangs of ruffians and knaves. Most notorious of these were the gang called the Mohocks. They were known to attack any person found out after dark. Women and men had been brutally assaulted by them. There were stories of Mohocks running their swords through the sides of sedan chairs, of Mohocks pulling men from coaches and slitting their noses with razors, or slicing 'em with knives. There were rumors that the Mohocks lived underground and could not be killed by any known weapon. Further, there were whisperings that they cut their victims to get at their blood, which they drank at foul subterranean ceremonies. They were an evill and frightening cohort.

Geo wished to slide into an alehouse, a move that would serve the double duty of getting us off the street and allowing us to quench our thirst. I pointed out, however, that as we were both well smeared with horse shite and the smell might draw some attention, even in the sweaty confines of a tavern.

After we had crossed many streets and were confident that we were no longer pursued, Geo spoke. "So it was Lady Chase who sent the note that summoned me."

"There is no doubt of it. I saw her — quite a lot of her

— all too well."

Geo looked at me, smiled and then guffawed. "Aye, you dog."

I could not help but laugh as well. The two of us chuckled for some minutes. I described her surprised look with her diddeys and commodity in plain sight.

"Perhaps she is secretly enamored of you," Geo suggested with a smirk when we resumed walking. "You certainly had no problem talking her out of her clothes."

I waved away his ridiculous suggestion. "Lady Chase used the coach and footmen of her sister, Lady S., the very woman we saw at Monmouth's today."

"Indeed. And while we were convinced the countess was inside the coach, Sir Francis clearly expected Lady S. to be its occupant."

"Fanny Chase hatched this entire affair to draw you into her arms," I said. "You are something of a breeding bull, Geo. At this rate you could father your own country."

"Oh shut up. I do not care for the wife of another man. I must see Sophie again, D. I am heartsick for her."

"But she is a countess and you are merely a man of fortune. Steadily rising fortune, 'tis true, but you have no rank, no station and only a small fraction of the money you would need to support such a lady. I know that does not sit well with you, but it's the meat of it."

"Then I must rise faster. I must acquire a title and an estate, just as the Baron Mowenholtz promised me in Barbados. I must have it now."

On our arrival at No. 4 Julian Square, we stripped off our dirty coats, waistcoats and breeches and threw them in a wash tub in the yard. We padded inside in our small clothes and were about to ascend the rear stairs when Prudence accosted us.

"Washington! This note was delivered when you were away," she snapped. "Come on, take it. I need to sleep."

Geo hurried to grasp the note from her hand. After quickly reading it, he looked to me and broke into a silly smile. "It requests a meeting on the morrow." Then to Prudence: "There is no name upon this. Who is this from?"

Prudence shook her head. "Don't ask me. It was dark

and I could not see her face. And she didn't give her name."
Prudence brusquely turned to go to her quarters. "She had a
lovely voice, though," Prudence threw over her shoulder as
she clomped away.

Geo would get no sleep that night.

Chapter Fourteen
Chips Tell the Tale

WHEN I AROSE in the morning, I noted Geo's room was empty. He had already arisen — if he slept at all. Finding him was not difficult. I merely followed the sound of chopping. I sensed Geo would be agitated this morning. And when the young Virginian was anxious or out of sorts, he took up his hatchet and began an assault upon the trunk of some unfortunate tree.

On this warm morning, I could hear the drumming of the blade against wood, but Geo was nowhere to be seen in the back yard of No. 4. This was not surprising as Geo had succeeded in felling every tree in the baron's yard. We no longer threw them over the wall any more as the baron seemed to take no notice of his house's plantings. The rear yard of No. 4 was strewn with the horizontal victims of Geo's hatchet.

With no trees standing, Geo had opened the gate separating No. 4 and No. 6. and brazenly entered the neighbor's yard to chop. For Geo, this carried no sense of ill-feeling. He simply needed a tree to chop whilst he thought through a knotty problem.

Not everyone, however, was so sanguine about losing trees. I scurried through the wide-open gate and called out in a low voice. "Geo, you fool, stop that chopping."

I saw that he had nearly severed the trunk of this latest tree. No one from the house next door had yet taken notice, however. I adjudged there was still time to retreat with honor. "Geo, stop that and come back into our yard."

He was not easily dissuaded, however, when so close to victory. He ignored me and continued to strike. The tree gave up the ghost and dropped.

Just then the rear door of No. 6 opened and out strode a portly man. He was well dressed and had spectacles and a fine wig. "What's all this?" he demanded.

I swung into action. "Well, you know, suh, we heard some noise like choppin' and we done come out he'ah and seen this he'ah tree been cut right down, yahz suh. We didn' see no one, suh. And my friend he'ah, he done jus' picked up that there hatchet that somebody done drop as they run away. Yahz, suh, master, suh."

The man nodded. "So neither of you chopped down my tree?"

"No suh. We ain't done no such thing, suh."

"All right, then," the man said, satisfied, and turned to go back inside.

I shot Geo a wink. But Geo did not look pleased. He appeared to have second thoughts about a harmless stretching of the truth.

"Excuse me, sir," Geo called.

The portly fellow turned back in surprise and not a little concern — was he to be ill-used in his own garden by these young ruffians?

"I cannot take part in a lie," Geo began. "Look at my clothes and shoes, I have wood chips all over my person. How could I have just come in here and picked up this hatchet after the tree was already cut down and yet still be covered with chips?"

The portly fellow came closer to Geo, adjusted his glasses and looked more closely at Geo's shoes and then his clothes. "Hmm, I see," he said. "An excellent point, corroborated by evidence."

"And so I must admit 'twas I who chopped down this crabapple tree."

"You are mistaken," the man countered.

"I am not, sir. I am positive I cut it down."

"Ah, no, I speak of the genus of the tree. 'Tis not a crabapple but a cherry tree," the man corrected Geo.

"Cherry tree?" Geo wrinkled his brow. "Those are most unfortunate cherries."

The man advanced on Geo with a purpose. He grabbed Geo's hand with both of his and administered a hearty shake. "I will not press charges with the magistrate. In point of fact, I wish to thank you, young sir."

"To thank him?" I said.

"Indeed. That tree was a gift from my mother-in-law. My wife insists we serve the cherries whenever her mother comes to visit — which is damnably often. And truth be told, I hate the bitter, shriveled things!" He smiled most prodigiously and repeatedly raised his eyebrows in exaltation. "I am James Bradley," he said with some expectation of our recognition. Geo and I merely smiled pleasantly, hoping he told us a bit more.

Bradley held his pose and then, seeing no recognition, he prompted us, "I am the Astronomer Royal."

"Ah, yes." I said happily. "You calculate the ephemerides that describe the positions of the sun and moon for the days of the year, as used by navigators such as myself for finding our position upon the sea. You are the superintendent of the Royal Observatory at Greenwich."

"I am the same!" Bradley replied. Then he turned to Geo. "And your name young sir?"

"Washington. Mr. George Washington of Virginia."

"Well, Mr. Washington, you have done me a great service and your honesty lends me to think most highly of you. Perhaps some day I can repay the favor."

"Perhaps so, Mr. Bradley. May I introduce my colleague, companion and second, master mariner Darius Attucks."

Bradley shook my hand but he said to Geo, as if I could not hear him or was not there at all. "I am sorry, I rather imagined him to be your slave, given his ignorant speech and manner. But his being a sailor explains both his knowledge of navigation and his deceitful nature in pretending to be something he is not. At any rate, I must depart." He bowed slightly and hurried back into his house.

"Even after I informed him that you were not a slave but a free man, he did not so much as look at you," Geo said. Then he looked at me. "He did manage to discern your essential nature, though."

"My clever efforts to absolve you of blame were wholly successful. Mr. Bradley only uncovered my deceitful nature due to your galling need for honesty. 'Tis a childish habit of yours, Geo. You must shake yourself of it to advance in life."

"I was unable to lie to him." Geo admitted. Then scratched his head in puzzlement, "How could so unobservant a man be the foremost observer of the realm? 'Tis unnerving."

"I would say rather that he is focused on his singular task of observing the heavens, not assaying the shoes and breeches of some colonial."

"You had better hope so."

"Now, about this chopping, you are clearly unsettled on some matter. Even for you, this early morning hatchet work is unusual. Before breakfast you often do your work in bed."

Geo looked down, ignoring my comment regarding his assignations with Lady Montagrave, or perhaps feeling a bit ashamed of them. "That association is over. You know of my feelings these days."

We walked back to the garden of No. 4 and I dragged the corpse of the cherry tree from Bradley's yard and shut the gate. "Aye, I know that you are smitten with the French countess. Do you wish to become attached to her?"

"I barely know her. Though that is not so much the bar to our connection as the regrettable poverty of my social and financial standing. It seems impossible that a man in my position should win the heart of so noble a lady."

"What bull shite, Geo. What of the dash you spoke so strongly of early in our acquaintance? Has it deserted you? Or are you simply afraid of long odds? If you insist on only backing sure things, you will not succeed. Stop whining about how you are unable to win the young lady and charge right in. Even should you fail to win her, the campaign for her affections will provide good training for future Herculean efforts."

Geo, who had been walking with his hatchet cradled in front of him, agreed that this was a perfect occasion for him to display on the outside the dashing person he was sure resided within.

Geo and I departed No. 4 Julian Square for his meeting with the mystery woman. In her note, she requested a meeting at five o'clock at the Covent Garden market. Though her name was unknown, Geo hoped she was none other than the Countess Sophie.

We could not have the benefit of the baron's or Sir Gerald's counsel on this matter, or indeed any other matter, as they and Lady Montagrave were often out of town on business. Important matters in Kent, to the southeast of London, seemed to occupy them much these past days.

As we walked, I recalled Geo's encounter with the Astronomer Royal. "That was quite memorable, what you said to Mr. Bradley."

"Of which do you speak?"

"Your declaration of conscience to him." I then mimicked his Virginia accent: 'Twas I that chopped down the crabapple tree.'"

"Cherry tree," Geo corrected.

"Very well, 'Twas I who chopped down the cherry tree.' That works just as well. The point being that such a display of honesty is affecting. People are moved by such a story."

Geo looked at me with a furrowed brow, "'Twas no story. It did truly happen."

I permitted myself a chortle. "I know that. I was there, as you may recall. I am merely saying that one could take that story and make good use of it."

Geo shook his head. "How does one make use of a story? Sometimes I think you are mad."

"Not at all. Now listen to me. If one wanted to heighten one's reputation, if one wanted to ensure people thought about one in a certain way, then that story could come in handy. Have a few people repeat it around. Have it printed up on handbills. Perhaps befriend a newspaper scribe and get him to write about it. Seems it would not be too hard to make sure people knew about it."

"To what end? Why would I spend my time spreading stories about myself?"

"I am simply saying, wait on that story, store it away. It might become useful."

I expected another outburst from Geo, but instead he walked for some time immersed in thought.

By and by the day grew more fair. Warm sun and a pleasant breeze lifted our spirits and we had little issue with the smell of the gutters or the raucous shouting of the orphans, the flashing knives of the cutpurses or the clatter of horse and wagon. It was a fine day to be young and a free man in London, truly the keystone of the world.

We had some diverse tasks to which we attended and the day grew on, the sun first shining bright, then resting his brilliant wings behind banks of passing clouds. Geo was agitated at the late progress of our affairs and by the afternoon was undone to hurry to Covent Garden and see what fate would meet him there.

Chapter Fifteen
The Mystery Orbits Align

IN THE PAST few weeks I had taken some time to talk to Prudence and Hawkins while they performed their domestic duties. They had answered my queries regarding London, telling me what they knew of the city's history and development. According to Prudence and Hawkins, Covent Garden was an area that had once been quite popular with people of quality. But as London had built westward towards Westminster, those people of wealth and position had moved west to the more fashionable precincts of St. James and Hanover Square. The area around Covent Garden declined from its exclusive heyday. It saw the influx of disreputable groups like gin shop proprietors, beggars, pawnbrokers, thieves, harlots and theatre people.

In the central square of Covent Garden was located an open air market that bustled with vendors of all manner of greens, of coffee and tea, of fruit, of grains and beans and peas and a hundred other necessaries. It was noisy and crowded with many people coming and going. After nightfall the vendors closed their booths and the square changed: it became the ground for bawdy women who engaged their customers amidst the labyrinth of stalls, and it was a feeding trough for scurrying rats and other vermin who gnawed on the leavings of the day.

The busy square was a suitable locale for those who wished to meet in public and yet be shrouded by the flow of humanity. A challenge to any rendezvous, however, was locating the other party in the crush. Geo's mystery woman had made provision for this, however. She indicated in her note that Geo was to walk around the square "against the clock." She, meanwhile, would circle clockwise and eventually the known and the mystery orbits would align.

So Geo and I began our circuits and before we had made half a turn, we spied Lady S. approaching. I saw Geo's face fall. He had been certain of Sophie's affection and the appearance of Lady S. dashed his hopes. She walked toward us with a devilish grin and a purposeful gait. We continued our counterclockwise rotation, though there seemed little point to it now.

As we drew closer, however, it became apparent that Lady S. was not looking at Geo, but rather to Geo's left. My suspicion was confirmed. She eyed a young man, not much older than Geo, who wore a green coat, vermilion waistcoat and shiny silver breeches. He posed with his silver-tipped cane and fancy wig much bedecked with purple ribbons. Lady S. walked right past Geo — truly she never saw him. She stepped up to Silver Breeches and kissed him quite immodestly on the mouth. Lady S. and the young man then sauntered away and were soon lost to sight.

"Well, that was a false alarum," I said happily. "Let us continue our circumnavigation. There is little reason to think Lady S. sent you the note. She was intent on that young fop from the first."

"So it would seem," Geo said, but he did not move.

"Let us continue then," I prompted.

Geo looked at me and then smiled. "Yes, of course."

After a complete rotation round the square, we did not sweep up any woman waiting to meet Geo. I insisted upon another circuit, however. And so we began again. We finished a handsome quarter turn when we saw her. She seemed to glide toward us, her simple blue dress showing off the glistening waves of her dark hair. Geo spied her instantly and increased his gait. This was a natural invitation for me to drop back and give them some time to sail in convoy together. But, given my role as official chronicler of this adventure, I could not leave them alone without first taking a few soundings.

"Your ladyship," Geo said as he bowed low.

"While I may be a lady, I am most certainly not a ship," the countess said with amusement. "Stand up and talk to me, Mr. Washington."

Geo straightened up from his bow, his face suffused with happiness.

"Now one thing I must make clear from the start — unlike the last time we met, there will be no lifting of my dress in public."

Geo blushed deeply.

Sophie looked at me, giggled and winked. "Shall we walk? I would like to hear about life in America."

"Excuse me, my lady," I quickly interjected, "but Mr.

Washington can only tell you about life in Virginia, which I can assure you bears no resemblance to America."

"You are a saucy one, Mr...? I do not know your name."

"Oh, pardon my rudeness," Geo blurted. He looked genuinely pained at his bad manners. "Countess, this is Darius Attucks, master mariner. He is my associate and my second."

I took the young lady's hand and kissed it gently. "I am honored, Countess."

"Now I must walk with Mr. Washington," she put her arm though his. "You will excuse us, Mr. Attucks?"

I nodded and withdrew. I felt a bubble of ill will suddenly rise and burst within me. She was a beautiful woman, a titled woman likely with a fortune. I was suddenly jealous of Geo and all his good luck. I wondered why a man such as myself, a man of education, of knowledge, of culture and refinement, should not also be due some measure of good fortune. Did a man need merely be tall, handsome and white to succeed so famously? Naturally, the possibility that this was true soured my mood.

Once they had found each other, Geo and the countess evidently had no desire to part. They walked on in the counterclockwise direction, surely a retrograde direction for two of society's elect. Unaware of how long they would walk and talk, I leaned against the wall of St. Paul's church in the square. When they came around the third time, still arm-in-arm and laughing, I decided that brooding on the injustice of life served no purpose. I decided to retire to the nearest alehouse and jury rig my mood via drink.

I found a suitable establishment, The Bull and Chain, across Henrietta Street from the market. Smoky, dark and reeking of spilled ale and overcooked meat, it was a tavern of the sort I most enjoyed, both for the air of wanton license and of besotted affability. I took a seat that afforded me a view of the square. I had no sooner procured a mug of ale than a fellow at the next table breached the air of affability. He declaimed loudly to anyone who would listen about "the nasty blackamoor" in the establishment. Several men laughed and applauded the fellow, who went by the name Old Jim.

One of the beneficial aspects of traveling alongside Geo was that those people most bloody minded about Africans naturally assumed that I was Geo's slave, or at the very least his servant. While it was galling to a free man such as myself to be considered some white man's property, the misconception was a useful one in that it kept the most ignorant and nastiest Englishmen happy and they did not hasten to annoy me.

Making an appearance without Geo, however, was yet another story. Some preening popinjay or beetlebrowed cretin like Old Jim would challenge me and I would on occasion be forced to demonstrate techniques used to keep rebellious ship's crew in line. They soon saw how quickly I could force them to humbly apologize. So the goading of this Old Jim fellow did not concern me. He was, however, backed by several others who would grow bolder if I failed to reply. Before I could begin my assault on them, however, a man at my table, a stout fellow with large, doughy features proceeded to upbraid my attacker. My defender had a large nose and an even larger wit. He silenced Old Jim with a few choice words.

I turned to my defender but he stopped me with an upraised hand.

"Think nothing of it," the man replied. "I abhor small minds and the petty hatreds they engender. However, simply because I have assisted you does not mean I think you less a fool than any other man."

"A sour sentiment that's sweet to my ear. I am Darius Attucks, master mariner."

"My name is Dr. Samuel Johnson," he replied flatly.

"I am most grateful, Dr. Johnson. Are you a physician?"

"Hardly. My doctorate is of the literary variety. Which is, unfortunately, not quite as well paid as the doctor of physic — he who cuts a man nearly in half to make him whole again."

"Yes," I agreed, "to make a man wholly fit, they first cut a hole in him. A literary man, however, runs little chance of being hanged for ill practice."

"Most writers deserve the noose, so badly do they butcher the language."

"If folks were hanged for poor writing, the hangman

would get little rest," I replied.

"Aye, and the first to swing should be the members of Parliament. For the writing of an unconscionable law that is an affront to every Englishman's birthright."

"What law is this?"

"That very writ which robs from every man, woman and child the most precious commodity of all: time. Our Parliament has ordered us to jettison 11 days! We are to change from the virtuous Protestant calendar of Julius Caesar to that papist concoction, the Gregorian calendar. By dint of this switch, we will make an irrevocable break in the great stream of British history, we will forever lose our natural connection to all that came before."

"Losing 11 days to institute a more accurate calendar seems but a small price to pay," said I. "'Twill bring Britain into tune with the motions of the celestial bodies and assist commerce."

Dr. Johnson would have none of it, however. "It is not simply the 11 days, 'tis the loss of the rhythm, the heartbeat of our history, our connection to the founding of the Roman city of Londonium."

I was surprised at the vehemence of Dr. Johnson's opposition. But to a man of letters, a man of history, such a break would seem the worse thing. Besides, I sensed that perhaps the good doctor enjoyed the role of contrarian. I suspected that should Parliament argue for the permanent enshrinement of the Julian calendar, Johnson would bitterly agitate for the introduction of the Gregorian version.

"Yes. I see your concerns regarding this change from Julian to Gregorian," I said. "It is a momentous endeavor."

"This hellish switch has got me all in a bind," Johnson said with some exasperation. "I cannot bring myself to write anything."

"But a man who expresses himself as well as you should never worry regarding his mastery of the written word."

Dr. Johnson laughed. "Mastery indeed. I am puzzling over a saying I have just concocted. I cannot seem to get it right. 'Tis most vexing."

"Relate it to me, that I may help."

Johnson looked me over and then began. "Very well. It goes like this: 'When a man is tired of bread pudding, he is tired of life.'"

"Hmm," I mused, tapping my finger on the table. "Well, the principal problem is that were one to eat bread pudding every day, one might, indeed, become tired of it. Yet at the same not be at all tired of the many other things in life."

"I saw that, too, of course," Dr. Johnson admitted.

"What if you replaced 'bread pudding' with something that is so varied and contains so much promise and excitement that no one would easily grow tired of it?"

"Yes," said Dr. Johnson. "How about this: 'When a man is tired of potatoes, he is tired of life?'"

"Potatoes are exemplary, to be sure, but..."

"When a man is tired of sweetbreads?" Johnson offered.

"No."

"Of haggis?"

"No."

"Sheep's pluck?"

"No."

"Lark in aspic?"

"No."

"Treacle duff?

"No. Perhaps think more widely than food alone."

"When a man is tired of joint stock companies?"

"No."

"Theatre?"

"No."

"Public speaking?"

"No."

"The House of Lords?"

"Certainly not."

"Books, handbills, newspapers and circulars?"

"No."

"I have it! — Dictionaries!"

"Perhaps, but no. What is big, has many people and is bursting with energy?"

"Ahh, yes, bursting, many people, energy and excitement. Now I grasp it. 'When a man is tired of Guy Fawkes Night, he is tired of life,'" Dr. Johnson said triumphantly.

"Hmm, not exactly. I was thinking thusly: 'When a

man is tired of London, he is tired of life.'"

Dr. Johnson made a face. "What absolute tripe. What a ridiculous aphorism," he snorted. Johnson yelled over to Old Jim. "Hey, you. I should have let you thump him," he said as he jerked a thumb at me. The doctor got up abruptly, drawing the attention of everyone at the long table. "Good day," he said loudly. "I have the meeting of my club at the Turk's Head. I shall not tarry here with men of no account."

The surrounding men grumbled at the insult. But Dr. Johnson hurried out giving them little chance for a retort. After the literary man had departed Old Jim turned to me. With a shrug he said, "Ain't he a tosser. Here now, I'll buy you an ale."

Meanwhile, out in the square, Geo and Sophie had completed many more circuits. It seemed each felt they had discovered the person for whom they had been searching. Sophie admitted to Geo that she found him a most attractive man, young and virile, dashing, yet polite and in every possible way the man who she had long sought. When she first saw him at the Falling Inn, she said, she felt like the world had changed and that a new sun shone on her. It was, she confessed, as if a seed had been planted, for a flower which no eye had yet beheld. Over time, she had heard more about Geo from the baron. When she met Geo at the Maestro Handel's house, the seed had burst forth.

"But that was when I lifted up your dress," he said sheepishly.

"Which mistake I found charming and which only served to endear you more to me."

Geo was like a sailor swept overboard. He felt himself floating round the square in a turquoise sea under a loving sun's caress. He could do little else but relate his own feelings of love and devotion. He confessed he had thought of little else but her from the first time he saw her. "I chopped down many a tree thinking of you."

"I do not know what that means," she admitted, "but it sounds delightfully improper and very endearing."

Emboldened by her response, Geo asked her the question that burned in him, like a Promethean fire delivered of Heaven. "Do you love me as I love you?" he asked.

She reached up and threw her arms around his neck and kissed him, "Yes, I am quite sure I do."

Geo was ecstatic in that place beyond words. Yet he also calculated. He had landed a woman who was beautiful to the eye, pleasing of disposition and who was of noble blood. His sour-souled mother had forbidden his plan to join the Royal Navy — even after his brother Lawrence had arranged for a midshipman's berth. But now she would take notice. She who was never pleased by his efforts to make something of himself, could not fail to be impressed. And not only was he smiled on by Venus, but the spirit of commerce was also his new-found benefactor. He had a firm promise from the baron, seconded by Sir Gerald, that soon he was to have a title and an estate. So ensconced, with Sophie as his wife, he would have achieved more than that he could have hoped. What he imagined as a long, difficult ascent, from younger son status to that of titled man of means, now seemed a wide, level road, on which he rode in a coach and six.

To Geo it seemed only a moment had passed since he and Sophie began their circuits of the square, so happy was he with Sophie on his arm. But, in truth, the day had fled and the dark of night was falling fast. On this evening, the Duke of Richmond and several others of the highest rank had arranged for a celebration of His Majesty, George II's 24 years on the throne. This took the form of a fireworks display from barges anchored in the Thames opposite Somerset House, some ways downstream from Westminster Bridge.

An orchestra was deployed in the Somerset House garden, which fronted upon the river. The musicians were engaged to play Maestro Handel's score for just such an occasion. Adding to the rockets and bombs set on the river barges, still more fireworks were arranged on the rails of the terrace along the Thames. The Somerset House garden was busy with many people of fashion, while the king was aboard his royal barge with his mistress. They were joined on the river by a swarm of boats and watercraft that hovered about the royal barge like gnats round a mule.

Geo and Sophie followed the crowds that left the market square and walked down Southampton Street, across the Strand and into the lanes leading to the river: Salisbury Street, Cecil Street, Dirty Lane. By a stroke of good luck they fell in with a party that showed them the way to the Savoy

Stairs. From this perch on the river, they could see not only the fireworks barges and the king's vessel, but a bit of the Somerset House gardens as well.

The happy couple had just sat down as the first notes of the fireworks music floated over the water. The crowd grew quiet so as to hear every measure. At the same time the colorful fireworks began. The walls and balustrades of the Somerset House gardens were outlined in sizzling red, with many great wheels of smoking fire interspersed. The initials "GR" burned in red and white letters 20-foot-high on the face of Somerset House. Meanwhile, red and white and yellow fountains of sparks popped skyward. From the barges in the river were lit a great profusion of rockets and mortar bombs that rose above the river and detonated. Soon the music was barely to be heard over the roar of rockets and the whine of shells exploding in reds, greens, blues, yellows and brilliant white, the effect of these chromatic flowers accentuated by the scattered reflections thrown back by the waters of the great river.

From the many thousands watching on shore there escaped loud exclamations of awe and delight. Geo and Sophie sat at the water's edge, with the Virginian enclosing the countess in his arms. As the rocketry filled the sky with light, Sophie said softly, "See the red glare of the rockets."

To which Geo replied, "Yes, and the bombs that burst in mid-air. They are most beautiful, yet they pale next to your brilliance."

Sophie leaned her head to touch his and he hugged her closer, their eyes dazzled by the light on the river. "This is perfect, my love," Geo said a bit awkwardly, still the backwoods surveyor not wholly comfortable with the courtly ways of the city gentleman.

From Sophie, however, there was a hesitation, a small silence, a looking away. Geo noted it immediately. It was as if he had come upon a deadly cliff while treading a gentle trail. "Why do you look away?"

She pressed his big hand in hers. "Do not worry. But there is something that must remain unsaid and unbidden. I must not discuss it, and you must not ask me of it."

"What is this thing that remains? You must tell me or I will suffer greatly."

She put her finger to his lips. "Do not suffer. I will tell

you when the time is nigh. I only hope ..."

"What do you hope?" Geo pressed.

"I only pray you do not throw me over when you hear it from me."

This disturbed Geo considerably. He pressed her again to speak. Again she refused and became agitated. When he demanded again that she tell him, she broke away from him and ran off, disappearing into the crush. The happy crowd took no heed, drunk as they were on wine, gin and ale, and the blossoms of fire in their upturned eyes.

Geo moved to follow. However, unknown to Geo and Sophie, I had left The Bull and Chain and followed them surreptitiously through the crowd down to the river. I was, at this point, only a step away from Geo. I grabbed his arm and stopped him from pursuing the countess. He looked at me with anger and threw off my hand. "I must find her."

"You must not," I said. "Lieutenant Colonel Chase has followed you from the square. I have seen him reconnoitering. He means to ensnare us in some way."

"He is only keeping watch over his aunt, Lady S., whom we saw earlier."

"Yes, but we must not give him any opportunity to invent a charge against us. And besides, I sense there is something not quite right about Sophie."

At that moment, given Geo's roiling emotional sea, there were perhaps no more foolish words I could have uttered.

Geo reaction was swift. "How dare you question her, you ... you ..."

This was it; the dangling pause always followed by the reminder that, after all, I was an African man and could never be considered the equal of a white man.

"... you ... you who know my mind so well on this."

"My feelings for Sophie are fixed," Geo continued, "and I demand you respect them. You have wronged me, sir."

"Yo, ho, Geo, listen to me. I do not question you. It is *her* that I question. I believe there is something vital that she does not reveal. Something that could overset your happiness and dash your hopes." Throughout my life I have found that I am exceptionally keen at judging character.

"If you question her, then you question me. I had

thought that was abundantly clear. I will have satisfaction from you, Attucks."

With that Geo hurried off into the mob, which was now dispersing after the last rocket had detonated and its shards faded. I was left with a hollow stomach and a swirling heart. I had not only failed the charge entrusted me by Heaven, but I had also wounded to the quick an honest man — and my own good friend.

Chapter Sixteen
Princes, Dukes and Prelates

THERE WAS NO TIME upon my return from Covent
Garden and the Thames fireworks to talk with Geo and work
out our differences. The five of us, the baron, Lady
Montagrave, Sir Gerald, Geo and even myself, were invited
to a ball at St. James Palace given in honor of Prince George.
    That we had been invited and must go to the ball
seemed a matter of some concern to both the baron and Sir
Gerald. Why this was so, I could not fathom. I imagined the
possibility of meeting so large an assemblage of wealthy
nobles and persons of commercial distinction would be
viewed as a most opportune occasion for making further
sales of Ohio land.
    On the carriage ride to the palace I rode with the baron
and Lady Montagrave in one coach while Geo and Sir Gerald
rode in the other. This arrangement was arrived at as Geo
refused to ride with me and Sir Gerald refused to allow Geo
and Lady Montagrave to ride together.
    I put the question of enhanced Ohio land sales to Baron
Mowenholtz, though I first had to fend off the wicked Lady
Montagrave, who insisted on reaching her hand under the
fold of my coat and pinching by buttocks, making it
powerfully difficult to concentrate on my question.
    The baron, displaying a nervous agitation, asked me to
repeat the question as he fumbled with his snuff box. After I
asked once more, the baron leaned toward me and explained
in the thickest accent I had ever heard from him. "Ve must
not say anything regarding the Ohio sales. There are only a
few parcels left fur purchase. Und should the word spread
that these properties are available, there could be a terrible
rush und many people could be hurt. Und there is another
reason to keep this quiet. Due to certain changing conditions,
the price has dropped! So, if our previous customers were to
know that we sold them at the higher price, then I think it
would be very bad, indeed."
    "But isn't that the way commerce is conceived to
work?" I asked. "If I have purchased a thing and later the
price becomes less, isn't that my risk?"

The baron laughed, though it was more like a hacking wheeze. "It is obvious that you do not understand the manner in which the nobility thinks of these things."

There was such a multitude of carriages, coaches and sedan chairs assembled to convey the guests to the ball, that the streets surrounding St. James Palace were hopelessly tangled with vehicles, horses and finely dressed people of quality. In his agitated state, the baron was barely able to sit still. He abruptly opened the coach door and commanded us to walk the final stretch to the palace.

At the dowdy main entrance to St. James, with its quaint octagonal towers and faded brick, arriving guests were announced by a stentorian chamberlain. The baron, however, insisted that there was no need for so ostentatious an arrival. We followed him like ducklings as he found a side entrance. He furtively paid a servant to usher us in, urging us to "Hurry, quickly!" Once within, the baron found the lowliest corner of the hall, under dusty old portraits of some fellows named Henry, for us to make our stand. Since we were so far at the back of the magnificently attired crowd and in a particularly poorly lit corner, not a soul noticed us.

The music started and we began to dance. However, our little corner was so distant from the musicians and there was so much prattle by the guests that it was exceedingly difficult to keep in step.

After three or four minuets — or were they bourées? — I was not sure which dance was which and I refused to ask Geo and give him the satisfaction of seeking his help. The baron made his farewells to the friendly, if exceedingly plain, women who had been our partners. He needed only to leave a card at the door and the court secretaries would have a record that he and his party had, indeed, attended. It would not do to ignore an invitation from the prince.

His plans were overset, however, when a liveried servant appeared and announced that the Baron Mowenholtz, the Lady Montagrave, Sir Gerald Compliss and Mr. George Washington were requested to attend to and dance with the prince's party. Though I was not named, I took it upon myself to follow along.

Though the music and the dancing continued, there was naturally some strong interest from the other guests as we crossed the hall and made our way to the Prince's circle.

When we arrived, the servant announced us.

"Ah, 'tis true," young Prince George exclaimed when we hove into view. "You *have* come to our little gathering. Our master of ceremony assured us that you had not been announced, yet here you are. A happy discovery, indeed."

"Your Highness," the baron said, "there is no hazard, no stumbling block, no bar, no barrier that could prevent my humble party und myself from accepting your Highness' most gracious invitation."

"And we are pleased you have done so. Now, let us dance."

When Geo and I saw the prince during the mock ball at Kensington Palace, young George was a poor dancer, yet now his steps were in harmony and his moves graceful. Clearly the prince had learned a great deal in the interim. Perhaps the example of Geo had been instrumental in his rapid improvement?

The musicians set back to their sawing and so we danced. Geo was superb, light and smooth and with the grace that suggested he was of noble birth and standing.

The baron lacked Geo's fluidity, he held his hands before him in an odd way and was stiff in the Teutonic manner.

With her limbs moving a bit faster than the other more demure ladies, Lady Montagrave was vibrant and fiery on the dance floor. What she lacked in the precision of her steps she made up with a shining joy of movement.

Sir Gerald was the antipode of his mistresses' emotion. He moved with a cool aspect, too busy leering at the ladies and with little concern with any specific dance steps.

As for myself, I found English and French dancing pleasant enough, if a bit removed from the desires that prompt people to dance in the first place. My people, the African people in America, seem to hold themselves closer to the animating fire that burns in every man's and woman's heart.

Once again I felt the two-headed beast of amusement and anger rise up in me as I beheld the lusty curiosity or barely concealed horror shown by the English women who were required to dance with me. I was perhaps the first African man whose skin they had occasion to grip or whose breath they felt warm upon their face.

Between dances, we were surprised to see Lady Chase suddenly step up beside Geo, as if by prior arrangement she would be his next partner.

"Lady Chase," Geo said with some confusion as he bowed to her. "I am ... ah ... pleased to see you again."

She acknowledged his bow. It seemed that sales of custard had been very good as Lady Chase was dressed most extravagantly. "You will see rather less of me than on our last meeting near Marybone."

Geo knew not how to answer this in a gentlemanly fashion and so refrained from any comment at all. The music began, a stately sarabande, and Geo began to dance with her. Geo's feelings of discomfort could be readily interpreted in his awkward motions. Lady Chase was in an expansive mood, however, favoring those around her with her broadest smile. During the steps, the two spoke.

"Mr. Washington, as you know," Lady Chase began, "my son, Francis, is most determined to see you and your friend Darius swing. He cannot be dissuaded from the notion that you are Jacobite rebels."

"Nothing could be further from the truth. We are loyal subjects of King George, madam. And will loyally follow his son, Prince George, when he ascends to the throne."

"Perhaps that is true, but my son does not believe it. He can be a most formidable opponent, you know."

"I am sure of it."

"It need not be so. Should you do a good turn for me, I would gladly call him off."

"What is it you desire?" Geo asked hesitantly.

Lady Chase dropped her voice to a whisper, "I should like to have you between my legs, but that ship appears to have sailed." She smiled sweetly to the neighboring dancers then continued, "I wish the Prince of Wales to publicly name my custard as his favorite dessert, exclusive of all others. When he does this, I can assure you my son will no longer pursue you, Jacobite or no."

Geo was surely taken aback. "But, madam, I cannot vouch for the prince's taste. What if he favors syllabub or apple brown betty?"

"Then you had better see to it he has a change of heart." The dance ended and Lady Chase again accepted his bow and beamed. "Custard, Mr. Washington."

Geo simply gazed at her.

"Just to show you that I take custard very seriously," she said, "you may expect a visit from my son in two minutes." Fanny moved away, a picture of comely good grace.

The musicians paused to suck on their cache of gin. Lady Chase, meanwhile, was good to her word. Lieutenant Colonel Sir Francis Chase strode across the dance floor and stood before the prince. He had a particular sneer upon his face that suggested he was privileged in some way and would soon reveal the nature of his advantage in a manner that he thought would reflect well upon him.

The prince, perspiring from his spirited effort, rested in a chair two attendants placed for him on the carpet. He noticed Chase's preening and called to him. "Lieutenant Colonel Chase, pray tell us what canary you have swallowed that we may return the bird to its cage." The guests within earshot laughed at this. Even those too far to have heard the prince's comments joined in the laughter on the correct supposition that the prince had displayed wit and to be seen laughing would do no harm.

"If y-y-your Highness will grant me leave, I m-m-must speak regarding this m-m-man." Chase pointed at the baron. Only seconds after the raising of the colonel's accusatory finger, the other guests backed away and the baron found himself in a lonely spot on the floor.

"Speak, Chase, so we may get back to our dancing."

"Thank you, Highness. Th-th-this man," Sir Francis indicated the baron, "w-w-who claims to be Meissel Von Mulct, the Baron Mowenholtz of the principality of Farkenheine-Ausgas, is an imposter." The ball-goers gasped. "H-h-he is a fake because no such p-p-principality exists."

Icy silence spread through the hall. The baron said nothing but opened his mouth and abruptly closed it again. He may have looked relatively calm to those who did not know him, but to me, he seemed surprisingly nervous with this unexpected and clearly ridiculous accusation.

"What is this foolishness?" the prince said.

"This m-m-man cannot be a b-b-baron of Farkenheine-Ausgas as said principality does not exist," Chase repeated, puffing out his chest.

The prince said nothing but merely looked to his left

where stood Lord Dunkennut, Gentleman of Heraldy, Peerage, Garters, Gyrkins and Grain Flails, an official position in the Prince of Wales' household since 1337. Dunkennut stepped forward, bowed to the prince and cleared his throat.

"I am not often asked to declaim on the subject of the German nobility at court occasions, so I naturally am quite excited. I could easily speak for an hour or more and not even begin to scratch the surface of this fascinating and important subject." The crowd was crestfallen at this suggestion from Dunkennut. "However, in the interest of the prince returning to his guests, I will attempt to make this as brief and informative as possible." The ball-goers were relieved and many long faces turned to smiles.

"In a real sense, Lieutenant Colonel Chase is correct," Dunkennut began. "The principality of Farkenheine-Ausgas does not exist."

Chase nodded in satisfaction. A gasp rippled through the guests. The baron shifted his weight.

Dunkennut continued, "Farkenheine-Ausgas was occupied by the Prince of Salm-Salm in, I believe, 1712 regained its independence in 1726 when the Prince of Salm-Salm lost the province — and a finger — in a drunken game of mumbledy-peg with the Papal Nuncio. After 1726, in a further series of gambling transactions, Farkenheine-Ausgas passed through the hands of the various Princes of Lobkowitz, Mompelgard, Schwarzenberg, Anhalt-Zerbst, Anhalt-Dessau and Anhalt-Bernburg, finally coming to rest with the Duke of Saxe-Coburg-Saalfeld-Gotha-Altenburg-Dinkelsbühl-Bopfingen-Rottenmünster,   where   the principality now resides."

Chase was triumphant while the baron looked like a man who had not reached the privy in sufficient time.

"Yet, it must also be said," Dunkennut continued, "that given the unique legalities of German principalities, dukedoms, bishoprics, imperial cities, electorships, baronies, margravedoms, councils of abbots and colleges of prelates, we can say that Farkenheine-Ausgas *does* exist — since any baronial titles granted by its prince at any time continue to hold sway and have authority in both Germany and in Britain, as recognized by Parliament in 1732 via the Noble Continuency and General Protection of Aristocracy Act.

Which I believe your late uncle co-sponsored in the Commons, Colonel."

"Th-th-the *what* act?" Chase snapped.

"May we resume our dance, Colonel?" Prince George said. "Or do you have any other noble persons you wish to denounce? Perhaps you would like to question the fitness of my title? It, too, has a German connection." The assembled guests again laughed heartedly.

Chase was clearly without a counter of any kind. He bowed stiffly to the prince, stared malevolently at the baron, then turned and quick-timed out of the hall with a twisted grimace.

"We believe you are well within your rights, Baron Mowenholtz, to ask for satisfaction from Lieutenant Colonel Chase," the prince announced. "Not, of course, that we would sanction the illegal practice of dueling. We would suggest something more modern: a law suit with a claim against Sir Francis' purse?"

The baron bowed to the Prince and then straightened his slightly askew wig. "Thank you, your Highness," the baron said in a reedy voice. The young prince watched him with interest, amused by the German's reaction. The entire room of nobles and notables also silently watched, their white faces and white wig powder and white dresses forming a pale knot of brocade and silk.

Mowenholtz took a deep breath and when the baron spoke again, he sounded more like his normal Teutonic self. "Your counzel is always of great service, your Highness. I will engage a solicitor at once." With that, he backed away from the prince, then turned and departed the room.

Geo dutifully danced and conversed with the prince and the ladies, but it was clear to me that his heart wasn't in it. We left the ball and met the baron, who was sitting quietly in one of the coaches, scribbling notes in a note book with a well-worn pencil. On the return to Julian Square, Geo again refused to ride with me and when we reentered the house, he retired immediately. I can only surmise that his anger at me was exacerbated by the absence of Countess Sophie from the ball. Which absence must have suggested to him the grievous possibility that he would never see her again.

Chapter Seventeen
The Bounds of Good Breeding

WE STOOD UNDER thick clouds, a medium rain steadily wetting us to the bone. No sunlight flashed from the blades of our swords to lend an air of heroism to the endeavor. There was only the dull gray light and insistent rain. I took the latter as a clear statement of Heaven's disapproval. I had, after all, been bonded by the almighty as guide, companion and second to this man, not as his butcher.

Geo stood opposite me, his blade unsheathed, ready for the contest. My sword was also ready, though I desperately sought an excuse not to employ it.

Apparently not a man to idly threaten, Geo had made good on his demand for satisfaction. He had arranged for us to meet this wet morning on the field of honor. He now stood ready to commence the bloody fight, though he did so with tight-lipped determination, not a hint of excitement nor zeal.

"Are you ready to begin, Mr. Attucks?" Geo asked, as impersonally as he might.

"I am ... almost."

"What, if I may ask, is preventing you from readiness?" Geo asked with some irritation. "Is your weapon ready?"

"Indeed, it is."

"Is it your waistcoat that hinders you, then?"

"No, my waistcoat, though wet, is otherwise quite comfortable."

"Is it the rain in your eyes?"

"Nay, my hat does protect my eyes from the drops."

Geo whipped his blade through the air in frustration. "Pray, then tell me what makes you unready. Perhaps I may be of assistance."

"I delay in the hope that you return to your good senses. Are you so ready to duel and get cut bloody?"

"*You* will be cut bloody, sir." Then he lunged at me. With ease, I knocked his blade away. Geo was a Virginia backwoodsman, 'tis true, but I had fought my way through a dozen pirates to escape with my life at Tortuga, had led a boarding party that recaptured our ship at Tangier, had even fought off an entire company of actors in New York. In other words, I had experience with deadly hand-to-hand combat and had never been bested ... save for a few nasty gashes.

"Geo, listen to me. I bear no grudge against Sophie."

"Then why do you defame her?" He lunged again. This time I sidestepped him and landed a kick on his arse as he went by.

"I seek no defamation," I replied as I squared up to face him.

"You will not keep us apart." He lunged again.

"I have no reason to." I hooked his sword with my own and he lost his grip. It flew away and skittered into the tall grass. He looked at me, a little unsure of what to do next.

I shook my head in disbelief and then pointed to where his sword lay. "Well, go and fetch it."

Geo scurried over and began looking for the sword in the wet undergrowth. "It must be right here. Where can it have gone?"

"I saw it slide in a little bit more to the left — your left. No, over there!"

Geo shook his head. "Could you lend a hand?"

Soon we were both pawing through the wet grass. "I hate to lose that sword, it was quite costly," Geo said.

"Yes, with all the swords lying around in armorers shops, you wouldn't think they would cost so bloody much. Ah! Here it is." I picked up the weapon and handed it to him. He took it, bowed and then suddenly hacked at me. I retreated, stumbled and fell, losing my sword. "That was decidedly ungentlemanly," I protested.

Geo smiled. "Yes. Wasn't it just?"

I scrambled to my feet again. "Geo, this is all a terrible miscarriage."

"Why?"

"I am merely repeating, in a different form, what she had already confided to you."

"She did not!" Geo swung at me again.

"Yes, yes. When she said there was something that she dare not tell you and that you dare not ask."

"Did she say that?" He swung weakly at me and again I parried the blow.

"She did. Do you not remember?"

He paused a while. "Yes." He admitted. "I think I do."

With that, he took a handkerchief from his pocket and wiped down the wet blade. Then he carefully placed it back in its scabbard. This seemed to relieve him greatly. "I was deathly afraid I would damage the thing. But luckily, not one nick."

I put up my own blade. "But how could you have damaged it? You barely swung it."

Geo gave me a sharp nod of agreement. "That was entirely by design, I can assure you. It might have been badly damaged, or even broken if I had put any strength behind it."

"You were concerned about damaging your sword?" I asked incredulously.

He nodded.

"But your good friend, your humble companion and trusted second, if he were cut, nay, if he lost his arm, that wouldn't concern you?"

"Perhaps I did make a small error in judgment," Geo allowed.

"An error in judgment, indeed. You have dishonored me, Geo." I drew my sword. "I must ask for satisfaction."

Geo looked at me out of the corner of his eye, unsure for a moment. Then he blurted, "Oh, shut up. Besides, you cannot challenge me. You are my second. It is ungentlemanly."

"But what of you challenging your own second? Surely that is beyond the bounds of good breeding?"

Geo shrugged. "Sometimes, I suppose, the rules need to be broken. I have never been much on breaking the rules, but perhaps I should begin."

And so I again learned from my charge. I took this lesson to heart. Indeed, we both decided that propriety and decorum could stand a holiday. We procured ourselves an ample supply of gin and toasted our great and good friendship at a downstairs gin shop. After the rain stopped and the late afternoon sun swept through the streets, we paid a ready sum to a bored farmer transporting a load of hay to the market. He allowed us to hop aboard his wagon.

We rode back to Julian Square, drinking and shouting. We became so drunk that we soon were dropping our breeches to show passersby our behinds. Some turned their heads in prudery. Others laughed and threw a rotten tomato or a dead rat at us. One street vendor hit Geo with a goat's head, knocking him flat in the hay. A young chimney sweep ran up to me with his face blackened, grunting and growling and jumping around as if he were an animal. I grabbed his dirty shirt collar and hauled him up in the air where he flailed his arms and legs and screamed bloody murder. He ordered me to let him go. So I did, into a pickle barrel — he went in soot-faced and emerged green and sputtering.

When we returned to No. 4, the effect of the gin had rendered us insensible. We lay outside the front door for some time. One merciful passerby believed us to be dead and said a short prayer. Prudence and Hawkins found us at last and we stumbled inside. The house creaked and groaned like never before, as if it was angry over something and wished to speak out. As I drifted off to fitful sleep in my little room in the attic, I became convinced my ship was adrift in a great storm of wind. I was unable to do anything to help her avoid the rocks and reefs of dire fate.

Chapter Eighteen
A Younger Son No More

WHEN I AWOKE, my head throbbed with pain. I lay abed listening to No. 4 creak in the wind. Downstairs, I saw that the baron and Sir Gerald had returned from yet another trip to Kent. They sat with Geo at the table and were engaged in a discussion of some import. I certainly wished to join them, but I also yearned for a cup of tea. I entered the kitchen and asked Prudence. As I was eager to join Geo, I made to leave. Hawkins then asked if I would like anything else with the tea. "Perhaps a bit of muffin or a hunk of bread?"

"No. The tea will suffice."

"We could get you some nice herrings to go with," Prudence offered. "Hawkins here wouldn't mind heading out to the shops."

"Thank you, but no."

"What about some tongue?"

"No."

"Hawkins," Prudence barked. "Go get Mr. Darius some nice hocklings from that shop on, what's that street? Always just flies right out of my head."

"You mean Grindleman's."

"Yeah, that's right." Prudence smiled at me. "It won't be no trouble for Hawkins here to set off and bring back some crispy hocks."

Thinking now that I had missed everything going on between Geo and the baron, but not wishing to give offense to Prudence and Hawkins, I gently declined the hocks.

"Grindleman's has got some very fine sheep's brain. Hawkins can gather some of that. What d'ya say?"

Hawkins then said, "I might fetch you some very nice sheep's brains."

"Hawkins, I just told 'im 'bout them sheep's brains," Prudence shouted at him. "Don't you listen?" Then to me she said, "He worked for a long time as a goldsmith, made 'im a bit mad in the head."

I nodded my understanding, but begged off the brains.

"Some eel jelly, then per'aps?" Hawkins pressed. "Fancy some pigeon sausage? Sweetbread pie? Sheep's eyes in lemon aspic? — that is to say, are you hungry?"

"No, I confess I am not. I will forgo the tea, as well. If you will excuse me." I exited the kitchen as quickly as I could. Without asking for leave, I sat down near Geo. As his counselor and second I had my rights to advise him.

"You indeed have done excellent work, Herr Washington," the baron said. "With that I completely agree."

"By your own admission, we have amassed a sizeable sum in payments," Geo pointed out.

"Don't forget that the baron has expenses he must meet," Sir Gerald said roughly. "This very house, the victuals that you and your darkie friend eat in great volume. These are all monies that come from the baron's generous purse."

The baron raised his hand. "Now, then, Sir Gerald. I am sure Mr. Washington understands that we have expenses. Und he has been most helpful in so many ways."

"Then it is time for my efforts to be rewarded," Geo pressed. "You quite clearly promised me a title and an estate. I mean to collect, your Excellency."

"Ja, ja. I understand. I have made numerous enquires regarding zis. Und I am quite close to securing for you just such a combination of a noble title und a country house. That is good, ja?"

Geo hungrily agreed.

"So. If you will excuse me, I must get to this problem immediately." The baron stood up and the other two men rose. "In the meantime, I wish you to go with Sir Gerald to meet with a potential buyer. Quite possibly our last buyer, so it is vital that you give him the best possible attention, ja?"

"Yes, of course, my lord."

Sir Gerald had a carriage ready and soon Geo and I were about to climb aboard. Sir Gerald had other ideas, however.

"Do you think you are going to bring that blackamoor in my carriage?"

"I am convinced I am, yes," Geo replied. Geo climbed aboard, then turned to offer his hand to me. I took it and scampered up. Sir Gerald was not happy. "I would suggest that he step down now. Or I will certainly have satisfaction from you, sir."

"I will provide you with a duel whenever you wish, Sir Gerald."

The big man hesitated. Certainly he had impressive physical size. And his demeanor was gruff and sinister. However, it appeared Geo had succeeded in calling Sir Gerald's bluff. He gave me a nasty glance but boarded the carriage. "It is only because the baron would be displeased if we dueled that I am letting this pass for now. Otherwise you would be facing my pistol."

"I have no desire to get anywhere near your pistol," Geo said. I could not help but snicker at this, which brought a further withering look from Sir Gerald.

"We shall duel when our business is completed," Geo said.

"You may count on it."

Needless to record, the carriage ride was not entirely convivial. On previous occasions when Sir Gerald let some of his dislike for us show, he would soon thereafter adopt an air of avuncular affection and common cause or become drunk such that he did not seem to mind us. This time, however, something had changed. He made no such effort at reconciliation. Instead, he maintained a stony silence, speaking only to remind us that the baron would not join us on this appointment. 'Twas a long trip, as it seemed to me that we took a roundabout route, going hither and thither. Almost as if the intent was to fritter away time. At long last, we arrived at the Janus Coffeehouse.

In a small back room we met the man the baron said would be our last buyer of Ohio land. He wore a rich, plum-colored coat with much gold filigree and elaborate stitching. His golden waistcoat was so filigreed the man might have had stolen it from one of Prince George's chamberlains. His jeweled rings, lace cuffs, golden lace cravat and ruby-jeweled cravat pin only further signaled he was a wealthy man and could easily afford to buy the last Ohio parcel, even if it wasn't at a reduced price. One odd aspect was the man's bushy head of red hair and overgrown beard. Beneath and behind all the hair the man seemed nearly lost — we could not make out his features. He remained seated as we entered. Sir Gerald went to him and bowed as deeply as I suspect he was capable.

"Ah, my lord Duke," Sir Gerald said with great

enthusiasm and volume — the crowd in the main room of the coffeehouse were screaming at each other over the coming change in the calendar that would rob everyone of the 11 days. "I am most honored that you have consented to meet with us."

"Nonsense. I know a good deal when I hear of one," the duke replied with a Scottish accent. A Scottish duke would, of course, explain the untoward amount of red hair the man possessed. "And this is most assuredly a favorable deal. I am greatly interested in purchasing any remaining parcels."

"Yes, your Grace. The price we discussed is more than generous. You may consider your purchase to be official and final. You may forward your down payment at your convenience."

The tumult in the next room reached a crescendo as various parties to the argument tossed their coffee at their opponents. Chairs were upended, crockery was smashed and fisticuffs ensued. The noise of the fighting became nearly overpowering.

"NONSENSE!" the duke yelled over the tumult. "I SHALL HAVE MY PAYMENT DELIVERED TOMORROW."

"AS YOU WISH, YOUR GRACE," Sir Gerald shouted in reply.

The duke looked to Geo and beckoned the Virginian to come sit by him. Geo bowed and sat down. The fight in the next room had devolved and now the fighters were smashing chairs, upending tables and crying foul and perdition.

"SO, YOU ARE THE YOUNG MAN FROM VIRGINIA, MISTER WASHINGTON?"

"YES, YOUR GRACE," Geo said as loudly as he could while trying to maintain his decorum. Sitting with a baronet was one thing, but an audience with a duke, even only a hairy Scottish duke, was an honor.

More crockery was broken and something sailed through a window with a crash. Now the great iron pot in which the coffee water was boiled could be heard crashing to the floor.

"THE BARON MOWENHOLTZ HAS TOLD ME OF THE EXCELLENT WORK YOU HAVE PERFORMED FOR KING AND COUNTRY. SETTLEMENT OF THE

OHIO COUNTRY WILL ADD IMMEASURABLY TO THE WEALTH AND POWER OF THE KINGDOM. I BELIEVE YOU SHOULD BE REWARDED FOR YOUR SUPERB EFFORTS, YOUNG MAN."

Geo nodded and smiled.

A large group of the fighters could be heard running out of the coffeehouse and relative quiet ensued. Geo was able to lower his voice, "Thank you, your Grace. I would be most appreciative of any help you may be able to — "

An even larger group of fighters surged back into the coffeehouse and the mayhem resumed. Geo was again forced to shout, "ANY GOOD WORD YOU MAY BE ABLE TO SAY ON MY BEHALF WOULD BE MOST APPRECIATED."

The broken dishes were broken into smaller pieces and another window was smashed. The clopping of horses hooves on the floor could be heard, followed by the rumble of a wagon and then the thumping of a heavy object hitting the floor. The horse snorted in terror and then a horse hoof with shoe attached punched through the adjoining wall sending shards of plaster flying. The horse's leg was withdrawn and through the hole, I could see that the heavy object was a small keg of gunpowder. And one of the coffeehouse customers was running about with a blazing torch.

The duke seemed not the least perturbed by the raucous doings in the next room. He turned to Geo: "I AM NEARLY CERTAIN THAT I WILL BE ABLE TO RUSH THROUGH YOUR REQUEST. I FEEL FORTUNE WILL SMILE UPON YOU, YOUNG SIR. NOW I MUST BE OFF. I GO TO PLEAD YOUR CASE AT COURT.

"THANK YOU, YOUR GRACE. THIS HAS BEEN A MOST PLEASANT AUDIENCE," Geo offered in a full-throated roar. At that moment, an explosion knocked us to the floor and the room filled with a dark, choking atmosphere. It seemed entirely possible that none of us would ever see sunlight again.

Our impending death was propitiously thwarted when one section of the coffeehouse wall collapsed due to the concussive effects of the explosion. While this might seem a dangerous event, it was, in fact, a godsend in that the smoke and foul air was immediately drawn from what was left of the room and replaced with fresher air that allowed us to resume breathing.

The massive hole also allowed us to easily exit into Burnhampton Court and thence onto the nearest street. After staggering out of the room a bit dazed and askew, the duke quickly rallied and when he left, he was in full fettle and looked fully recovered.

Sir Gerald, Geo and I took ourselves to the nearest tavern and cleared our dusty throats with flagons of stout, ale, porter and cups of gin. With business clearly performed to his satisfaction and with sufficient gin in him, Sir Gerald could almost be called a good companion, our previous disagreements forgotten. We ate several meals, gambled at cards, smoked clay pipes, shouted and sang, partook of much loud and boisterous argument, engaged in good-natured shoving, back slapping and gesticulation, silly faces and mock horror. We entirely lost track of time. Sir Gerald finally staggered upstairs in the embrace of a young woman who, after prompt payment, promised only the most felicitous of attentions towards his person.

When we emerged from the tavern, Geo and I again found ourselves in the night city. We traversed dark streets and bumped down inky alleys as we struggled to find Julian Square. The dark was challenge enough. We were further hampered, however, by our evening's companion: John Barleycorn. He made us to stumble and he slurred our minds.

On several occasions I looked behind and was nearly certain I saw a shade pacing us. But I shook it off, attributing it to the effects of drink.

Thus,'twas a rude shock when another shade suddenly appeared to block our path. He wore no coat, only a black waistcoat over a charcoal blouse. His black breeches were tucked into black boots. His eyes were covered by a black mask — such as is worn in Venice at carnival. At his side hung a black-sheathed sword. While he wore black, he was no African like myself. He was as white as Geo and just as tall.

"Greetings, sirs," the black-clad man said in seeming good humor.

"What d'he say, 'Green tea is served?'" Geo slurred, "What does that mean?"

I heard a noise behind us and turned to see another

black-clad man. Any thought of Geo and I attempting to overpower one blackened knave fled when the second fiend showed himself.

"Please follow us," the first man said, with a black-gloved hand on his sword hilt.

Since Geo was in no condition to overcome even so much as a kitten, I assured our dark interlocutor we would follow him, and that there was no need for violence.

He led us through narrow passages, hidden alleys and winding stairs. We moved through nighttime London as shades in a brick underworld, never taking a main street. Instead we passed unseen as if traveling via the deepest caverns of the earth. After some time we arrived at a sunken graveyard. We stumbled over a crumbling wall and our feet sunk into the soft soil of fresh graves.

In a corner I heard the scraping of a shovel. The weak light of a stub candle suggested bent figures hauling a coffin from the soil. The grave robbers took little heed of our passing but continued their devilish work.

Ahead was a small chapel, its stones stained by ages of coal smoke. From within, a flame flickered. The chapel's windows threw tombstones of light on the dead man's ground. Our dark guide brought us to the door of the chapel and a voice from within bade us enter.

Geo led me past the half-opened door. Arranged inside was a rough gang of men, well-armed and of a sinister aspect equal to our two guides: they also were swathed in black and masked. The fairest one, a man with light brown eyes and brown hair, held position in the center of the group and seemed the leader. He spoke.

"We grant you safe passage this night."

"And what — 'scuse me — who, are you to grant us such?" Geo stammered.

"We are the rulers of the night," the handsome one replied.

It was then I supposed who these men were. We had been granted an audience with none other than the Mohocks. These were the fearful ones who were whispered to perpetrate odious deeds in the dark.

"Why safe passage for us? We do not even know you," I said. I was doing my best to cast off the effects of drink and gather my wits.

"Let us say we have a mutual friend," he answered. "That will be enough for now. One of our own will see you back to Julian Square. But realize that it is only our mutual acquaintance that saves you from our wrath."

"Tell us who you are and why you rudely threaten us?" I pressed.

He put up his hand and shook his head. "We have done you this favor. Mark me that some day you will return this favor to us."

Then another of the masked Mohocks led us out of the chapel and into the maze of streets till we were on the very doorstep of No. 4 Julian Square under the watch of a million stars. When I turned to thank him, he had already slipped away.

The next day Geo and I were in a most aggrieved state. We resolved that only several perambulations round Julian Square were sufficient to excise the poisons we had consumed the previous night. As if we both hoped that we had merely imagined it, neither of us made mention of our odd audience with the fearful Mohocks.

Usually Geo was fastidious to avoid the sheep shite that often littered the square. This morning, however, his ill-feelings caused him to plow right through 'em.

But that morning, Geo received the most exciting news of his young life. Awaiting us upon our return were the baron, Sir Gerald and Lady Montagrave. They were gathered in the drawing room, where the chandelier glowed with freshly trimmed candles. Newly cut blossoms graced every table. After Geo and I made our way into the room, Prudence and Hawkins appeared and hovered in the doorway. They watched the proceedings with interest and, it seemed, with some pride.

The baron sat in a chair near the fireplace, nobly attired in an ochre silk coat and waistcoat, with generous lace cuffs and a purple neck cloth. His face was bright, his skin hale and pink, as if recently scrubbed. His freshly powdered wig was adorned with a wide orange ribbon. Only the mud spattered on his shoes rendered his ensemble less than perfect. He welcomed Geo to him like a proud papa, holding a shiny, new silver-tipped cane aloft like a standard won on the field of battle. Sir Gerald lowered himself onto the divan, where perched a smiling Lady Montagrave. I grabbed a spare wooden chair from the rail and perched upon it. Geo took his seat next to the baron. Though Geo did his best to present the air of noble reserve that seemed his natural countenance, there was little doubt of his inner excitement.

Prudence and Hawkins and two servants dispensed brandy in crystal glasses and the baron took out his silver snuff case for a generous pinch of the fragrant tobacco. When all were equipped with brandy — even, I noticed, Prudence and Hawkins — von Mulct gave a toast.

"To my friends und associates und all who gather here. When I furst made the acquaintance of young Mr. Washington in Barbados, I was immediately struck by his intelligence, his affability, his candor und his propriety. Add to this his experience as a surveyor in the American wilderness und I vas sure he would make an excellent business associate. This he has become und more. I have seen him ripen into a man of character und importance. Und so, because of his efforts, the holdings of Great Britain will increase in population and commercial vibrancy. The court of His Royal Highness George II, therefore, has bestowed upon him the following title and grant of land." The baron stopped to put down his brandy glass and take up a long document from which dangled several imposing seals and ribbons. "Henceforth and forward, George Washington of Virginia shall be styled the Viscount Washington and shall take his seat at Braddock Hall in the county of Kent."

Geo beamed and then looked down at the floor for some moments. When he regained his composure, he looked at each of us in turn. The others, myself included, clapped and cheered at his great good fortune. The baron, Sir Gerald and I lined up to bow to the new viscount.

"Shall I kiss your ring?" I asked Geo.

"Not yet," he replied earnestly. "Having just been informed of my title, I have not obtained a proper signet."

I shook my head at his thickheadedness. "Ring kissing is for bishops, not viscounts, you dolt."

"Ah, yes. You're right," he replied. At first I thought my criticism of him rested on a fear that he would become a self-important ass. However, I must confess a further realization: I felt a sharp pang of envy. Geo had advanced and I had not.

I stood aside so that Geo might step past me and receive a congratulatory, and passionate, kiss from the seated Lady Montagrave. So enthusiastic was her congratulations, I wondered if she might pull him down on top of her and initiate a general boarding of his ship. Even Sir Gerald offered his good wishes, though he refrained from a kiss. Prudence and Hawkins bowed and curtsied to Geo in happy agreement. Then we joined in a round of toasts for the new-minted nobleman. Several bottles were opened and the level of good feeling rose ever higher.

During these rounds of congratulations, Geo and I felt the call of nature and headed to the privy in the back yard for relief. Geo, as befitting his new status, used the privy, whilst I let fly into the pile of dead ornamental trees that Geo had dispatched with his hatchet.

"I must say I am delirious at this turn of events," Geo said as he made water in the privy.

"I can only imagine," I replied.

"My brother Lawrence is the one with all the good fortune. I have only been able to get scraps from the table. And to think I now will have a table finer and more esteemed than anything he has in Virginia."

"But I thought you came from a family of some wealth."

"Wealth is a relative thing, D. Lawrence is a man of means in Virginia and does have the estate at Mount Vernon. However, compared to men of means here, Lawrence is a mere farmer and Mt. Vernon a cottage. I set out to rise in this life and I have succeeded beyond my wildest hopes, past my most fervent fantasies. There is only one more thing that can make my joy complete."

"You speak, I imagine, of Countess Sophie?" I asked as we walked back into the house, re-tying our breeches.

"I do." Then he stopped and put his hand on my arm. "I must thank you. I would not have achieved this exalted status without your help."

I smiled at him, my pangs of jealousy twined with bonds of friendship.

Geo wasted not a moment in going directly to the baron and asking him as to the whereabouts of the countess. "I insist you send word to her at her lodgings that she might come and join us."

The baron rose from his chair and walked past Geo, saying as he passed, "I will not."

This caught Geo with his sails aback. He hardly knew how to respond. He followed the Baron into the front hall and blocked him from further retreat.

"My Lord, I must insist on this point."

"I will not summon her und that is final." The baron raised his nose and pursed his lips in defiance.

Sir Gerald, Lady Montagrave, myself, Prudence and Hawkins all moved into the front hall to watch the proceedings between the new Viscount Washington and the Baron Mowenholtz.

"This thing I ask is no great hardship," Geo said, wavering a bit.

"Simply because you are now a Viscount does not mean that you can order whomever you like to do whatever you wish. I will not summon her, it is impossible."

"Such a thing is not impossible," Geo retorted.

"It is," the baron said. "I cannot summon her ... because she is already here." The baron turned and raised his arm to present the countess, who was descending the stairs toward us, more beautiful than ever in a yellow silk dress, her neck illuminated by a necklace of silver, diamonds and rubies, her dark hair elaborately coifed, held in place with combs of silver. Geo stood with a sloppy smile upon his face, utterly transfixed. When she reached the bottom stair, the baron spoke.

"My dear countess. May I present to you his Excellency George, the Viscount Washington, lord of Braddock Hall in Kent, to which we repair on the morrow, ja?"

Sophie and Geo said nothing for a few moments. They floated in their own world, held in the air by their interlocked eyes, their eager hands and expectant bodies. Geo tenderly took the countess's hand and raised it to his lips then held it lightly against his cheek.

"I am so very pleased for you, Viscount Washington," she said softly.

"Your presence renders this moment complete," he replied.

The baron cleared his throat. "Und so, now we dine,

ja?"

Thus the party adjourned to the dining room where a handsome feast was served. I would be very surprised if Geo or Sophie spoke again that night; so intent were they in gazing into each other's eyes, so far were they beyond words.

Chapter Nineteen
Master of Braddock Hall

THE COACH LEFT London town very early in the morning. Two of its occupants, the baron and Sir Gerald were bleary-eyed and a bit grumpy at the early start. Two others, Geo and the countess, were oblivious to any mishap or discord. They sat with hands locked and their bodies pressed together, barely noticing the two men in the coach with them, nor, indeed, the vast city of London passing by the coach windows. I sat outside the coach, upon one of the precarious seats at the top rear provided for footmen and servants. Lady Montagrave had elected to stay in bed in London. She did not arise to see us off as lately she was said to not feel well in the morning.

We lurched and rolled to the southeast of London into Kent, staying on the Dover road. The day had dawned pleasantly warm with processions of puffy clouds that heralded nothing more sinister than a stretch of fine weather. For Geo it was the perfect match to his blue-sky outlook. For me it meant a pleasant ride through charming countryside.

After passing through many a town and village, we turned off the main road onto a short carriageway that led to a great house. The prodigious mansion was easily three times the size of No. 4 Julian Square. As I have performed considerable investigation into the subject of architecture, and have read numerous tracts on it, I can safely say that I am something of an expert on the subject.

The house in question was an old one. Unlike the winged Palladian villas so popular among men of power and taste for some decades, Braddock Hall was a grizzled veteran. By my eye, it was built in the reign of James I in the early 1600s or so. Constructed of sturdy and pleasing red brick, the hall displayed two imposing symmetrical faces, both standing three stories, not counting their high round chimneys. Each story was provided with tall runs of leaded windows, each level's windows aligned perfectly with the windows of the story below. Running from bottom to top and enclosing the many-paned windows were slim pilasters carved in a most pleasing Flemish style. A sandstone parapet surmounting the eaves was pierced with a series of charming rosette designs. The grand front entrance was set back somewhat from the windowed faces. A broad fan of stone steps led upward to the imposing oak door, which was placed equally between the two forward-thrusting fronts, as if to adjudicate the opposing wishes of two headstrong children.

"Viscount, Countess, Sir Gerald, I give you, Braddock Hall," the baron said with a flourish. One can only imagine the towering wave of joy and excitement engulfing Geo. We rolled to a stop in the paved yard at the house's front. All of us aboard the coach marveled at the house's grandeur.

As we climbed down, a wizened servant tottered out. His hair was silver white and he raised and lowered his eyebrows with nervous anticipation.

"May I help you, sirs and lady?" the old fellow rattled. "I am Simperton, the butler and overseer of this estate. We are not receiving guests these days, as the master is not in residence." Simperton wrung his hands and shifted his weight from one foot to the other. After some years living largely by himself at Braddock Hall, Simperton had become uneasy in the company of strangers.

"Don't be ridiculous," the baron replied. "The master of this house stands before you." Von Mulct waved his arm at Geo.

The old servant looked quite distressed. "But, sir. My master is Sir Digby Eggleton. He serves the crown in India. He is commercial secretary to the Viceroy."

"Ja, und a better commercial secretary there could not be, Simperton," The baron replied. "Look at this house, Sir Digby is a genius with money, ja?"

"Well, yes, that is so. But why do you say that this man is the owner?" Simperton asked. Sweat had broken out on the old fellow's forehead.

"Because, Simperton, he *is* the new und rightful owner."

The baron produced a small, leather-bound portfolio and opened it smartly to a sales contract and registered bill of sale. "It is clearly indicated here that Viscount Washington is the new and rightful owner, having purchased the property through Sir Digby's London agent."

"May I see those papers?" Simperton asked.

"Indeed you may." The baron held out the papers.

"You may peruse them at your will." As Simperton reached for the portfolio, though, the baron tucked them back under his arm in one swift motion. "Just as soon as ve have taken a look around und unpacked the Viscount."

Simperton, exasperated and in over his head, nodded and then tried to keep up with the group striding toward the house.

"Is not Braddock a Scottish name?" asked the countess as she stopped, balanced upon the highest step, reticent to go further.

"Ja, Sir Digby's mother was Scottish — from Perthshire, as I remember," the baron answered smoothly as he stepped past her and swung wide the heavy oak portal. Von Mulct led us into a front hall thickly decorated with oil portraits, marble busts, gold leaf and defrocked deer antlers.

Inside, the rooms were dusty, but not so much so that it took one bit away from Geo's pride and happiness at how far and how quickly he had risen in the world. He decided that one of the first things he must do was to write to his mother and to Lawrence in Virginia and relate to them his astounding news. It could be fairly said, Geo ruminated, that the younger son had eclipsed the firstborn in the prosperity of his establishment.

After a brief tour, which served to further cement the impression of wealth and luxury, the baron announced to Simperton a further provision of the sale, viz all of Sir Digby's personal possessions — the paintings, sculpture, objects d'art, furniture, musical instruments, clothing, tapestries, linens, silver and china, and other items of value — were to be immediately removed and brought to London for storage until Sir Digby's return from India.

No sooner had the baron announced this than a score of workmen, led by a smiling foreman Boyle flooded into the house. The baron and Sir Gerald walked about, putting little red flags on those items to be taken away. This planting of flags seemed altogether unnecessary since nearly everything sported a red ensign. The workers then began stripping Braddock Hall. Sir Digby's possessions were rapidly packed, crated and carried out the front entryway before being sweated aboard five ample wagons that had recently drawn up outside.

The disintegration of the estate that he had overseen for

more than 18 years caused the elderly Simperton some considerable level of distraction. He retired to his quarters below stairs to write a letter to Sir Digby's sister, Lady Ledelia Rashersome. Lady Ledelia lived not five miles from Braddock Hall and, being a commoner who did well to marry a wealthy baronet, was a jealous guardian of her brother's good name and bank account. Simperton finished his letter and called for the stableman to mount one of the estate's four horses — the other 16 having been sold off by Lady Ledelia and the proceeds invested for her brother's return.

Simperton instructed Braden, the stableman, to take the letter to Sir Digby's sister.

Braden made ready to do so, but he was very surprised that a postman chanced to stop at Braddock Hall delivering a letter and asking if there were any posts he might convey. Braden was delighted to hand over the letter and return to his duties in the barn, which consisted mostly of sleeping, brewing and drinking ale — which led to more sleeping.

Meanwhile, Geo and Sophie and I walked around Braddock Hall, trying to not get trampled by the remarkably enthusiastic workers, who seemed eager to finish the removal job as rapidly as possible.

Geo, Sophie and I discussed the views and prospects afforded by the various windows, debated the proper furnishing and the assignment of the assorted rooms. In our imaginations we turned Braddock Hall into the finest estate in Kent, and, quite possibly, all of England. Any house, of course, without furniture and accoutrements provided one with a dizzying array of possibilities for arrangement — most of which plans must be thrown out, however, when the oafish dimensions of real furniture are introduced and the rooms are found to have shrunk considerably.

At one point in our rambling around the estate we found ourselves alone in the overgrown herb garden by the kitchen door. I watched a playful pair of finches flitting through the shaggy plants when Geo turned to me. "Mother Geechee's prophecy was correct. Did she not say I would be a titled man and live in a big house? Look all around you, has it not come true?"

I pondered this. "'Tis two-thirds true. What of the 'riv-ah'? I remember she said you would live by a 'great riv-ah.'"

Geo was irked by my memory. "Well, there must be a

river around here somewhere." He turned his head this way and that, as if a wide river flowed by the garden wall and he had somehow missed it. "England is graced with many rivers," he said sharply. "One can't take these prophecies too literally, after all." Then, quickly, "Where has Sophie gotten to? I must find her." With that, Geo sank back into his rapture and strode off to find his lady love.

No more than a few hours later, the job was done. Braddock Hall was empty. All of the house's most beautiful contents were tightly packed on board the wagons. That which remained were some of the more practical items, such as the stairs and the bricks. The baron assured Geo and Simperton that he would return on the morrow to bring gifts for Geo's new household. Before Geo and I left London, the Baron had suggested that we would need to bring necessary clothes and kit for an overnight stay; those bags had already been removed from the coach and placed in Braddock Hall. Von Mulct told us he would bring the rest of our things from Julian Square upon his return.

"However, we need to get this load of goods back to London and properly stored. So we must leave immediately," the Baron explained.

Sir Gerald stepped up to Geo and gave him a perfunctory bow. He smiled quite broadly, in a great show of mirth. "My best regards to you, Viscount Washington. You have my congratulations on your new house and I wish you and the Countess every happiness." He took Sophie's hand and gave it a lingering kiss, as he looked up into her eyes for an uncomfortably long time.

Sir Gerald turned to me next. He only gave me a cold nod, however, before striding outside where he mounted a horse and departed. He rode down the drive and swung left on the London-Dover road to return to the city.

The baron grabbed Geo's hand and shook it vigorously before clasping him in an embrace and kissing both sides of his face. It was a heartfelt farewell and certainly more emotion than we had ever seen from the German. "I will miss you, George. You have been a profitable associate und a reliable friend."

"But why do you say you will miss me? Will you not

return tomorrow?"

"Ja, ja, of course," the baron replied quickly. "I only meant that as you are living here now, we will most likely not be seeing so much of you. That is a shame. However, life must go on, ja? Und you have your new estate und I suspect a new bride soon, hmm? Make the most of your chances, George. That is what I have always tried to do." Then he turned to Sophie. "Goodbye, your ladyship. I wish the best of luck to you." To which Sophie curtly nodded and looked away.

Before he walked out, he glanced over at me. "You have made a good addition to our efforts. I thank you for your help." Unlike Sir Gerald, the baron knew how to be cordial. He was an honorable man. I admired him for that. "You are welcome, Baron Mowenholtz," I replied. "I have been honored to assist in my small way."

We walked to the steps and watched with warm feelings as the baron left Braddock Hall and climbed aboard the coach. Geo, the countess and I looked on as the baron leaned from the coach window and waved to us. The coach and the wagons rolled down the drive to the main road. When they reached the London-Dover road, the heavily laden convoy swung to the right.

"Is there another road to London?" Geo asked idly as we watched the coach and wagons disappear in their own dust, heading southeast toward the port town of Dover.

Chapter Twenty
Alarum and Flight

A QUARTET OF MUSICIANS played while finely dressed dancers moved on the floor in graceful unison. Dozens of candles in crystal chandeliers added warmth to the perfect scene unfolding in Braddock Hall. There, at the head of dancers was the Countess Sophie, and alongside her the Viscount Washington. Together they presided over a ball that was unmatched in every way: in the quality of the guests — there was the Duke of Cumberland chatting with the Prince of Wales and over there, the Tsarina of Russia affectionately rubbing the neck of her horse; in the beauty of the dancing; and in the splendor of the house in which the gathering transpired. Truly, this was the best ball in the best home with the best hosts. The gathering was as close to perfection as had ever been seen in this world.

The Viscount Washington loved to dance at balls such as this. He also loved to gather with his friends and smoke pipes while they acclaimed him with shouts of "George! George! —"

"George! Wake up!" Sophie shouted at Geo, driving away his wonderful dream. "George, we must get up and dress immediately."

His dream now shattered, Geo sat up. He saw the alarum on the countess' face and he leapt from their improvised bed — a mattress laid across some boards in one of the many upstairs bedrooms. "What is it? What is the matter?"

The countess pulled on a simple dress over her small clothes. Geo had a sudden vision from the night before — her body stretched out beneath his, her naked skin soft and willing, her hair fanned across the pillow like spokes of dark light. That had been no dream, he was sure of it.

"We must fly from here," she blurted out, "lest we be captured."

"Captured by whom? Have the French landed?"

"Men! You can't do two things at once. Get dressed

while you talk!"

Geo obliged by grabbing his breeches and pulling them on. "We are close to the coast, is King Louis's army nearby?"

"No. We flee from the local authorities. They make their way here even now. We must depart with all haste."

"But why should I flee? I am the Viscount Washington and Braddock Hall is my home. Why would I wish to desert it when I have only just secured it?"

She had wormed into her dress and now was slipping on shoes, she did not answer his question. Geo stopped again and touched her arm. "Why do you not answer me? Why should I need to flee mine own house?"

Sophie also stopped. They stood gazing at each other as the warm light of a new day streamed through the windows of Braddock Hall — he frozen in confusion and she in locked in confession.

"Do you not know? Have you not realized by now what is afoot here?" Her eyes were wet with tears. She cried for herself, of course, but more, she wept for him and the end of his titled dream. She had known all along this moment was coming, but it had been so fine to playact it yesterday, to discuss the furnishings and the dishes and the nursery....

"What are you saying? I must confess I do not understand."

She hugged herself and looked down at the bare floor, its Persian rug long since carted away by the baron. "George, you are no more a viscount than I am. And this house was never yours, but belongs to Sir Digby Eggleton still."

"But the baron informed me the house was mine. He said so. And I saw the papers that clearly indicated that I am the owner. I also saw the papers that clearly stated I am the Viscount Washington. There must be some error."

"If but there was," Sophie said bitterly. She had spoken the truth and now the spell was broken. She hastily threw her few clothes into a bag. "George, pack your things. Quickly, we must go." Sophie was again in control of herself. She pushed her emotions aside, as fate had forced her to do so many times in the past. She ran to my room to wake me.

When Sophie returned, Geo was sitting on the floor in a shaft of sunlight, his knees clasped to his chest. Sophie went to his side and shouted at him: "You have been deceived, George. It does no good to further the injury by hanging. We must flee."

I entered the room with my bag packed and saw that Geo was still sitting on the floor, quite immobile. It was time for quick action. "Yo, ho, Geo! Yo, Geo! I beat your arse in our duel. You couldn't beat me and you won't stand a chance against Colonel Chase. He will beat you bloody and leave you for the dogs!"

Sophie looked at me as if to say, "That will never work." But sure enough, I saw Geo stir and then look at me. "You never beat me," he said "You never beat me because we never had a proper duel. If we were to duel right now, you would not defeat me." But still he did not move. So I did what I knew would draw a reaction. I stepped over to him and punched him on the cheek with my closed fist.

Quickly, he was on his feet, "You miserable bastard, you punched me," he said, rubbing his face. I laughed and nodded — happy to see Geo's tall body on its feet. Sophie shot me another look as if to say, "I *knew* that would work."

I hastily agreed that we had never properly dueled and suggested to Geo that he quickly dress. He did so and every moment that passed he regained more of his former steady countenance and dependable manner. Sophie and I threw his things into a bag and the three of us ran down the wide staircase, our steps echoing in the empty house.

In the stable we saw Braden the stableman was sound asleep amid a pile of hay, empty bottles scattered on the floor. We encountered no resistance from him in quickly saddling and making ready three horses. Just after mounting the steeds, however, we heard the voice of Simperton call us from the barn doorway closest to the house. "Stand your ground or I'll pepper you well! You'll not add horse thievery to your crimes." He held a short-barreled fowling piece leveled at us.

Geo spoke up: "We have coin, Simperton. We can pay for these animals."

"They are not for sale."

I broke in, "Here now, mate. Let me point out some of the realities of your situation. Since you don't have that piece cocked, I'd wager you forgot to prime the pan. Getting that done will take a shake or two. And unless you've double-charged that gun, you have little chance of hitting us before we ride out yonder passage and get out of yer range." I pointed out the open doors to Geo and Sophie on my immediate right, on the side of the barn away from the house. "But if you *have* double-charged that old blunderbuss, there's a damn chance it'll blow up in your face. So why not be a good man and let us pay for the mounts and go our way. What do you say?"

Simperton's face and body suddenly drained of all bravado. He dropped the muzzle of the piece and croaked, "In my haste, I poured in so much powder, I must a' triple-charged it." His sudden change of heart left him looking very much an old man. It was hard not to feel sympathy for the fellow.

"You have proved a worthy adversary," I said. "How did you manage to spread the alarum?"

"I wrote a letter to Sir Digby's sister Lady Ledelia, who lives not five miles away. I had to protect my position, after all."

"Of course," I agreed.

"My mistake was giving the letter to Braden. He —"

"D, we must away from here," Geo interrupted.

I gave him a low wave to quiet him. "Braden was not helpful?"

"He gave it to a postman, but why it wasn't delivered I don't know. I resolved to write a second note and gave this to Braden to deliver. The drunken fool rode in a large circle and returned here with the letter undelivered."

"So you rode it over yourself."

"'Tis the only way. Lady Ledelia raised an immediate alarum with the local magistrate." Simperton paused, looking thoroughly disconsolate. "I dislike Lady Ledelia immensely, if you must know. She married well and now the cow thinks herself a duchess. But I had to do my duty to Sir Digby."

"He will be proud of you."

Simperton spoke up again, "you should know that a Lieutenant Colonel Chase of the Prince of Wales' Life Guard was already scouring the countryside for you before my note to Lady Ledelia. Chase is accompanied by ten dragoons. I don't know what you've done, but they aim to catch you."

"That is their aim, but we shall have no problem evading them, this back road is clearly the one to take."

I saw Simperton tilt his head slightly to one side as if

he had something he wanted to say, but then thought better of it. I knew that I had him on the line; now to set the hook. "It couldn't be simpler, we just stay on the track headed west and take the main road to London."

Simperton could not hold his tongue. "You don't want to get caught, do you?"

"Oh?" I asked.

"That road joins with the London road where the London road dips to the south. If this Colonel Chase doesn't find you here, he will likely backtrack on the London road and catch you up in no time. The better way is to take this road to the first stream crossing, then head south in the stream bed till you come to a bridge. Make a right turning onto that road and ride west. When you come to a hill nearby a windmill, climb the hill and strike overland, due north. That'll take you directly into London by way of the fields till you fetch Blue Anchor Road. Follow this route and you'll avoid the London Road."

"We are in your debt, Mr. Simperton. Geo, pay the man."

Geo looked pained. "Whilst you were speaking I checked my bag and have discovered that my coin is missing. Its weight has been replaced by pieces of lead."

I quickly felt through mine own bag and also found that what I thought was the weight of coin consisted of lead slugs used by setters of type. "It appears I have also been robbed by our friend Von Mulct. Fear not, we will find a way to return the horses to you."

Simperton looked to his right and saw the scarlet of the dragoons coming up fast on the London road. "The red coats are coming," he said excitedly. "The red coats are coming!"

"And so we are gone." We kicked the flanks of our horses, clattered under the archway and took the path through ornamental bushes and trees 'til it dove into a wood that swallowed us up. We were hidden from the eyes of Chase and his dragoons.

"Is it best to return to London?" Geo asked gruffly.

"When we arrive in London, I have some money and I have friends who can help us," Sophie said.

I offered, "And I can get us a ship in London to carry us back to America."

Geo nodded grimly. "Very well, to London, then."

We rode in silence after that, through the stream and onto the westbound road. It was not until we led our horses to the top of the hill marked with the windmill that we stopped to drink some water and rest. As a man of the sea, I was unused to riding and already suffered from the hard effects of the saddle.

From our position underneath a dead oak, too rotted and twisted for the shipwright's axe, we could see the fields all around us. Even a stretch of the London Road was visible. We saw no signs of Chase and his troopers. The dome of St. Paul's was a distant lump on the horizon, showing us the way to the city.

Perhaps for reasons of shame, chagrin and embarrassment, no one had broached the painful subject of the baron, Sir Gerald and Lady Montagrave during our ride from Braddock Hall. We had used the emergency of our flight from Colonel Chase as a suitable pretext for silence. But now, with London in sight and having not been apprehended, we could no longer take refuge in the immediacy of danger. Still, Geo sat looking south and Sophie reclined against the tree gazing north. It fell to me, then, to begin the accounting.

"Sophie, much has taken place since only yesterday. As you can imagine, we are in a state of some confusion. Can you help us to make some sense of these events?"

My entreaty did not fall upon deaf ears. She spoke immediately but was somehow both conciliatory and defiant in her tone. "I'll tell you what I know. There is no point in any further deception."

Geo, eager for the truth, turned to face her. He even managed a smile — an impressive effort for a man who, in less than 24 hours, had won and lost a title and a country home.

"Firstly, as you have no doubt surmised, Meissel von Mulct, the Baron Mowenholtz, is nothing of the kind. He is not a baron and he is certainly not German. He is an English charlatan and swindler whose real name is Thomas Tryingdare. He learned his profession from a young age. His parents were small-time gamblers, pickpockets and footpads who abandoned him on the Continent when Tryingdare was a young man. He fell in with a German charlatan from whom he learned the business of deception. Tryingdare speaks many languages and can pass for a German, a Russian, a Frenchman, a Venetian, or a Turk to name a few.

"While in the Caribbean he hatched an idea of selling faked land parcels to wealthy Londoners. Originally he planned to sell fake parcels in Jamaica, but when he ran across George in Barbados, he was ecstatic at having a colonial who actually had done surveying in the Ohio lands. It added immeasurably to the appeal of the sale. So he changed the nature of the swindle and concocted faked parcels in America. And he immediately incorporated George into his plans. Though you did not know it, Tryingdare traveled with you on your ship from Barbados."

"No, he did not," I retorted. "I was one of the ship's officers. I am something of an expert on nautical affairs and knew of everything that occurred on board."

"He was a member of the ship's company —"

"Impossible," I interrupted.

She pressed on. "He was signed on as the mute sailor, Simon Gull."

I was momentarily speechless.

"That is why Gull joined the crew only hours before sailing," Geo said.

"And why he was such a worthless seaman," I added vehemently. "Barely knew a knot."

"But how can all this be true?" Geo said angrily. "I saw the papers, I examined the plot plans, they were entirely convincing."

"Tryingdare is a master of forgers and forgery," Sophie said. "A document, after all, is nothing more than paper and ink, wax, seals and ribbons. He knows forgers far and wide who can concoct the most convincing faked documents."

"He appeared such a man of nobility and breeding," I mused. "And his German accent was so thick."

"It was over thick," she said. "Tryingdare was making clever use of English prejudice. The English think themselves better and see Germans as buffoons. By speaking so, Tryingdare tricked his victims into dropping their guard."

"But I sat with him, talked with him. I looked into his eyes and read his face. He cannot be so thoroughly devious and monstrous," Geo insisted. "Nor I so foolishly credulous."

Sophie smiled sadly. "Remember that he has had many years to perfect his art. And he has fooled men of every station, from the lowest to the highest. But you should know, that he did, in fact, value your friendship. He told me so much at a time when it gave him no advantage."

Geo was not ready to forgive. "I have been utterly deceived by this Tryingdare," said Geo through gritted teeth. "Were he here, I'd cut out his heart and feed it to him."

"For his victims that is the most infuriating aspect of his genius. He always makes his escape. He has never been apprehended, nor spent one day in gaol."

"What of Sir Gerald? — if that is his real name," said a more subdued Geo, coming to grips with the depths of the deception.

"It is his true name, in fact," She replied, "He is a long-time associate of Tryingdare's. The pair work well together. Sir Gerald has connections to many titled persons and men of property. A cabal of informants keeps him abreast of their affairs. Sir Gerald, too, always manages to escape the law. He engineers events to appear as if he has lost money and been swindled by Tryingdare just like all the other victims."

"So that is why Sir Gerald returned to London alone," I said.

"And Tryingdare?" Geo asked. "When we last saw him he was headed toward Dover with five wagonloads of Sir Digby's goods."

"I don't know all the details of Tryingdare's affairs, but I can imagine he had a ship waiting. He has no doubt sailed to Amsterdam where he could sell the items for a profit. I do know that Tryingdare and Sir Gerald spent considerable time in Kent scouting for the right estate. It seems Braddock Hall fit the bill as Sir Digby was a man of considerable means, was in India for some time and had no relations other than his sister Lady Ledelia."

"By whom we nearly came to grief," I said.

We fell silent for a moment. I felt Geo's eyes on me and when I glanced at him, I knew what was in his mind. He had a question that he wanted to ask Sophie, but which so far had been occulted by the easier questions that burned for answers. But those were passed, now was the discomfiting time when it had to be asked. I thought perhaps it would be easier for Geo if I framed the question.

"Sophie, you have explained much of Trydingdare's and Sir Gerald's actions. What we must know now is how you are aware of these things?"

Her eyes met mine. Cool, even cold, blue, they showed the calculation of the charlatan and the cunning of the footpad. In that sight I had my answer. Though, of course, I had already known from the moment she woke me this morning. In fact, I now remembered that I had most probably had something of a glimmering of things not being quite right all along. I was almost nearly positive of this, now that I remember back, I think. Geo, young and not as experienced in the ways of the world as myself, had, of course, been thoroughly taken in.

"I am not a countess, nor am I French, though my real name is Sophie."

"Well, that's something on the truthful side of the ledger," I said hopefully. Geo looked at me as if I should shut up. Sophie seemed to agree. So I said nothing more.

"I am an English woman," she continued. "While my story is a sad one, it is not unlike many others of my station. Poverty and death do not make the kindest nursemaids. My father was unknown to me, my mother long since passed. When my mother died I fell in with those who live by their wits, and who abandon common morality. I learned many tricks and turns, but all the while I longed for the stage. To trod the boards and act at Drury Lane or Covent Garden was my dream. But it is also the dream of many and I had no patron to smooth my path. And so, I took to acting charades of a less reputable nature than Othello. And in doing so I half-convinced myself that I was practicing the craft of acting, in preparation for someday taking my place before the footlights."

"What of Tryingdare?" I asked.

"I have known him my whole life. To be truthful, he has often helped me through difficult times. And also to be truthful, he paid me to keep George interested in the scheme, but not so interested that he asked the wrong questions. And... " She trailed off.

"Is there more?" I prompted.

The coldness left her eyes. She was not so good at acting this part.

"Yes. I was also hired by Tryingdare to romance George. I was to stay close enough to pique his interest, but far enough away such that he continued his pursuit."

Clearly affected by her latest revelation, Geo stood up and walked away from us to where the horses grazed.

Though her face maintained its firm composure, her eyes were now soft. She looked imploringly at me. "Darius, I worked for the money, 'tis true. But now I do care for him. Can you tell him? Can you help him realize the truth?" She broke off and gazed toward distant London. "I know it sounds hollow now."

I went to Geo as he looked over the horses. He said nothing.

"Geo, I would speak to you."

"Very well, speak," Geo snapped.

"She's done a cruel thing in deceiving you. But, I believe she does care for you. And she is willing to stay with us. If we were caught right now, she would be hanged as a horse thief the same as us. She needn't have done so, she could have struck off on her own. But she did not."

"What would you have me do?"

"Just treat her well, at least until we can get aboard a ship and get back to America. She could come in handy, 'til then."

He considered my request. Like Sophie, he, too, gazed at the distant dome of St. Paul's. "I will do as you ask."

I considered it his finest hour.

The rest of our trip across the fields was strained. Geo helped Sophie onto her horse. As he was doing so, she looked down at him — possibly for a sign of forgiveness? But Geo was the great stone face; he gave her not a single indication of his feelings. He maintained the same steady visage throughout the remainder of our passage. And even though Geo's attitude told her nothing, his unswerving approach seemed to calm her; she seemed to draw strength from him. And, I must confess that the sight of Geo, with his tall frame, sitting ramrod straight upon that horse, his countenance a picture of quiet determination and inner grit, affected me as well. I was astounded to find that I, too, drew strength from him.

We found the Blue Anchor Road and from thence quickly made our way across London Bridge and through the city's back streets, alleys and yards to the house of Sophie's friends in Whitechapel.

After we arrived, Sophie paid a small sum to a friend to ride down the Kent Road and find a wagon driver who would consent to return the horses to Sir Digby's barn. Such honor, while common among men of the sea, did most certainly surprise me coming from thieves and charlatans.

Geo and I sat in the kitchen of the house and ate gamey meat pie and drank stale porter; but we were of such hunger and thirst, it mattered not. Sophie was to join us, but she never appeared 'til some minutes later, her face drawn with care. There had been a knock upon the door, she said. 'Twas a man sent by Sir Gerald — he knew of Sophie's friends. Indeed, the man said, there were few places in London she could go where Sir Gerald's spies couldn't find her. Sir Gerald knew our predicament, of course. Via this intermediary, Sir Gerald sent word that it was his duty to assist us in leaving the country. We were to meet him at the Drury Lane theatre that very night.

Chapter Twenty One
In the Grip of the Pox

TO OUR JUBILATION we discovered that Sophie had sufficient monies to pay for a small hackney cab to Drury Lane. We had no wish to go all the way by foot. The three of us were a bit cramped in the cab, but it was apparent that Geo and Sophie were not unhappy with the close quarters. The tight fit made their recent reconciliation that much more pleasing to them.

Their reunion had occurred like this: After our lunch in the kitchen, I was sufficiently tired that I lay down in a corner and slept. It seems, however, that Geo and Sophie began talking again. At first formally, carefully, then with increasingly tender regard. Finally, they had gone out for a walk. When they returned, the creaking of a loose bed awakened me. Their renewed passion made sleep difficult so I went out to find a tankard of ale.

We were ushered into the backstage of the Drury Lane Theater by one of Sir Gerald's men. For Sophie, being backstage was clearly magical.

"Had you imagined the innards of the theater to look like this?" Geo asked.

"I am too excited to perceive more than a blur," she said as we wove our way through the actors and musicians, costumers, stagehands and hangers-on. There were so many turnings and changes in direction, I found myself lost. However, as to the art of the theatre, I had read some thick volumes on the subject and seen a few plays such that I most humbly judge myself something of an expert on matters theatrical.

While admiring the cogwheels of illusion, we were rudely surprised. Geo and I were collared by two hardy fellows too big and insistent to deny. Sir Gerald appeared from behind a scrim painted to depict the underworld. He congratulated the two men in their speedy arrest of our persons. Sophie stepped in front of us and faced Sir Gerald. "Alright, you have taken us," she said. "We surrender."

Sir Gerald laughed. "Don't be silly, my dear," he responded to Sophie. "You need not be taken into custody. You will accompany me to my private box for the play, while these two knaves are dealt with by the magistrate. I should think they will swing before the month is out."

No matter how strenuously she insisted that she, also, should be taken to the magistrate's court, the two law officers ignored Sophie. They led Geo and I away. Sophie stood alone on the stage door steps watching us go, a picture of distress. Both of the law men were of a brusque demeanor. They were hardened by regular contact with truly desperate men — killers, thieves, highwaymen and husbands.

"Considering the case in its entirety, I thought I did rather well," I remarked to Geo. We rode in the stern of a waterman's wherry on the Thames.

Geo looked at me with what might have been a measure of irony, or perhaps it was simply the roll of the boat from small waves in the river. We were fettered at our wrists and our ankles. One of the magistrate's men sat with us, while the waterman worked the boat's sweeps as he rowed us down stream. Though it was a sad occasion — we were prisoners bound for jail — it must be said that the views of the city were unmatched. The great proliferation of houses, the multitude of church steeples, the wharves and jetties, docks and quays, warehouses and depots were all o'erlooked by the soaring dome of St. Paul's. From the many stairs on either side of the river, a skittering traffic of boats, launches, gigs, wherries, hoys and punts carried passengers, mail, small cargoes and produce to and fro in an endless dance of commercial intercourse.

Even the river itself seemed alive. In the reflections upon the moving water I could imagine naiads and nereids, nymphs and water spirits plying the murky depths, carrying the directives of fate to the great city's inhabitants.

We were nearly knocked out when we passed "Pudding Stairs." The city's foulest leavings flowed down to the waterside and gathered at this point, forming a great brown "pudding" whose smell was beyond description.

We approached ancient London Bridge — the buildings built upon it were like swollen ticks on a hound.

The water raced as it squeezed through the bridge's many arches. We found ourselves in a curl of rapids, beset by the roar of white water in the enclosed arch. Our waterman was deft, however, and we shot underneath the bridge into calmer water. Great rafts of anchored ships, like oaken islands, choked the stream. On the north bank I spied the prison fortress of the Tower — 'twas a great relief to pass safely by the place where so many had lost their heads. But another sight soon loomed — decaying bodies hanging from the gibbet at Execution Dock. Pirates and criminals were hanged here. Their bodies were left to rot and lose their eyes to crows. Our waterman seemed to take pleasure at the sight and slowed as we passed beneath the yellowing flesh.

A hazy fog settled upon the river, casting the great woodlot of ships' masts in a forlorn gloom. Faraway shouts were muffled to mumbles, while nearby voices wandered disembodied. Presently, a squadron of hulks emerged from the mist. Anchored in the river with only the paltry poles of their lower masts still in place, the ships' hulls were distended with odd porches and balconies, vestibules and sheds tacked on in a piecemeal fashion. These were prison ships, blighted with their poxy carbuncles, never to sail again. I feared the sight of 'em. If we entered these floating jails and we would surely languish unto our deaths.

"Yes, you were most memorable in the court," Geo said, when we reached the hulks.

"I'm pleased that you think so highly of my efforts to defend us," I said. "I believe my hours of reading law books at sea helped me immensely. I imagine that I know as much as any lawyer."

"Oh, yes. It showed in your learned comments," Geo replied. "I am disposed to give you a hearty thank you. However, my hand and leg irons preclude it."

"No matter," I replied. "A hearty 'huzzah and well done' is payment enough."

"No, no, I insist," Geo replied vehemently. "When we arrive at our destination and these irons are removed I will assuredly provide you with a most memorable thanks."

As we neared the prison hulks we noticed a great tumult had erupted along the nearby quay. A wagonload of the prisoners' biscuits had overset, spilling the rations willy nilly across the filthy boards. People now charged the scene to grab at the rock-hard bread. Shipless sailors and rotting drunks, threadbare harlots and fish wives; they all pushed, punched and fell in the battle over the manna. Some unhappy souls lost their struggle and were pitched into the thick Thames mud — the state of the tide being at its lowest ebb. These mudmen — blackened head to toe by the foul ooze — sloshed and squished up the nearest river stairs. Too dispirited to rejoin the fight, they disappeared in down grimy alleyways.

The sergeant of the guard and his men set to driving back the mob, liberally administering coaxing blows with their clubs along with loud exhortations to respect crown property and to "fuck off!" Meanwhile, every hole and hatch on the hulk filled with the faces of prisoners, like rats peering from holes in a wall. They watched with the glee of men with few chances at amusement.

The last biscuit snatchers scrambled away with their treasures as we landed at the quay. A young naval ensign, of no more than 14 years, greeted us with a surprisingly generous gift of a shilling piece each, which he pressed into our hands before announcing himself as Ensign Howe. He led us to a waiting Royal Navy boat where four sailors manned the oars, ready to row out to our new home on one of the prison hulks.

After our hearing in his court, the magistrate spoke to us in happy terms of our status as colonials. "Were you citizens of London, I would have had little leeway but to send you to one of the city's prisons: the notorious Newgate, or the spawling Fleet. But as you are from America, you may be housed in the Navy's prison ships riding upon Thames water. You will have fresh breezes and a truly commanding view of the city."

Our cheerful new escort, Ensign Howe, further expanded upon the good fortune of confinement to the prison hulks. "You are fabulously lucky," Howe assured us. "Had you been consigned to one of the city prisons you might be forgotten entirely. You might spend decades in rags. However, here aboard His Majesty's ships *Hades* and *Diablo*, you will be subject to summary naval justice. 'Tis a blessing, really."

Geo was unsure of the significance of this status. "What is summary Naval justice?"

"Oh well, on board a ship, the captain has complete authority, of course. That is, we don't follow the usual slow, land-based procedures for punishment. No, no, we can get you in a noose in no time in the Navy. Instead of moldering in prison for years, you can swing from a yardarm almost immediately following a verdict. In fact, in conditions of extremity, captains will often hang a crewman first and hold their court martial later at some more convenient time."

"That is barbarity," Geo said.

"Not at all," the ensign responded. "'Tis the height of naval efficiency. It's well known that hanging a sailor or two serves to encourage the others."

"But we are not enlisted in the Royal Navy," I said, knowing that I'd trumped him. "Thus, we can't be executed by the Navy no matter how expeditiously said procedures are performed." Again it occurred to me that I ought to practice law, as I had a natural flair for it.

Ensign Howe smiled. "Tell me, what do each of you hold in your hand?"

Geo and I looked at the shilling Howe had given us at first meeting.

"'Tis the King's shilling," Howe said. "You have both accepted it of me and thus, are duly enlisted."

"That is little more than tyranny," Geo said. "A great nation's navy should not be composed of men cheated by a coin trick."

"Be it tryanny or no, you will not find a judge in the kingdom to dispute it."

The boat came to rest alongside the hulk and Geo and I climbed a rope ladder to its noisome decks. We were in the odd position of enlisted men in the Royal Navy, duly signed crewmembers of the prison hulk *H.M.S. Hades.*

The long lower decks of the former warship *Hades* had been segmented by a number of bulkheads so as to produce a warren of cells. It was in these that prisoners were to sleep in filthy hammocks with little to do save gamble, fight, or carve model ships from beef bones.

Geo and I were the recipients of some luck, however, as we were assigned to a cell with a porthole, formerly a gunport, facing the quay on the closer, northern riverbank.

We could see the coming and goings of people on the quay and in the streets beyond. Our fellow cellmates were a man of African descent like me, save he was from Haiti and spoke a patois that was nearly incomprehensible, and a surly Frenchman who was sure that he would be hanged within the hour. He continually said goodbye to us, as if the executioner loitered just outside the door. He endless cycle of "adieus" drove Geo nearly to violence. Geo vowed he would execute the Frenchman himself if the man did not shut up.

In addition to a general disposition of ill humor, which, after some thought, I determined might be connected to his imprisonment, Geo also felt great sadness at his separation from Sophie. Even though she had participated in defrauding him and bruising his young reputation, Geo still felt deeply for her.

So it was a great occasion on the second day of our hulk imprisonment when Geo grabbed me from my writing and called me to the porthole.

"Who do you see upon the quay?" he asked me excitedly, his face bright.

I gazed out onto the city scene before me and had to admit that I saw many people.

"Yes, of course," he said with obvious irritation. "But look there. Who is that?"

"A fat cooper rolling a worn-out barrel?"

"No, not that one. Look over there."

"A bone-picker digging through a pile of offal?"

"No, no, no, the woman standing just to the left."

"The bone picker's left or our left?"

"Our left, you fool. Why would I use his left as a frame of reference when he could turn around and that would require me to re-label right-as-left and left-as-right?"

"Exactly. Thus, my question."

"No, your question was pure idiocy borne of too much sun on your brains," Geo snapped.

"That can hardly be true as I regularly wore a hat when I stood the deck during my days as a ship's officer. My brains experienced little in the way of extraordinary heating."

"Pardon, monsieurs," the Frenchman cut in, "Adieu. Adieu."

Geo rolled his eyes. I imagined that the Frenchman's brains would soon be gathering too much sun.

"Oh! *That* woman," I said, seeing the young woman with the blue shawl who stood staring out at the hulk. "I believe that is Miss Sophie!"

"It is, indeed," he said with surging confidence. Geo leaned out the port hole and waved to her. "She does not make me out. Here, you stand immediately to the right—"

"Your right or her right?" I interjected.

"My right!" He snapped. "How did I ever agree on you as my second?"

"There was no one else on that Irish beach available to save you from the shipwreck?" I thought it was an honest question, so I gave an honest answer.

"Very well, point taken. All right now, you lean out right alongside me. There can't be another pairing of a white man and a dark man on this vessel. When she sees my white face and your dark face, each alongside the other, it will be as clear as a navy signal flag."

I approved of his nautical reference and so we both leaned out the porthole and waved our hands. It did not take long before Sophie was waving back to us. Geo, now more excited than ever, decided he must send her a message.

"Nearly every thing I had gained here in England I have now lost. I must not lose her," Geo said. He drew a scrap of paper from his pocket and scribbled a note to her using a piece of charcoal. He then asked me for something to wrap it up with.

"I have a handkerchief," I said as I offered it to him.

"No, you fool, I need something with weight, something that will carry."

"You still have the King's shilling given you by Ensign Howe," I offered.

Feverishly, he retrieved the coin from a waistcoat pocket. He wrapped the note around it. I had already drawn a bit of string from the lining of my coat. Geo accepted it with thanks and did a very appreciable job of tying up paper and coin into a tight package. Now he faced his toughest test: to stand at the porthole and throw the bundle to the quay where Sophie stood. He backed himself up and looked at the porthole carefully.

Then with a hop, step and a hop followed immediately with another step, he threw the package expertly. I could hardly believe it; 'twas a throw for the ages. "You threw a shilling across the Thames." I said, near breathless with amazement.

Geo brushed me off as he watched Sophie. "I did no such thing. I threw a shilling not even a third of the distance across the river."

"That may be true," I said. "But my way of saying it is much better."

The package landed on the quay not 10 feet from Sophie's shoes. She saw it fall and moved to pick it up. A brown pug dog, prowling the quay for rotting fish heads, saw Geo's missile land and instantly snapped it up. Sophie attempted to grab the pug, but he trotted smartly to the far side of the quay. She stalked him, pretending to have no interest in him whatever, while at the same sidling as close as possible. But each time she turned her head to look at him, the pug moved.

Needing a distraction for the dog, she circled around to stand in front of a passing food vendor, his cart full of roasted pigeon on a stick. Sophie blocked the vender's way. He stopped and took up one of his crunchy treats, ready to give it to her when he received payment. But rather than hand over the coppers, she pulled down the front of her dress to present her round young breasts in all their glory. The lark vendor was enraptured — Sophie' beautiful bosom was an easy reach away — and he paid no attention to his wares. Sophie moved with brazen speed. She grabbed the roasted bird from his hand and deftly tossed it to the pug. For his part, the dog was unable to resist the smell of the bird meat. He dropped Geo's package and lunged for the fragrant roasted bird before one of the wharf rats could get it.

Sophie covered her breasts, spun on one foot and scooped up the now abandoned package from the quay. She saw its purpose immediately and untied the package to read the note. When she had finished she waved and nodded and clasped her hands together over her heart as she gazed across the water toward Geo.

In the meantime, the food vendor began loudly complaining that she had stolen from him. Sophie turned, bared her breasts once more, took his hands and guided them to her teats. He cupped them and lapsed into a contented silence. She then backed away, covered up once more and disappeared around a corner. The pigeon seller stood wistfully for a few seconds. Then he resumed hawking his birds.

Geo turned to look at me, a broad smile upon his face. "She is wonderfully clever, is she not?"

I nodded in agreement, but was also a bit chagrined. "I agree that she is a quick thinker."

"Yet?"

"She had plenty a' opportunity to let *me* give her teats a tug, yet never did so," I said.

"Oh, clamp it," Geo said with a laugh. "You're a horny dog, D."

"I suppose I *am*."

"She gave the vendor just enough to shut him up. 'Twas brilliant."

"You're not concerned with a greasy pigeon vendor pawing Sophie's diddeys?" I asked with genuine interest.

"Not at all. To see it in a nautical vein, she was maneuvering in a close quarters fight, determined to carry the day. I'd say she did so with colors flying. She is magnificent."

Geo's happiness and enthusiasm was impossible to resist. I soon was smiling, too. "Aye, she is quite a woman."

"Indeed!" Geo agreed.

"No doubt!" I added.

"Unquestionably!" Geo roared.

"Unfailingly!" I responded.

"Adieu!" said the Frenchman, caught up in the enthusiasm.

"Absolutely!" Geo said.

"Guaranteed!" I yelled.

"Adieu!" the Frenchman bellowed.

"Yes," Geo said wanly.

"Unswervingly!" I screamed.

"Adieu!" the Frenchman barked, his eyes closed and his head thrown back.

Geo said nothing.

"Unremittingly!" I boomed.

"Adieu!" the Frenchman thundered and stamped his feet.

Geo's face had fallen and his eyes were droopy puddles.

"Remorselessly!" I said.

"Adieu!" the Frenchman shouted with his tongue hanging out. "Adieu! Adieu! Adieu! Adieu!"

Geo slowly lay down on the deck, utterly withdrawn.

I fell silent, too, sad for Geo and his lost love.

The Frenchman grasped my concern for my friend. He finished with a final, tentative, " ... Adieu?"

Sophie returned to the quay every day, in London rain, fog or shine, to gaze out at Geo and I. But Geo only raised himself up to look back to her for a few days, then he refused to get up.

The reason for his poor spirits became apparent soon enough. He became inflamed of a fever. Then round marks appeared upon his face. Geo was in the grip of smallpox. He was taken from our airy cell and delivered to a place deeper in the hulk. It was a dank, fetid, airless hole where sick prisoners were consigned to die or recover, dependent upon their inclinations and the tender mercies of the almighty. I was barred from attending him in this place. My commission from Heaven to be Geo's advisor and helpmate was overridden by a greater power: Royal Navy regulations.

For some days, extending to more than two weeks, I heard nothing of Geo. I must admit I slipped into a state of unhappiness, which is to say utter despair. Not only had I failed in the dictates of Heaven, but I had lost a friend with whom I had attained a rare connection. It is sufficient to record here that for the fortnight in question I abandoned all pretense of maintaining this account. My Geo saga had ended.

A sea of faces turned toward me when the cart topped the rise. Spread before me, in the golden sunlight of morning, were thousands of people. They were high born and low, English and some Africans, young and old, men and women. All had gathered to see me off. I must say I was flattered by their attentions. That so many had left the potter's wheel spinning, the hops still brewing and the money uncounted just to send me on my way, made me love the good people of London, who so often are said to be selfish, cruel, money-grubbing creatures, consumed only with their own pleasure and cold to the misfortune of others. Did not this crowd put the lie to such defamations?

Much drinking of ale and gin and bottles of wine provided opportunity for salutes from the crowd as I passed. Other vendors supplied the people with tripe in a cup and turtle stew and jellied eels. The folk shouted of a happy "collar party" that would soon ensue. I had no knowledge of such occasions, but their good cheer buoyed my spirits and I hoped that soon I would similarly quaff brew and back slap my fellows.

Only as my squeaking cart approached it did I notice the odd triangular structure that stood at the focus of the crowd. From one of its stout yardarms a lone rope dangled. I also took notice of the rough hemp strands binding my wrists. Further, it occurred to me that I was standing tied to a post in the middle of the cart. At this juncture I became concerned that I was not about to enjoy a fine London lager. My unquiet increased when I was led down from the cart and pushed to a position directly under the dangling rope.

The sky clouded over and the assembled mob took up a chant,

> "Nigh, nigh, under Tyburn sky,
> the blackamoor will surely die!"

After some consultation between magistrate, bailiff, members of the watch and lieutenant of the guard, the rope was slipped o'er my neck and an executioner appeared. He wore dark clothes and a hood that allowed only his eyes to show. Belying his fearsome appearance, he very gently urged me to step up on a foot stool. When he spoke, there was something familiar about his voice. Yet I could not place it.

All was in readiness for the great event. And I must admit I, too, grew rather excited at the prospect of witnessing some public spectacle, 'til I remembered that I was the entertainment. I looked out over the people and saw them laughing, heard their chanting and witnessed their wild abandon. The executioner slid a black hood over my head, plunging me into darkness.

Amidst all the shouting, chanting and carrying on, I could make out the voice of the executioner speaking to me. His voice was damnably familiar as he called my name, "D!

D! Wake up, D!"

The darkness left as the hood fell away. I blinked my eyes and saw that I was in my cell in the prison hulk. And kneeling alongside me was no executioner. It was none other than Geo. His was the voice I heard calling to me. The pox had departed him — he had survived!

"Geo! You have prevailed o'er the pox!" I was so overjoyed that I embraced him with all fervor. And he returned my brotherly regard with equal measure.

Then he smiled at me and nodded. "'Tis true. I am somewhat weak, but otherwise no worse. I had a most informative physician. He explained the disease has two forms and that I had contracted the milder illness. Thus explains my recovery."

"It is yet another sign of favor from Providence. You are destined for some greatness, of that I am convinced."

"And I am convinced that you have gone mad in my absence," Geo replied. "What greatness can I occasion while rotting in a prison ship?"

To this I had no answer.

"Surely I am pleased to be alive," Geo said as he sunk to the deck, his countenance sinking also. "But there is no mistaking that we are forgotten here and are unlikely to ever depart this ship save wrapped in a shroud."

Chapter Twenty Two
Ghost Boats

THE NEXT MORNING was predictably misty, with London city obscured by curtains of opaque fog; only a ribbon of the river ran clear of the vaporous condensation. I rose from my rude pallet and gazed upriver through our porthole. I was immediately put in mind of a visit my ship had once made to St. Augustine in Spanish Florida, where I saw many Indians upon the river in their canoes. They silently and brusquely paddled to and fro, often disappearing into the green folds of the river as it snaked toward strange interior habitations.

Now aboard *Hades*, I again saw a troop of Indians, but they were gliding in muscular unison upon Thames water. The effect was most unnerving. As if I had been transported many thousands of miles back to the Americas whence Geo and I had come. Or perhaps these shades I watched approach were messengers from beyond come to take me to the next world in their ghost boats.

It then occurred to me that perhaps the many days of confinement in the decrepitude of the prison hulk had twisted the sinews of my mind. The ligaments had snapped and I was inventing fantastical scenes and visions.

The only thing for it was to rouse Geo and determine if he, too, saw them or if these sights were mine alone to behold.

"Yo, ho, Geo," I said as I gently roused him. I endeavored to be as quiet as possible so as not to wake the Jamaican nor the mad Frenchman.

"Eh? Adieu," the Frenchman grunted, yet still slept.

"Geo!"

"Sophie? Is she here?" Geo sat up suddenly and rubbed his cheeks. Amazingly, the pox had not heavily touched his face and I imagined he would not be disfigured.

"No, no. She may be upon the quay, but it is too misty to make out. Still, there is something you must see."

Geo hung out the porthole to look, but now there was little doubt the Indians were no shades: a rising chorus of war whoops — "Woo-woo-woo-woo!" — resounded in the spaces of the hulk. The Indians were climbing aboard and seemed to be moving ever closer to us.

"How can American savages be staging a raid on a ship in the Thames?" Geo asked. "Have they the ability to cross oceans in canoes? Is England under attack?"

I admitted that I knew no answers to these baffling questions. But we had little time to wait, as two Indians appeared at our cell door. They wore headbands and feathers and their faces were painted with lines and designs. And they were the palest, whitest Indians I ever saw. They peered in and when they saw Geo and I they whooped and hollered and one of them ran off. Soon a cohort of the Indians returned and unlocked the cell. Geo and I were hustled out and taken above decks.

As we reached the main deck we saw a group of the pale savages were clustered around their chief. When the group opened to let us pass, I was most surprised to see that the leader of the invading Indians was no red man. He was none other than the young Prince of Wales. When he saw us, his face assumed a cheery countenance. "Ah, Washington, here you are!"

A stupefied Geo and I bowed to Prince George, but neither of us could make out why the heir to the throne stood before us in a deerskin loin cloth and blouse, his arms and face painted in ocher and crimson paint and with a trio of white feathers sprouting from a headdress. Next to him stood Lord Blathingwell, the prince's normally foppish aide-de-camp. Blathingwell looked quite uncomfortable in his deerskin leggings, scallop shell cuirass and purple paint.

"Are you very surprised?" the Prince asked excitedly, clapping his hands. "We had hoped you would love our little expedition. A little taste of your Virginia home? Fighting the savages day and night, eh? Isn't it jolly?"

Geo looked around at the company of Indians in utter amazement. They had taken over the hulk. The small, beleaguered force of Royal Navy guards were gathered amidships and were themselves now under guard by a squad of pale-skinned braves armed with large clubs and "George Rex" cartridge boxes slung over their shoulders. Since Geo appeared to have lost his wits, I spoke up. "Your Highness, I know I speak for my colleague, Mr. Washington, when I say we are most pleased and surprised to see you."

"Oh, good, good," the prince said. "Putting this little

folly together was bit of work, eh Blathingwell? But no matter that, we are here now, no need to fret."

"We are honored by your presence, your Majesty. Even if we do not fully understand its significance."

Prince George's eyebrows rose in surprise. "Well, we have come in response to the entreaties of a lady, of course. She has informed us that you and Mr. Washington have been improperly imprisoned and that justice requires you be set free. We certainly could not ignore the plight of my Indian-wrestling friend George from Virginia, and besides, we had no sooner received her request than we imagined what fun it would be to rescue you. You know, an Indian raid at dawn and all that. An exciting bit of business." Then he leaned in close to Geo and me and remarked quietly, "You have no idea how stuffy our affairs can get, cooped up with our grandfather. All that mindless prattling in German."

"May I ask, your Majesty, which lady informed you of our plight?" Geo questioned. It was good to see him recover his tongue.

"Well, yes, you may. She was a titled French woman, what was the name Blathingwell?"

"Some obscure French title, your Highness. The Marquise d'Abbeville?," Blathingwell asked uncertainly.

"The Countess d'Abbeville," Geo corrected.

"Oh, I suppose," Blathingwell replied with a shrug. "I never remember those Frenchy titles."

"No matter what her title, you can count yourself well served by her friendship, Washington," the prince said. "She made a most persuasive case — as did her affianced."

"Her affianced?" Geo asked with trepidation.

"Blathingwell?" Prince George demanded again.

"I understand she is engaged to Sir Gerald Compliss."

Geo reeled from this news.

"Your Highness, if I may ask, is Sir Gerald a regular at St. James?" I asked.

"He enjoys what you might call a 'commercial relationship' with many gentlemen at court. Blathingwell knows him particularly well," the Prince said with a chuckle as he swiped Blathingwell's head with the fringes hanging from his deerskin blouse. "Go ahead, tell them."

"Sir Gerald is an accomplished card player and I am in his debt," Blathingwell said with tight-lipped irritation.

"You mean you owe him 500 pounds!" the Prince burst out. "Our wet nurse plays cards better than you, Blathingwell!"

"Perhaps, your Majesty, these gentlemen are not interested in hearing about the situation with your — *ahem* — 'wet nurse.'"

The prince, suddenly grasping Blathingwell's meaning, replied with some embarrassment, "Oh, yes." He hastily changed the subject. "So, Blathingwell, what is our *plan de manoeuvre*?"

"Since we have freed the prisoners, we may now beat a hasty retreat. Lieutenant Colonel Chase is, no doubt, already in pursuit, attempting to locate us."

The prince frowned at this plan. "But would it not be more like a real raid by dangerous Indians if we smashed things up a bit?" The Prince turned to Geo. "You are our Indian expert, Mr. Washington, what could we do to make this a more satisfying Indian raid?"

Geo looked around a bit blankly and then turned to me. "D, what further mayhem may we undertake here?"

I replied directly to the prince, "Your Majesty, this hulk is barely afloat. I don't imagine you wish to do much to it, lest you sink a crown asset."

"Heavens, no. My grandfather would be most annoyed with me were I to sink one of his ships."

The Prince, however, was not satisfied that a proper job had been accomplished. If he was going to roam about playing Indian, he wanted to do it right. The cloaking mists seen earlier in the morning had now lifted. Using a small spyglass supplied by Lord Blathingwell, young Prince George noted a ship anchored nearby in the bend of the river, off the Isle of Dogs. "Blathingwell, is not that ship owned by the merchant James Stamp?"

Blathingwell took his turn with the glass. "Indeed, your Majesty. That is his company signal at the upper truck of the main."

"Ah, well, we think we shall pay Mr. Stamp back for his shoddy support of his king and country."

Geo and I looked to Blathingwell and he responded, "Mr. Stamp's trading company was known to have engaged in business with the Spanish during the last war with Spain. He is said to have made a considerable fortune trading stockings and small clothes via the Austrian Netherlands."

We joined the prince, Blathingwell and the Indians as they climbed down the side of *Hades* and went back aboard their boats. These were not true Indian canoes, but English boats propelled by paddles in lieu of oars. The flotilla of boats pulled down river to the ship owned by Stamp. Bobbing in the prince's boat, we watched with fascination as the Indians swarmed aboard Stamp's ship, a stout merchantman named *Charles*. They grabbed the eight or so crates that had been stacked on the deck and tossed these crates into the river. As one floated by on the flooding tide, I noticed it was East India Company tea.

Blathingwell was upset with the whole affair, but the prince hushed him with the assurance that Stamp had lost very little. "In an earlier time, Mr. Stamp would have felt the headsman's axe for his treachery to the crown," the prince remarked. "In these present days, when a king is restricted from fully embracing his people, Mr. Stamp merely loses a few crates of tea."

Later that day the action of the prince's Indians on the river became widely known when various accounts of the affair were written up in London's penny papers. One newspaper headlined the story: "The Stamp Act, or the particulars of a Tea Party on the *Charles*." It occasioned much discussion in the town's coffeehouses, many of which debates ending with hot coffee poured over the heads of speakers on both sides of the question.

For the prince and his party, however, there was the unswerving pursuit of Lieutenant Colonel Chase to consider and so we stayed on the move lest we fall into his clutches.

Chapter Twenty Three
Rabbits, Comets and Craters

SINCE AN ESSENTIAL element of an Indian raid is surprise, the prince ordered the pale-skinned Indians back to the boats and to pull for the southern shore of the river. We made land in Greenwich, on the broad lawns of the Greenwich Naval Hospital. As a widely read man of the sea, I was fully aware of the facts pertaining to the buildings. They were built in 1694 largely due to the prodding of William III's co-regnant, Queen Mary. The hospital saw to the needs of wounded Royal Navy sailors. It also provided a home for disabled and retired seamen, the first such in the world.

As our company walked along the east side of the hospital, the sight of a troop of men dressed as Indians perambulating past the stately buildings was sufficient to bring its residents forth. Many of the sailors who greeted us had been mutilated in the War of Jenkins Ear against Spain. These moved as best they could, as some were missing a leg or two. A direct hit from a cannonball or from razor-sharp wooden splinters had taken their legs. Some particularly sad souls were missing arms and some had doleful combinations of missing legs and arms. The limping, shuddering mass of invalids seemed a hydra-like beast making its halting way with mumbles, groans and cries. I had not the heart to tell these brave men, now broken by war, that Capt. Jenkins had lost his ear to a jealous wife, not to an attacking Spanish officer. I could not bring myself to explain that the war for which they had sacrificed so much had been a lie from the start.

The invalids were most appreciative of the attention and kind words from the Indians. Upon learning that we were hungry and parched, they called forth the orderlies to produce a meager offering of flat beer and stale bread. Though in our current state, even this seemed a feast. Soon we were on our way to a chorus of farewells that could have been the exaltations of a foreign tongue, so misshapen were the exclamations due to sailors' patriotic injuries. Throughout our short visit the prince kept his lower face covered with a

cloth so as to maintain his anonymity from these sailors who
had served his royal family so well.

Directly up a long, grass-green hill stood the
Greenwich Royal Observatory. This site was well known to
me who had benefited from its investigations into the
motions of the sun, stars, planets and moon. The
Observatory's celestial calculations are compiled into
almanacs that assist navigators, but into which I shall not
delve here. All aspects of navigation are kept mysterious to
the average seaman lest they realize how straightforward and
simple the art truly is and we navigators find ourselves cast
aside.

Geo and I, indeed our entire party, was still in the grip
of a powerful hunger and thirst that the moldy and flat
offerings of the invalids had not served to quench. The prince
had a solution to our predicament, however. "My grandfather
pays substantial sums for the upkeep and advancement of
that place," the prince said, pointing to the buildings on the
hill. "It would seem they could provide us with some victuals
and wine." Thusly, we trooped up the broad hill towards the
Royal Observatory.

As we walked in the hot sunlight of the fully formed
day, the prince admitted that his Indians were not natives to
America at all.

"Don't know if you noticed, but those are not, in fact,
Indians," Prince George said as we trudged up the hill.
"They're lads from our Irish regiment. They're barely under
control when employed as British soldiers. They make much
better savages. Our cousin the Duke of Cumberland may
have put the Scots down at Culloden a few years ago, but
we'll never get the bloody Irish to lay down. They'll fight us
forever. It's more likely that we let you Americans go your
own way then we give the Irish their freedom, eh?"

"I would hope, your Highness," Geo offered, "that we
would all remain your happy subjects forever."

"And so do we, Mr. Washington. Would be a damnable
thing to break apart so prosperous and enlightened a kingdom
as that reigned over by our grandfather. Indeed, this matter
touches upon another item that we would put to you."

"I am at your disposal, your Highness."

"We are aware, of course, of the college in Virginia
named for King William and Queen Mary. This William &

Mary school is pleasing, to be sure. They have that wonderful intertwined W & M symbol that we much love. However, we would also like to acknowledge the beneficent rule of my great grandfather George I, my grandfather George II and, of course, my future reign as George III, by instituting a new college to be named "G, G & G." We are thinking that perhaps the symbol could be equally clever as the William and Mary symbol and would gain wide acceptance when cast in metal for use as a tea trivet or a door knocker or some such. We wish you to found such a college in Virginia upon your return."

Geo was taken aback by the Prince's request but agreed that he would do his best to found G, G & G college. Poor Geo was still out of sorts from the shocking knowledge of earlier this morning that his lady love, who by her own admission was no lady, had agreed to marry the corrupt gambler and friend of charlatans, Sir Gerald.

"Perhaps," the prince offered, "it might be called 'The G's Three' for short?"

Geo nodded offhandedly while I ruminated on this example of the enlightened nature of George II's kingdom.

We had nearly traversed the open flank of the hill and entered the grounds of the observatory at its summit, when we noted the speedy approach of a troop of horse.

Our Indian braves protectively circled the prince, while Blathingwell scurried quickly behind young George, who, though only 13 years old, was tall for his age and afforded some measure of protection. Prince George noticed Blathingwell standing behind him and glared at his aide-de-camp, who sheepishly stepped out of the young prince's shadow … until the prince returned his gaze to the approaching riders, whereupon Blathingwell scurried behind him again.

Riding at the head of 10 dragoons with two riderless horses in trail was none other than Lieutenant Colonel Sir Francis Chase. Late morning sun glinted from the polished buckles of the dragoons as they slowed to a trot and then stopped in a proper line. Colonel Chase's black charger, Pip, pawed the ground as Chase looked over our party. When he spied the prince, he dismounted with a jump and pushed his way past the Irish/Indian braves.

"Chase, you have run us to earth again," the prince said

with some irritation.

"Y-y-your Highness," Chase bowed. "G-g-good day, Lord Blathingwell." When Blathingwell heard his name, he stepped out from behind the prince. Though chagrined, Blathingwell did his best to present an air of noble superiority. Chase turned back to the prince. "Y-y-your Highness, the king has been wondering as to your whereabouts in light of reports of a marauding band of American natives loose in London."

"Oh, we were just having a bit of fun with our Irish lads," the prince responded jauntily, unable to hide his joy at the uproar his "Indians" had caused.

"Th-th-the king wishes you to return to the palace. He deems it most unseemly for a Prince of Wales to traipse about the capital in the dress of a savage."

Young George sighed. Apparently even his grandfather did not understand his youthful requirement for tomfoolery. "Very well, Chase. We shall return with you. But we don't see why we cannot play the savage. After all, what is the point of Great Britain going out into the world conquering savage peoples if we can't dress up like them and have a bit of enjoyment now and again?"

"I'm q-q-quite sure, your Highness, that my rank is insufficient for me to answer that question," Chase replied carefully.

"Stop angling for a promotion, Chase. We were only engaging in a rhetorical flourish and did not expect an answer. Come along, Blathingwell."

The two spare horses were brought forward for the prince and Lord Blathingwell. The Irish troops were instructed to return to their barracks on foot.

Chase cast a prejudiced eye at Geo and me. "D-d-does your Highness wish that these Jacobites be returned to their confinement in the prison hulks?"

The prince seemed tired of this question. "We have on good authority to suppose they were wrongly charged. Both Sir Gerald and that French woman have spoken to this point, as we remember."

Just then a coach bounced up the wide lawn. Emerging from the coach were Sir Gerald, Lady Montagrave and Lady Chase. The big man bounded from the coach, his face red with anger. Nearly knocking Chase to ground in his effort to get past him, Sir Gerald marched directly to the prince. "Your Highness," Sir Gerald said with a well-executed bow. Then he stood, looking up to the Prince astride his roan horse, waiting for leave to speak. For her part, Lady Montagrave made her way down from the coach more gingerly. She searched out Geo. The look of longing and regret that she showed to him was breathtaking. Lady Chase also looked to Geo and then to me. She did not regard us in an unfriendly way, but neither did she display her former warmth towards us.

"Ah, Sir Gerald, we were just speaking of you." The prince looked to Lady Montagrave. "Good day, Madame."

"Your Highness. I am Lady Antonia Montagrave, at your service."

"We are pleased to see you again." Then he noticed Lady Chase and whispered to Lieutenant Colonel Chase. "Sir Francis, your mother is here. Do avoid the subject of dessert, will you?"

Lady Chase approached the prince, "Your Majesty looks stirring today. You make a fitting Indian warrior prince. You could be the symbol for a flavor of custard . . . nutmeg-cornmeal, perhaps."

"We think we thank you, madam." Then to the big man, "So, Sir Gerald, have you come to collect from Lord Blathingwell?" the prince asked with a smirk.

"The matter of which I must speak is far more serious than the mere payment of a gambling debt, your Highness," Sir Gerald said severely. Blathingwell positively lit up at not having to pay his debt.

"Do tell us what that it is? We are late for our return to our grandfather's domain."

"Some days ago a woman claiming to be the Countess d'Abbeville addressed you on behalf of those two." He indicated Geo and me.

"Yes, yes. Get on with it."

"I can say now that the woman is a poseur," said Sir Gerald. "She is not of noble birth, but instead was born to a night soil man from St. Giles. She only pretends to nobility."

"How shocking," the prince replied with a yawn. "We *are* feeling a bit tired. Had a rather early morning today."

"This c-c-countess, is she not your b-b-betrothed?" Lieutenant Colonel Chase was confused.

"*Was* my betrothed, sir," Sir Gerald corrected huffily. "She and I have no further connection."

"This is all quite fascinating," the prince announced flatly. "But we fear we know not why you have made such haste to tell us this."

"I do so, Highness, to ensure that those two guilty men are properly punished."

"I-I-I am surprised," Colonel Chase observed, "to f-f-find that a man who profits so much from the gambling of others should have so refined a sense of justice."

"Don't judge Sir Gerald's motives, dear," Lady Chase admonished her son. "He is a wonderful patron of my custard shops. Sir Gerald has recently experienced a sizeable profit from a commercial venture in Kent and he has just invested handsomely in my custard enterprise."

Sir Gerald was ill at ease with the mention of Kent. He looked quickly around the group but made no answer to Lady Chase's statement.

At the Royal Observatory on the top of the hill, a small group had gathered. Servants and workers of the observatory, even the Astronomer Royal himself, gazed down on the prince and those surrounding him. A passing rabbit vendor had paused on the walk leading up to the Observatory and watched the proceedings with great interest.

The prince addressed Lady Chase "Can you think of any subject that does not lead back to custard, madam?"

Lady Chase smiled warmly, thought a moment, then announced triumphantly, "I cannot, your Majesty."

"So we supposed. Well, we are off to the palace. Chase, if you must pursue this, detain them in the observatory and call for the local magistrate. He can sort this out. As for us, we are taking our leave. Mr. Washington, our best to you. Do not forget our charge to you regarding 'the Georges Three College.'"

With a royal wave to all assembled, George, Prince of Wales, heir to the throne of Great Britain and Ireland, crown prince of the house of Hanover, future head of the Church of England and protector of the faith, charged down the hill. He headed toward the great expanse of London, which lay curled along the Thames like a giant beast digesting its last meal. Eight of the dragoons immediately followed the prince at the gallop, while the Irish lads padded quickly after them. The

Celtic savages discarded their headdresses as they went, leaving a feathery trail down the Greenwich Park hillside.

This left Sir Gerald, Lady Montagrave, Lieutenant Colonel Chase, Lady Chase and two dragoons to confront Geo and me. Sir Gerald immediately drew his sword and advanced on us. "You knaves shall not escape." Then to Chase, "We shall take the Prince's advice and lock them in yonder conservatory."

Lady Montagrave shook her head in disgust. "It's the Royal *Ob*servatory, you twit, not the *con*servatory."

"Don't play me for a fool, Antonia, or you shall be very sad to have done so. I care not what the buildings are named nor what takes place in 'em. That they will serve as a temporary lock-up is all I know." Then he demanded that Geo and I proceed uphill. The rabbit vendor, who had seen all this with sharp eyes, scurried up the hill ahead of us and disappeared.

Lieutenant Colonel Chase, his mother and the two dragoons, meanwhile, prepared to depart and gather up the magistrate. Before she climbed back aboard the coach, Lady Chase remarked to Geo, "If you had only spoken to the prince regarding my custard, all this might have been avoided."

"Madam," Geo replied, "this may seem revolutionary to you, but custard is not the keystone of human events."

"Well," Lady Chase sniffed before she climbed aboard her coach, "perhaps it ought to be, Mr. Washington."

Geo and I were herded inside the observatory and locked in a closet. After some time, our eyes adjusted to the dark, aided by light filtering in from a small window set high on the wall.

We saw it was a large closet used for storage. Piled on some shelves were a number of models of various astronomical machines and devices. I immediately recognized some of these strange devices as proposed methods for navigators to find their longitude at sea — a most vexing problem not yet solved. Parliament had even offered the staggering prize of £20,000 for anyone who might devise a suitable method of determining longitude.

The models and miniatures within the closet were obviously designed to demonstrate their inventor's ideas.

One model was composed of some 100 tiny ships arranged on a wide cotton wool sea. From each ship there arose a diminutive rocket. I had heard something of this proposal, which called for specially equipped rocket-launching ships to be anchored in a line across the Atlantic. These vessels would then fire their rockets at precise intervals. Passing ships could determine their distance off these reference ships by the delay between when they saw a ship's timed rocket explode and when they heard it. There were some questions as to lengths of anchor chains for ships moored in mid-ocean and other small details, but, in general, the proposal seemed quite sound.

Another more fanciful suggestion involved the construction of a very precise clock to be taken aboard ship. With such a clock navigators could carry the time of Greenwich along with them. This idea, put forward by an untutored clockmaker from Lincolnshire had little to recommend it. As everyone with any knowledge of clocks knew they were too big and unreliable to ever be carried on board a ship. This clockmaker, who went by the name of John Harrison, was clearly a charlatan.

While we were in the closet, Lady Montagrave called in to Geo and me, but mostly to Geo, and asked if there was anything we needed. He replied that some ale or wine would be most appreciated. But we heard Lady Montagrave arguing with Sir Gerald, who refused to allow us anything at all.

Then Geo and I heard a curious sequence of events play out. First was a loud exclamation of surprise, then a crash and the breaking of glass, then some urgent whisperings and furtive bumps. Finally, we heard a key scraping in the lock.

The door swung open and Lady Montagrave and an unknown man dragged the inert person of Sir Gerald into the closet. "Make way, make way," said Lady Montgrave. The unknown man was dressed in the rough and dirty clothes of a street peddler. Once Sir Gerald had been tugged fully inside the closet and the door hastily closed to hide us inside the closet, the peddler straightened up so that his dirty face was visible. When he did so, Geo breathed in sharply and then grappled with the man and began kissing him most passionately. For a moment, it looked as if they would fall to the floor. I could see Lady Montagrave's obvious discomfort at this astounding display of affection.

At last their lips parted and I saw that 'twas no man Geo embraced. It was Geo's beloved Sophie. She was expertly disguised as a rabbit vendor. This clever ruse allowed her to move about unimpeded and for her to gain entrance to the kitchen of the Royal Observatory.

Lady Montagrave spoke up with some irritation. "We must depart before the arrival of the magistrate."

Just then a loud knock came upon the closet door.

Geo and Sophie were stirred from their tender embrace and froze in anticipation. Indeed, our entire party except, of course, Sir Gerald in his unconscious stupor, was apprehensive of the slightest movement. Lady Montagrave stepped forward to the door latch and said brusquely to all of us, "Remain silent, I shall speak."

She swung wide the door and revealed a bespectacled man of ample proportions. "I was passing and saw the broken glass and heard noises within. Is everything quite all right? Has the magistrate yet arrived?"

"Ah, no," Lady Montagrave said calmly. "However, we have the situation well in hand, here."

I realized that Lady Montagrave did not know the man standing before us. Since I did, I pushed past her.

"Astronomer Royal Bradley, I am most happy to once again make your acquaintance," I said as I bowed to him. Perhaps my dirty clothes and unshaven face did not present me well, or perhaps the Astronomer Royal did not remember me. No matter. "And also happy to see you again is my colleague Mr. George Washington of Virginia." I grabbed Geo's arm and pulled him forward. "You may remember we met on Julian Square when he chopped down the cherry tree given you by your mother-in-law, thus freeing you from the need to eat its distasteful fruit."

Bradley looked at the equally unshaven and unkempt Geo and then broke into a broad smile. "Oh, yes! 'Twas I who chopped down the cherry tree,'" Bradley said. "Such charming honesty! And at the same time such a help to me. I am pleased to see you again, young Mr. Washington."

"As am I to see you, esteemed sir," Geo replied.

"So where are the fugitives?" Bradley asked. "Those for whom the magistrate has been summoned? I have been at work and not had opportunity to check on the prisoners."

Lady Montagrave stepped forward then. "Not fugitives, sir, but only a single escaped prisoner." She pointed at the still supine figure of Sir Gerald. "We were forced to knock him cold when he attempted to escape again."

Bradley looked down at Sir Gerald. "He seems unaccountably well dressed and presentable for an escaped prisoner."

"Aye, that's the slippery nature of this affair," said I. "He's a clever one at throwing off the authorities. But a man of your highly developed perceptions, one who can mark the slightest deviations of the planets and stars from their traces, will surely not be led astray by this criminal."

Bradley nodded quickly. "No, of course. I was not fooled in the smallest portion."

"As one would expect from a man of keen scientific thought, without peer at the very pinnacle of his profession," Lady Montagrave purred. Geo, Sophie, Lady Montagrave and myself stepped out of the closet into the hall. I closed the door and turned the key to lock Sir Gerald within.

Astronomer Royal Bradley nodded again at the compliment but soon his face clouded. "I am flattered, of course, by your kind words. However, I must ruin this happy occasion and call you on your attempt to conceal the truth."

Lady Montagrave, usually the most composed of characters, looked at me in barely concealed alarum. "We have not passed any deceptions to you, sir," she said. "We have been wholly above board."

"You have not," Bradley rejoined, "and I must expose your dishonesty."

It was at this juncture that I considered simple flight might be our best strategy, as I could not bring myself to strike an Astronomer Royal, a man who every day endeavors to improve the knowledge of the heavens and thus aid the ocean navigator. And so I sidled a few steps toward the door, trying to catch Geo's eye that he might follow me. Geo, of course, had eyes for no one save Sophie.

"Your dishonesty," Bradley began, "consists of this: You say I am without peer at the highest precipice of my profession. And while 'tis true I have climbed high, there is one summit that has so far eluded me. There is one man who stands above me. One whose accomplishment shines brighter than my own and pains me greatly." Bradley clutched at his heart in case we might have missed his point.

"Pray, tell us," Lady Montagrave swept in close and placed her hand on his arm, "what is the source of this pain?"

Bradley paused, his head thrown back and his eyes closed. Then with much emotion he uttered a single word. "Halley."

"Halley?" Lady Montagrave was mystified.

"Do you mean the late Sir Edmund Halley, the previous Astronomer Royal?" I offered.

"The same," Bradley confirmed. "Sir Edmund Halley dogs my every step as surely as Sirius paces Orion across the sky. I have done superlative work in calculation and observation, I have discovered the aberration of starlight, have measured the nutational variation of Earth's orbit. I have won the Copley Medal and been named the Astronomer Royal and have the favor of the king and parliament. Yet he has that one achievement that marks him forever above me."

"And that is?" Geo asked.

"He has ... *a comet!*," Bradley burst out. "Bright and majestic, it returns to the Earth in periodic glory. Its shining light will forever remind generations to come of his name! I have no comet, nor anything named for me. And I despair I never shall."

"There are so many stars in the sky, why not just name one after yourself?" Lady Montagrave asked.

Bradley shrugged off Lady Montagrave's suggestion as unworthy of response. But I thought there might be a way to reach him and at the same time secure coach fare to Portsmouth and a ship back to America. Staying in London to secure a ship was now out of the question.

"Mr. Bradley, while 'tis true Mr. Halley has his comet, perhaps I might offer another path to scientific immortality?"

Bradley looked to me with interest. "I assure you I would entertain it."

"There is said to exist in the western lands of America, a magnificent and capacious crater formed by the impact of some great celestial traveler falling upon the earth. I'd wager that you have looked upon the surface of the moon and seen the craters there?"

"What astronomer would I be had I not?"

"Indeed. Well, this crater is said to be as big or bigger than the hulls of a fleet of ships laid stem to stern. It is said to be so big that London town, Westminster and the Thames across to Southwark could fit within it and still have room for Dublin too. This stupendous hole in the earth has never been seen by any person but Indians and so has no name whatsoever in the manner that we reckon names."

Bradley's eyes widened. "I see."

"Now, if Mr. Washington and I were to return to America armed with reasonable funds, we could mount a most effective expedition to find the crater. As you may remember, I am a navigator and Mr. Washington is a surveyor. Once we locate the crater, we will name it for the man whose vision inspired and succored the search. How fitting would it be for posterity to forever remember you via 'Bradley Crater.'"

"Yes," Bradley said breathlessly.

"Furthermore, you are yet a young man. Continue your search for comets and there is the possibility you will find one to rival Halley's. Halley will have only his comet, whilst you will have both comet *and* crater."

Bradley tapped his finger upon his hand a few times in consideration and then readily agreed to my proposal. Bradley went to his safe and happily dispensed a tidy sum for the use of the American Bradley Crater Expedition.

We departed for Portsmouth not long afterwards. With so generous a subsidy from Astronomer Royal Bradley, we were able to engage a coach and ride in some style. Geo and Sophie sat together while I sat opposite them. Lady Montagrave had no desire to sail to America and so she said her farewells to us at the Dusquenne Inn, the coach stop nearest the Royal Observatory. That is, until it came time for her to say goodbye to Geo. She took him aside to an alcove in the tap room. They spoke for some minutes before Lady Montagrave leaned close to Geo and whispered in his ear. He blanched quite visibly and seemed at a loss for words. She kissed him gently and with much evident feeling, an expression of sorrow and regret briefly passing her face. Then she was gone and Sophie was back on his arm. We rushed to board the coach and depart.

Though Geo was clearly happy to again be with Sophie, he had a reserved air that lingered. As we were not alone, I was unable to ask Geo the nature of his disquiet.

However, the long ride did allow me the opportunity to discover the particulars of how Sophie rescued us from the outlandish longitude projects storage closet of the Royal Observatory.

It seems Sir Gerald was adamant in his designs upon Sophie. He wished to marry her, both because he was captivated by her physical beauty, but also because he saw in her a fitting successor to Lady Montagrave — who Sir Gerald thought was losing her appeal and her usefulness as she grew older. Sir Gerald told Sophie she could be the greatest female charlatan who ever operated in London and that working in concert they could amass great wealth and influence.

For her part, Sophie wanted only to be with Geo, but she realized that Sir Gerald was so given over to his feelings towards her that he could be used as an instrument to free Geo and me. So Sophie agreed to marry and partner with Sir Gerald. But first he must use his influence at court to have us released. Sir Gerald did as she bade him and together they appeared before Prince George and treated for our freedom. This was a great risk. Had Sophie been discovered as an imposter, she would certainly have found herself imprisoned in Newgate.

Their entreaties were successful, however, and the prince agreed to free us. But Sophie now undertook her plan to slip away from Sir Gerald. She disappeared into London's underworld, all the while keeping watch upon the prison hulk for the signs of our release. She followed us across the river in the guise of a rabbit vender and was in position to see us brought into the Royal Observatory. She entered the observatory kitchen and interested the cook in a few of the rabbits from the sling she carried around her neck. Then she slipped into the hallways of the observatory. Coming upon Sir Gerald and Lady Montagrave, she knocked Sir Gerald out by cracking him across the noggin with a rare Venetian telescope reputedly once used by Galileo.

Lady Montagrave was already aware of Sir Gerald's plan to toss her over in favor of Sophie. She had resolved to bow out of the charlatan game and retire to her country estate. So she instantly agreed to drag Sir Gerald into the closet wherein we were all reunited.

Truth be told we were tired from our long day and so we dozed and slept for much of the rest of the long ride to Portsmouth. We were sure that we had wholly escaped. Little did we realize that others followed in pursuit.

Chapter Twenty Four
A Barbary Corsair

OUR COACH CLATTERED into the streets of Portsmouth, winding its way down to the waterfront. It was a far less impressive port than London. Portsmouth was far from matching the forest of masts that jammed the Thames at Wapping. Still, there were ships in Portsmouth and some were headed to America.

We were feeling some measure of contentment at having escaped London and the clutches of Sir Gerald and Colonel Chase. Geo and Sophie retired to a tavern whilst I made inquiries as to gaining passage to Virginia.

Without much effort I found a ship bound for America, the 139-foot *Sulgrave Manor*. Its captain, a pock-faced Walloon named Joop Dementian, refused to sign me on as a mate, saying he could not believe that an African man knew a single jot of navigation. So it was ordinary seaman or nothing, with Geo working off his passage as assistant steward. Sophie was not assigned a duty, but she could assist the assistant.

I took the happy news of our newly secured berths aboard *Sulgrave Manor* back to the tavern where Geo and Sophie were taking their ease. I was sure they would be greatly pleased. As I pushed through the smoky air, I was struck by a sight most unexpected: Seated on the long bench not two tables from Geo were Prudence and Hawkins, Thomas Tryingdare's maid and butler from No. 4 Julian Square. With the precipitous flight of Tryingdare to the continent, these two must have been left high and dry. But, surely they could have procured new employment in London. Why were they here in Portsmouth? I presented myself to them.

"Prudence and Hawkins, it is I, Darius Attucks. I am happy to see you once again."

Prudence looked quickly at Hawkins, who smiled slowly and offered his hand. "Many felicitations, salutations, and great good fortune be visited upon you — that is to say, hello."

"G'day," Prudence agreed, seemingly flustered.

Geo and Sophie had been watching for my return, but had somehow missed the old couple, who sat with their backs to Geo and his lady. We quickly joined with them at the table. Prudence's expression turned to apprehension as her eyes swept across each of us before coming to rest on Sophie. Crossing her arms, Sophie presented a hardened expression that caused Prudence to drop her gaze.

"Ma'am and Mr. Hawkins," Geo said with a warm smile. "How extraordinary to see you here. I would imagine with the unfortunate departure of your employer, you had found yourselves without a position."

Hawkins nodded rapidly, or rapidly for him, at any rate. "Unexpected and sudden, events happen unbidden, life flows ever onward — that is to say, we are adrift."

Sophie shook her head at this. "You needn't continue the charade, Mr. Tryingdare. Surely you remember that I was also a player in the recent play in London with your son Thomas."

Geo was taken completely by surprise. And while I may have seemed equally surprised to the casual observer, I am sure I had doubts about Prudence and Hawkins, though I cannot pinpoint exactly when they began.

"Do you mean to say that Hawkins is Tryingdare's father?" Geo asked Sophie before turning to Hawkins. "Is this true?"

Hawkins blinked at Geo and then shot a quick glance to Prudence, who nodded glumly. He took a deep breath and responded.

"Charades and deceptions, confidence and betrayal, many players wearing a mask — that is to say, yes."

"And Prudence his mother?"

"No, no. His mother is long gone now," Hawkins replied. "Prudence is most certainly a friend to him, however."

"So you left London, left Julian Square?" I asked.

"Indeed, we were forced to do so. Sad to say, but No. 4 Julian Square left us."

"It has been let to another tenant?"

"Rumblings and grumblings, growlings and tearings, a great tumult and then nothing — that is to say, collapsed."

"The house fell down?" Geo asked.

"'Tis true. It fell in on itself. The morning after we received communications from Sir Gerald that Tom had sailed for the continent, the house made a great series of noises and shudderings — "

"We was awfully scared," Prudence interrupted.

"Yes. My wife and I ran out into the square only in time to save ourselves. All the floors came crashing down like a house of playing cards. Threw dust upon everything for a block round and we did choke mightily in its pall."

"That thug Boyle who buried us alive must have wrecked the house when he undertook Trydingdare's orders to rebuilt it," I said. "So what did you do?"

"Prudence and I have friends in that great city. We returned to sift for our meager baggage, but the pile of wreckage had already been turned over by footpads and rag pickers who seized all items of value. Whilst there, however, we occasioned to overhear that the property was to be sold. And this point I think you may find of interest. The buyer is a successful merchant from the town of Boston in the colonies. This American has pledged to build an entirely new house at No. 4 Julian Square, to be placed on a solid foundation and built with the finest materials and a plan of three balanced parts such that a collapse in the future will not be possible. The house will stand for many generations as a stately beacon of enlightened construction."

"That is all fine," Sophie said brusquely, "but what of Tryingdare's fortune? All the coin he fleeced from the moneyed folk of London?"

Hawkins shrugged. "He had already moved much of it out of London to various locations in Kent. But I imagine he collected it prior to his departure. On our way here Prudence and I checked one place he was said to have a cache, but we found it quite empty."

"So you have no money? What are you to do here in Portsmouth?"

"We shall not tarry here. We are off to Gibraltar with the tide."

"Why Gibraltar?" I asked.

"'Tis well known as a place of charlatans and mountebanks, liars and shifty men. Stem of poisoned fruit, vine of venomous grapes, more is the subterfuge, thievery, and dishonesty accomplished in Gibraltar's shadow.

Moreover, we shall greet Tom there within the quarter year."

"But now, alas, the tide turns, the river runs, sea birds take to the wing — that is to say, we must depart." Hawkins picked up a traveling bag, helped Prudence to her feet and then draped a great cape across his shoulders. He walked very slowly and it seemed that his great age made him labor. Sophie watched him closely. We said our goodbyes and Hawkins and Prudence were walking out when Sophie motioned that we should follow them.

Once we made the street, Sophie quickly caught up to the couple. With one easy motion she slipped the cape off Hawkins shoulders. Hawkins turned to express his alarum, until he saw it was Sophie and that Geo and I were backing her up. "May I have your knife?" she said to me. She took it and sliced open the lining of the cape. Inside the glint of gold sovereigns was visible even in the weak light of late afternoon.

"We are foiled, unmasked, done in by cruel fate and its sharp-eyed handmaiden — that is to say, you have uncovered our boodle."

Sophie stared at him as she held the cloak. When neither Hawkins nor Prudence said another word, she spoke. "Had I found your only treasure you would surely be more anxious and excited. Indeed, Prudence would be yapping unbearably. Since you take this discovery in your stride, I can only surmise you have more coin secreted elsewhere. D, lift that bag, would you?"

I did so and reported that it was unnaturally heavy.

"As I imagined it would be," Sophie said. Then to Prudence and Hawkins, "You may keep the bag. We shall take the cape. Enclosed herein is certainly only a token of that which we earned through your son's illegal trade."

Hawkins shrugged and then gently took Prudence's shoulder and turned away. In the golden light, they walked down the quay, not once looking back.

With the cape and its sovereigns in our possession, we made our way toward a boat tied to the wharf. Once aboard we would row out to our ship and be on our way to America.

Then two figures appeared around a corner and blocked our path. They were on foot and with the setting sun behind them, they were little more than silhouettes. When the larger one spoke, we knew well enough who he was.

"Stand and put up your hands," said Sir Gerald.

"Y-y-you are apprehended under the authority of the king," said the second, who from his halting speech we knew to be Lieutenant Colonel Chase.

'Twas true that three of us faced two of them. The woman in our party was an accomplished charlatan and no doubt could handle a sword as well. Except that we had not a single sword amongst us.

"I am open to suggestion," Geo admitted honestly, though not helpfully, to me.

I had not one idea of the proper gambit, yet I said it not, as I didn't wish my fellows to lose heart.

At that very moment, we heard footfalls and emerging in our sight were two more men. These also formed dark silhouettes in the horizon light. We assumed that these two were in the camp of Colonel Chase and we were now outnumbered four to three. Nothing could be further from the truth, however.

The new arrivals drew their swords to engage Sir Gerald and Colonel Chase in spirited battle. It was only as they turned and lunged that we saw the two were clad entirely in black and wore masks to hide their identities. They were none other than two of the dark-clothed tribe we had met in London — the Mohocks. Were they engaging Colonel Chase and Sir Gerald to allow us time to make our escape? 'Twas difficult to discern in the twilight, but one of 'em looked very much like the handsome, well-formed fellow who spoke to us that London night. He turned quickly to us and with one quick motion of his hand he bade us to flee.

Sophie was already backing away, calling Geo and me to follow. The young Virginian and I exchanged a quick nod of agreement, then escaped. We had no idea of why these Mohocks were assisting us, but we were only too happy for it. Perhaps some day we will discover the reason for their efforts.

Not a quarter hour later, we were aboard *Sulgrave Manor* in the harbor. The sailors sang a chantey as they paced round the capstan, raising the anchor, whose chain clanked as it rumbled aboard. On the foremast, the fore topsail had been wrung out, while the main topsail was broken free of its gaskets and given a taste of the northerly wind.

Geo, in his strength and enthusiasm, had joined the sailors at the capstan. Since I was signed on as a paid hand, I was right there alongside Geo, my hands on a capstan bar, pushing hard.

"It was most unfair of us to steal from Prudence and Hawkins," Geo grunted to me as he pushed. "We must return the sovereigns to them. For, no matter how they were obtained, the coins were in their possession."

I was poised to grunt back my answer when I saw a gig approaching. Four men worked the oars while two others sat at the stern. If my eyes were not deceiving me in the fading light, the stern men were none other than Sir Gerald and Lieutenant Colonel Chase. Somehow they evaded the Mohocks. I called to Sophie, who had donned some slops and now looked every bit a sailor, save for being the most beautiful sailor aboard. She lingered by the capstan and I was forced to break my messages to her into bits — one for each time I passed her while trudging round the turning capstan.

"Sophie, Sir Gerald is aboard yonder boat ..."

"... and Chase with him ...."

"... use Hawkins' cloak ..."

"... to coax the captain to keep ..."

"... us on course and not stop."

The anchor was free of the bottom and now cleared the surface, making its own wake as the ship ghosted forward, picking up speed as the sails filled.

Sophie had retrieved the cloak and moved quickly to the quarterdeck where stood the phlegmatic Walloon, Capt. Dementian. He focused his saturnine eyes at Sophie just as Colonel Chase called up from the launch.

"C-c-calling the deck, there," Chase bellowed. "I am L-L-Lieutenant C-C-Colonel Chase of the Prince of Wales' Life Guard. I would speak to the captain."

The anchor, dripping gobs of foul mud, now hung at the cathead, nearly secured for the voyage. Sophie pulled her knit cap down on her head and sidled onto the quarterdeck. She whispered to the captain and then placed a shiny gold coin in Dementian's hand before she retreated to the fife rail at the mizzen mast, taking cover in the mass of lines there.

Finished with the task of raising the anchor, we stowed the capstan sheaves. Geo and I then tried our best to stay out of sight.

Dementian moved to the quarterdeck rail and yelled down to Chase in the boat, "Captain Dementian, here. What would you have of me, sir?"

"I c-c-call upon you to heave to and let us aboard. W-w-we have business with some of your crew."

Dementian considered this and then looked over to Sophie at the mizzen. She took another coin, placed it on the deck and slid it toward the captain. When it got close, Demetian's foot came down upon the piece of gold, holding it fast. He looked back to the launch. "Is it the king's business? Or of a more personal nature?"

"Y-y-you have no leave to question me, captain," Chase said with irritation. "B-b-backwind your sails and hold fast whilst we come on board."

This time Sophie did not wait for Demetian to look her way, but merely slid another coin to the captain as expeditiously as possible. It hit a rough plank and bounced. Before it could roll astray, however, Demetian deftly trapped it. He then calmly replied to Chase. "I am but a servant, sir. The owners of this ship have given me my orders and I am loath to ignore 'em. You speak of backing my sails, yet you will see that they draw a favorable wind and that my anchor is catted. I have begun my passage as per my masters' wishes and can do none else. I pray you good fortune for your return to the quay, and I bid you farewell." He leisurely bent down, picked up the two gold coins under his foot and pocketed them with a clink, his eyes still droopy and his face betraying no hint of joy.

Chase and Sir Gerald could only fume in the lowering twilight. Sir Francis stood up to yell at our captain, but lost his balance and fell into the water, thrashing and kicking. *Sulgrave Manor* slipped out of the harbor and into the waters of the English Channel. Sir Gerald and Sir Francis looked very small and of no consequence as the gig dropped far astern.

The calming rhythm of the hull rising and falling on the waves lent an air of serene expectation. Smiles were seen all around. Sailors lit the stern and side lanterns and Dementian called out to the mate, "Keep her south by west,

Mr. Lee, loose the main course and ready the ta'gallants. I
fear this wind will go light on us a'fore the midwatch. I shall
return after I've supped." And with that he disappeared
below.

Geo, Sophie and me ate our boiled beef and bread with
the crew. The first few nights of a passage are the best for
eating and drinking aboard a ship. The beef is only starting to
spoil, not like weeks into a passage when it is so rancid a
sailor must choke it down as best he can. And in the
beginning the ale is yet nearly fresh — after two weeks
sloshing in the casks it is musty and flat. So we had a fine
supper that first night as a fair wind sent us south and west
toward the mouth of the Channel and the Atlantic beyond.

Sophie had the third mate's berth, while the displaced
third mate made do with a corner of the captain's day room.
As a steward, Geo had a berth just aft of the galley, but the
berth was built for a small boy of twelve and Geo could not
fit. He made do with a hammock in the aft hold. As an
ordinary seaman, I had rights to a berth in the fo'c's'le with
the rest of the crew. But some took offense at an African man
sleeping in their midst. That often happened when I found
myself on a new ship and the crew had not yet seen that I
could charm the sheets and halyards like a swami with a
snake. I set up my hammock alongside Geo's.

It was dark in the hold when we slept, the only light
from a single guttering candle in a dusty lamp. For this
passage to America the ship's cargo was items of cast iron.
Every night we heard the iron clink as, with each roll of the
ship, it moved in the bins.

On the morning, we had a breakfast of salt pork and
half-stale bread, not forgetting a cup of ale. The day was
clear and bright, with a deep blue sky. The wind had shifted
to the east, which suited because we had turned west
sou'west. Captain Dementian had ordered all canvas set and
so *Sulgrave Manor* charged forward with a bone in her teeth.
It was one of the those fine days of sailing that made every
hand aboard forget about storms or rocky shores and imagine
a sailor's life to be nothing but a jolly ride to leeward.

As nicely as the ship moved in the steady breeze, she was, after all, a fat merchantman and was not built for speed. Early in the morning the watch aloft sang out, "Sail ho!" It was the sail of ship a few miles off. During the next hours the sail grew larger till before noon it was clear enough that the other ship was o'ertaking us. This seemed of little note, as the other vessel also flew a British ensign.

As the unknown ship drew ever closer, it was obviously on a collision course. I strode aft to warn the captain that the ship overhauling us on our port side was no ordinary merchantman. Just as I reached the quarterdeck ladder, a large black flag burst forth from the highest truck of other ship's mainmast and a cannon boomed for our attention. But the flag's halyard had evidently not been properly secured. No sooner was the black signal set to the breeze than it flew away and became entangled in the ship's fore shrouds. There was much shouting on the deck of the other ship, which was now nearly alongside us. A second black ensign was unfurled from the top of the foremast, but it, too, broke free. It flew into our rigging and became ensnared. Further heated shouting was heard and it was clear that these were no Englishmen.

I was up the ladder and onto the quarterdeck when the mystery ship turned sharply towards *Sulgrave Manor*. Our helmsman attempted to turn away to starboard but the other vessel struck us amidships and we all fell down.

"Captain," I yelled from where I sat on my arse, "'tis my belief these are Barbary pirates."

Dementian nodded soberly from where he lay on the deck. "Yes," was his entire response.

The pirates scrambled aboard soon thereafter, with only a few falling into the sea or getting tangled in ropes. The captain of the pirates walked upon our deck with a deliberate step, almost as if he were picking his way amidst the filth of a London street. Standing a full hand higher than his crewmen, he presented a curious tottering effect when he moved. The leader, who called himself Al'Zaazeez, was an Egyptian from the fallen kingdoms of the Nile. His clothing was a curious mix of Barbary Arab and classical Egyptian. Unlike the dark hair and beards of the other pirates,

Al'Zaazeez showed the fairest brown hair. The Egyptian carried an orange with him that he sniffed regularly to relieve his nose of the rancid odors from our vessel.

We were now prisoners of the corsairs. We were gathered at the mainmast and guarded by Al'Zaazeez's men, who surrounded us with their swords drawn. For all their fierceness, however, they smiled and made faces at us — unless they saw Al'Zaazeez nearby, and then they assumed their most cruel countenance.

After a quick tour of our ship, Al'Zaazeez ordered his men to carry a few of the crates from the hold and place them on the deck. The iron items proved to be hatchet heads (for trading to friendly Indian tribes that they might harvest the scalps of unfriendly Indian tribes) and manacles (for securing slaves until they were broken of their unruly nature). Al'Zaazeez showed little interest in the hatchet heads, but the manacles produced smiles and exclamations. He ordered his men to haul away all the crates of the manacles onto their own vessel.

Captain Dementian nodded and said. "We have a slave trade, the Arabs have a slave trade. We take crates of manacles and chains from Arab ships, they take 'em from ours. We all use the same tools of the trade."

"Yes, same tools," Al'Zaazeez said in English, his smile bright with several gold teeth. "Someday Arab meet Englishman in middle of Africa. Between us, we take every last African. Whole of land empty of Africans."

Then Al'Zaazeez took a close look at all of us. He directed us to form lines, shoulder to shoulder. He was looking into Geo's mouth, getting a sense of his teeth, when a series of shouts went up. There was a scuffle below and one of Al'Zaazeez's crewmen appeared, dragging Sophie up into the sunlight. When the Barbary pirates had first unfurled their black flag, Geo had taken Sophie below and attempted to hide her in the captain's spirits locker. He assumed that since followers of Mohammed are forbidden by their holy book to drink wine or whiskey or other spirits, they would not search there.

The Barbary leader examined Sophie. He proclaimed himself delighted with her beauty and her spirit. She had taken a swing at Al'Zaazeez but missed and decked one of his attendants. He proclaimed that Sophie would fetch a great price in the slave market in Algiers or perhaps he would give her to the Bey of Tunis to whom Al'Zaazeez admitted he owed a gambling debt. He ordered Sophie taken aboard his ship. Thus did Al'Zaazeez seal her fate — and Geo's as well.

Sophie, a woman of much experience in the world, knew how savagely fate can plait life's cord, making snags and snarls. She had been dealt bad cards before and she knew there was nothing to do but play them. Still, no matter how tough her manner, she was a young woman of passions. Her feelings for Geo were keen enough to squeeze tears from the edges of her eyes and for her mouth to break into quivering. As the pirates hustled her down the deck and through the bulwarks, she turned her head this way and that, catching her last glimpses of Geo before they were parted forever.

Geo attempted to stop the thieves from stealing his love, but the pirates only pressed their phalanx of swords in closer, many sharp points only inches from his face.

"Sophie! Sophie!" he raged, his eyes brimming with water, his face red, his throat filled with wordless lamentation.

His fellow crewmembers and I struggled to restrain him, but so strong was the young man he nearly wriggled free. We managed to protect him from having his head separated from his neck by one of the Barbary pirate's broad cutlasses.

Al'Zaazeez was not bluffing; the manacles and Sophie were all he took from *Sulgrave Manor*. The pirates cast off, bumped our vessel one more time and nearly snared their bowsprit in our port fore shrouds. But even with those mishaps, Al'Zaazeez and his crew still possessed sufficient seamanship to sail their ship away — and to crush Geo's heart.

Chapter Twenty Five
In Consideration of Liberty

WITH THE DEPARTURE of the Barbary pirate ship, our weather turned dark and gloomy. We started our passage with blue skies and a following breeze, now we labored into head winds, rain squalls and thick seas. The spirits of all aboard were dulled by the fall of the glass.

These feelings, however, had no comparison to the despair that seized Geo. He barely spoke. He maintained a grim countenance, with lips set and eyes focused on some far off horizon. His duties he performed silently. Barely supping and drinking little, he spent many an hour swinging silently in his hammock, in a half world between sleeping and waking. He was inconsolable. He knew there was little chance he would ever see Sophie again.

As I pondered Geo's situation, it occurred to me that there was another aspect, perhaps equally painful as the loss of Sophie, with which Geo wrestled. He had arrived in London with his prospects bright, with a firm philosophy of dash and direct action. He was convinced he would succeed as a man and a younger son through the application of his will and his courage, sweeping all obstacles away. Subsequent events, however, had put the lie to his cherished plan and left him at various points poor, imprisoned and separated from the woman he loved. Now, he would need a new philosophy. He would need to construct a *modus vivendi* for reconciling himself with the tricky adversary that was life. For Geo, it surely brought back to him the early death of his father Augustine — a death that left him without his greatest advocate. How his path had been molded by that loss. A path that led him to his present situation: wandering in an arid land of defeat and loneliness.

Some of the crew became convinced Geo's soul had been stolen by Al'Zaazeez when he took away Sophie; that only the profane husk of Geo's body remained. Try as I might, I was unable to communicate with him. He did not answer my questions and so I ceased to ask them. A chilly gulf opened betwixt us.

The weather, Geo's strange behavior and the

superstitions of the sailors made *Sulgrave Manor* an unhappy ship. Some aboard said she was cursed. At night lightning would reveal great armies of storms surrounding us. By day a greasy sun mixed with gunsmoke clouds. An aspect of imminent doom gripped the vessel.

Then heaven showed its hand.

I was on deck for the midday watch. The wind was squally and we had handed the main and fore course, reducing sail since the captain wished to fly only the topsails and ta'gallants. Truth be told, I had been increasingly out of sorts for several days. After the change of the watch, I felt an illness grasp me fully. Feverous chills racked me and I staggered to the deck. An itch erupted across the skin of my face and neck. I scratched and writhed and lost all sense of my person.

My shipmates looked upon me and recoiled in horror and fear. Soon Captain Dementian was called and he concurred that I had been taken by the pox. The crew gathered and there were demands for action.

Though I was adjudged by all hands as a knowledgeable and trustworthy seaman of stout courage and nimble limb, and though not a man jack of 'em said they thought for one moment 'bout my African skin, they all decided then and there to toss me by the boards. 'Twas necessary, they said, to save the infection from spreading throughout the ship. This decision was affirmed by all aboard. The crew was caught up in ever-louder cries and exclamations.

"Throw the blackamoor over!"

"His heart is as black as his skin, toss him over afore he blackens us all!"

"Drown the Jonah and save the ship!"

They formed a steadily tighter knot around me, their shouts raising their courage to o'ercome their fear of the pox. They pressed in on me and I was lifted into the air by many hands, held high like a pharaoh on his catafalque. The body of sailors moved crablike toward the starboard rail, readying to toss me into the opaque sea.

Amid the shouts and threats, no one noticed a pale man of considerable stature arise, seeming to float from the shadow depths of the midships hatch. It was Geo stirred from his stupor. He crossed the deck and stepped boldly alongside

Captain Dementian. Geo deftly grabbed the captain's sword and swept the thick cutlass blade in a wide arc. The bare metal flashed across the eyes of the rabble. Sailors saw Geo and fell back, his stature and the grim purpose of his advance inducing fear. They deposited me not in the waves but again upon the deck. The closed knot loosened as the sailors retreated.

In a moment Geo was alongside me, supporting me with one arm while the other held the cutlass in an iron grip. He threatened them all with the blade.

"You shall not throw him by the boards," Geo announced with calm certitude. "And should you try, I'll lay off your arms and heads."

The frozen moment of shock and surprise was thrust aside by a new rage of shouts and threats.

"Are you mad? He has the pox!"

"If he stay aboard, we shall all die!"

"Put 'em both over the side!"

The crew was fiercely worked up, but none dared be the first to test Geo's mettle. It wasn't dash and drama he showed that day, but unyielding resolve. And every man upon that deck saw in Geo the fire-tempered iron of a born captain. Soon their ardor cooled and the shouting gave way to grumbling and a foul temper.

"I've had the pox," Geo announced. "Since I cannot be harmed by the disease any further, I will tend to him."

Dementian had watched with open admiration Geo's effort to hold off his crew (a merchant ship captain must always hold a disparate crew in line or find himself stabbed in his bunk). The captain resolved to defuse the hissing bomb. "We shall accommodate you, Mr. Washington. You may take Darius with you below."

At this the crew raised further howls of protest.

"However, you will take him deep into the ship, to the captain's hold. There you may nurse him and see him through his malady," Demetian declared, "or there you both shall perish."

Geo, great beads of sweat running down his face, nodded, stood up and let fall the cutlass. Its point dug into the oak deck, the blade swaying slowly from weather rail to lee scupper in a glinting oscillation.

In the very depths of the ship, beneath the captain's salon, under the steward's rooms, nestled atop the stern end of the thick keel timbers, was the captain's hold. With its paltry dimensions, the hold was little more than a large box given over to the storage of precious goods, like gold, silver, brandy, or the captain's wench (hidden away during departure, once the vessel cleared harbor she came up to live in the captain's cabin to give him succor during a passage).

For many days Geo spent his waking hours fetching me drink in the form of ale from the ship's casks and hard biscuit and a bit of boiled beef. I was in no condition to eat nor drink but Geo forced this sustenance upon me and so saved my wretched body and soul.

For my part, I was in a delirium and could not converse nor could I read, but only lie in the sweaty confines of the captain's hold while my unfailing companion did his best to help me.

Whether 'twas induced from the fever or was the second sight Moher Geechee saw in me in London, or the influence of my twin Jabbar, I cannot say, but at some time during my crazed state, I saw images, like paintings in the sky. I saw Geo as an older man in a fine general's uniform, astride a white charger and leading a great army. And another vision showed me multitudes of people in strange clothes in a towering city. There stood a massive statue of an older Geo and people carried around green notes with old Geo's face upon it.

Later, when some of my strength had returned to me, I resolved not to speak of these things as I became convinced the visions arose from nothing more than the overheated state of my mind. I could place no stock in 'em. Perhaps these dramatic sights only suggested my own death. I had fulfilled Heaven's task and shepherded Geo through his trials and adventures in London, perhaps now my life was to end as the Almighty called me home.

Once my pox broke and my tortured skin began its healing, Geo would read to me. Captain Dementian, though a steady fellow and well-trained by experience, held little regard for books and so had none in his cabin 'cept for some treatises on navigation and a French book with engravings of men and women in various configurations of pleasure. So, save for a moth-eaten Bible — which was in no danger of being read by the captain or his profane officers — there was nought else to read but a solitary volume of philosophy by John Locke. This book had been left aboard by one of the ship's previous passengers, a young printer from Philadelphia who was returning to America after a stay in London.

So it was from the Bible and this Locke book Geo spoke aloud to me as I recovered. We had some stimulating discourses on the topics Locke addressed, such as the rights of man and the consent of people to be governed, which stood in opposition to the divine governance of kings.

At first, Geo thought these ideas to be ill-advised. Yet upon further discussion, I impressed on him the necessity for the people to have a robust say in their governance. And he began to agree. I pointed out that the Virginia House of Burgesses was, after all, a representative body and that the citizens of Britain's American colonies had developed a sound tradition of self-governance.

I also made it clear, in case he had forgotten, that Geo had attempted to ingratiate himself into English society and had not only failed to procure a title, an estate of any size or a fortune, but had managed to get himself imprisoned and had fled the country as a fugitive. His further efforts in England would be viewed with little merit.

As I was often delirious or otherwise insensible during the height of my infirmity, the time elapsed while Geo and I were in the captain's hold seemed but a day or two. For Geo it was another matter entirely. He was trapped, as in a jail, with no release, save for either my death or my salvation.

Lucky for me and for Geo, I did recover. I became well enough for us to leave the captain's hold and return to our hammocks on the second deck. The captain gave me three more days to rest and then I was to return to duty. While lying in my hammock, I thought about my time with Geo and his early formulation for himself. He had previously decided that dash and elan, the headlong rush into action, were to be his watch words. Yet I suggested to him that a more measured, serious manner might better suit his naturally phlegmatic character.

"So you think that I should abandon the life of the man of action and take up what?" Geo asked. "Perhaps become a banker or a religious hermit?"

"Not at all," I gently disagreed. "I counsel as much action as you may handle. I suggest that rather than present yourself as a hare-brained hothead, that a calm, reasoned sangfroid more naturally suits you."

Geo composed his face into a solid, unflinching mask with his lips puffed out and eyes squinted shut — his representation of reasoned sangfroid. He held it such until he could no longer. Then we two burst into laughter. Geo agreed that perhaps my suggestion had a measure of good counsel.

For his part, Geo returned immediately to his duty as the tallest assistant steward ever to sail the North Atlantic. The poor fellow was nearly bent double in some of the ship's spaces. To help him get straightened out again, we would sit and talk on the foredeck, where Geo could stretch out on a coil of line. Happily, these sessions in the fresh sea air also helped him dissipate some of the gloom at having lost Sophie.

We spoke of many things, but on the third day we were back to the subject of governance.

"I have been thinking of that Locke fellow all morning," I said.

"Oh?" Geo answered as he tried to untwist his cramped back by some stretching, "And what have you concluded?"

"Something quite important. Consider three salient facts: Firstly, Parliament has no American members elected to represent American interests, nor does the king have an American advisor at court; secondly, there are long delays in communications with Parliament and the king and; thirdly, Americans have excellent experience at democracy and self-rule. From these facts what obvious and inescapable conclusion can you draw?"

"That you should go back on the watch schedule and haul some ropes so you will not have time to construct arguments regarding political philosophy?"

"No, think of the three points," I said. I also tried my best to ignore a badly trimmed jib sail that luffed with percussive exuberance.

"Very well. You are saying that king and Parliament do not consider the interests of American colonists; that due to the long distances involved, even if they did so, governance from Britain is inherently impractical; and that Americans have developed considerable experience at self-governance and could manage to do more given the chance."

"You have got it."

"Got what?" Geo asked flatly.

He wanted me to say it and so I did. "Separation from Britain is the only answer. America should declare its independence and become a sovereign nation."

I had expected hot dispute from Geo at this suggestion — after all, it was a dangerous idea, sedition, a hanging crime. However, he did not do so. He only seemed to calmly think over the prospect. Then he stated his response. "I have three points for you: Firstly, this is treasonous talk and I ought caution you to be careful in the voicing of such sentiments; secondly, Great Britain is the mightiest military power on the globe while America is a backwater and cannot hope to oppose London's will; thirdly, there could not be a more pointless discourse with less potential for a happy resolution than a discussion between an African mariner and a younger son of no estate and even fewer prospects. In short, the proposition is illegal, impossible and pointless."

I listened as the ship's bow worked though the waves amid a bubbling flux of white water. Then I said, "I take it, then, that you approve of independence?"

Geo did not reply, but showed a face of such imperturbable calm and stolid confidence, with just a hint of a deadpan grin, that I felt entirely vindicated as to my comments on his proper countenance. I was also suddenly not a little excited about the future prospects for America if young men like Geo would rally to her cause.

But America's future was not our immediate concern, it seemed that there had been a mistake in the calculation of our position and we now approached the entrance to Delaware Bay, rather than the Chesapeake Bay. This was a problem as Annapolis on the Chesapeake was our intended destination. Captain Demetian was understandably concerned as to the prospect of running aground. To gain further insight into our navigational situation, I was discretely called aft to the captain's quarters. The captain decided it was only slightly less humiliating to take navigational instruction from an African man than to run *Sulgrave Manor* onto the beach.

Chapter Twenty Six
To Each, Fate's Portion

AFTER A SHORT inquest, I was able to solve the captain's navigational troubles. The ship's octant needed adjustment and I simplified Demetian's sight reduction calculations. On the strength of this improved navigation, we smartly doubled Cape Charles and entered the Bay of the Chesapeake. Only a mile from the bank of the Potomac, Geo and I and were ready to disembark in one of the ship's boats when the wind slipped from a fair southwesterly to a dead calm. Prevented from making any further progress north, Captain Demetian anchored near the mouth of the river. He conducted a farewell celebration for us who had, on the whole, been good shipmates.

The celebration consisted of the crew drinking every last drop of rum aboard, while Captain Demetian and the mates drained many bottles of wine and brandy. I hazard that Geo and I had a few draughts as well. But rather than cause Geo to delay our departure, it seemed to make him more eager to get on land. So we engaged Caleb, the ship's bosun, to row us ashore. A short man of substantial girth, Caleb was an ardent participant in our departure celebration and was under the influence of drink when we boarded the ship's boat.

The last crimson embers of the sun glowed upon the still water of the river. The bosun's oars dipped holes in the reflected sky as we made for the Virginian shore. Geo called out that he saw a good place to beach the boat. This was a mistake, as Caleb, who was rowing and thus facing aft, turned quickly to see what had aroused Geo's interest. His corpulence prevented him from making a full turn, however, so he leaned back to see further forward. Drink-addled, he fell backwards against the starboard gunwale with a rumbling exclamation of surprise. This sudden shift of weight affected the balance of the boat and it overset, dropping the three of us into the river.

"D!" Geo yelled loudly out over the water as he held onto the capsized boat. "D! Where are you?'"

I was directly behind him and in fine shape as I am a

strong swimmer. I reached over to tap him on the shoulder. He spun around to see me smiling behind him and was clearly chuffed at my playfulness in the face of almost certain tragedy. "Caleb has sunk," Geo said with some irritation. "I will slip under and search for him." Just then there was a sound like a great whale blowing its spout. "Damn — went under for a bit," Caleb gasped.

We swam the boat to the shore, poured out the water and set it right. We thanked Caleb for his efforts and gave him a push back toward the anchored *Sulgrave Manor* — from which lantern light suffused and the sound of ragged singing and laughter drifted across the river.

Meanwhile, Geo and I turned from the bank and toward the woods. We were soaked to the skin, but it was a warm summer night and we were happy to be on American soil once more. We set off, walking upstream, excitement in every step. At least our bellies were full and both of us still felt the warm glow of recent drink. We had a long fetch to reach Mount Vernon.

A day later, after purchasing two old plough horses, we were on a path along the river that ascended to a bluff. On the top of which promontory stood the humble house that Lawrence Washington had dubbed Mount Vernon. One and a half stories tall, with no more than four or five rooms, I could not help but compare it unfavorably to the stately elegance of Braddock Hall in Kent, the estate of the short-lived Viscount Washington.

This simple wooden construction built on a fieldstone foundation would not serve even as an out building at Braddock Hall. And to add further to Geo's discomfort, this new-world estate did not belong to him. It was the province of his half-brother Lawrence and would remain so until Lawrence died.

As we approached the house, Geo's mother, Mary Washington, espied us and came out to offer greeting, after a fashion. She was a tall woman and in her countenance she most nearly resembled Geo. She presented the natural physical command that I had lately seen from Geo, though without the grace. Geo's father, Augustine, must have been the dancer.

"Where have you been?" She chastised Geo from her first breath. "You depart Barbados with some German lord and then sail for London? You abandoned your infirm brother when you fled." To this, Geo made no reply and his mother added, "Come in quickly, Lawrence surely lies upon his deathbed." Before Geo could respond, she brusquely turned and returned to the house. Geo stood still for a moment, his mouth tight and his body tense. I did not know if he was more concerned with his recent talk with his mother or at the greater prospect of losing his half-brother. He walked purposefully to the house.

I followed Geo within, but Mrs. Washington took offense at an unknown African man in her stepson's house and bade me to wait outside. Lawrence's wife, Anne, was kind to come out and speak with me — though I suspected perhaps she did so as a needed diversion from her mother-in-law.

Lawrence's consumption had not improved and now he lay abed, coughing blood and in a delicate state. Were Lawrence not to recover, Mary informed Geo, he would inherit Mount Vernon. This was of considerable importance to Geo as, although the house was not imposing, the entire estate was of substantial size, running to many thousand acres.

I was assigned a bunk in the slaves' quarters, but rejected it immediately. Though I had every sympathy and solidarity with my fellow Africans, I had no desire to join them in their lodgings. To do so would put me in significant legal danger: I could be named a slave again for spending even one night in slave's quarters. I had no intention of once again becoming another man's property.

Anne was gracious to offer me a plank berth in the cellar of the house, the only stipulation being that I use the lower stairs to enter and leave the cellar, and not show my face in the house proper.

For several days I remained at Mount Vernon, spending time with Geo as he waited for some resolution to Lawrence's illness. This extended stay also afforded me time to finish this very manuscript.

At last, following nearly a week, I had completed the work to my initial satisfaction. As Geo had already agreed to my suggestion that I write this diary of our adventures, I gave the roll of pages to Geo for his perusal. I was happy and not a little excited. I knew of his high moral standards and was quite sure he would be pleased with the rigorously true manner with which I depicted his actions and character.

On the next day, Geo returned to me. Some other person might find the young man's moods difficult to read, but as I had now spent considerable time with Geo in a variety of circumstances, I prided myself on knowing him. He was clearly pleased with my efforts.

"D, I am aghast at this," Geo said, holding up the manuscript. "My brother may yet live, but he is so weak he will certainly not survive the winter. Which means that this estate will fall to me."

"And so you will finally have your estate," I said snidely, hurt by his reaction. I rolled the papers and placed them inside my shirt. Then, "You really did not like it? Was it one particular part or the length or the number of chapters or —"

"You must understand, D," Geo hurriedly explained, "that when I was a younger son with slim prospects, I could suffer such an account to be published in New York and read by the few people of low character who pay attention to such things as books. However, as the future proprietor of the first-rank plantation I intend Mount Vernon to become, such an account would be injurious to my reputation and the reputation of my family. Were our London business agent to know of this account, he would certainly use it against me and my family. As such, I cannot allow you to publish this. In fact, I demand that you destroy this manuscript forthwith. From this day forward, we must act as if none of it ever took place." Geo looked at me with eyes of resolution, but also some sadness. He appeared to appreciate the work that had gone into the recording of this adventure. And I believe part of him wished very much for people to know of his scandalous, yet genuine love for Sophie. Not to forget the general acclaim, notoriety and coin that a successful literary work can confer.

"That is shite!" I snapped. "I cannot destroy the fruit of my labor, Geo. And furthermore, the world should know of your most beautiful affair of the heart with Sophie." I placed my hand upon his shoulder to demonstrate my sincerity. Then I added offhandedly, "There is, of course, the chance it might sell many copies, producing a tidy sum, which I would split with you in our agreed-upon fashion."

He took my hand, clasped it warmly in his hands and then turned to pace the porch, in a state of great emotional agitation. He wiped his brow, clasped his arms about him and paced with head down. I looked around and saw the full summer fruitfulness of the Virginia land. This fullness overspread every prospect of the eye, from the waving branches of the apple, peach and cherry trees to the ripening crops in the surrounding fields. Nature had made this land rich — aided by the effort of 100 African slaves owned by the Washington family.

While I gazed upon the land's bounty I espied three ride riders approaching. By the roughness of their clothes, their mud-spattered boots and their hard-bitten countenances, I guessed these were not gentlemen farmers come to call. They rode swiftly into the yard with the two younger men performed flying dismounts, hitting the ground while nearly at the gallop. One of the men could not stop, however. His legs windmilled and he fell face first into the mud near the water pump. The other fellow chuckled at this, grabbed a stool and rushed to the horse of the third man, who was of substantial proportion and had some difficulty dismounting. Geo shot me an apprehensive glance before stepping to meet them.

"Aha, I see young Master Washington has returned to Mount Vernon," the fat man cackled as he struggled to the ground. "I am Vrinelle Dewey, young sir. I rose to the office of sheriff during your long absence in Barbados."

"I am pleased to meet you, Sheriff Dewey. Why have you occasioned to visit us?"

Dewey, his waistcoat bulging, squinted toward where I stood upon the porch. "That dark one is my cause." He pointed with the cane his young assistant had lately placed in his hand. "I have been informed that he is a runaway slave and as such, needs be placed in irons forthwith."

The corpulent man nodded and his clean young deputy — the other was muddy and still dazed from his recent fall — rushed the porch to seize me bodily. His action was so nimble that I fell wholly into his grasp. He roughly pulled my off the porch and into the yard. But now, Geo roused himself into action. He grabbed a hold of my free arm and dug in his heels.

"You shall not take him. He is no slave but a freeman from New York."

Dewey chortled. "There are a hundred men of property here in Virginia who will swear he is one of their own. Unhand him, Master Washington."

Geo only dug in harder. The muddy deputy joined his fellow and pulled. My arms, yanked one way by Dewey and the deputies and the other by Geo, registered acute pain. Now Geo's sister-in-law, Anne, rushed forth from the house and joined Geo, equalizing the pull somewhat. But then Dewey joined in. The three officers of the law were stronger and were slowing dragging us toward their horses. I shook and shimmied in an attempt to shake them off but they held fast.

The next thing was something that humbled me and filled me with pride. Three young house slaves, who risked being sent into the fields if they incurred their master's displeasure, issued from the dwelling and joined the fray. Unluckily, they did so in a line that attached itself to Geo's waistcoat. They stumbled and swung around like the child's game of crack the whip. Geo held on, but he also stumbled, accompanied by Anne. Like nothing so much as a miniature solar system, the entire assemblage of persons swung in a staggering circle, all of us in orbit around the massive bulk of Sheriff Dewey who formed as solid a gravitational center as the sun provides the planets.

Other slaves now were drawn into the staggering, spinning knot like passing comets captured by gravity. They swarmed into the scrum, so late to the affair as to know not a whit of its origins or purpose. They grabbed on and swung with equal effort for our side and for the deputies. The lumbering mass had grown so large as to produce an unintelligible chorus of grunts, shouts and exclamations. Further, the participants now grabbed a hold of each other from nearly every angle and part. One astounding result of this was my nearly complete freedom inside the churning mass. My arms were released. Thus, when I stumbled and fell, I was ignored. I took immediate advantage of this state by crawling toward the thick copse of trees that edged the river bluff.

Soon I was deep into thick bushes and shrubs and quite invisible. Nearly three minutes passed before the realization dawned that I was no longer in the center. This idea worked like gravity's opposite, the various pieces of the mass flew rapidly apart. Dewey's deputies assumed I had run and was running still. They hastily helped the big man to his horse. They didn't wait for him to take his saddle, however, but instead pushed him athwart the horse like a sack of potatoes. They took to their mounts and led Dewey's horse away. Dewey departed delivering a stream of invective directed alternately at his deputies and at Geo. The field slaves returned to their work and the house slaves went back to their toil.

From my place deep in the bushes, I could just see Geo escort Anne back to the house. He then paused and looked around carefully. When he was sure that Dewey and the deputies were gone, he moved toward where I crouched. When he came sufficiently close, I whispered to him. "Geo, I am here." Soon he was in the thicket beside me.

"Even I did not see you disappear," Geo said. "'Twas a conjuring act worthy of an eastern magi."

"I just crawled."

Geo leaned back and sighed heavily. "What a farce. You see what I must deal with. Sheriff Dewey is a minor potentate overcome with the small measure of power he receives from the crown. All such royal endorsements are foul things that corrupt their bearers. When I am master of Mount Vernon such men will lay siege to this place. I shall have no peace and no protection from these petty emperors. You, however, will have the freedom to sail the world. To go to any place a ship is sailing. That is an enviable life, on the open ocean, free of all this."

He suddenly raised his head and I saw a feverish glimmer in his eyes. A wild idea had grasped him.

"I have the answer — take me with you," Geo said, leaning forward eagerly.

"WHAT?"

"Take me with you," he insisted. "I'll accompany you to New York. We shall procure berths aboard a vessel bound for who knows where. We shall be free men, making our way in the world. Together, with our knowledge of earth, sea and sky, we could find Sophie and bring her to America. Rescue her from slavery and perdition. Perhaps even find that crater for Astronomer Bradley!"

I hardly knew what to make of this. The young fellow who had striven for a title and an estate in England, would now give up a colonial estate to roam the seas with an African man? Was it to save Sophie from slavery to the Barbary corsairs? — or to save himself?

In an instant I imagined us aboard a fine ship with white-topped waves and a steady wind; I saw Geo and me exploring the ancient temples of the Indies; bedding Italian women in Naples, Egyptian women in Alexandria, Spanish women in Cartagena; in the mysterious lands of the Mohammedans; spending a clear morning at anchor in New York; watching a moonrise at sea. 'Twas a glorious vision.

"Would you sail away from your family, from Mount Vernon, soon to be yours?"

"Yes. I would."

I looked at him and shook my head gently. "No, Geo. This is where you belong. You can free more than Sophie from slavery should you stay here and do what is right and just. You know of what I speak."

His eyes cast down now and his face sunk into his hands. "I would avoid such trials and troubles if I could. I would away with you and find Sophie. Surely it can be done."

"I would not know the first place to look. Nor have the monies to purchase her freedom nor the army to fight for it. Rescuing Sophie is a worthy goal, but you must stay and make a better world right here."

He sat glumly, a picture of dejection. There was one thing that might make him feel better. I reached into my shirt and felt the wispy pages of the manuscript. I faltered, then gathered my resolve and pulled the paper roll into the light. "Geo, you are giving up your dream of finding Sophie, 'tis only right I sacrifice something as well." I held the manuscript out to him. "Take this account of our travels and destroy it. You need never fear its contents will be revealed."

"No, I cannot take that from you," he pushed my hand away.

"I insist you take it."

"I shall not."

"You must, you fool," I demanded.

"Keep it," he said with some heat.

"You take it," I barked as I tossed it into his lap.

"I said I didn't want it," he retorted as he threw it back at me.

"It's yours, you oaf," I offered the paper again.

Geo suddenly held up his hands in a gesture of acceptance. "Very well. I will take it from you. But hold it for a while more and finish any parts of it you will. When it has grown dark, I will return here with some victuals and wine. You may make your way down the bluff to the river. There is a boat there. Row across the river and you will escape Sheriff Dewey, who surely will patrol the roads roundabout, seeking you. I will take the manuscript from you before you depart." He stood up ponderously, as if taking some monstrous weight upon his back. I did not envy him. Then he paused for some time. "We had quite an adventure, did we not, D?"

"We did," I said with a rueful smile.

He grinned back at me, his eyes soft with regard. An expression of feeling I shall not forget should I live 100 years. At that instant of brotherly affection, I nearly spoke out. I nearly agreed that he should accompany me back to sea. That he should abandon this house and its burdens and join me in freedom. But before I could say the words, he turned and departed.

I confess I was most amazed; both at Geo's desire to abandon his family and at my willingness to relinquish this account, into which I had poured so much care. Both decisions seemed both wholly correct and utterly dismal. I considered how far we had come together since that day when I saved his life upon the Irish beach. Heaven had given him to me and I had shepherded him safely through both great events and small back to his ancestral home. Though I did not consider myself a pious man, I am well read in the rites of the Christian church, indeed being something of an expert on spiritual matters. I was certain Heaven was pleased with my actions.

Even that pride did not assuage the deep sadness I felt at leaving Geo's side. We had become true friends, as shipmates who have been through thick and thin often do. Leaving him raised the specter of loneliness, as if I were leaving a newly found part of me.

I am yet a young man, however — surely I will have further exploits to record. I can hope Geo and I will see each other again. I am a man of the sea and its waves touch upon many lands — most especially the shores of adventure.

Afterword
by Professor Edward G. Portobello

IT APPEARS that Washington was the last man to hold the manuscript the day Attucks left Mt. Vernon. Thus, it follows that George Washington, not Darius Attucks, sealed the manuscript in the mansion's foundation. Where it remained for more than 250 years until the day I chanced upon it.

We have no account of Attucks' and Washington's final meeting. The historical trail left by Attucks is an exceedingly slim one. Indeed, there is nothing in traditional sources to suggest Darius Attucks existed at all.

Therefore, we must remember Darius' regular admonition to Geo that he was "a man of the sea" and look toward the accounts of seafarers. Here there are faint traces. A look at ship's log books in the collections of the International Museum for the Maritime History of the African Diaspora and Jazz Syncopation in Bozeman, Montana, reveal several tantalizing entries. From the 1754 log of a brig named *Sassafras*, there is a mention of an African American second mate who not only was adept at running the ship, but who "had the navigation." From a 1755 log of the full-rigged ship *Apollo*, we read of a second mate who would command the vessel when the captain and the first mate were both incapacitated after over-imbibing "flip" — a popular drink among sailors that mixed ale, molasses and rum. The second mate in question went only by the initial "D." (There is also an intriguing account of an African American jazz Sousaphonist named Darius arrested after a drunken brawl in Brooklyn that began as an argument over the musical significance of Sammy Davis, Jr. But, as the fight occurred in 1964, it may not have been Washington's Darius.)

While neither of the above examples can be considered definitive, I remain convinced that after further digging into these and other archives, I will discover a fuller picture of the master mariner and George Washington's friend, Darius Attucks. Further, and even more intriguing, I have uncovered indications, the nature of which I am not at liberty to disclose, that Attucks composed another manuscript detailing a second saga with his friend "Geo."

What that account describes and where Darius and Geo traveled together, I do not know. However, I am diligently searching for this lost document and have high hopes I will locate it soon.

#

About the Author

In addition to writing books and working as a magazine editor, I am one of the few remaining high priests of an obscure cult that uses bizarre instruments and consults rare manuscripts to learn cosmic secrets.

More about that below, but first a little about me.

I live in Portland, Maine. I'm the editor of a sailing magazine called *Ocean Navigator*, a magazine for sailors who enjoy crossing oceans (and sailing coasts, too). My wife is also an editor and I have three wonderful sons. Oh, and we have a black lab dog, who always seems to find herself on the wrong side of the door, especially deep in winter when opening the door is a chilly affair.

Now back to the cult. Once you know the rules of this cult you can travel anywhere on the globe using just three items: a clock, a *Nautical Almanac* and a sextant — sounds like magic, yes? (Oh, you'll also need some form of transportation like a boat, plane or camel). By now you've probably guessed it. I teach celestial navigation. I'm one of the few people in the world who still instructs folks how to find their way across the earth using just the sun, moon, planets & stars. Celestial navigation has become so arcane it's probably classified alongside alchemy!

In addition to mysterious, bizarre pursuits, I also like to sail, read, cook, make short films, hike, drink beer, draw, run, mess around with guitars, waste time on the web and watch movies.

Did I mention I open the door for my dog a lot?

Please consider writing a review of *George in London* on the book's Amazon page. Even a short review is valuable. It's a great way to help other readers find books.

Go to timqueeney.com for more info on *George in London* and possible *George* sequels. You can contact me via the contact form on my website or at rone@maine.rr.com.

www.ingramcontent.com/pod-product-compliance
Lightning Source LLC
Chambersburg PA
CBHW061557170626
46811CB00001B/236